Heart of Steel

"Rising star Brook has created two completely mesmerizing characters whose journeys in this gritty and treacherous world make for heart-stopping fun!" —*RT Book Reviews* (top pick)

"*Heart of Steel* is an exciting and stimulating read. Fast-paced, with plenty of humor and gripping action that grabs you at page one. While you don't lose any of the swashbuckling high seas, er, sky adventures nor Ms. Brook's superb world building, whose depth and heart makes this series, *Heart of Steel* isn't as emotionally dark as the first in the series—*The Iron Duke*. Which is perfect because these characters would never have survived that sort of story line. It's not often you can find a couple who complement each other as well as these two do. Yasmeen and Archimedes are a fantastic couple whose chemistry and dynamics are off the charts. Their steamy sexual games last well towards the end and provide us with plenty of entertainment." —*Smexy Books*

"Yasmeen and Archimedes were a fantastic hero and heroine and a solid couple. I haven't read many steampunk novels, but if the writing is half as good as it is in this series in other books in the genre, I really need to check out more." —*Paranormal Haven*

"The world that Ms. Brook has created with this series is incredibly fascinating, with a wonderfully intricate alternate history that adds such depth to the story. Archimedes is one of my absolute favorite heroes, and he and Yasmeen were truly perfect for each other. Recommended for fans of incredible steampunk, of adventuresome heroes with a truly romantic nature, and of kick-ass heroines who keep their awesomeness long after their hearts are engaged." —*The Romanceaholic*

continued . . .

"A straight-up adventure. Daring escapes, explosions, zombies, treasure hunting, and one man's quest to fall in love with the woman with a heart of steel . . . *Heart of Steel* has characters worthy of adoration, a gripping adventure, and a romance to cheer for."

—*Vampire Book Club*

The Iron Duke

"I loved it! As far as I'm concerned, with *The Iron Duke*, Meljean Brook has brilliantly defined the new genre of steampunk romance. From now on, everyone will compare other writers in the genre to her."

—Jayne Ann Krentz, *New York Times* bestselling author

"A stunning blend of steampunk setting and poignant romance—smart, sexy, breathtaking, and downright addicting. I'm ready for the next book or anything else Meljean Brook writes."

—Ilona Andrews, *New York Times* bestselling author

"Engrossing steampunk adventure . . . [A] complex, gripping read."

—*Publishers Weekly* (starred review)

"With adept writing and a flair for creating believable worlds, Brook's first in the Iron Seas series showcases her masterful storytelling."

—*Booklist*

"A high seas/airborne adventure that's filled with zombies, pirates, and deadly betrayal. Along with the pulse-pounding adventure, there's plenty of serious sizzle for readers to enjoy."

—*Romantic Times* (4 ½ stars)

"I absolutely loved this book . . . Everything from characters to world was done with care and precision . . . Any current fan of Ms. Brook has to read this one and those who aren't fans should. Steampunk has never been written so well." —*Night Owl Reviews*

Demon Forged

"Dark, rich, and sexy, every page makes me beg for more!"
—Gena Showalter, *New York Times* bestselling author

"Another fantastic book in a beautifully written series. [It] has all the elements I love in Meljean's books—strong, gorgeously drawn characters, a world so real I totally believe it, and the punch of powerful emotion." —Nalini Singh, *New York Times* bestselling author

"A dark, gripping read . . . The characters are brilliant, and the breathtaking romance, vivid setting, and darkly delicious adventure will immerse readers in this spellbinding world until the satisfying conclusion." —*Romantic Times*

Demon Bound

"An excellent entry in a great series . . . Another winner as the multifaceted Guardian saga continues to expand in complexity while remaining entertaining . . . As complex and beautifully done as always." —*Book Binge*

"Be prepared for more surprises and more revelations . . . Brook continues to deliver surprising characters, relationships, paranormal elements, and plot twists—the only thing that won't surprise you is your *total* inability to put this book down." —*Alpha Heroes*

Demon Night

"Meljean is now officially one of my favorite authors. And this book's hero? . . . I just went weak at the knees. And the love scenes—wow, just wow." —Nalini Singh, *New York Times* bestselling author

continued . . .

"Poignant and compelling with lots of action, and it's very sensual. You'll fall in love with Charlie, and Ethan will cause your thermometer to blow its top. An excellent plot, wonderful dialogue . . . Don't miss reading it or any of Meljean Brook's other novels in this series."

—*Fresh Fiction*

Demon Moon

"The fourth book in Meljean Brook's Guardian series turns up the heat without losing any of the danger."   —*Entertainment Weekly*

"A read that goes down hot and sweet—utterly unique—and one hell of a ride."   —Marjorie M. Liu, *New York Times* bestselling author

Demon Angel

"I've never read anything like this book. *Demon Angel* is brilliant, heartbreaking, genre-bending—even, I dare say, epic. Simply put, I love it."   —Marjorie M. Liu, *New York Times* bestselling author

"Brook has crafted a complex, interesting world that goes far beyond your usual . . . paranormal romance. *Demon Angel* truly soars."

—Jennifer Estep, author of *Widow's Web*

"Enthralling . . . [A] delightful saga."   —*The Best Reviews*

Titles by Meljean Brook

DEMON ANGEL

DEMON MOON

DEMON NIGHT

DEMON BOUND

DEMON FORGED

DEMON BLOOD

DEMON MARKED

THE IRON DUKE

HEART OF STEEL

RIVETED

Anthologies

HOT SPELL
(with Emma Holly, Lora Leigh, and Shiloh Walker)

WILD THING
(with Maggie Shayne, Marjorie M. Liu, and Alyssa Day)

FIRST BLOOD
(with Susan Sizemore, Erin McCarthy, and Chris Marie Green)

MUST LOVE HELLHOUNDS
(with Charlaine Harris, Nalini Singh, and Ilona Andrews)

BURNING UP
(with Angela Knight, Nalini Singh, and Virginia Kantra)

ANGELS OF DARKNESS
(with Nalini Singh, Ilona Andrews, and Sharon Shinn)

Riveted

MELJEAN BROOK

BERKLEY SENSATION, NEW YORK

THE BERKLEY PUBLISHING GROUP
Published by the Penguin Group
Penguin Group (USA) Inc.
375 Hudson Street, New York, New York 10014, USA

Penguin Group (Canada), 90 Eglinton Avenue East, Suite 700, Toronto, Ontario M4P 2Y3, Canada
(a division of Pearson Penguin Canada Inc.) • Penguin Books Ltd., 80 Strand, London WC2R 0RL,
England • Penguin Group Ireland, 25 St. Stephen's Green, Dublin 2, Ireland (a division of Penguin
Books Ltd.) • Penguin Group (Australia), 250 Camberwell Road, Camberwell, Victoria 3124, Australia
(a division of Pearson Australia Group Pty. Ltd.) • Penguin Books India Pvt. Ltd., 11 Community
Centre, Panchsheel Park, New Delhi—110 017, India • Penguin Group (NZ), 67 Apollo Drive,
Rosedale, Auckland 0632, New Zealand (a division of Pearson New Zealand Ltd.) • Penguin Books
(South Africa) (Pty.) Ltd., 24 Sturdee Avenue, Rosebank, Johannesburg 2196, South Africa

Penguin Books Ltd., Registered Offices: 80 Strand, London WC2R 0RL, England

This book is an original publication of The Berkley Publishing Group.

This is a work of fiction. Names, characters, places, and incidents either are the product of the author's
imagination or are used fictitiously, and any resemblance to actual persons, living or dead, business
establishments, events, or locales is entirely coincidental. The publisher does not have any control over
and does not assume any responsibility for author or third-party websites or their content.

PUBLISHING HISTORY
Berkley Sensation trade paperback edition / September 2012

Library of Congress Cataloging-in-Publication Data

Brook, Meljean.
Riveted / Meljean Brook.—Berkley Sensation trade paperback ed.
p. cm.
ISBN 978-0-425-25604-6
1. Sisters—Fiction. 2. Imaginary societies—Fiction. 3. Iceland—Fiction. I. Title.
PS3602.R64274R58   2012   2012022736
813'.6—dc22

PRINTED IN THE UNITED STATES OF AMERICA

10 9 8 7 6 5 4 3 2 1

Acknowledgments

To Jill Myles and Ilona Andrews: thank you so much for being there, holding my hand, and kicking my butt. I owe you guys so much tea. Special thanks to Telma Teixeira and Olguín Venustiano, who both assisted with foreign languages in the novel (and a belated thanks to Rosario, who helped many times before.)

To Monica Jackson, who fought to turn the world around: You flipped some of us. I truly believe that everyone else will follow, someday. I just wish that you were here to see it.

Chapter One

Before Annika had begun her journey, her mother had assured her that the people in the New World weren't all that different from the women in their village of Hannasvik. Annika's mother reminded her of how the peoples of Africa and Europe had sailed across the Atlantic four hundred years ago, fleeing from the Mongol Horde that had ridden from the east on the backs of their conquering war machines—just as Hanna and the Englishwomen had escaped the New World slavers and had made their home in Iceland a century before. She'd spoken of the enormous mechanical warriors that the New Worlders had built on their coastlines, sentinels that served a warning to the Horde, should that great empire ever develop a navy and follow them across the sea—just as Hannasvik's trolls protected their village and intimidated any enemies who might attempt to drive them from their home.

The Horde never followed the New Worlders, however. The sentinels stood for centuries, staring out over the open sea while wars over territory and trade routes were fought behind their backs, and they were slowly stripped of their armaments and engines.

And they were slowly falling apart. Annika glanced up through the drizzling rain and eyed the immense Castilian warrior guarding the gates to the port city of Navarra. In the four years since she'd left Hannasvik and joined *Phatéon*'s crew, Annika had come to accept the truth of her mother's words: Individually, the people of the New World weren't that different from those in her village.

The governments and rulers, however, must have been.

No elder in Hannasvik would have allowed Annika or any of the other engineers to neglect their trolls, not when lives depended upon their maintenance. The same obviously wasn't true in the New World, and Castile's sentinel was the worst. Aboard *Phatéon*, Annika had seen every machine still standing along the Atlantic coastline—from Johannesland's colossus in the north to the Far Maghreb's twin warriors, three thousand miles south of the equator—and the warrior in Navarra was by far the most decrepit. Rust ate away at its plate armor and crested helmet; corrosion pitted the iron around every bolt and rivet. Sand had drifted into the crevices, forming a solid mass at every joint, topped by grassy nests. Gray seagull dung crusted the spiked shoulders and gauntlets.

Once a marvelous and deadly machine, now it was simply dangerous. Even if the sentinel had still possessed the engines to walk, the great hinged knees would have buckled after a single step. Struts buttressed its lower half now, a framework of steel supporting the towering legs that served as Navarra's port gates.

What a horrible waste. If the Horde *had* come to the New World, they likely wouldn't have been intimidated by such useless machines . . . unless the New Worlders' defensive strategy was to crush any invaders beneath a rusted ruin. More likely, however, visitors to the city would be killed by falling pieces.

Visitors like Annika. Only an hour earlier, she had walked the north port road through the gate and into the Castilian city without being crushed—but while she'd been at the printer's office purchasing another season of personal advertisements, an icy breeze had begun to blow in from the ocean, stinging her cheeks with rain and sand. A strong gust might rip away the sentinel's giant hand or armored shoulder and throw it to the ground, squashing Annika in the street.

If a steamcoach didn't squash her first.

A horn blasted near her right ear. Two tons of rolling iron sped by, the front wheel whipping her skirts forward. With a yelp, Annika yanked the red silk tight to her leg before the rear wheel could catch the fabric and rip it away—or drag her along the sandy road behind it. That damned idiot driver. Only a blind man wouldn't have seen her walking along in a brilliant crimson skirt and canary yellow coat.

Though the coach was already lost from her sight beyond its dense trail of smoke and steam, she yelled after him, "You rotting rabbitchaser!"

Pointless, but satisfying—until she sucked in a lungful of the acrid smoke. Coughing, she pounded her fist over her chest, then glanced over her shoulder just in time to avoid the three-wheeled cart that rattled around a horse-drawn wagon and attempted to squeeze between the plodding beast and her leg. Her fierce scowl went unnoticed by the driver.

Well, hang them all. It was true that the row of shops that separated the north and south roads made narrow corridors of each street, leaving little room to maneuver—but they were headed in the same direction, and the port gates were only a hundred yards away. Was running her down to gain a few seconds truly necessary? Given the manner that some of them handled their vehicles, she suspected they were *aiming* for her.

Perhaps they were. Perhaps she'd broken some unspoken Castilian rule that no one aboard *Phatéon* had thought to warn her about. Perhaps she was unintentionally giving a message: Please crush me to a bleeding pulp alongside this road.

And now that the thought had entered her mind, it wouldn't

leave. She looked over her shoulder again. No vehicles were bearing down on her . . . yet.

Oh, and her mother would have been shaking her head now, telling Annika that her dread was a product of her imagination. That might have been true, once. Growing up, Annika's tendency to woolgather had been a source of consternation and amusement for the women in the village. Her imagination had continually gotten the best of her—and was precisely why she currently served as second engineer aboard an airship, flying from port to port, rather than eating supper every night in her mother's cozy earthen home. She'd often fancied dangers that weren't there and daydreamed when she should have been wary.

No longer, though. Within a few months of joining *Phatéon*'s crew, Annika had discovered that port cities in the New World each came with a unique set of dangers, and she'd learned to be wary until she was familiar with them. Manhattan City's entry inspectors didn't just examine the documents proving her origin and certifying that she wasn't infected by the Horde's nanoagents. They groped her legs and arms to make certain she wasn't hiding a mechanical apparatus beneath her clothing—and swinging a fist at an officer who groped too fervently would land her in a cell until her airship's captain bailed her out. Inside the city, a curse spoken within hearing distance of a constable resulted in a hefty fine; exposing a bare ankle or elbow earned a rebuke and a trip in a paddy wagon back to the port's gates, where her salacious behavior was reported to Captain Vashon and the airship threatened with docking sanctions.

In Oyapock, however, Annika could have walked naked down the paved streets without garnering a second look—and given the number of light-fingered war orphans who swarmed visitors entering Liberé's capital city, it was only by virtue of her trouser buckles that her pants weren't stolen off her bottom while she wore them. On her first visit to Oyapock, Annika might have considered

nudity a blessing, however. The city sat at the mouth of the Ori-
noco River; accustomed to colder climes, even Annika's lightest
clothing had seemed to suffocate her. But the urchins hadn't left
her nude on that trip—they'd taken her money and her hair instead.
She hadn't felt them lift the purse from her waist. A slight tug at the
back of her head had been the only warning before her thick braid
had disappeared and her curls sprang into a dark halo. With her
hand in her newly shorn hair, she'd stared in openmouthed shock as
they'd scampered away. She'd learned, though. Now she kept her
hair short and only carried as much money as she needed into
Oyapock, leaving the bulk on the airship.

Annika took her valuables with her in Port-au-Prince. Though
a Vashon airship was welcome at any of the French islands in the
Caribbean, *Phatéon* wasn't exempt from arbitrary searches by the
king's men looking for treasonous nobles or cargo left unaccounted
for on the tariff sheets. When Annika had reported her money
missing from her berth after a search, *Phatéon*'s old goat of a quartermaster had laughed before informing Annika that she'd paid *"le
fou de l'impôt."* She hadn't known enough French to understand
him then, but his meaning had been clear: Only a fool left her money
onboard when the king's men came. Annika preferred to take
it with her, anyway. Though many of the French cities seemed to
be sinking into an elegant ruin, all trading routes led through the
Caribbean, and the islands were ripe with spices and fruits unlike
any she'd ever had in Iceland. The fish seemed flakier and the mutton lighter when eaten in a French market, and the stalls were filled
with lustrous fabrics that she couldn't resist purchasing. King's
men or no, Annika always left the islands with an empty purse.

Now, Annika knew each city's quirks well enough that she
rarely felt trepidation passing through the port gates. Navarra was
no exception—and in many ways, was pleasant to visit. Entering
the city was painless, the inspection process consisting of a glance
at her papers and a wave through the gates. No orphans waited to

steal her money. The drapers sold cloth that matched the French markets' in quality, if not quantity; the food was bold and tangy, and the people she spoke with no more rude or friendly than in any other city, even when she stammered along in her butchered Spanish.

But she knew not to enter the city if any part of it was burning. She knew that if a crowd began forming in the streets, she needed to return to *Phatéon* as quickly as possible. The queen's guard wouldn't care whether she was actually participating in the bread riots—simply being in the area was enough to justify arrest, and Annika had never heard of any crew member of any airship returning from a Castilian gaol.

Since leaving home, she'd been as wary as her sense and instincts dictated. And if her imagination suggested a danger that didn't exist, no harm was done . . . except to her nerves.

A shout came from another vehicle, the words barely audible over the huffing engine—but she didn't understand much Spanish, anyway. Shoulders stiff in expectation of being run down, she glanced around. A cab driver gestured and shouted from two feet away, probably telling her to use the wooden walkway that ran along the front of the shops.

She would have used it, if there'd been room. But a church must have been distributing food nearby—men, women, and children with sunken cheeks and tired eyes stood in lines on the weathered boards, shuffling forward now and again, everyone quiet and orderly.

The fried sweetbread Annika had purchased near the printer's office suddenly weighed like a rock in her stomach. In many ways, the New World was *nothing* like Hannasvik. There was hunger in her village—oh, she'd known it many times, when the winters had been long and the nets empty, when the flocks had been thinned by the wild dogs, when even the rabbits seemed scarce—but if one person lacked food, then everyone in the village did. Here, she dared not even give any of the people the few coins left in her purse. If seen, she'd be arrested for inciting disorder.

And though she could imagine many ways to secretly pass the money to someone, she could also imagine the gaol too well if she were caught.

What a strange land, where giving a small bit of help might put a noose around her neck.

Oh, but she missed home. Longing gripped her chest—to see her mother, to feel the heat of a troll's belly as she stoked its furnace, to smell the sea and the smoking fish and the sheep. But she couldn't return, not yet. Not until she found her sister, Källa.

Until then, she was fortunate that *Phatéon* had become something of a home, too—and it was not far away now. She was almost to the port gates. Prudently, she opened her canvas umbrella to shield herself from the seagulls' rain that fell from the buttresses. Ahead, directly beneath the center of the sentinel, port officers watched the south road from a wooden guardhouse, making certain that no one attempted to avoid the inspections on the north road and enter Navarra via the southern gate. Beyond the guardhouse, the sand-strewn cobblestone road widened to accommodate the shops and pubhouses serving the aviators and passengers who weren't allowed into the city. Steamcoaches idled in front of the inns, the liveried porters loading and unloading luggage.

A strong gust blew more sand into her face. Around her, above her, the sentinel and the supporting framework seemed to shudder. With the sound of droppings splattering against the taut canvas, Annika didn't dare look up—and she resisted the urge to break into a run. Sense reminded her that the sentinel had weathered the hurricanes that roared up the coast every summer; surely it could survive a bit more wind.

On the other hand, how many times had she heard the story of the shepherdess who killed a giant with a single stone . . . ?

Annika quickened her step. Over the docks, the airships swayed and bobbed in the wind, pulling against their tethers like fat haddock fighting on fishing lines. A large cargo carrier, *Phatéon* didn't appear to move as much as the smaller airships, but Annika knew the mooring anchors groaned under the strain and the cables vibrated with tension.

Far ahead, dark clouds crowded the eastern horizon. If that storm moved in before *Phatéon* had been fully loaded, the night promised to be a rough one. They'd be jostled in their bunks and stumbling around the decks until the tether was unhooked.

Not so terrible, except that the second mate—who slept in the bunk above Annika's—tended to become portsick on such nights.

Another shout, this one from her left. Annika paid it no mind. If the person wasn't set to run her down, their business was none of hers, and the noise simply added to the cacophony on the road. Someone was always shouting near port gates; only the language changed. She thought it had been either Spanish or Portuguese, but was only certain the voice had been male.

Even that had become familiar. Since leaving Iceland to search for Källa, she'd become accustomed to new cities, a new life—and to seeing men everywhere. They were exactly as Annika's mother had described them: much like women, but hairier. And, when part of a group, stupider.

The shout came again. Closer, louder. Annika slowed. A uniformed port officer had left the guardhouse and strode in her direction, his thick mustache shadowing his frown. Annika glanced to the side. No one stood nearby. The guard's gaze had fixed on . . . her.

Annika's heart clenched, then began racing. *Oh, no.* But he was only one man, and not in a group. Whatever it was, surely she'd be able to reason with him.

A gray dropping splattered against his hat brim. The officer didn't seem to notice. He spoke again and *she* felt stupid. She didn't understand a single word. Most likely it was Spanish, but so quickly said that she couldn't make it out. Stopping a short distance away, he held out his hand, impatiently flicking his fingers.

He wanted something from her. But what?

Annika glanced down at herself, looking for the answer. She didn't carry anything but her umbrella, and didn't know how to ask him what the problem was. Her knowledge of the language didn't extend far beyond *No estoy infectada* and *¿Cuánto cuesta?*

Her fingers tightened on the umbrella stem. Her imagination didn't help her now. She could only picture the worst. Sudden nerves made her words loud and shrill. *"Parlez-vous français?"*

Annika had been forced to learn French when she'd joined *Phatéon*'s crew, and not just because Captain Vashon hailed from the Caribbean islands. French was the trader's language—and this was a port city. Surely he understood a little.

Dismay slid through her when his mouth firmed. Slowly, he said, *"Muéstreme . . . sus . . . cartas."*

His voice sharpened on *cartas*. Annika wracked her brain. Had she been blocking a cart or another vehicle? Was it something else? Not the identifying papers she had tucked away in her purse; she knew the word they used for that: *documentos.*

But they only asked for those when she was passing the inspection point on the sentinel's north side. Why stop her while she was leaving?

Once, she'd been briefly detained in Manhattan City when a constable had asked where she'd acquired her clothing. Even though he'd spoken English—an odd version of it, to be certain, even odder than she'd heard spoken in London—it had still taken Annika several minutes to realize that he suspected her of *stealing* the clothing, because the expensive fabric lay beyond a stoker's means. And despite her explanation that she'd purchased the silk on the cheap at the French markets and sewed the pieces herself, he hadn't seemed to believe her until a nearby group of women had come to her aid.

Laughing at the constable, they'd assured him that Annika couldn't have stolen the clothes, because no woman of quality would own anything so ridiculous as a white skirt over indigo trousers, pairing it with a lavender blue bodice.

No lady would ever be seen in a costume resembling a Liberé flag.

Today, Annika wore crimson and yellow. Perhaps the colors had marked her in some way—and she supposed that she *did* resemble a Lusitanian flag. But what of it? They weren't at war with Castile.

There were no women to save her now. She scanned the faces of the people nearby, hoping to recognize someone whom she could call upon. Though several travelers had turned to watch the encounter, she didn't see any of *Phatéon*'s crew members.

And what stranger would dare help? Not here, not in Castile.

Panic fluttered wildly in her chest. She faced the guard again. "Do you speak English?" As he had, she spoke slowly, trying to make herself understood. "Please tell me, what is the matter?"

With another sharp word and gesture, he shook his head. His hand shot out, seizing her wrist. He turned toward the guardhouse.

"No, please! Wait!" She dragged her heels, trying to slow him without openly resisting. Her heart pounded. Only with great effort did she stop herself from smashing her umbrella over his head and sprinting to the docks and *Phatéon*. Desperate, she tried again. *"Norse? Mælt kann norse?"*

"He demands to see your letters of entry."

A male voice came from behind her. She barely had a moment to feel her relief when the newcomer spoke again, but not in English—and not directed at her.

The guard looked around and stiffened, as if in alarm. He let Annika go, his hand dropping to the short club at his belt. *"¡Retírese, señor!"*

Whoever he was, the stranger apparently posed more of a threat than Annika did. She opened the purse tucked within her skirts, stealing a glance back. Beneath a wide-brimmed hat, the man wore a faint smile—not exactly an expression of amusement, she thought, but as if he'd heard an old, worn-out joke. A gleaming monocle concealed his left eye. Focused on the guard, he lifted his hands as if to show the officer that he was unarmed.

Oh, but he *was* armed. Annika's fingers froze around her folded papers, and she took another, longer look.

His right hand resembled every other person's—large, perhaps, with broad palm and long fingers, but proportional to his height. His left hand and wrist were of the same size, yet they were human only in shape; the skeletal limb had been constructed of steel. The fluid movement as he spread his mechanical fingers was indistinguishable from the same movement in his right hand, and spoke to the intricacy of the design—the contraption wasn't stiff, but responsive . . . and probably incredibly strong.

No, he didn't carry any weapons. But from the guard's perspective, the man's hand *was* a weapon—and the man himself a danger to Castile.

Prosthetic limbs were common enough in the New World; if not used by soldiers injured at war, then laborers who'd suffered accidents in the factories and fields. Those replacement limbs were often stiff and clunky, however—a hook for a hand, a wooden leg strapped into a boot—and only if replacements were used at all.

But there was nothing clunky about this man's elegant hand, which meant that it hadn't just been contoured around his arm or strapped on, but *grafted* on so that the steel contraption had become a working part of his body. Only the Horde's nanoagents could graft a mechanical apparatus to human flesh, making it as maneuverable as a natural arm. This man had to be infected with those tiny machines—the same machines that the Horde had used to forcibly graft tools onto their laborers. Most of those tools hadn't been designed to function or appear as human as this man's did, but Annika knew that it wasn't the hand itself that alarmed the guard. It was the nanoagent infection.

Although an infected person was stronger and could heal faster, the nanoagents had also allowed the Horde to control the populations in the occupied territories of England and North Africa, using radio signals from tall broadcasting towers. A few of the towers had been destroyed, freeing the people in England and Morocco—but many in the New World thought the revolutions were only a temporary setback in the Horde's inevitable advance across the ocean. Others in the New World feared that the nanoagents would reanimate their corpses after death and transform them into hungry, savage monsters, like the zombies who roamed much of Europe and Africa, leaving it uninhabitable. Others were revolted by the idea of tiny machines crawling around inside their bodies like bugs.

Annika knew too many of the infected to share the same fears, but the port officer obviously did not—or he knew many infected people, and still feared that the nanoagents might spread.

Brandishing his club, the officer gestured toward the nearest inn. Annika didn't need to understand his sharp commands to know that he was ordering the stranger to turn back, away from the gates.

The stranger didn't retreat. He looked to Annika, and the turn of his head offered a better impression of the features between his hat brim and gray wool scarf. He possessed a clean-shaven jaw, perhaps in the native style—or simply because a beard would never grow in evenly. Pale scars raked the left side of his face, with several wide, ragged stripes running diagonally from forehead to cheek. Oh! And that was not a monocle at all, but some sort of optical contraption that had been embedded into his temple, which shielded his left eye with a dark, reflective lens.

Utterly marvelous. What could he see through that?

"A noble was poisoned last week." He spoke clearly, the tones deep. She couldn't place his accent but had no trouble understanding him. "Rumor is that the assassin was a Liberé woman who carried Lusitanian papers."

So she *had* been marked—not just by the colors of her dress, but also by the darkness of her skin. Truly, if Annika were the assassin, she wouldn't have announced it so boldly. With a sigh, she unfolded her documents and presented them to the guard.

"Norway," she said, and because the officer seemed reluctant to look away from the stranger long enough to verify her origin, Annika helpfully pointed to the proper line. "Born in Bergen."

His gaze darted to the papers. Apparently not the least bit concerned about an assassin now, he waved her on. For a moment, she stared at him in disbelief. He could have so easily disrupted—no, *destroyed*—her life, as if she were nothing. Now he set her free in the same dispassionate manner. It did not engender grateful thoughts, yet she still managed a *"Gracias, señor."*

It did not come out as genuinely as she intended, but he didn't seem to note the bitter anger lacing her reply—and Annika was not a fool to wait around long enough for him to recognize it. She turned and set a brisk pace, her heart still hammering. The stranger waited, as if making certain that she wouldn't be further disturbed, before falling into step beside her, his hands clasped behind his back.

Since coming to the New World, she'd often been told that her manners were coarse, but Annika thought that the application of genuine gratitude could never be found lacking.

"Thank you, sir. I can't express how much I appreciate your interference."

He nodded. She thought that would be the end of it, that now he would return to the two men waiting in front of a nearby inn, and who were obviously his companions. Dressed in the same style of wool overcoat that buckled asymmetrically across the chest, long trousers, and sturdy boots, the men watched them pass. The young one sporting a pointed red beard and curling mustache seemed to make a remark; the elder shook his head and laughed, his breath puffing in the cold air. Beside them, porters loaded crates onto a lorry.

They all must have been standing there when the port officer had shouted for her to stop, she realized. Her rescuer had heard her desperation and come to her aid.

She glanced up at the stranger again. He walked to the left of her, his eye contraption only visible as a glint of metal beyond the bridge of his aquiline nose. His hair was as black as hers, though without a hint of curl. The straight ends touched his shoulders, the forward strands drawn away from his face and contained by four steel beads tucked behind his ears.

Did he intend to accompany her all the way to *Phatéon*? Surely that wasn't necessary. "I'm out of danger now, if you wish to return to your people."

"My people?" His brow rose, and he glanced toward the men. "Ah. They'll manage without me."

And she wouldn't? She ought not to say that, however, not after he'd rendered such an incredible service to her.

She ought not say it, and so of course she did. "But *I* can't manage without you?"

His sudden grin was nothing like his earlier smile, which had seemed a weary response to an old jest. This appeared to burst through him as if he knew laughter was the only reply he could give.

Annika had to smile in return, and then laugh when he asked, "I trust you were *not* hired to kill a Castilian noble?"

"Perhaps I was," she said. "If I were a clever assassin, I'd carry fraudulent papers that claim I was born in Norway, not Lusitania."

"Are they fraudulent, then?"

Yes. Not for the purpose of assassination, however, but for the purpose of mobility. This exchange had become unexpectedly fun, however, and so she played along. "Oh, of course."

"And what is your true origin?"

A hidden village on Iceland's western shore. But even as a joke, she could not risk exposing her people, and chose the farthest location away from them. "A smuggler's haven in Australia."

That seemed to disappoint him. His grin had already faded to a pleasant, amused expression, but now she detected a hint of frustration in the tightness of his mouth and the intensity of his gaze. He was truly looking for an answer, Annika realized. This was not simply polite conversation to pass the time; he wanted to know where she was from.

Or was that just her imagination? She had guarded the truth of her origin for four years. Perhaps the constant vigilance made her suspect everyone of trying to discern it.

When he didn't respond to that lie, she covered her unease with a dramatic sigh. "In truth," she said, "Australia would be far more exciting, but alas, Norway it was—and is where I am bound again."

"You fly out immediately?"

Perhaps Annika imagined the sudden tension in his voice, but she couldn't mistake the way his gaze moved over her face, as if searching for the answer—or hoping for a specific reply. "The airship departs later tonight," she confirmed.

The stranger's lips tightened before resolve seemed to firm his expression. He nodded. "En route to Bergen?"

Eventually. *Phatéon* was scheduled to fly to the Norwegian port within a month, but it would not be a direct flight.

"Yes," she said, her unease deepening. Why did he ask so specifically? Perhaps he was only making small talk, but she wasn't comfortable with the direction he'd taken. Best to change the subject.

And if this truly *was* conversation, it was time that she held up her part and made intrusive inquiries of her own. "Will you also be departing soon? Or do you make a habit of waiting near port gates and running to a stranger's aid?"

"No. Typically, I run after erupting volcanoes."

"To study them?" Annika guessed. She couldn't think of any

other reason to do such a thing—and only if it paid well. "That is your profession?"

When he nodded, she studied *him* more closely. What sort of person made a living from such a thing? She had witnessed eruptions in Iceland before, and would have said that only a reckless fool would go chasing after one. This man didn't appear foolish, however, and his manner seemed too contained to be reckless. Something else must be driving him to pursue such a dangerous occupation, something that he didn't readily show.

Asking him to reveal that reason, however, would require Annika to venture beyond the boundaries of intrusive and into unforgivably rude. Even she couldn't cross that line. She settled for, "I didn't realize volcanoes were so fast that one had to run after them."

His amusement returned. "In truth, I more often run *away* from them."

She arched her brows and glanced at his mechanical hand, still clasped behind his back. "Not always fast enough?"

"No, that was another sort of explosion." His gaze narrowed. "You've spent time in England."

"In England? Well—Yes?" Confusion tripped her up. What an odd response. She *had* spent a little time in that country when *Phatéon*'s route took her there. But why would such a statement follow hers . . . *Oh.*

Fierce heat bloomed in her cheeks. Prosthetics and mechanical apparatuses were so common in England as to be unremarkable. But in the New World, such topics were handled with delicacy, if not outright avoided. Her insensitive comment must have distressed him, though he hid it well. Perhaps that was an indication of his fine manners; he didn't point out her lack of them, though he had every reason to.

She had long come to terms with her failings, but Annika hated knowing that she might have hurt someone with them. "I am so sorry. How horrid of me to make light of injuries that must have been painful."

He shrugged. "And long ago."

Was he dismissing the topic or her apology? He didn't seem distressed, but rather uninterested in discussing himself—and examining her features as if interested in *her*. Well, if he wanted to know what sort of woman she was, he was soon to learn that she had difficulty letting anything go without proper resolution.

"Whenever it happened, I am sorry for my words now," she said. "I'm often told that I don't possess any proper sensibilities, but that doesn't excuse—"

"Who tells you this?"

"Everyone," she said ruefully, and the stranger laughed before subjecting her to a considering look.

"If you wish to make amends," he said, "eat supper with me now."

That was *not* an offer she expected to come from someone with manners. Not offended, but incredibly surprised, she shook her head. "Pardon? I believe I misheard."

"Share a meal with me at the inn," he said unmistakably, before softening his expression with a smile. "I wouldn't take advantage of a woman's obligation to me, but I have no choice. If you leave this evening, I'll have no other opportunity to enjoy your company, and I want to know you better."

The intensity of his gaze deepened as he spoke, as if the entirety of his being had focused on gaining her consent. Annika stared up at him, uncertain how to respond. She'd have liked to spend more time with him, too. She wanted to know why he chased volcanoes, and what had possessed him to come to her aid—and there was nothing that forbade her from sharing a meal with someone. But her instincts were ringing, and she couldn't ignore the alarm they raised. She had been propositioned before. She'd been flirted with before. This was . . . different. Though she couldn't have articulated why she felt the need to be wary, Annika was certain that this man wanted something from her—but not company, not courting, not even to share a bed.

"I'm sorry," she said, feeling very stiff. "The captain has asked that we all return to the airship early, so that we're aboard before the storm hits."

He nodded, but she saw the clench of his jaw, the frustration that suddenly shadowed his expression. Annika continued her brisk pace. The stranger remained at her side, but as they crossed from the cobblestones onto the wooden docks, the rumble of lorry engines and the shouts of the stevedores made further conversation impossible. Annika walked in silence, her thoughts in tumult. Perhaps she'd been mistaken? Perhaps she was only wary because his offer had been so unexpected. Perhaps she'd just insulted him again.

If so, nothing could be done now. With relief, she reached *Phatéon*'s mooring station. The cargo lift had been raised against the side of the airship, but the ladder hung down to the docking boards.

Annika stopped and folded her umbrella before turning to the stranger, who had tilted his head back to look up at the airship. She had to tilt her head back to look at *him*. Oh, he was quite tall—and so close. Rarely did Annika feel small, but standing next to him, she did. "Thank you again."

His gaze lowered. Though his smile had not returned, she thought he seemed pleased. Satisfied, perhaps. "You travel aboard *Phatéon*? I've heard that she's a fine ship."

"Yes." She caught the rope ladder, steadied it. "Very fine."

He nodded. "I will leave you, then. I wish you a safe journey, miss."

"I wish the same for you."

Politely, he touched his hat—and stood, waiting . . . for her to climb safely aboard, she realized, and felt silly of a sudden. All this way, he had only been helpful. It had been kind of him to stay with her until he'd made certain that she'd arrived at her destination unharmed. It had been kind of him to offer a meal.

Still, Annika sensed his gaze on her as she climbed the ladder—and could not shake the feeling that the stranger hadn't gotten what he wanted, and that he wasn't done with her. That she would see him again, that he would be waiting for her in Bergen . . . or somewhere else.

But perhaps that was only her imagination.

Chapter Two

For twenty years, David Kentewess had searched for his mother's people. He'd finally found one of them.

The small woman ascending *Phatéon*'s ladder didn't physically resemble his willowy mother in any way, but her unusual, burred accent had been the closest he'd come to hearing Inga Helgasdottor's voice since she'd lain beneath a burning pile of rubble and whispered a final, agonized plea.

David would be damned before he failed her. But for years, he'd despaired of being able to keep his promise.

Until he'd heard this woman's desperate words—first in French, then English, then Norse. *Norse*, for Christ's sake. Who spoke that anymore? Only scholars—and few of them at that.

Certainly no one in Bergen. David had been to that Norwegian port several times, and he'd never heard anyone with an accent like hers. Perhaps the language was still spoken in some remote village—but not in any of the villages he'd visited. He'd almost given up hope of ever knowing his mother's origins.

Perhaps this woman didn't hold the answer. Perhaps he imagined the similarities to his mother's voice. Perhaps he was mistaken.

David didn't think so. And—

Hell. He'd forgotten to ask her name.

With a sudden grin, he watched her climb. The shock of hearing her peculiar accent near the gates had stolen his brains. Before he realized that they would be traveling on the same airship, he'd been so determined to keep her in his sight that he hadn't even thought to ask that simple question. He'd find out soon, though— and everything else he wanted to know.

What incredible luck. If he'd left the inn a few minutes later, or if she'd been on any other vessel but *Phatéon* . . .

But she wasn't on another ship—and instead of a bird shitting in his eye at the port gates, an answer to an old prayer had landed in his lap in the form of a vibrant woman. Such *mad* luck. Wild elation lifted through him, rising with every step he watched her take, but he quelled the shout of laughter swelling within his chest. Perhaps she wouldn't hear his laugh over the noise of the docks, but he wouldn't give her reason to look down and see him cackling like a drunken rotbrain.

His grin would likely scare her, anyway.

That thought erased his smile. He'd have to be careful about how he approached her. She hadn't seemed disturbed by his mechanical hand or mangled face, but he hadn't given her the opportunity to take a close look yet. While walking with her, he'd deliberately positioned himself so that only his unscarred profile was on display.

When was the last time he'd made such an effort to present his good side to a woman? Hell, when was the last time he'd thought about *having* a good side? Too long. He'd have to be certain not to forget, and try not to scare her away . . . again.

Though she'd been polite about it, he had no doubt that she'd run from him. Only crew members climbed the rope ladders; passengers waited for the cargo platform, particularly if they wore skirts. And she *must* be a passenger—no aviator dressed in silk from head to toe.

So he'd unsettled her . . . but not because of his scars or his nanoagent infection. She hadn't fled until he began asking questions. Why?

He'd soon figure it out.

She'd almost reached *Phatéon*'s deck. From his angle on the ground, her voluminous skirts swallowed her figure, aside from a flash of yellow now and again when the crimson material parted to show the trouser legs beneath. Odd, wasn't that? David had been too focused on her lively features and her voice to take note of her dress, but now it was all he could see. He recalled the purple scarf warming her neck and covering her corkscrew hair, the number of ribbons adorning her sleeves and hem. He'd passed frippery shops with fewer bows displayed in the windows than the woman had worn, and though he knew nothing of women's fashions, he couldn't remember seeing such a combination of colors and shapes at any of the numerous ports he'd visited in the past ten years. A glance along the docks and a scan of the other ladies' dresses confirmed it: Her clothing was odd.

Good. *Odd* fit the sort of woman he was looking for.

When his family had lived in the mountain-builders' city at the confluence of the Inoka and the Great Muddy rivers, both the white settlers and his father's people had said Inga Helgasdottor was odd, too—not because she'd worn silk and ribbons, but because she'd possessed an unusual manner and lacked any proper sensibilities. His mother had laughed loudly, and at strange moments. She'd made shocking observations, suggested things no polite woman would have. She'd swaggered, even when David's aunt had coaxed her out of homespun trousers and into a skirt. And whenever someone had asked where she'd come from, his mother only replied with a smile.

As a boy, David had never asked. She'd been with him, she'd been fierce in her love, and that was all that had mattered. Only later had he discovered that his father had asked often—terrified that she'd leave and he wouldn't know where to find her.

But his father had lost Inga Helgasdottor anyway. They both had.

Now David had found a woman who didn't swagger, who didn't appear as strong or as wild, but who seemed similar in essentials, as full of life—and he wouldn't lose this one.

Despite that certainty, sudden fear squeezed his lungs when she reached *Phatéon*'s deck and disappeared over the side. *She was gone.*

David forced himself not to chase after her. His mechanical legs had been designed to provide stability over rough terrain, but balancing his feet on drooping rope rungs was another matter. Climbing the ladder would be a precarious and awkward pursuit—and unless she could fly, there was nowhere else for her to go until *Phatéon* docked in Iceland, anyway. Better to wait for the cargo lift.

It wouldn't be a long wait. A steamcoach rumbled up to the mooring station. Seated beside the driver, Dooley scowled down at David in a way that said he wasn't truly upset. When Patrick Dooley was angry, his pale face became as hard and as red as a brazier.

With the grating squeal of rusted brakes, the vehicle stopped. Dooley hopped to the ground, a little less spry than when David had met him eight years ago, just before their first expedition. Since then, most of the digger's abundant brown hair had migrated from the top of his head to his jaw, with gray threading through it. A heavy mink hat protected his now bald pate, and the furred bulk offered the impression of a disproportionately large head sitting atop Dooley's wiry body.

His scowl deepened with every step he took toward David. "You've made a liar out of me, Kentewess!"

Not likely. David had never met any man as proud of his own honesty as Dooley was—or who so often hid his amusement with a frown. His friend often attempted to appear hard and cynical, yet rarely succeeded.

No surprise, then, that David liked him so well. "Did I?"

"You did." The digger glanced back at the coach, where Regnier Goltzius gave directions to the stevedores who would unload their equipment. "I just wagged on to the Dutchman that you were incapable of speaking to a female for more than three minutes."

Unlikely to speak to a woman, yes. But *unable* to? "I'm capable."

"Not that I've ever seen." The scowl cracked for a moment, revealing the amusement beneath. "You're incapable—or too terrified. The answer is yours to pick."

Christ. How would he get out of this one? Dooley always turned every opinion based on observation into fact, and only hard evidence could counter it. Problem was, David couldn't easily recall *any* conversation of late that had lasted more than a few minutes, unless it was with a member of a recent expedition or a colleague.

Ah. There was his answer. "Inoue Nanami."

"The madwoman who floated a jellyfish balloon over Krakatoa?" Dooley swept his hat off and knocked it against his leg, shaking free a shower of raindrops. More drizzled onto his head. "You listened as she gave a lecture to the Society. That's no conversation."

"I spoke with her."

"You tossed questions at her when she'd finished—and every one of them was relayed through her translator. As I see it, you were only speaking to *him*."

Damn it. With a laugh, David shook his head. "But now you've seen me with this woman for twice that length of time. So did I prove you wrong or make a liar out of you?"

No reason to let Dooley know that although he'd walked with the woman for more than three minutes, the noise of the docks had prevented them from speaking for a good portion of it. Their conversation had been long enough to make David certain that she had answers, and brief enough to make him frustrated that he couldn't solicit them from her.

Dooley took the less offensive choice. "I'll admit I've been proved wrong."

"Good man," David said. "When I've reached your great age, I hope I'll admit defeat as gracefully as you do."

The older man snorted. "If you've brains enough to survive as long."

"So it was your brains that saved you after the earthquake on Tzapotépetl? I'd say it was my hand that pulled you out of that crevice."

"It was me with the sense to reach for your hand, wasn't it?"

David conceded with a grin. The man could talk his way around almost anything. Bolstered by his victory, Dooley lifted his hat back into place and winked at Goltzius when the young botanist joined them.

"As Kentewess was so quick to abandon us while the steam-coach was loaded, I say we ride up top to share a bottle and leave him to watch the unloading."

Goltzius's only response was an open, good-natured smile—a diplomatic response, to David's mind. As the newest member of their team, joining David and Dooley after only a week's acquaintance, Goltzius hadn't yet known them long enough to participate in the back-and-forth of a friendly ragging, let alone take sides. David thought that camaraderie would come, eventually. Goltzius had been a good fit so far, bright and determined, and weathering without complaint the delays in securing supplies and the cramped accommodations aboard the airship from Johannesland to Castile.

If such trivialities had frustrated the botanist, no doubt this expedition would have been hell for him—for *all* of them. David had once spent six months in the company of a linguist who'd whined over every insect bite. By the end of it, he could have cheerfully strangled the man—and he'd have strangled him with his right hand, just to prolong the pleasure of it.

He hoped Goltzius wouldn't arouse the same murderous compulsions. As it was, his addition to the team had already aroused a few, though Goltzius wasn't to blame for them. Politics were.

When David and Dooley had proposed this nine-month survey to the Scientific Society of New Leiden, they'd picked botanist Mary Longcreek to accompany them. Experienced, dedicated, and familiar with plant growth recovery following volcanic eruptions, she'd been the ideal choice for their team. The previous week, she had still been preparing for their departure when the Society directors had abruptly assigned her to an upcoming two-year expedition to determine potential sites for rubber tree plantations in the Pacific islands. They'd replaced her with Regnier Goltzius, a recent Academy of Sciences graduate.

The directors gave a sound reason for the change: Longcreek's experience made her a better choice for the long and potentially perilous journey. David wasn't fooled, however. She wasn't the only experienced botanist available to the Society—but unlike Goltzius, she wasn't the youngest son of a cousin to the Grand Duchess of Erie, one of the Society's most generous patrons. Immediately placing Goltzius on an expedition no doubt pleased Her Highness . . . and the directors didn't risk her anger by sending him to his death. Exploration societies were no strangers to fatalities among their ranks, but danger was less likely found in Iceland.

Resigned to the change, Longcreek had turned months of research and notes over to the young man. To his credit, Goltzius had seemed to recognize the machinations behind his placement, and had appeared both frustrated and embarrassed during their first meeting. He hadn't apologized, however, which had furthered David's good impression—as had Goltzius's keen interest in their survey of the abandoned island.

But at this moment, Goltzius's interest was directed upward. "Was all well with the young woman?"

"Yes." Until David had chased her off—but he glanced up, too, hoping to see her again. A *whirring* click sounded in his ear. The vision in his left eye blurred and sharpened as specialized lenses rotated into place beneath the tempered glass shield—the nano-agents aiding him in his search. Whenever he didn't see an object that he was looking for, the mechanical bugs helped him find it. Now, their assistance didn't make any difference. The thermal lens slipped into place, showing him bright orange heat concentrated around *Phatéon*'s boilers and the yellow eddies of steam rising from the vents. No people were visible; though warm, they didn't emit enough heat to register through the hull, and even his nanoagents couldn't help him see through solid wood.

"You be careful with those, now!"

With alarm, Dooley abandoned them to look after his own interests—the clockwork dogs that would pull their supply sleds. David turned to watch, his default optic slipping back into place, matching the vision of his left eye to his right. At the steam-coach, Dooley fluttered about until the stevedores carefully set the dogs' crate on the cargo lift platform.

Goltzius frowned. "Are they so fragile?"

"No." David's equipment for measuring ground tremors and their surveyors' tools were more likely to be damaged than those dogs—and a good thing, too. Iceland was green for a good portion of the year but earned its name in winter; those dogs were invaluable in the snow and over the glaciers they planned to survey. When spring came, they only had to roll the sled's runners into wheels, and the dogs would still be useful. "They wouldn't be any good to us if they couldn't survive a fall or two. But listen to Dooley, and he'd have you believe they had brains instead of gears, and that they'd cry over pebbles in their paws or shiver in the snow."

"I hear that, Kentewess!" Shaking his head, Dooley rejoined

them. "And agree with every word. You tell me now, young man: What difficulty would it have been for the blacksmiths to put a fur coat over their bare metal bones?"

"How could they, when most of the fur left in New Leiden already went into your hat?" As the older man snorted, David looked to Goltzius. "The first snowstorm, he'll toss us out of the tent to make room for those dogs."

"You striplings will be better off outside than those pitiful mongrels would. They don't have any heat to share, whereas all you've got to do is shuck your clothing and snuggle up together."

Goltzius's mild alarm over that statement changed into determined humor. He sized up David with a glance. "I *did* come looking for adventure."

David grinned. With a response like that, there was no doubt the young man would fit right in during these next few months.

The huff and rattle of another steamcoach drowned out Dooley's reply. A man of average size emerged, tipping his felt hat forward against the drizzle and buckling a brown shearling topcoat. In the crook of his arm he carried a polished walking stick with a silver wolf's head. Chips of amber glittered in the eyes.

Dooley turned away, his lips pursing. In an aside to David, he said, "Now there's a fancy one."

God forbid that a man ever possess money, unless he also supported the Society with it. But David had to suppress the ribbing that Dooley deserved—the gentleman approached them with an easy stride, his stick apparently just for show.

Dooley's mouth flattened, his immediate dislike firmly set.

Until, with an amiable smile, the man said, "I believe it's three Society men that I'm seeing, yes?"

His accent immediately marked him. Dooley gave a wide grin, extending his hand. "It is. And a fellow countryman to me, I hear."

"Sure I am." His smile widened, and he eagerly pumped Dooley's hand, his as dark as the other was pale. "Komlan, of Monaghan and the town itself. And you're a western man?"

"I am. Patrick Dooley, of Ballyduff. Standing here with me are my colleagues David Kentewess and Regnier Goltzius—though neither one had the same fortune to be birthed on God's own favorite land."

"Upon such a happy meeting, even that sorry failing of character can be forgiven." As Dooley laughed, Komlan glanced over at the supply crates loaded on the lift. "Are you to Iceland, then, or on to Norway?"

"Iceland and the town of Vik, to begin."

"On the southern rim? I know it. We've men working west of there, laying rail from Smoke Cove to Höfn. Eventually, it will run through Vik, as well."

"Rail for a locomotive?" Goltzius frowned when Komlan nodded. "To what purpose?"

David wondered the same. A century before, in the years following an eight-month fissure eruption, the Mist Terrors decimated livestock and crops. Ash fell in thick layers over the land, and toxic volcanic gases poisoned half the island's inhabitants. The remaining population had been forced to flee or face starvation. Except for a few ports and fishing villages, Iceland had been abandoned for a hundred years. A locomotive around the southern rim of the island wouldn't serve any purpose that an airship or a boat couldn't provide more quickly or more cheaply.

"For the purpose of providing work, lad," Komlan said.

A shout from the airship stopped Goltzius's response. They all glanced up, then over at the cargo lift, where a stevedore waited. "The coach is empty, sirs. Is there anything more to be loaded before we send her up?"

"Just us. We'll ride up next," David said. "Mr. Komlan?"

"No 'mister,' son. The name alone was good enough for my

forefathers, and it's good enough for me," he said. "Go on and send that lift up. My cargo is already in the hold—and likely already being fed."

"You're taking livestock, then?"

"Men." He smiled as David and Dooley exchanged a glance. He raised his voice over the clanging of the chain when the lift began to ascend, and clarified, "Labor of the paid sort."

"You're hiring here?" Color crept up Dooley's neck. "Back home, there's many an Irishman hurting for an honest day's work."

"And not a one of them will work for as little."

"Hurting enough, they would for almost nothing."

There wasn't a kingdom or a country that couldn't be said of, David knew. But Castile was different in one important respect. "Are they as unlikely to complain about it?"

"Never has that been said of an Irishman," Komlan agreed with a grin, then shook his head. "I'm only a working man, same as those in the cargo hold. I've no say over a business that's not mine to own, or how they earn their profits; I go where I'm told to go and hire men who'll give their labor in exchange for the price the boss has offered. It's not much, but in return they'll also receive meals, clothing, and a warm place to rest their heads—all of which is in scarcer supply here than about anywhere else."

"It's truth, that is," Dooley admitted with a sigh.

"An unfortunate one." Komlan echoed his sigh before asking, "Have you been long from home?"

"That I have. Too long."

Not as long as Dooley might go on about it, as David had discovered on their first expedition together. Goltzius had already been given a taste of the same on their journey here. He glanced at the botanist, who watched the two men with an expression reflecting troubled thoughts. His frown smoothed when he noted David's attention, replaced by a wry smile.

Moving in closer, Goltzius said, "Shall we wager on who out-lasts the other?"

David would put his money on Dooley. But he shook his head. "There's no point to it. *We* won't last long enough to find out who won."

In truth, he didn't care to last even a minute more. David left them to their reminiscing, suddenly impatient for the cargo lift's return. There was only one person whose origin interested him—and she was already aboard the airship.

Aside from the enormous white balloon hovering over-head, the main deck of *Phatéon*'s wooden cruiser looked much like the sailing ships that David had been on. Tethered to the docks, it swayed much like a ship did, too. The bobbing forced him to stop and adjust to the motion before he could take a step without stag-gering. The ride would smooth out as soon as the engines fired and the airship was under way. Until then, he had to be mindful of his shifting weight.

He didn't see the woman on deck, but wasn't surprised. A storm was headed in, the wind icy and the deck boards slippery with rain; she'd be warm in her cabin by now. Within the hour, how-ever, she'd probably sit at the captain's table for dinner, along with any other passengers. He could wait until then.

Captain Vashon herself welcomed them aboard, a tall and impressive woman with iron threading through the black hair at her temples. Hailing from a family of French aeronauts made famous by their military exploits and made wealthy by their mer-chant activities, she had a reputation to uphold. She did it well, David thought. He'd heard nobles who'd have been hard pressed to match the cultured tones of her speech, had seen heads of state with less immaculate uniforms.

She eyed David's face and hand without comment, which he expected. Few people remarked on his prosthetics, no matter how long they stared. When her attitude toward him didn't change afterward, that was just as rare—and he liked her for it.

Her welcome was followed by a query whether they had any other needs or concerns to address before their departure. Though David burned to ask her about the woman, he didn't dare. Men didn't ask after unrelated female passengers. If the captain suspected any untoward interest, he'd likely spend the entire journey separated from her.

When they all responded in the negative, Vashon's gaze fell on him again, and she anticipated the question he *would* have voiced. "There is a lady aboard who looks forward to seeing you, Mr. Kentewess."

A woman with whom he would easily spend more than three minutes in conversation—his aunt by marriage, and the only family he had left. Lucia Kentewess had been serving as ship's physician aboard *Phatéon* for ten years now. "Thank you, Captain."

Her dignified nod could have rivaled a queen's. "It is my pleasure. Monsieur Dubois will show you to her quarters. Dubois?"

A young man with a scraggle of a mustache appeared at his side. "This way, please, monsieur."

David took his leave and followed Dubois to the companionway that led to the lower decks. The wide stairs were easy to maneuver, far easier than a ladder. Dubois all but skipped down them, as if he never gave such considerations a thought. At his age, David couldn't have even descended to the second deck without assistance.

Sick bay lay all the way at the front of the ship on the third deck; Lucia's quarters were in the adjoining cabin. Dubois rapped at the door and announced his own name, then opened it with a flourish when she called for him to enter.

Vashon had arranged a surprise, David realized. His aunt hadn't been expecting him—at least, not at this moment. The remains of an afternoon tea still lay on her small table, a thick physician's volume open beside them. Her overcoat was slung across her bed. Sitting at her desk, Lucia glanced up at Dubois with an expression of polite inquiry. When her gaze moved past the boy and into the passageway, she suddenly stilled, staring.

David waited, his throat unexpectedly tight. Her face had softened a bit over the years, and a few new lines had formed, but everything else was so familiar. She still rolled her blond hair at her nape. She still kept a watch pinned to her breast. Her neckline was higher, but the flower-sprigged cotton of her dress was just as simply cut, just as pretty. The black streak at the top of her right ear might have been the same mark from ten years ago, when she'd absently tucked a loosened curl away with ink-stained fingers. No, her appearance hadn't changed much at all.

His had.

"David?" Now her hand lifted to her mouth, eyes filling with tears. "Oh, David. *Look* at you."

He came into the cabin, and those small steps seemed to push her over, the tears spilling. She rose from her chair, hands extended. Behind them, Dubois quietly closed the door.

She caught his face between her palms, greeted him with a kiss to both cheeks before stepping back, her hands clasped in front of her chest. Joy shone through the tears, lighting her face with a wide smile. "Oh, I cannot believe it. Captain Vashon told me that you were delayed—that you wouldn't board until later this evening."

"No." The lump in his throat had grown, making it difficult to manage even that. The warmth of any touch was so rare that David never noticed the absence until he felt it again—and his aunt touched him so freely, without reservation.

"Well, you are here, and I am not about to let you escape quickly. Give me your hat and coat, and let me see you."

Obediently, he removed them both. She hung the coat in her

wardrobe and turned to look at him again, her gaze openly curious as she studied his eyepiece.

"It is not at all like you described in your letters," she said. "I had imagined something more . . . bulbous, perhaps, similar to a magnifying goggle."

A giant eye, staring at her. "I probably exaggerated the details. It seemed enormous when they first grafted it on."

All of the prosthetics had seemed enormous, alien. Heavy legs that he couldn't walk on for months, a cold hand that crushed anything he tried to grasp, and the strange views through lenses that the nanoagents altered at random, until he'd learned to control them with subtle motions of his jaw and cheek.

"You did make it sound rather bulging and grotesque. But I must say, David, the effect is actually rather dashing."

He had to laugh. No doubt she was sincere, but her love for him obviously impaired her vision as much as an exploding window had damaged his. He had seen too many strangers recoil upon seeing his face to believe it.

Truth or not, however, her opinion mattered more to him than any stranger's ever could. "Thank you, Aunt. I will have to practice my heroic leer to complete the effect."

"Go on." Laughing, she looked to his hand. "May I?"

"Of course."

He sensed her touch there, too—the warm slide of her skin over steel, the soft pressure of her palm against his. She gasped softly when he interlaced his fingers with hers.

"It's so marvelous," she breathed. "Can you feel anything?"

"Temperature, pressure, some textures." All dull, compared to his other hand, yet a miracle that he could feel anything at all. "It's not the same. The sensation is clear, but less intense. Muffled."

"I have always wondered. None of the crew is infected, and although we have had a few passengers, I could never ask. But I wondered what they felt, and if it was the same for you. And your legs, too? Oh, but you are *so* tall. Would you have been so tall?"

"The Blacksmith took measurements and compared them to men of similar size," he said. "Perhaps I might have been an inch shorter or taller, but this is near to my natural height."

"And both your father and mother were tall. Your mother in particular. I always felt quite the little girl next to her." With a sigh, she squeezed his hand. "Well, let us sit. There's a biscuit left, if you'd like to have it, though we'll eat dinner within the hour. I've drank all the coffee, but I can put on more. Or, I have a lovely bottle of—Oh, where is it?"

David pulled out a chair, that sense of familiarity descending again as she began opening cupboards at random, muttering as she searched. Dinner notwithstanding, he helped himself to the biscuit, a sugary confection that crumbled down the front of his jacket. He hastily brushed the wool clean before she turned around.

Yes, some things never changed.

"Here we are! On your left, those glasses on the shelf? Ah, yes." Lucia grinned as he set the two goblets on the table. "I know nothing of good wine, but after I lanced a boil that was giving one of our passengers—a French count, no less—horrible fits every time he tightened his corset, Captain Vashon gave this to me. It must be worth something; for months, our chief engineer sent envious glares and made hints to share it. Oh, it's quite dusty, isn't it? I should find a rag—"

"We don't plan to lick the bottle," David said.

"No, we don't." She poured the deep burgundy liquid almost to the rim. "We shall see how distinguished our palates are."

Not very. David rolled the wine around on his tongue, and wished he had another biscuit, instead. Pure sugar would have been less sweet.

"Oh, my." Lucia set her glass aside. "I should find a funnel and pour it back in before giving it to the chief. If I don't tell Leroux, he will enjoy it just as well. And you?"

"He can have mine, too."

"It's a pity. Oh, but—I have heard, David, that the infected are more susceptible to drink. Will you be all right?"

"Some are more susceptible than others. I need more than one sip for it to affect me . . . but I also save money in the taverns."

She smiled at him, resting her elbows on the table and cupping her chin in her palms. "It is simply all so incredible. You heal more quickly, is that true?" At his nod, she wondered, "Did it heal your eye, then?"

"No. That damage is permanent." Just as the nanoagents couldn't regrow his arm or his legs or erase his scars, the bugs couldn't repair an eye that had been mutilated years before the infection. "But where I could only see light and dark on that side, the nanoagents use different lenses and focus for me. There *is* a bulging lens behind the shield, in fact. I use it like a microscope."

"And your hand is so intricate, like an anatomical sculpture. Is it better than the hook?"

No question of that. "Yes."

"And worth selling your father's shop to pay for them?"

That wasn't so easy to answer. David hadn't just sold the velocipedal shop and the house where he and his father had lived in the years following the Inoka Mountain disaster; by infecting himself, he'd also made it impossible to ever live among his father's people. There were days when David was absolutely sure he'd done the right thing—and he thought that Lucia hoped this was one of those days. But the unequivocal "yes" wouldn't come.

"Oh, David." Her voice gentled. "Was there anything for you in that town?"

That was easier to answer. "No."

No job. He couldn't have continued his father's work. No status, no future, and no desire to stay.

"Then you've done what your father would have wanted."

"And what he told me to do." His father's last wish. David had fulfilled that, but not his mother's.

Soon, though.

"And it was the first time you obeyed without adding an impertinent remark, I imagine." She smiled again when he laughed. "I'm sorry that I've never made certain our paths crossed before. How can ten years pass so quickly? And yet, here we are."

"Whenever I came back from an expedition, I always anticipated your letters." The only personal correspondence that David received. "They were the best part of my return."

"As were receiving yours. But there was no mention of a wife?"

With a chuckle, he shook his head. "No."

"You cannot let that girl stop you."

His former fiancée, Emily. David hadn't thought of her in a few years. "She won't," he said. "I've had no time to court a woman."

And hadn't met any women who wanted to be courted.

"You've said Dooley is married."

"And met his wife while he recuperated from bullneck fever. Will you wish that on me?"

"Lesions aren't as dashing as prosthetic eyepieces, but if it was successful for Dooley . . ." She trailed off when he laughed. As she watched him, her eyes softened, and her smile seemed to tremble. "I'm sorry. Seeing you now, like this . . . Oh, you were such a joy to us—to your father and me, after the disaster. You were so fearless, so unstoppable. Some of my very best memories are of you driving your little cart around town."

He cupped her hands between his. "Those are some of my best memories, too."

"You were so happy."

Yes. "But only you and my father believed it."

Everyone else believed he must be miserable and had simply worn a brave face. They must have also thought him a brilliant actor; David knew he wasn't.

"All those damn fools." Lucia shook her head. "And now, are you still happy?"

"I get along." Whether in a cart or on mechanical legs, nothing had been the same after his father had gone. He'd once been filled with laughter, bursting with possibility. Much of that had seemed to leave with his father's last breath.

Perhaps that exuberance had simply been youth. David enjoyed his work, was continually excited by it. He had fine friends to share meals and conversations with. Still, he sensed that something was missing . . . or unfulfilled.

Such as his promise to his mother. Was he only lacking that? He hoped so. When he spoke with the woman whose accent so closely matched hers, maybe he'd be closer to fulfilling that promise, and he'd discover whether anything else was absent in his life.

The silence between them had gone on for too long. He saw Lucia's concerned gaze, and smiled in response.

"I'm well," he reassured her.

She nodded, and seemed to hesitate before saying in a rush, "One of Paolo di Fiore's men is aboard *Phatéon*."

David's chest tightened. Paolo di Fiore—the man who'd attempted to build a machine inside the heart of an artificial mountain. In a land devastated by territorial disputes, the great device would filter the soot-laden air and clean the polluted river waters, and bring the warring peoples together in a common goal. He'd intended to bring renewed life to an entire region but had instead destroyed the mountain and half a city. His mother and his uncle had both died in the disaster, along with thousands of others. David had always counted himself fortunate that he'd only lost his legs, an arm, and part of an eye. Others hadn't been as lucky.

Di Fiore had survived, but David had never thought the man was fortunate. He'd read the newssheets following the trial; by all accounts, grief and horror had broken the man.

"I didn't realize that he'd been released from the insanitarium."

"About five years ago. Of course the newssheets reported on it, but I believe you were in Aztlán. You heard nothing of it?"

"No."

But he wouldn't have. He'd been away for almost a year during that time. Who would have mentioned it to him when he returned? His colleagues would have either assumed he already knew, or refrained from talking about it out of courtesy. Knowing now, how did he feel about the man's release?

Nothing. He'd thought anger would fill him, but there was none. Only mild curiosity. "Di Fiore's man . . . is he on the crew?"

"A passenger. I only know because Captain Vashon asked whether the reminder would be too painful. She would have arranged passage for him and his laborers aboard another ship."

Ah. So Komlan was di Fiore's man—and they were apparently building a locomotive railway in Iceland. Perhaps the man hadn't fully regained his sanity, after all.

He squeezed her hands. "I won't think anything of it. And you?"

"No." She exhaled a long, shuddering breath. "It *is* painful. Not to have him aboard, but to see . . . to *know* how it all changes with hardly more than a blink. Oh, David. Do you know I have not stepped foot off this airship in three years? Because every time I go down, I see less and less of the world I shared with your uncle, and feel everything from that time slipping away."

Then David had arrived at her door and brought the change to her. He couldn't be sorry for coming—and knew she wasn't, either—but he could be sorry that it hurt her.

"Oh, I'm a foolish old woman." She laughed through her tears when he shook his head. "Yes."

He held on to her trembling hands. "You're not."

Almost everything from that time *had* slipped away—and they were left to cling to what they could . . . or hunt down the remains.

When she nodded and smiled at him again, he gave her fingers another squeeze and leaned back. She wiped her cheeks, then lifted the watch at her breast.

"Oh, now look. You'll barely have an extra moment to ready for dinner."

David glanced down at his jacket and trousers. They were rough, but the best he had with him. "I'm ready."

"No, my dear. That was my polite way of shoving you through the door so that I can repair the damage that all of this weeping has done to my face."

Laughing, he stood. "You're still beautiful."

"And you're forgiven for lying."

She turned her cheek for his kiss, which he happily bestowed. At the door, however, he couldn't help himself. Hat in hand, he faced her.

"I spoke with another passenger on the docks, but I forgot to ask her name. Have you met any of the others aboard?"

"A woman, David?"

He heard the laugh in her voice. "Yes. Young, vibrant."

"Beautiful?"

Rather pretty, but with such lively expressions that her features appealed to him far more than any beauty's. "Yes."

Lucia nodded. "There is one such young woman aboard. She's bound for Heimaey, in the Vestmann Islands."

She spoke the name as if it should have some import, but David didn't recognize it. "Heimaey?"

"Hymen Island."

"Ah." Heat filled his cheeks. The island off the south coast of Iceland was inhabited only by women, and was where some Catholic families sent their unmanageable daughters, keeping them pure for advantageous marriages. Rumor was, however, that the women were simply left there—and since no men were allowed to set foot on the island, distasteful stories of virgin cults and women who would steal a man's virility had begun to spread. "Her family requested that she be taken to the island?"

"Accompanied by her nurse, yes. They have the stateroom on the second deck. You saw her on the docks?"

"Yes."

"I hadn't realized that she'd been allowed to leave the ship."

Perhaps she hadn't been. David hadn't seen how the trouble at the port gates had started, but he felt certain that her birth documents were false. Had she been trying to escape?

Maybe he should have helped her. "Do you know her name?"

"Maria Madalena Neves."

"Lusitanian?" That couldn't be right. She hadn't spoken Portuguese at the gates.

"I believe so. She boarded *Phatéon* in Nova Lagos—though I do recall she said that her grandmother was from one of the northern kingdoms. Sweden, perhaps."

That might be the answer, then. If she'd been unmanageable, she might have been sent away before, to family in the north. Would she know *his* mother's family? "Will she be at the captain's table?"

"She has been these past two nights. I can see to it that you have a seat next to her, if you like."

"I would."

His aunt nodded, but a hint of uncertainty weakened her smile. "David, I hate that this must be said, but I hope that she has not misled you in any way. It hasn't happened on this ship, but I've heard that some of these girls will attempt to make themselves . . . ineligible. And they'll use any man to do it."

David grinned wryly. "She must not be that desperate. I asked her to join me for dinner at the inn. She refused."

"She *refused*—?" Lucia seemed to stumble, at a loss for words.

"Ah, well. Perhaps she will be desperate enough to seduce you after we are under way." When David began to laugh, she raised her hands to suddenly pink cheeks. "Oh. No, dear. That is *not* what I mean. Only that her fate will seem more inescapable at that point."

He'd known what she meant. That didn't make the other any less true. "Is it inescapable?"

If so, he would offer to help her escape it.

"No. The Vashons receive a fee from the family, and so the captain will fly the girl to Heimaey. But on *Phatéon*'s next docking at the island, she'll receive free passage away if she doesn't want to stay."

"Do the families know this?"

"Of course not. But here is something you won't expect to hear, David: Of the fifteen girls we've taken, only two have left." With a sly grin, she patted his hand. "Perhaps this one will have reason to leave, too?"

He'd dug this hole, hadn't he? "That's not what I—"

"Hush, now. And make certain to comb your hair." She turned away from him, unpinning her own hair. "If you can tear yourself away from Miss Neves after dinner, I would like to introduce you to the crew in the wardroom. We're rather starved for new company, and so passengers are always welcome—and there is one person in particular who I think would interest you."

Only Maria Madalena Neves interested him, and if what he suspected of her origin was true, Lucia would certainly understand why. "I will see you again shortly, then."

"*Comb your hair,*" was her only reply as he left.

David's cabin was on the second deck—and, he realized after asking for directions—only a few steps from the stateroom. His heart pounded when he stopped at his door, and he stood looking down the passageway toward hers. She might emerge at any moment.

What would she think of seeing him there, after she'd run from him on the docks? What would she think of suddenly facing him across a table? Perhaps he ought to prepare her. He could look in on her, inquire that she was all right after her ordeal at the port gates.

Everything would be proper. Her nurse would be in the state-room. He wouldn't even enter the cabin, but simply make his inquiry from the passageway.

Oh, he was a fool. Knowing that, he still combed his fingers through his hair and approached her door. And if by some terrible chance, she was alone and desperate enough to invite him into her bed . . .

He wouldn't say no. Hell, he'd like to spend the entire journey there, even if only to watch her face as she talked. Even if she insisted on the dark, even if she insisted that he didn't kiss her or touch her skin more than necessary, he could still watch her face through his light-enhancing lens.

God. He shook his head. Who was desperate, here?

Maria Madalena Neves wasn't.

A few seconds after his soft knock, the door whipped open—and yes, she was absolutely beautiful in a blue silk gown that would have been more suitable in a ballroom than at a captain's table. Her hair was long, dark, and curling. Plump lips pressed into a tight line. Two spots of red appeared high on her pale cheeks.

"What do you want, senhor?"

Nothing, now. But he had to make certain. "Excuse my intrusion. You are Senhorita Neves?"

"Yes." She tossed her head, blue eyes flashing. "I know you as well, Senhor Porco. I know what you've heard about me, and why you have come crawling to my door. Do you truly think I could ever be so wretched that I would lower myself enough to let you touch me, pig?"

She stepped back. The door slammed, shuddering against the jamb. David stared at the wood for a long moment, then pushed his fingers through his hair again, mildly surprised that her ire hadn't burned it away.

So that hadn't been her. Damn.

He knocked at Lucia's door. Powder puff in hand, she opened it, looking up at him curiously. "David?"

"Don't sit me next to Miss Neves," he said. "The woman I met had short black hair and an enormous red skirt over yellow trousers. Do you know her?"

"Yes." Lucia gave a merry laugh, nodding. "Yes, I know her. That is Annika Fridasdottir. I meant to introduce you to her tonight."

Annika. Perfect. "Who is she?"

"Oh, David. I have been trying to discover the answer to that mystery for almost four years." She batted his nose with the puff. "We'll see if you do any better than I have."

Chapter Three

When her stomach rumbled a hungry complaint half an hour before supper, Annika wished that she'd taken the stranger up on his offer. She lay facedown in her bunk instead, with a hollow belly and a pillow over her head, trying to sneak in a few minutes of sleep.

Sleep wouldn't come. Her mind spun out waking dreams, refusing to rest.

What sort of supper would they have eaten? For a week, she'd been craving roasted mutton; surely the inn would have served that. And a thick, salty gravy that she could sop up with crusty bread. She could have devoured an entire haunch and still had room to lick her fingers after.

Oh, and she had to stop imagining this before she drooled into her mattress. It still faintly smelled of the sweet straw beneath the cotton cover, and nothing soured a bed as quickly as moisture seeping into the stuffing. She would dream of the stranger, instead, and of what his answers to all of her queries might have been.

Though she still couldn't imagine a good reason to chase after volcanoes. To study them, he'd said. What was there to study that couldn't be viewed from afar? They shook the earth and terrified the sheep and ponies. They spewed ash that turned the daytime sky to gray and the nights to red. They poured lava down their snowy sides, sending up billowing steam that could be seen for miles, melting ice into rivers of mud that destroyed everything in its path. Everyone in Hannasvik knew to keep their distance from an eruption.

So there must be another purpose. Annika had once imagined herself descending into the mouth of a volcano—but she had also been five years of age and her ears still ringing with tales of dragons who hoarded their gold in mountain caves.

Perhaps that was what the man sought. Not dragons, because no sensible person believed in them, but glory. That seemed almost as foolish as searching for a dragon's hoard, but perhaps the stranger was like Sigurd, who'd been manipulated by Reginn to carry out that dwarf's revenge upon his dragon brother. Perhaps he'd been led to believe glory could be found in such pursuits.

She didn't like to think that her rescuer could be so easily manipulated, however. She didn't like to think of him resembling Sigurd the Deceiver at all. She preferred her heroes to resemble Brunhild, who took her bloody revenge upon the Deceiver after he'd misled and taken advantage of her.

Annika should have been as bold as Brunhild, too.

With a sigh, she turned over and stared up at the bottom of the shadowed bunk overhead. Now she doubly regretted refusing his invitation to supper. She'd never know why he ran after volcanoes. She'd never know whether her instincts had been correct and if he *had* wanted something from her other than company. Maybe he'd only wanted to know more about her, as he'd said—or had wanted to share her bed. That would have been easy enough to refuse.

Unless she hadn't refused.

That was difficult to imagine, too, though she tried. She had the memory of kisses to draw from, a caress of her breasts. Her own explorations had taught her the brief ecstasy of release. But to lie with someone, to fully give herself over to that person . . . she would need to feel more than those things. She would need to know the rending need and longing that her mother had told her came hand in hand with passionate love, as if her guts had been riveted together and the only way to ease the pain was being with that person. Annika had no memory of such emotions to rely upon as she dreamed.

The rest was just physical pleasure, and she could do that for herself.

Not here, though. Few places on an airship offered enough privacy to attempt it, so it did her no good to imagine bedding the stranger. She'd only end up frustrated.

With effort, she pushed those thoughts away. Daydreaming did her no good, either. It never had. In Hannasvik, she'd never been responsible for tending the sheep, but she'd still earned the name Annika the Shepherdess—because she was always gathering wool.

Sleep would have served her better, but there was no hope for it now. The cabin door squeaked open, followed by the tread of boots across the boards and the scratch of a spark lighter at the washstand. The brass lamp's flickering flame danced across the second mate's fair cheeks and glinted gold in her chestnut hair. Elena wound the oil pump and the wavering glow from the burner softened, steadied.

Elena's index finger marked her spot between the pages of a closed book—apparently she'd abandoned the wardroom to enjoy a few more minutes of reading here before her watch began. Across the narrow aisle, the other two bunks were empty. No surprise that Marguerite was gone; the steward's assistant reported to the kitchen before breakfast and would be running ragged through supper, but was the only one of the four women who ever got a full night's sleep. Mary Chandler ought to have been in the upper bunk, catching rest while the first engineer was on watch. No doubt Annika would hear an earful from her later, going on and on about how tired she was.

Glad that it was Elena who'd come in, Annika rolled up on her side and propped her chin on her fist. She liked Marguerite well enough, but her conversations with the older woman never seemed to range beyond food and the weather. Mary preferred to gossip, which was fascinating when Annika knew the person under discussion and unbearable when she didn't. Since Mary had recently received letters from her family in Manhattan City, Annika knew from experience that it would run to unbearable over the next few days.

She never tired of Elena's company, however—and a good thing, too, given that they'd shared a cabin for almost four years. Annika had joined *Phatéon*'s crew as the third engineer shortly after Elena had become the third mate. Their friendship had become fixed in the first months, with Elena spending every free moment teaching Annika to speak French and serving as her guide to the New World.

The loneliness of leaving home had been easier to bear with Elena—and initially, Annika had hoped that friendship might become more. But the passionate longing she dreamed of never developed and her guts never felt riveted, no matter how much Annika would have welcomed it at the time.

Perhaps it was for the best, though. Like most New Worlders, Elena probably wouldn't have welcomed any romantic advances—and if found out, Annika would have lost her position on the airship . . . or worse, if she was reported to anyone other than the captain.

In any case, as the years had passed, Annika had grown to value Elena's friendship more. Love could wait until after she found Källa—if it ever came at all.

Elena turned away from the washstand and stopped abruptly, spotting Annika. "Oh!" Apology tugged her lips into a grimace. "I didn't mean to wake you. They started bringing dinner into the wardroom, and with the jolting, I couldn't bear the smell."

Her friend did appear a bit bald around the beak. Annika hadn't even noticed the airship's rough rocking, or that the storm had come in. Yet another reason to stop herself from daydreaming. "I wasn't sleeping."

"How could anyone in this? I hope we cast off soon. The cargo's almost all up and most of the crew aboard; we're just waiting for the mail, and of course the post delivery is late. Did you just come back from the city?"

"A little while ago."

"Have you spoken with the chief yet?"

Chief Leroux, the head engineer. Annika hadn't seen him since her return. "Why? Did he send for me while I was out?"

"And got Mary, instead. She was steaming mad, too, having to take García's watch."

The first engineer ought to have been on duty now, not Mary. "Why did she have to?"

"Because García's off ship. His wife came to visit. Five minutes later, he turned in his papers and decided to stay in Castile." Elena's arched brows and gleeful tone told Annika that she wouldn't like whatever her friend had to say next. "And that makes *you* the first engineer."

Oh, blast. Annika hoped not. García had twice as many duties as she did.

Elena laughed at her expression. "Look at you. Anyone else would be happy to take another step closer to a chief's ticket. I'd be dancing for joy if I was dumped into the first mate's position like this—and wouldn't stop pushing until I was master of a ship."

Yes, but Annika wasn't here to make a career out of it. "Leroux will bring someone else aboard as first. Neither Mary nor I know the electric generators well."

"You could learn."

That was Elena's answer to everything. "I'd rather spend my time sewing than studying schematics."

Elena cast a critical look at Annika's voluminous crimson skirt. "You *could* use the practice."

Annika gasped and narrowed her eyes at the other woman, but wasn't the least bit upset. Elena often wore the less elaborate pieces that Annika had given her. Her skill with a needle wasn't in question; her taste was. Annika loved her clothes, however—and considering that her mother had often said the same of Annika's penchant for bright colors and ribbons, the teasing simply felt like home.

"Say that again the next time you rip out the seat of your trousers and come looking for me to fix it."

"And be pricked in the derriere for my honesty? I'll hold my tongue until you're done." With a grin, Elena climbed the short ladder to her bunk. "Was there any word from your sister?"

Annika shook her head. In four years, there hadn't been a response, though she'd regularly placed personal advertisements in every newssheet from Sweden to Far Maghreb. She'd have to soon find a different ship, a different route. *Phatéon* traveled from the tip of the southern American continent to the Scandinavian kingdoms, England, and Ireland, but avoided the more dangerous waters near the Ivory Market in Africa and the smugglers' havens of Australia. Annika didn't think that Källa would have ventured so close to Horde territory, but her sister had been infected with nanoagents since she was young. Even if she'd managed to secure fake letters of origin, perhaps she hadn't been able to find a place in the New World—and though Källa could have made a home in the countries around the North Sea, temper might have driven her as far from Iceland as she could go.

Annika didn't want to leave *Phatéon* any more than she'd wanted to leave Hannasvik. Finding her sister was more important than those wants, however.

But until she left, her job needed to be done. With a sigh, she scooted to the edge of the bed. "I'd best find the chief, then."

On the third deck, she pounded on Leroux's door, but the old engineering chief wasn't in his cabin. Perhaps the engine deck. As she turned toward the companionway, the ship's physician came out of her quarters. Lucia Kentewess carried a bottle of wine and wore a bright smile—a lovely look for the woman, whose smiles were usually tinged with melancholy.

Annika liked Lucia very well, and preferred her company to everyone's except Elena's, but she suspected that the doctor sought her out for conversation in the wardroom because she viewed Annika as something of an amusing oddity. Which Annika supposed she was, and so didn't mind the woman's attention. The New Worlders were often amusing oddities, too.

"Annika! Is the chief in?"

"No. I'm looking for him myself."

"Ah, well. I shall give this to him after dinner, then." The doctor glanced at Annika's skirts, then swayed as a gust of wind jerked the ship around by the mooring tether. "You aren't on duty?"

"I'm on the eight to twelve today." Unless García's leaving would change that, as well.

"Oh, that is perfect. My nephew, David, is aboard. If we can get away from the captain's supper, I'd love to introduce you."

So that explained the bright smile. His aunt had spoken of her nephew before, and had once shown Annika a ferrotype photograph of a grinning boy sitting in a small steam-powered cart, wearing a hook on his arm and his trousers tucked around missing knees. A tall native man and Lucia had stood on either side of him. If Lucia hadn't told her what had happened to the boy's mother and her own husband, Annika would have assumed that it was a portrait of a happy family, not one torn apart by a disaster.

Annika vaguely recalled that he had traveled since then, but she better remembered Lucia's pride when she'd spoken of him than any specific stories. David Kentewess likely wouldn't find Annika as interesting as his aunt seemed to, but she didn't mind meeting him, especially if it added to the new joy in Lucia's smile.

"I should be in the wardroom unless there is a change to my watch schedule. García left *Phatéon*, so I'm on my way to discover that now."

"Oh, of course. Go on, then."

Annika did, gathering her skirts at her knees to descend the ladder. The distant *thud* of the closing cargo doors echoed up the companionway. They were done with the loading, then, and might soon be under way. *Phatéon* couldn't carry as much weight as a sailing ship, but was often stuffed to the deckheads with perishables and mail. On this run, they carried laborers to Smoke Cove; crates of dry goods and foodstuffs bound for the island of Heimaey filled the rest of the cargo hold, and mail drops would be made at a few coastal communities in between.

Annika didn't participate in any of the loading or unloading. Her job was simply to make certain that *Phatéon* arrived at her destination by tending the furnace and engines at the heart of the ship.

She caught sight of the chief outside the engine room, his white hair easy to spot even in the dim passageway. Almost seventy, his face deeply lined and tall, bony frame stiff, he had difficulty going up and down the ladders to this deck. He usually sent instructions and messages from his quarters, relaying them through García.

"Fridasdottor! There you are, girl!" His voice boomed down the corridor. Leroux always shouted—as one had to do in this part of the ship when the engines were engaged. They were silent now, but he still yelled. Too many years in an engine room had destroyed his hearing.

"Chief Leroux!" she shouted back. "I've heard that García turned in his papers!"

"That boy did, and ran off." Leroux didn't care that García

was a forty-year-old man, just as it didn't matter that Annika wasn't a girl any longer. "You'll be acting as my first on this run."

"Yes, monsieur."

"Eh?"

"Yes, monsieur!"

Thin lips pursing, he gave her a considering look. "I've never had a girl as first."

Annika smiled in response. Before Leroux, she'd never taken orders from a man, either.

His eyes narrowed. "Always smiling, you are. We'll look over that generator together tomorrow. Don't think I haven't noticed how you've avoided learning about it."

That erased her smile. "Yes, monsieur."

"The captain doesn't want to take on any new men until we're back to Port-au-Prince. Until then, you'll be a two-section watch and splitting the third's duties with Chandler. As first, you'll decide how to split them. Don't take the worst jobs for yourself."

Maintaining the privy pipes and flushing systems. "I won't, monsieur."

"All right. You know what you ought to be doing now?"

What would García typically be working on before they left port? "I need to perform the engine checks before we fire her up again, and make certain the balloon warmers are in order."

Leroux nodded. "We don't want that envelope deflating the moment we fly into arctic weather."

And didn't want a spark from a badly maintained warmer igniting the hydrogen. "Yes, monsieur."

"Then get to it, girl." With that, he was off, his walking stick thudding against the boards.

Even though Mary had opened the portholes, the engine room was stifling. Humid air continually rose through the open hatch in the deck floor that allowed for easy access to the furnace and boilers on the deck below, the vapors condensing on the pipes and propeller shafts overhead. A rhythmic rasp from the boiler room told her that Mary was stoking the furnace, which was never allowed to go out. The copper pipes carried heated water through the ship, warming the cabins; another bank of brass pipes carried sound from the quarterdeck, for commands shouted throughout the ship. Usually the engine was too loud for the stokers to hear those orders, so they relied upon the telegraph dial instead. The setting on its face matched the dial on the captain's bridge, allowing Vashon to order them back or ahead under partial or full steam. Currently, the indicator arrow pointed to STOP.

The great steam engine filled most of the room, a hulking beast fabricated from iron and ingenuity. She lay sleeping now, her oiled pistons that drove the propellers at rest, the turbines quiet rather than screaming. Beautiful, but Annika liked her best when she woke and worked.

The scraping from below ceased. Mary climbed up out of the furnace room a moment later, the freckles of her hands and face concealed by a light dusting of coal. A blue paisley scarf covered vibrant red hair, the same shade that Annika remembered her mother's had been before gray had dulled it. Since her mother had been stolen as a young girl from a Horde crèche in England, however, no relation likely existed between her mother and the third engineer despite that resemblance. Annika had a better chance of being a blood relation to the woman. Only a few years older than Annika, Mary had also been born in Manhattan City; unlike Annika, however, she hadn't been living alone on the streets and taken by a woman from Iceland.

Mary also spoke English—not the sort that Annika had grown up hearing, or the sort that she'd heard on her visits to England, but she enjoyed speaking with someone without having to first think of every word.

Annika still had to watch everything she said, however, or find that Mary spread it to everyone aboard.

With a damp cotton rag, Mary wiped her face, scrubbed her bare arms. "So you've heard about García turning in his papers?"

Annika nodded, moving to the engineer's station, where the repair dockets and manuals were neatly stacked. García would have left the engine checklist here. He'd been so familiar with the process that he wouldn't need to use it, but Annika did.

"I'm wagering that his wife didn't like him going from port to port." Mary hooked the rag into the waist of her trousers. "She'd rather keep him at home."

"Perhaps," Annika said, but thought that Mary was only telling her own truth, not García's. Annika had never seen evidence that the first engineer took any lovers, but Mary had lain with many other men than her husband. Considering how devoted García had been to his wife, and how the rioting in Castile worried him, Annika thought he'd left because he couldn't bear to leave her alone any longer.

But Mary wouldn't have assumed that. People never believed of others what they couldn't imagine of themselves.

The other woman sniffed, as if disappointed that Annika didn't have any more to add. "Well, that's it for him, then. Did you receive word from your sister?"

"No."

Mary pursed her lips—probably to stop herself from saying, "Of course."

Annika had to stop her own laugh in response to that expression. She knew what Mary suspected: that Annika wasn't really looking for her sister, anyway. Mary believed that she was Liberé, a descendant of the Africans who'd fled across the ocean to escape the Horde. According to the other woman, Annika disguised her accent and pretended to hail from Scandinavia so that Captain Vashon wouldn't discover that an enemy of the French worked in her engine room.

Mary wasn't completely wrong; her papers were faked. But Annika wasn't Liberé.

Perhaps she had been, once. Annika didn't know who her blood parents were. A warm, dim memory of a woman's soft voice and tight arms made her think that she'd been orphaned rather than abandoned, but she couldn't be certain. She only knew that at two or three years of age, she'd been found wandering the streets of Manhattan City, hungry and dressed in rags. Now she was one of the Huldrene, the hidden women of Hannasvik. That mattered more to Annika than blood ever could.

She found the checklist at the bottom of the stack. All menial tasks, but they would take her at least forty-five minutes. Do them now or later?

Probably best to do them now. Mary wasn't supposed to have been on duty, and a little more than two hours still remained until first watch. They both needed to eat—and as acting first, Annika decided who would go now.

"You run up to supper, then." Her belly rumbled at the same time she spoke, as if to protest the choice she made. "I'll work through this list while you eat, then we'll start our rotation at first watch—and we'll use the same dogged watch schedule as the deck crew so that we'll both get our suppers in on equal time. Make certain to sleep while you can."

Dismay filled Mary's voice. "So we're just the two of us?"

"Until we return to Port-au-Prince." Only a month, but they'd be exhausted by the end of it. Four hours on duty, then four hours rest, with only a little variation at the two-hour dog watch. At full steam, they'd be stoking the furnace until they were all but dead on their feet. "I'll ask the chief if he can find a boy to help shovel."

"That new Black Irish boy was eyeing a stoker's apron."

"Who?"

"Sula, I think they called him. One of James's boys."

Ah, one of the children who served the senior aviators and learned the ropes. If he was hoping to secure an engineer's license later, they might as well bring him down here now. "All right. I'll suggest him to the chief, and if we're lucky, the deck can spare him. Either way, I'll take the first's duties, you've got the second's, and we'll share the third's."

Mary was the third now. Expression hopeful, she asked, "Who will have the privy pipes?"

"You."

Her face fell. "Hornblow over it all."

Was *that* English? Whatever she meant by "hornblow," it probably wasn't the sort of noise that Annika associated with the word. "What does that mean?"

"Annika." Her name was a remonstration. So it must be something vulgar, then. Something she'd have been fined for saying in Manhattan City. When Annika only looked at her, waiting, Mary's cheeks reddened. She leaned closer and said under her breath, "*Poop.*"

Well, yes. Annika supposed that it was.

Annika infinitely preferred sewing to studying. It seemed ridiculous, as those two tasks were almost the same. Both required her to sit in the corner of the wardroom, in the armchair near the brightest lamp, yet she still seemed to squint as often over small print as she did a seam. With enough time, bending over a page or a garment stiffened her neck and made her wish for one of the more comfortable chairs beside the bookshelves, or a seat at the game table, where the players stretched while moving a mark or tossing a card, rather than sitting in one attitude for an eternity.

When she sewed, however, none of that discomfort seemed to matter. Studying, she had to force herself to focus, or be easily distracted by everyone else's activities.

She turned the page of the generator manual, and stifled a sigh as another diagram introduced a host of new words. She already understood how the electrical generator worked, but didn't know the French terms for most of the components. As much as she disliked taking the time to learn them, however—an armature coil and a *bobinage d'induit* performed exactly the same function, no matter what she called the thing—she would dislike appearing completely ignorant in front of the chief even more.

Luckily, many of the words were similar, because she wouldn't have much time to look over them. Less than an hour remained until first watch began.

It was still more time than Annika might have spent if Doctor Kentewess hadn't asked whether she'd be in the wardroom after supper. If not for that—and if Elena hadn't been clinging to a bucket when Annika had returned to their cabin to dress for dinner—Annika might have taken the advice she'd given to Mary and attempted to sleep again.

If she didn't fall asleep here. How long had she been looking at this diagram? And the room was so warm. Fighting a yawn, she blinked quickly, trying to concentrate. Her final blink turned into a long, slow nod with her eyes closed.

Voices in the passageway shook her out of it—the doctor's voice among them. Oh, good. She gladly closed the manual and looked to the door.

A young man with a pointed reddish beard entered. Oh, she'd seen him before—but where? The older man behind him appeared just as familiar, though she recalled him laughing. Had it been on the docks? That seemed right. He'd worn an overcoat and an enormous hat, and he'd been laughing as she and her rescuer walked past their steamcoach . . .

Oh.

Her stomach dropped through the seat of her chair. She knew who the third man would be, but couldn't account for the leap of her pulse upon seeing him. His presence surprised her, yes. But why the sudden impulse to flee?

Before his long legs carried him a full step through the door, his gaze had scanned the wardroom and locked on hers. She heard the doctor introducing the three to the navigator and the players at the game table, but Annika had already realized who he must be: David Kentewess. Not in a little cart at all—and no longer a boy.

He was still looking at her. Just *watching* her from across the length of the room, his face unreadable and the intensity of his gaze like a strong grip that prevented her from glancing away. She stared back, heart slamming against her ribs. Oh, but surely there was no need for this panic. The impression she'd had before—of him wanting something from her, that he would follow her until he got it—had just been her imagination . . . hadn't it? What could Lucia's nephew want from her? He must be as surprised as Annika was.

But, no. Why would he be surprised? He'd escorted her to *Phatéon*'s mooring station . . . and hadn't said a word that he would soon be traveling aboard the same airship. Why refrain from telling her? Had his silence been some New World courtesy that she didn't understand? Or had he deliberately withheld the information?

Perhaps she would never know. But at least now she could ask why he chased volcanoes.

He looked away when the men at the game table stood and extended their hands to his companions. Oh, *finally*. Annika took a moment to steady her nerves and to study him—a study that was far more interesting that a schematic had been. His legs were likely the same sort of skeletal prosthetics as his hand; unfortunately, his wool trousers concealed their design. Dinner gloves hid his hands now, too—but the absence of the garments he'd removed since she'd last seen him revealed more.

Without his brimmed hat, no shadows obscured his features. More ragged scars cut through the hairline at his left temple and bisected the eyebrow over his gleaming lens apparatus. His black hair was combed straight back from a broad forehead and skimmed the bottom edge of his collar. The overcoat he'd worn on the docks added bulk he didn't actually carry—as did his jacket now. The heavy tweed fit him horribly. His shoulders were wide, his torso tapering to lean hips, but his clothes might as well have been cut to fit a box. She hoped he had not paid much money for them.

Perhaps he would soon win enough for a new jacket, though. At the game table, the first mate gestured to the patolli board, inviting Lucia and the passengers to join them. The older man responded eagerly, friendly avarice in his tone. *Oh.* Annika glanced down at the generator manual, surprised by her disappointment. A moment ago, she'd wanted to escape. Now she wished that there was enough time before first watch to join the game.

She looked up and found David Kentewess's gaze on her again. A moment later, the older man's eyes lighted on her. He blinked and turned to the doctor, then to her nephew. Annika couldn't hear what he said, but she saw Lucia's quick glance in Annika's direction. After a word with those settling in around the game table, the doctor started across the wardroom.

Kentewess left the others and accompanied her. Standing, Annika forced herself to look away from him and greeted his aunt, who responded with a curious arch of her brows.

"Mr. Dooley wanted to know whether you'd had any additional trouble from the port officers. I wasn't aware that you'd had any trouble at all. Is everything well?"

"Oh, yes. I was detained at the port gates. Your nephew bravely rescued me."

"*Rescued* you? Why, he mentioned nothing of it."

When his aunt slanted him an inquiring glance, Kentewess flushed. "It was nothing, Aunt Lucia. Only a miscommunication."

"Nothing to you, perhaps," Annika said. "But considering what might have happened if that miscommunication hadn't been resolved, it meant everything to me."

He seemed to still, holding her gaze. "Did it?"

"Perhaps not *everything*," she had to admit, and looked to

Lucia. "He's right to question me. Only minutes after he risked himself to confront the port officer, I rejected his company."

Oh, she must have exposed her lack of proper sensibilities again. Lucia's mouth opened, but she seemed at a loss for words. With wide eyes, the woman looked to her nephew, who didn't appear taken aback.

"I told her that you did," he said to Annika. "But at the time, she thought I spoke of someone else."

And Lucia likely felt awkward now for asking to introduce them. Well, there was no reason for that. "I began wishing that I hadn't rejected your offer shortly after I boarded—and I wished it all the more after I saw what Cook sent up for our supper."

The right corner of his mouth lifted. "Will you accept the company now?"

"I will be happy to." Though only one other seat had been grouped in this corner. Not enough for the three of them. "Give me one moment to drag the extra chair over from the library—"

"I'll do it," he said before she could take a step.

Lucia stopped them both with a lift of her hand. "David, you go ahead and sit, dear. I intend to win a round at the table."

She left them with a smile and swish of her skirts. Kentewess glanced at Annika's chair, then to the one on her right—reluctantly, it seemed, as if he'd have rather chosen her seat. He sat after she did, his back ramrod straight. The light from the lamp on the small table between them glinted off the thin steel casing of his eyepiece and reflected in the lens. Not speaking, he simply looked at her.

His obvious discomfort sparked her own. Suddenly uncertain, Annika searched for something to say, and could only come up with, "Thank you. Again."

"You shouldn't. I've taken advantage of your gratitude, after all."

"You haven't forced me to eat supper with you."

"My goal wasn't to eat, but to remain in your company."

Oh, yes. So that he could know her better. "Well, you are in

luck. You see the two things that compose almost all of my life now."
She gestured to her dress, then to the generator manual. "Making
whatever sort of clothing takes my fancy, and those schematics."

"You sewed that one?"

"Yes." She touched the high neck and the stiff, pleated lace ruff.
"I'm told that such finery is only for nobility and royalty. But I like
the look of it so well, I can't resist making my own. Do you mistake
me for a queen?"

He hesitated, as if deciding whether to answer diplomatically.
When he chose honesty, she liked him all the better for it.

"No," he said.

"Then no harm is done. If someone ever did mistake an engine
stoker for a noble, then his idiocy will cause him more problems
than my ruff ever could. Why do you wear gloves now? No one else
in your party did."

Though his expression didn't change, the fingers of his left hand
curled slightly. "I never know how people will react to the prosthetic. Tonight, at least, I didn't want to ruin my host's dinner."

"People fear it?"

"Some do."

"Do you take off your eyepiece, too?"

But of course he couldn't. She could see now that it was also
grafted to him, a seamless meld of flesh and steel.

That brief, one-sided smile flashed again. "No."

"So they must realize that a metal hand might be there, despite
the glove. In fact, they might think that both of your hands are
metal."

"Yes."

Ah. So he was saving idiots from themselves. "I'm usually more
afraid of what I can't see, because that threat is the unexpected
one. Do you like being feared? It seems a powerful ability to make
someone quake in your presence without any action on your part."

"It's better than pity."

"What isn't?" Pity only served the person who felt it; generosity better served the person who needed it. "I'd prefer everyone to fear me. Though that must be alienating."

The port officer hadn't been able to send him away fast enough. She assumed that others did, too. They likely used varying degrees of politeness to do it, but the effect would be the same.

"It can be, yes." His admission held no self-pity, however; he sounded baffled. "You don't fear them, though. Have you seen many like this in Norway?"

"Oh, yes." No, not truly. Prosthetics were common enough in the Scandinavian port cities, and the kingdoms allowed people infected with nanoagents to settle there, but her familiarity came from home.

With one exception, all of the women who'd founded Hannas-vik had been infected, and their bodies had undergone the Horde's modifications. Though the same augmentation was rare among the women now, many were infected—and still others needed their own prosthetics after accidents or wild dog attacks.

None were as brilliantly made as Kentewess's, however. His devices would have inspired envy in her village.

Realizing that he was watching her, waiting for more, she added, "And *Phatéon* has been to England several times, of course."

"Of course."

A probing look accompanied that easy reply. Annika paused. The sense of unease that had come over her on the docks had returned—the certainty that he wanted something from her.

Perhaps she was mistaken. Still, it wouldn't hurt to direct the conversation away from her fabricated past. "I'm sorry to say that those two things are truly all there is to know about me. Our supper would have been a short one."

"No." He leaned toward her slightly, bracing his elbow on the arm of the chair—finally settling in. "I'd still want to know more."

"It would have been a boring supper, then. I'm already intimately familiar with the topic."

"Then I'd have asked you to talk about yourself until I was bored, too—though I doubt I would have ever been."

Oh, but she liked his smile. And as unsettling as that intense focus was, Annika enjoyed how direct he was and how his gaze never wavered. She couldn't fathom why he was intent on discovering more—perhaps it was just politeness and a desire to please his aunt—but his attention flattered her. Usually the passengers who visited the wardroom took one glance at Annika's clothes and decided she was either absurd or simpleminded. It felt absolutely lovely that someone thought she might be fascinating, instead.

But she was more interested in him. "I think we should talk about you. Why volcanoes? Do you travel often? Have you ever had to fight zombies as you climbed to a mountain peak? Oh, it all begins to sound like an Archimedes Fox adventure."

"With fewer villains?" His warm, quiet laugh drew her in. "It is nothing so exciting—and I'm also familiar with this topic. We should talk about everyone else in this room instead."

He was joking, but it sounded like a fine idea to Annika. No doubt whatever he shared of his companions would also tell her more about him. And she enjoyed listening to him—the rhythm of his words sounded like a pony at a trot. Duh*dum*duh*dum*. His speech was much more pleasant than riding at that pace, however, with no sense of being bounced around.

"All right, I will begin." She leaned in, lowering her voice. "Did you see the young brown-haired man sitting at the chair beside the bookshelf?"

He didn't look away from her. "Yes."

"That is Mr. Otto, the navigator. While he sits, he listens to everyone talk—he listens to your friends now—but rarely speaks on his own. He pines for a woman instead, carving tiny flowers into that whalebone busk. Since I have been aboard, he has carved over a dozen of them."

"For one woman, or for many?"

"I don't know. I don't even know if he has met one yet or merely waits for love to come along. But hopefully she will wear a corset, or that busk will be only good to pry open another crate of whisky. He's rather fond of that, too. And if you ever have trouble sleeping, ask him whether a homolographic projection is superior to a sinusoidal projection, and you will nod off in minutes."

"Map projections? Goltzius might engage him in that debate."

One of his companions. "Is he the younger or the older?"

"Younger."

"And?"

"I believe he fell in love with Miss Neves the moment she sat at the captain's table."

"I can't blame him." Though Annika doubted it was love. "I've seen her."

"So have I." He seemed about to say something more, then shook his head. "Goltzius also prefers coffee to tea."

"Who does not?"

"Me."

"Oh." She sat back. "I must end our acquaintance now."

This time, he didn't just offer the one-sided smile. He grinned in full, and Annika's delight warmed her from head to toe. "Will you absolve me of my sin if I tell you that I never drink it? On an expedition, the weight of every item is carefully considered, and I was overruled by a two-to-one vote. So our sleds will carry coffee."

"Then your abominable taste is forgiven."

"You said that as well as a queen." He glanced at her neck. "Goltzius's cousin could wear that ruff without question. His is one of the great Dutch families that settled early in Johannesland."

"Which one?"

"They are the Great Dukes of Erie, now. I don't know what they were before." He paused, watching her face. "What is it?"

She shook her head. How could she tell him that his friend was a relation to the man that Hanna and the Englishwomen had killed to secure their freedom? A prince's son—and the reason they'd fled to Iceland.

That had happened more than a century ago. The women of Hannasvik no longer had reason to fear the repercussions of that murder . . . but they had other reasons to stay hidden now.

So Annika had reasons to keep that secret. In response to his concern, she shook her head.

"Nothing. Something that I ate disagrees with me." Judging by his stifled laugh, that wasn't the sort of admission one made. Ah, well. He already knew that she often flung propriety around by the nose. "Please, go on. Why is such a lofty person traveling with you now? What kind of expedition are you on?"

"We plan to make a survey of Iceland. Goltzius is our botanist."

"*All* of Iceland?"

"Yes." The glow of the lamp reflected in the dark, flat lens of his eyepiece, creating the illusion of depth—and making his gaze seem all the more penetrating. "That upsets you?"

"No," she lied. "It is just dangerous, yes? The wild dogs. And . . . and . . ." Oh, what else? What else would he *believe*? "And the boiling mudpots!"

"I intend to study the mudpots, and we're prepared for the dogs. Have you been to the island?"

"Only where *Phatéon* has been: the ports at Smoke Cove and Höfn, and a village on the southern rim. But I have heard of people tumbling into the mud and unable to pull themselves out while they are cooked alive—and of others torn apart by the damned stinking dogs. What purpose does your survey serve?"

"Primarily, to measure the current volcanic activity and to

determine the effects of the fissure eruptions on the soil and plant growth. We're only there to record our observations."

"Then you'll leave?"

"We will," he said, but her relief was short-lived. "The society that funded us always has another goal in mind beyond scientific pursuit, however—and it isn't difficult to imagine what they hope to find now. The Dutch had claims on the island before it was transformed into the northern defense against a Horde naval fleet. They probably hope to settle there again."

Annika pressed a hand to her roiling stomach. Her supper was genuinely disagreeing with her now. "Unless your survey shows that the island can't support a population?"

"Yes."

It could. Perhaps the land wasn't as rich as in Johannesland, but with effort, a living could be scraped out of the soil and drawn from the ocean.

How horrible that a relative of the murdered prince would determine the fate of Hannasvik—and that killing him to prevent it would do no good. The society would likely just send another expedition. Even more horrible, he was a *scientist*. Superstition and fear had long protected Annika's people, but those stories would not stand up to rigorous observation.

She would have to warn her village. If the women knew these three men were coming, perhaps they would have time to hide. Or perhaps *something* could be done to persuade the men that Iceland still wasn't habitable.

Perhaps if her people were very lucky, there would soon be another terrible eruption.

"Now our survey makes you smile?" Kentewess asked, watching her face.

Annika shook her head. "I just had a ridiculous thought. Too ridiculous to share. You were telling me about your companion?"

"I don't have much more to say. I haven't known him long."

"You're very bad at this."

At gossiping about Goltzius, that was. He'd shared much more important information about the expedition, however, so Annika didn't mind at all.

"I am," he agreed easily. "It is your turn again—and the crew in this room outnumbers our group. You should tell me about two of them for every one of mine."

"All right." She looked to the game table. "The older man with the gray hair and the jacket that won't buckle over his stomach is Monsieur Collin, the purser. He likes to read French poetry aloud, and is convinced that Josephine Ayres is a man, because no woman could have such subtlety of mind and rhyme."

"Do you argue with him?"

"Oh, no. His opinion is too obviously stupid, and I become too frustrated. Your aunt often engages him, though, and she is better equipped to use other poets as evidence. But I think he *wants* to believe it, and nothing would persuade him otherwise, even if Ayres appeared in front of him."

"He sounds similar to many scientists I know."

"Truly?" Annika laughed when he nodded.

"When we decide to bore each other with stories about ourselves, I'll tell you of the time an astronomer once challenged me to a duel."

"A duel? Why?"

Smiling, he shook his head.

"Oh, you are cruel. All right, then." She glanced at Collin again. "He cheats when he plays patolli—but only if he knows you well, and only in ways that will get him caught. For example, he'll hide a piece in his trousers and when he stands up, it will fall onto the floor. Half the fun of playing with him is trying to guess when he will take the piece and where he'll hide it. Once, I found it on my lap. I didn't feel a thing when he put it there."

His brows rose. "And this is the ship's purser?"

"Yes. Despite his opinions of poetry, however, I don't think he's foolish enough to do the same with Captain Vashon's money."

"Not when he'd hang for it."

"And not when so many would be eager to see it." On her first visit beyond a city's port gates, she'd seen men hanged for much, much less—with the spectators just as willing to watch. But that memory made her stomach churn, so she pushed it away and carried on. "The woman talking to your aunt is the steward, and married to Collin. She couldn't form one of Ayres rhymes, I'm sorry to say."

"So he has reason to believe that women can't."

Her withering stare was met with his deep laugh, attracting the notice of the navigator, the first mate, and Kentewess's companions. Oh, she didn't want to share him with the others yet. She leaned in closer, turning her body as far toward him as the chair would allow, and was pleased when he did the same. Only someone more socially inept than Annika would interrupt them now—and as no one in the room fit that description, they would be left alone.

"Madame Collin's voice is also more beautiful than any other I've ever heard. When we are all pushed into the chapel on Sunday morning, I only pretend to sing so that I can listen to her." Also because she didn't know any of the hymns, but that was beside the point. If she'd known them, she would have still listened to the woman. "She likes sunrises better than sunsets—she is always on deck shortly after dawn, even in the rain, but I've never seen her on deck to watch the sun go down. She likes to drop rosewater onto her hair. She always smells lovely, which is well appreciated on a ship."

"Is it? I should splash a bit over myself."

Annika drew a long breath. If he had an odor, she couldn't detect it. With some of the crew, across the room wouldn't be far enough. "You smell all right, at least from this distance."

He didn't smile as she expected. His posture stiffened slightly, his gloved fingers curling against his palms. After an endless moment, he finally answered. "From this distance, you do, too."

She couldn't smile, either. Her chest tightened, her breath feeling heavy and quick all at once. Suddenly aware of the inches separating them, she wanted to lean closer—close enough that she *could* scent his hair, his skin. Would he smell like soap, smoke, sweat? Something completely unexpected?

Even she couldn't breach propriety so blatantly, though. With effort, she forced herself to stop imagining her face against his bare skin.

Perhaps it would be easier if he stopped looking at her mouth. Her heart pounded, and she waited, *waited* for him to look up. How could she move her lips when he watched her like that? Oh, but she had to try.

"So that is Madame Collin," she said in a rush. Annika hoped that she had given him enough; she could barely remember what she'd said about the woman. "And now your man. Dooley, I think your aunt called him? Have you known him for very long?"

His gaze finally lifted to hers again, but she still felt a bit breathless, as if she were on the edge of a laugh. Nothing about this was funny, though—except her attraction to him. Why here, why now, and why a man who might expose her village? It was ridiculous.

Perhaps it was the gods who were laughing at her instead.

"I've known him for many years now," he said. "Dooley is the digger in our group, which sounds exactly like what it is: he digs up bones, looks through rubbish piles, pieces the dead and the buried back together, and attempts to tell their story with them. We'll try to locate some of the earliest settlements marked on the old maps, and visit the allied outposts as well."

They wouldn't find much there. Once, an alliance between the French, Dutch, Irish, and Portuguese had established a naval stronghold in Iceland, guarded by enormous sentinels and icebreaking, engine-powered ironships. The alliance served as a first line of defense against any Horde attempts to cross the Atlantic. But that had been before the invention of airships, before the discovery that no Arctic sea passage connected the great oceans—and before the number of giant, armored sharks in the northern waters made traveling by ironship too dangerous. The alliance had already begun to disintegrate before the fissure eruptions; the outposts were completely abandoned not long after, and much of the machinery left behind.

Until Hanna and the Englishwomen had discovered it. Each sheet of metal and bolt had been salvaged, each engine and boiler had been used to construct their village's defenses—a village that they'd built as far from the outposts as possible.

"Those outposts are all in the southeast," Annika said. "Is that where you'll start?"

"At Vik, on the southern rim. Then north and east."

Taking them away from Hannasvik—giving her village more time to prepare. "You'll travel along the coast?"

"Across the glaciers, first."

She stared at him. Was he mad? Did he want to *die*?

Her expression must have amused him. With a laugh, he said, "There are volcanoes beneath them."

"*Under* the glaciers?" She hadn't known that. Obviously there were volcanoes in the region. But *under* the ice? "And you intend to study them?"

His eyebrows rose. "To answer that means we must talk about me instead of Dooley."

"Blast it." But she didn't truly mind. The more they spoke about him—or anything else—the more she wanted their conversation to extend beyond the minutes they had left. "I'm enjoying your company. *Very* much. If I'm not on duty, I intend to monopolize your time until you leave the ship."

That seemed to stun him. His gaze searched her face, as if he suspected a joke. After a moment, he cleared his throat. "I'd like that, too."

"Good. Now, tell me more about Dooley. At the port gates, when we passed by him, he was laughing at you. Why?"

"Because I don't often run to a woman's rescue."

"Why did you?"

"Why did *you* need to be rescued? Why were you at the gates?"

"I'm looking for my sister, Källa. I use the personal advertisements in the newssheets to search for her. I was in Navarra paying for another season and checking for replies."

He paused, as if surprised that she'd shared that information. There was no reason not to, however. Everyone on board knew it.

"Why did she leave?"

"Because I lit a fire when I shouldn't have." And nearly exposed their village. But that memory shamed her too much; she didn't want to share any more of it. "Dooley?"

His mouth compressed with disappointment before he said, "He's fond of dogs, but on our first expedition to the Yellow Rock Mountains, a bear killed his wolfhound. He hasn't owned one since. Not a live one, at least."

"What other sort is there?"

"Clockwork. They're in the cargo hold now."

Incredible. "Will you show me?"

"I will." His quick smile said that he was as pleased by her request as she was by his reply. "Now?"

Regretfully, she shook her head. "I'm on watch soon."

"Tomorrow, then." He leaned back and looked to the game table, his gaze thoughtful on Dooley. "He has a slow temper, but it's something to see when it fires."

"Has it fired at you?"

"A few times. Not often."

"What sparks it?"

"Stupidity. He doesn't mind the company of fools, except when they put others in danger. An abusive word against a fellow countryman will also do it, though if he's of the same opinion of that person, it takes a miracle for him to admit that person was Irish. He'll suggest misbreeding or claim it's the fault of the Brits—those from Manhattan City, not England."

Some old hatred lingered there, begun when the English tried to flee the Horde centuries ago. Annika didn't know the story of it, but Mary Chandler often blamed the Irish in the same way. "Does he really believe it?"

"No. He just hates to be disappointed by the people he wants to like."

"Who doesn't hate that?"

"A cynic. They'd enjoy being right." He met her eyes again, matched her smile. "Dooley isn't a cynic by any stretch. And he's honest, but not to a fault. If the truth hurts someone, he won't say it unless necessary. I don't know if he'd save himself with a lie—but I think he would save someone else with one."

"You haven't had reason to find out?"

"Luckily, no."

"Would you lie?" Annika would in a heartbeat. She didn't enjoy lying, but she did it all the time. Lives depended on it.

"Yes." He didn't hesitate. "I'd rather be ashamed of a lie than ashamed for not helping someone. So would he. He can't stomach it when the strong take advantage of the weak. I think it's why he prefers expeditions to life in a city."

So that he wasn't surrounded by people taking advantage of each other? "Animals do the same," Annika pointed out. "Dogs, especially. They single out the weak prey and tear it apart."

"But he doesn't expect animals to feel compassion, so he's not disappointed by them."

Ah. That made more sense. And Kentewess had been quick to defend him. Since Dooley seemed like a good sort of man, that spoke well of Kentewess, too.

"You like him very much, don't you?"

"I do." He glanced toward the game table again and tilted his head as if trying to catch a bit of their conversation. Annika ignored the others in favor of watching Kentewess's changing expression— fondness, at first, then a flash of humor, as if he heard something that amused him. He looked to her again. "Ah, yes. And there are the stories—Dooley loves any fable or tale, the sort passed down through generations, and to pick out any variations. That's partially the reason we chose Iceland for our next expedition: His mother used to collect and record the whalers' tales about the trolls and witches, especially those that flourished after the fissure eruptions. Since her death, he's made it a hobby to trace their origin. I'm sure he'll speak to some of the old fishermen in Höfn and Smoke Cove."

Dooley wouldn't find the origin of the stories there. Though some of the fishermen might claim to have lain with a witch or two, it would have only been in their imagination. Most of the women from Hannasvik went a bit farther for their seed.

She couldn't resist asking, "You don't believe in witches and trolls, Mr. Kentewess?"

"No. Do you?"

"Yes. But we aren't talking about me."

"I'd like to make you talk, Annika Fridasdottor."

Oh. That softly spoken statement and his steady gaze seemed to flip her stomach over, a thrilling little jolt of desire that ebbed into a warm flush beneath her skin. His response called for a smart reply, but she couldn't think of anything except that she'd been wrong, so wrong. She'd thought his interest wasn't in bedding her. She'd thought he'd wanted something else from her.

Now Annika thought the bed was exactly where his interests lay. That he felt the same attraction she did.

How would he make her talk? A kiss? Something more? Oh, she wanted that. She wanted to know what it was to need someone so desperately that she would promise anything for another kiss, another touch.

But she couldn't. And she couldn't let this attraction go any further than flirtation. Pursuing this wouldn't be fair, not when she couldn't let anything come of it.

With regret, she looked away from him. *No more of this.* They would have a fun conversation and nothing more.

What had they been talking about?

Dooley, she remembered. But it was her turn now. Only one man at the game table was left to discuss.

"The tall, thin man is Mr. James, the first mate. He's very good at his job." She paused, searching for something else to say. What did she know of him? "He has a wife and two children, I believe."

Kentewess didn't speak for a moment. Then, with a slight frown, "That's all?"

"He enjoys playing patolli—and winning."

His gaze narrowed. "You don't like him."

"No, it's not that." She didn't know him well enough to dislike him. "I avoid him when I can."

"Why? What has he done?"

"Nothing. He's not rude or unpleasant, but I never know how to respond to him, and that frustrates me." Until later, sometimes, and thinking of a reply when it was too late frustrated her even more.

"What does he say?"

"When we pass each other in a companionway, he will make a comment like, 'So you are here again?' in a friendly way. But his question always makes me feel as if I shouldn't be there. And when I answer honestly—'I'm returning to my cabin'—I feel like I should have been cleverer. Then I resent him for it. I hate feeling stupid, but I always do when he speaks to me. So I avoid him."

He nodded, his gaze on the first mate. "I understand that."

"You've felt stupid?"

"No." He grinned when she wrinkled her nose at him. "I've avoided people who made me uncomfortable, even if they were always polite."

She hoped never to give him reason to avoid her. "So, that is everyone. Shall we talk about you now?"

"No. You've yet to tell me about my aunt."

"You know her."

"I know what she tells me in her letters."

Annika wouldn't have thought that a man who hadn't visited his aunt in ten years cared very much, but Kentewess obviously did. A quiet plea lay in his words, to tell him anything that she hadn't told him herself. Did he hope to ease his aunt's sadness? Perhaps he could. Judging by Lucia's smiles, he already had.

"She's often melancholy. I think she must have loved your uncle deeply."

"She did. It was returned." His gaze was troubled as he looked across the room. "Does she get along well alone?"

"Yes. She has friends here." His aunt was sad but not broken. Annika never worried that she'd fling herself over the side of the ship. "She's very proud of you. I wasn't aboard more than a week when she showed me a photograph."

"She says she doesn't leave *Phatéon*."

"It's true. If she needs anything, though, she doesn't hesitate to ask for it. Elena—the second mate—and I often bring back items for her in the port cities." Annika pursed her lips. "Except she doesn't let me pick out her ready-made dresses. She relies on Elena for that."

His gaze returned to Annika's. "What would you pick for her?"

"A gown of deepest green. She once told me that she enjoys flying over the forests better than the water—she likes looking out over the trees. A damask, I think. It would be heavy and warm, which is always welcome on the deck of an airship, and the fabric has such a lovely texture when you run your hands over it. I think such a gown would make her happy just to wear it. She wouldn't need the bows or the lace—but of course, that is what she fears I'd bring her."

"Do they make you happy?"

"Oh, yes. They're so pretty, aren't they? If possible, I would wear nothing but a bow every day—especially if it was silk. Nothing compares to silk." She'd never felt anything like it before coming to the New World . . . but they weren't talking about her. She looked to Lucia again. "A year ago, *Phatéon* carried a passenger who fancied her—another physician, he was. She took him to her bed, but though he proposed a marriage, she wouldn't leave with him. She was even more melancholy for a while after that. I'm not sure if she regretted her refusal, or if she was sorry that he hadn't been your uncle."

Perhaps it had been a combination. For as long as Annika had been alive, her mother, Frida, had suffered from similar regret and grief—even though her lover still lived, and only a stone's throw from their home. That they'd shared a fierce love had never been in doubt, but Hildegard had also wished for a child of her blood. She'd claimed that lying with a man would mean nothing; even the goddess Freya had taken many lovers without regret, and Hildegard's heart would remain with Frida.

But it had mattered—at least to Annika's mother. A terrible row had parted them, and even after Hildegard had returned a year later with the infant Källa, Frida hadn't forgiven her. She'd refused to take Hildegard back into their home. After asking one of the other women to bring her a daughter from the New World, she'd poured all of her love into Annika instead.

It hadn't been enough. For two decades, Annika bore witness

to her mother's silent longing, her pain—and the two women had remained apart.

She and Källa had grown up as sisters, regardless. Everyone in Hannasvik knew that their mothers belonged together, and that they were both too stubborn and prideful to do anything about it. Heartache ruled them instead.

So it was for Lucia, but stubbornness couldn't be blamed. Her love was dead. And even if she tried to find another, love didn't always come.

Silence was Kentewess's only reply. When she glanced at him, a flush had darkened his face. He seemed at a loss for words.

Well, his aunt had not likely written that in her letters, had she? "Will you reprimand me for my impropriety?"

"No." Embarrassment receding, he shook his head. "I wasn't prepared to think of her in that manner."

He preferred a warning? Very well, she would give him one. "Then prepare yourself for this: If you hope to take me to your bed, please understand that I cannot. It may be easy for others to take a lover, but it isn't easy for me. I understand that I might enjoy it. But I would rather not take the chance of regretting it afterward. I'm not very adventurous."

He stared at her, his face unreadable. When he finally spoke, his voice was low and rough. "You are bold in other ways."

"Not in that way." Even though she couldn't stop imagining what bedding him would feel like. She was quite, quite certain that she *would* enjoy it. But that wasn't enough. "I'd be sorry that you aren't someone that I love."

"Is there someone?" It seemed dragged from him.

"No. But there might be, one day." She met his gaze squarely. "Is that what you want from me? Is that why you're spending time with me now?"

He looked at her for a long time, his jaw clenched. A struggle briefly moved across his expression. When he spoke, resignation filled his reply. "No," he said quietly. "That wasn't what I wanted."

"But you want something else?"

"Yes."

Heavy disappointment weighed in her stomach. She shouldn't feel it. His lack of interest was better for them both, because until she loved, Annika wouldn't bed him. Until she found Källa, she couldn't commit herself to anyone.

Still, she'd liked thinking that he'd fancied her, too.

"What *do* you want, then? Why did you rescue me?"

He didn't immediately answer. His mouth hardened, and he looked toward the game table. Frustration tightened his expression. He glanced back at her and seemed to wait.

Annika frowned, then realized that he wasn't delaying. He was waiting for her to respond to someone else. She heard her name from across the room. The first mate had mentioned her—and now everyone at the table was looking their way.

"Go on, ask her," Mr. James said. "She's seen them herself. Haven't you, Fridasdottor?"

Irritated by the interruption, Annika shook her head. "I wasn't listening, I'm sorry. What have I seen?"

"The trolls on the island." The first mate gestured to Dooley, whose keen eyes had fixed on her. "This one here is asking about any stories we've heard. I told him that you haven't just heard of them, you saw one—or so you've said."

So she had. Aware that Kentewess's focus had sharpened on her profile, she nodded. "Yes. I did."

Dooley twisted round in his chair to face her. "I've never heard an observation from someone firsthand—only from fishermen who were relating a story they'd heard from someone else."

"What have they said?"

"Legend is that the fissure eruption broke open a passage to the

Underworld. That all of those creatures you hear of in northern widows' tales came through: the trolls and dwarves, the invisibles, the hidden folk, the witch women with hollow bodies and fox tails who seduced sailors and stole infants."

Some of that was true. No community could survive without children—and a community of women had to steal them, or find seed.

"The only things that came out of those eruptions were ash and volcanic gases," Kentewess said. "Whatever the basis of the stories, they originated elsewhere."

Yes—from women like Annika. Everyone who left Hannasvik did their part to spread the tales, in the hopes that superstition would keep others away. They *had* kept people away for a century . . . but never before had they been told to someone who would travel around Iceland, searching for scientific truth.

Dooley wouldn't be able to discern that truth now. There was no reason not to tell him. But Annika wasn't certain the stories served their purpose anymore, anyway. In just the few years since she'd left Hannasvik, more people had begun to settle in Smoke Cove. *Phatéon* carried more men to the island now. Kentewess's expedition would undoubtedly lead the three scientists near her village . . . and if the Dutch eventually returned, more communities would sprout.

Annika felt the sick certainty that her village wouldn't remain hidden for much longer, trolls or not.

"Annika?" The gentle nudge came from Lucia.

Madame Collin rapped one of her wooden game pieces against the tabletop. "You weren't worried about looking like a fool when you told us of it. I suppose now you're worried your tale might send that young man running."

Chuckles rose from around the table. Annika's cheeks blazed. Oh, how they looked at her. Some with amusement, others with pity. Had her interest been so obvious? Or did they laugh because they knew he hadn't returned it?

If only she could crash through their group with a troll now.

Beside her, Kentewess said, "I don't run."

The laughter abruptly fell into uncomfortable silence—except for his aunt, who covered her smile and looked heavenward. Dooley's eyes seemed to sparkle with humor, crinkling at the corners when he glanced from Kentewess to her.

"Will you please share your story with us, miss?"

She had little choice. A glance at the clock offered no help; a bit of time still remained before she needed to leave for her watch. With a sigh and a nod, she said, "It was four summers ago. I was aboard *Freya's Cloak*—a sailing ship—on route from Norway to Smoke Cove."

That was a lie, too, though *Freya's Cloak* often took that route. Annika's tale would stand, though; the ship was captained by one of the Huldrene, a woman who'd found Hannasvik too small for her. Ursula Ylvasdottor hadn't abandoned the village, however. Using *Freya's Cloak*, she'd carried the village's wool to market and procured items that they couldn't produce themselves—including false letters of origin.

Annika had never been aboard the ship. She'd traveled most of the distance to Smoke Cove in her troll and walked the remainder of the way, accompanied by her mother and her friend Lisbet. In Smoke Cove, they'd met with Captain Ylvasdottor, who'd given Annika her identifying documents, an engineer's license, and a personal reference, then pointed her toward *Phatéon*.

"It was August, I think," she continued. "We sailed around the north of the island because of the number of megalodons reported to the south."

"That was a bad year," Collin broke in, nodding. "Four years ago, I remember. You still hear the whalers talking about it, how they'd find themselves a pod, then the moment their harpoons drew blood, they were caught in the middle of a feeding frenzy. The megalodons would ram the hulls of any ship nearby, attacking them whether they ran their engines or not. Any little sound would bring those sharks. They sank two dozen ships that year—maybe more, because there were others that went missing, and no one knew what happened to them."

Annika nodded. "The captain never ran her engines, anyway— that was why I wanted an airship. Aside from the stoking, there wasn't much to do aboard a sailing ship, so I spent most of my time on the deck, watching for icebergs. When we came around the island, we sailed as close to her shore as possible. Oh, but I remember the hills. They were so green, like a blanket of velvet beneath the sun." She didn't need to lie about that, or fake the wistful note in her voice. Her home *was* beautiful, from the black sands to the craggy, barren peaks. "I saw the troll then, sitting not far from the beach."

Dooley leaned forward eagerly. "What was it?"

A machine covered by seal- and shark-skins, with a ruff made from the fur of a great Arctic bear and tern feathers collected from the nesting grounds near Hannasvik. Four times as tall as Annika, with squat legs and a square body, it had been built from the salvaged remains of the sentinels and war machines left by the defenders waiting to intercept the Horde's navy. Its giant head could house a seated driver, who was surrounded by levers. It had enough room in the heart for three people to sleep and cook. A belly full of coal fed the troll's furnace, and an ass made of a boiler and a steam engine moved it.

"At first look, I thought it was a rock—black and brown and mottled. But it must have just been warming itself in the sun, because it stood." She came up out of her chair and bent over, her hands on the deck and her bottom in the air. "On four legs, like an Arctic bear, but bigger. Much bigger. Then it rose on two legs, like this. The belly was gray and smooth. Its breath steamed, and I'll never forget how it roared. I've never heard anything so terrifying before or since. Then it walked away, with long arms swinging."

She sat again. Dooley's mouth had fallen open.

"It's an animal?"

"I don't know. It had a big, shaggy head, but I couldn't see its face properly. I only had the impression of a creature that was lumpy, disfigured—particularly when it was sitting. If it hadn't moved, I'd have never known it wasn't a rock." She paused and looked to the clock. Only a minute or two more. "If you're looking for personal accounts, you can ask the captain of *Freya's Cloak*. She saw it, too."

The first mate huffed out a laugh. "I'd wager anything that what you both saw was a bear washed in on an iceberg. And I can tell you the explanation behind what you think you saw is aboard this ship." James waited until everyone looked at him. "It's Hymen Island, and the virgins who live there. You want to keep men away, you spread those rumors about witch-women and spirits. And when people see a bear washed up on an iceberg, they assume it's a troll."

Dooley was shaking his head. "The Church has only been using Heimaey for forty years. And though there've been tales of this sort for centuries, the lore specific to Iceland and those fissure eruptions dates from almost eight decades ago."

"So you believe she saw a troll?"

The first mate's disbelief fired more color into Annika's cheeks. That specific story *was* a lie, but she'd been familiar with the machines her entire life. And blast it all, she didn't like his suggestion that she was too stupid to know the difference between a bear and an enormous, lumbering troll.

"She obviously saw something." Dooley smiled. "Unless she's having her fun with us."

"I'm not." None of this was fun anymore. "And I'm sorry to leave you, but I must prepare for my watch."

Annika stood and dared a glance at Kentewess. He was studying her; she suspected that he'd never taken his focus from her the entire time she'd been speaking. She didn't see any doubt in that searching gaze now, only pointed speculation.

He still wasn't done with her, she realized. He still wanted something from her. She couldn't imagine what it would be.

Now she wasn't sure that she wanted to know.

Chapter Four

When describing his friend to Annika Fridasdottor, David had forgotten to mention how loudly Dooley snored. The man's sawing drowned out the noise from *Phatéon*'s engines, which had fired up not long after she'd left the wardroom. Finally untethered and under way, the airship no longer bucked against the wind, but despite the calm, David couldn't find sleep.

He couldn't blame Dooley for that. Months spent sharing a tent had accustomed him to the man's snores. A half hour spent with a pretty engineer was responsible, instead.

Annika Fridasdottor was more of a mystery to him now than when he hadn't known her name, and one David desperately wanted to unravel. Sitting with her, speaking with her had been like taking a deep breath at the top of a mountain after a month spent choking down the air in a port city.

Every word they'd shared echoed in his head. He couldn't stop picturing her smile, her laugh. Her worry when he'd told her about the survey. Her tension when she'd recounted her story of the troll.

Her unwavering stare when she'd asked if David wanted her in his bed.

God.

David *did* want her. But he'd have to be a fool to hope for anything of the sort. Twice, he'd paid to be with a woman. Both times had been disasters—the first awkward and uncomfortable until she'd poured oil onto his erection, telling him any woman bedding a man who was part machine would always need extra help, and flinching when she felt his steel hand. He'd gone to the England for the second, where the prosthetics wouldn't matter. She'd needed help, too. She hadn't flinched when he'd touched her, but she'd turned her gaze away from his face, her teeth clenched as she bore his body's advance.

He hadn't been able to finish with either of them. He'd quickly left—for a time, feeling more grotesque than he'd felt since the prosthetics were first grafted on. That, because of the reaction of two women whose names he'd never learned. He'd rather not know how it would feel to have someone like Annika cringe away from him and grit her teeth when he entered her.

Abandoning sleep, David sat up. His photomultiplying lens clicked into place over his left eye. Though still dark, the cabin appeared illuminated with a cool blue light. Dooley lay on his back, his mouth open and blanket shoved to his hips in the heated room, his chest covered by a thin nightshirt. David reached for his trousers, then tugged his boots on over the thick cotton that padded his steel prosthetics and prevented them from slipping around inside footwear designed for people with flesh over their bones.

A glance at his pocket watch told him that it was almost midnight. Annika's shift would be over in a few minutes . . . but he wouldn't seek her out. Her intention to spend every moment of this journey with him probably didn't include the moments in the middle of the night.

If it did, however, he'd gladly alter his schedule to fit hers. At this hour, they'd have the wardroom to themselves. She wouldn't lie with a man without love, but by God, she didn't have to lie with him. Her company, given freely, had already proved more pleasurable than those earlier encounters had been. For a few hours of privacy with her, he'd happily sacrifice the sleep.

He pulled on his jacket and left the cabin. The airship's main deck would be cold, windy—perfect for clearing his mind and cooling down the rest of him.

His mind cleared halfway up the companionway.

What the hell was he doing? David *needed* Annika Fridasdottor, but not as a friend. She held answers, and he had no more hours to waste. A week wouldn't be enough if she never told him what he needed to know. He'd already spent too much time trying to secure those answers—and going about it in the wrong way.

He should have known. Should have realized. His mother had simply smiled whenever someone had asked where she'd come from and who her people were. For years, David had assumed that she'd hidden the truth in order to sever ties to that place—perhaps to forget some shame she'd endured, or to escape her past. He'd assumed that she concealed the truth to separate herself from her people . . . not because she'd wanted to conceal *them*.

But his mother hadn't even told his father, someone she'd loved and trusted, and who would've loved her no matter what secrets she might have revealed. And in all this time, it had never occurred to David that his mother's smiles might have served another purpose.

A smile allowed her to remain silent. A smile meant that she didn't have to lie to his father. A smile suggested that the answer was a game or a puzzle to figure out; a smile allowed her to keep a secret without suggesting that his father couldn't be trusted with it.

But his mother had never needed to work aboard an airship, where a smile alone wouldn't have secured a job. His mother had never had to maintain a lie that might be picked apart by a man who'd lain awake with their conversation echoing in his head. His mother had never had someone tell her that they would soon be conducting a survey of Iceland.

Would she have been able to smile then? Or would she have appeared just as worried as Annika did?

David thought she would have.

If Annika was protecting her people, as he'd begun to suspect, and if she had reason to lie, a week of flirting wouldn't tell him where his mother had come from. He'd do better to tell Annika of his own reasons for wanting to know—and that she had no need to fear him—instead of trying to tease those answers from her.

Resolved, he headed down the stairs. Though most of the crew below decks was abed, finding the engine room was simple: he followed the noise. By the time David reached the door, he couldn't hear his own footsteps over the rattling and huffing. The boards vibrated beneath his boots, through his metal feet—a muffled, almost ticklish reverberation.

Years ago, he'd sometimes caught himself trying to scratch an itch below a knee that wasn't there. Now, nearly a decade after buying his mechanical legs, he still found himself surprised when something *was* there.

Ticklish, of all things.

A blast of humid air greeted him when he opened the door, the smell of hot iron and oil. Ahead, an array of six enormous pistons rapidly alternated in time to the huffing, the giant shafts cranking flywheels into a spinning blur. A woman in trousers stood in front of the engine, with her back to him. He recognized Mary Chandler's red hair before she tied a scarf over her head, carefully tucking away the loose ends. Coming onto watch, apparently. Had he missed Annika, then?

No. Arms akimbo, Mary braced her hands on her hips. She shifted her weight to one leg, revealing Annika, crouching sideways to her at the base of the engine . . . without a shirt. Just a thin chemise, almost transparent with sweat and steam.

Shock and desire pummeled David like iron fists. His body clenched, senses reeling. He should look away.

He couldn't.

Tiny sleeves capped her shoulders, leaving her arms bare. Spanner in hand, she tightened the bolt over a valve. Smooth biceps flexed beneath skin glistening with perspiration and darkened by a fine layer of coal dust. The same dust streaked her face, grayed her cotton chemise and buff trousers. A wide leather belt cinched her waist and held spanners of various sizes.

David's pulse pounded in his ears, seemed louder than the engine. With her profile to him, Annika glanced up at Mary Chandler. Like the other woman, she'd tied a scarf across her forehead and down around her ears, knotted at her nape; unlike the other woman's, it was a brilliant orange, seemingly untouched by coal dust and sparkling with sequins. Annika gave an absent nod, watching the woman.

Who was shouting, David realized when he heard his own name.

He shouldn't listen. Experience had taught David that he wouldn't want to overhear anything Mary Chandler had to say— and a few sentences confirmed it. He'd met Chandler in the wardroom not long after Annika had left. Judging by her comments now, he'd made quite the impression. Still, he wanted to see Annika's reaction to her words.

She didn't have much of a reaction at all. Tucking her spanner into her belt, she simply nodded again while Chandler spoke. She rose, caught sight of David. Her eyes widened with surprise. Full lips curved into a welcoming smile.

Chandler abruptly stopped shouting. She glanced over her shoulder. Red flooded her cheeks. She quickly turned away, patting Annika's shoulder and moving past her, deeper into the engine room.

Annika gave her a curious glance before starting toward David. His breath stopped. The damp cotton of her chemise clung to her breasts, revealing their soft shape, the darkness of her nipples. Jesus Christ, help him. The sight hardened his cock, thick and aching.

He forced his gaze up—and froze on her throat, at the necklace made from a leather thong and small bones inscribed with runes. He couldn't read them. His eyepiece clicked, cycling through his lenses as he tried to see the glyphs, but it wouldn't matter—the faces of a few runes lay against her skin, concealing the names there.

He resisted the urge to reach for his own runes, the names his mother had worn. Not here. He'd show her them when he told her his mother's story.

Elated by the discovery, he met her eyes, matched her smile.

Hers widened. With a sweep of her hand, she drew the scarf away from her head . . . and took a wad of cotton from each ear. David choked back a sudden laugh. So she hadn't reacted to Mary Chandler's comments because she hadn't *heard* them?

"Mr. Kentewess!" she shouted. "May I help you? If you're coming to ask us to quiet the engine, I assure you we can't!"

As he shook his head, his gaze involuntarily dropped to her breasts again. Her dark nipples had beaded, pressing against the thin cotton. *God.* She didn't even seem to realize—or didn't care.

If so, he liked her impropriety. But he absolutely wasn't prepared for it. He tugged the front of his jacket together, praying it concealed his body's turgid response.

Clearing his throat, he forced himself to look at her face again. "Do passengers often ask you to quiet them?"

"Never directly. But we hear complaints about the complaints!" She moved past him to a workbench, where she tugged the tools from her belt. With a twist of a valve, steaming water from a copper pipe overhead filled a basin. Dipping a cloth into the small bath, she glanced over her shoulder at him. "You can't sleep?"

"I wanted to continue our conversation!" he shouted back.

She nodded, then turned away from him to wipe down her face, her arms. A square swath of blue wool hung on the wall near the door, a hole cut in the center. When she dropped it over her head, the wool covered her in front and back from neck to thighs. She gestured for him to precede her into the passageway, then laughed when he held the door open, letting her go through first.

In the corridor, she turned to him. "I have to check the warmers on deck! Are you accompanying me?"

"Yes!"

She led him forward through the dim passageway, past the companionway he'd used to reach this level. When distance muffled the din from the engine, she looked to him. "We'll avoid waking everyone in the aviator's berth if we head to the forward ladder. Should I ask what Mrs. Chandler said? By her expression, it must have been about you. She loves to gossip, but never likes to be caught."

Who did? "You didn't hear anything of it?"

"No. Is it better I didn't?"

Probably. But he still wanted to see her reaction. "She told you that I asked after your watch schedule in the wardroom, and that Dooley teased me about being sweet on you."

"Sweet on me?" Her laugh wasn't what he expected. It could have been cruel, but was warm and inviting, instead—asking him to laugh with her. "I've never seen anyone fall in love who didn't know each other for years first."

"Truly?" He'd known several people who'd loved each other within days, his parents and Dooley among them.

"Yes." She slanted a playful look at him through her lashes, and he was sorry that they had no need for a stoker on their expedition. He suspected that she'd have fit into their group even more quickly than Goltzius had, and that he'd have enjoyed her company as much as Dooley's. "Are you sweet on me, Mr. Kentewess?"

"Not yet."

"Then whatever Mary said means nothing. *Did* she say more?"

Goddamn him for wanting to know. This shouldn't matter. It did. "She said that you ought to rethink your interest in me, because I'm horrid."

"You're horrid?" She stopped at the foot of a ladder. "What have you supposedly done?"

"I look horrid, rather. My face is melted and my hand is gone."

"Ah." She frowned. "That was rather horrid of her to say, wasn't it? That won't stand. I'll give her a talking-to."

Blast it all. While fishing for her reaction, he'd caught one he hadn't intended.

"That wasn't to tattle," he said. In the wardroom, he'd told Annika he'd never felt stupid. He did now.

"She won't know who it came from, Mr. Kentewess. By tomorrow morning, she'll have said the same to everyone." She studied his face for a long second. "Why would she say melted? It doesn't even look burned. Nothing like this."

Twisting around, she pulled up her shawl and showed him the back of her right arm, from the elbow to just below her shoulder. The ridged scar there was paler than the rest of her skin, mottled with pink.

"What happened?"

"I backed up against a furnace." She tugged down the wool again. "My mother always told me that someone with no scars was either very lucky or hadn't ever had to work very hard. This wasn't from working hard, but from daydreaming when I should have been. I learned a bit of a lesson, too."

"So you weren't lucky."

"No. My mother wasn't, either. She lost four toes to the ice one winter. Another girl I know had her nose torn away by a wild dog." She paused, her expression thoughtful. A small crease formed between her brows. "It could be said that she was very lucky, I suppose. The result might have been worse."

"Then I'm either unlucky or incredibly lucky, depending on how you look at it." He preferred to think he was lucky.

"Yes. And sometimes, I think it's not about luck at all; you lift your face to say a prayer to the gods, and the answer they give is a bird shitting in your eyes." She pursed her mouth, watching him. "What is it?"

David shook his head, unable to describe the ecstatic leap of his heart. In his life, he'd only heard one other person use that expression. His mother, whenever something unlucky had happened, would say that a bird had shit in her eye—that the gods had answered a prayer, but that the answer wasn't one anyone would like.

Finally he said, "I'm fortunate, then, that one of my eyes is always covered."

"Yes." She laughed suddenly, glancing at his eyepiece. Few people looked without staring—or without pretending that it didn't exist at all, looking everywhere *but* his prosthetics or his scars. She didn't do either. Her gaze moved to his cheek again. "Whatever Mary thinks, it's obviously not melted. Mostly, it looks like someone shoved your face against a rotary sharpener. Or you lost a tangle with a wolf."

"If I'm alive, I must have won that tangle."

She grinned. "Yes. So Mary doesn't think you're handsome?"

"Horrid, yes." David had to agree.

"And she's not any judge. In port, she once pointed out a man to me who she thought was handsome—and the moment I saw him, I looked for the nearest tree to climb, thinking that I'd just seen a bear." She preceded him up the ladder. By the time David reached the top, where she stood waiting, he was sweet on her. "I've never been able to determine what 'handsome' means. You aren't as hairy as most men. I think that's lovely. So that must be how *I* determine it."

He'd accept that, especially since she didn't seem to be stroking him on, hoping to spare his feelings. His gaze dropped to her smiling mouth. Perhaps this journey wouldn't only last a week. After she knew where he was headed, why he was headed there, she might want to join him.

"My aunt tells me that you've searched for your sister four years now," he said. "Do you miss home?"

She didn't need to answer; the wistful expression softening her eyes told him. She looked away, toward the companionway leading to the main deck. Faint lamplight spilled through the open hatch to the wet boards. With a sigh, she pulled the orange scarf over her hair.

"It looks like we haven't yet flown out of the wind and rain. Are you still coming up with me?"

"If I'm not in your way."

"You won't be."

"Then I will." When she lifted her chin to tie the ends of the scarf beneath her throat, he said, "The runes on your necklace. May I look?"

Her fingers stilled. After a long second, she nodded.

David wanted to step close to examine it, to lift the leather string in his hands and steal a moment against her skin. He didn't need to. She pulled the necklace away from her throat, twisting the small bones until the runes faced him. His nanoagents detected the shift of his focus and adjusted his lens.

"Annika, daughter of Frida," he said softly. "Daughter of Kára, daughter of Astrid, daughter of Agnes, daughter of Jane." He looked up, saw the surprise in the parting of her lips and widening of her eyes. She hadn't thought he'd be able to read the runes, and no wonder—he'd searched long before finding a historian who could teach him. With his gaze on her face, he unbuckled his jacket collar, tugged out his own runes. "This was my mother's."

Astonished, she sucked in a sharp breath and reached up, rolling the first bone between her fingers. "Inga." Her gaze jumped to meet his again, searching his features. For a resemblance? "*You are her daughter?*"

"Her son." Joy and triumph surged through him. Yes, this was closer to fulfilling his promise, the closest he'd been. He recited the runes from memory. "Inga, daughter of Helga, daughter of Sigrid, daughter of Ursula, daughter of Hanna. Did you know her?"

Dropping the runes, she let her hand fall to her side. The wondering light in her eyes faded. She shook her head, her expression closing. "No. I'm sorry."

Oh, no. He wouldn't let her shut him out now. "She died wearing these, Annika. She died saving my life. She asked me to bury them on her people's holy mountain so that her soul can find her mother's, but I don't know where that is. Help me. Please."

She cast a stricken glance at his runes. "I can't."

But his mother's request had affected her. Heart pounding, he stepped closer and said softly, "Whatever secret you're keeping, I won't expose it. Please, Annika. Please let me do this for her."

"I'm sorry. I can't help you." Hugging her arms against her chest, she backed up a step, then turned for the companionway. "Don't follow me up, Mr. Kentewess. You'd only get in my way."

He'd damn well get in her way until she gave him what he needed. David started after her—then forced himself to stop. Fists clenched, he watched her disappear up the stairs. She'd been taken off-guard and her defenses were up. He'd let her go for now, give her time to think.

But he wasn't done with Annika Fridasdottor.

It seemed only seconds after Annika had fallen into a fitful sleep that Elena nudged her awake again. Blearily, she glanced at the clock. Ten minutes until the four-to-eight watch began. A month of this would kill her.

Maybe she'd begin to sleep easier after David Kentewess left the airship. Annika doubted it.

Elena lit the lamp. With a sigh, Annika rolled over. Just two more minutes. Of course, her mind wouldn't let her have it. Closing her eyes, she could only see the hope on David's face after she'd spoken his mother's name. Could only hear him beseech her for help again. Giving up, she watched the flickering light dance across the bulkhead instead. So bright against the darkness—and from one small flame.

Five years ago, Annika had nearly exposed everyone in her village by building a fire. Such a simple act. She wasn't sure anyone aboard could have understood the harm she'd almost done. Secrecy had kept the women of Hannasvik safe for a century, and her fire had shouted their presence to the outside world.

She'd been woolgathering that day. Looking out over the sea and thinking about the women who'd first settled there. Every girl in Hannasvik had grown up hearing the story of how sixty laboring women had been smuggled out of Horde territory in England aboard an ironship. Rescued, some might have said, but no one taken from Horde-occupied lands was destined for anything but slavery and servitude—in the Lusitanian mines, most likely, but it was impossible to know what their destination might have been. Not a single sailor who could have told them survived the journey.

Not far from England, the smugglers had come upon a more lucrative bounty: a Dutch noble's ship, on a honeymoon journey from Norway to the New World. Kidnapping and ransom had long been traditional upon the high seas; typically, the hostages walked away alive and the kidnappers sailed away richer.

It all might have happened exactly as the smugglers had planned if Hanna, who'd been forced into a marriage with a prince's son, hadn't risked her life to free the Englishwomen chained in the ship's hold—and if the ironship hadn't sailed out of range of the Horde's controlling tower in the same hour. The signal that had stifled the women's emotions for decades had abruptly disappeared, over-whelming them with the strength of their own unfamiliar feelings. Led by Hanna, the ensuing revolt left everyone else on the ship dead, including her husband—who, it was said, had been the last man killed, and who had been locked in a cabin during the fighting.

After assuming command of the ironship, Hanna had taken the women to Iceland, abandoned only a few years before, and where no one would seek justice for the murder. There she helped them build a village of their own, and told them the stories that would give them a new history and shape their new lives—stories that were still repeated to their daughters.

Nine months after the revolt, seven children had been born; whether they'd been conceived before or after the women had been unleashed and their emotions hot upon them, Annika never knew. All of the babies had been girls, and it had been considered a sign from the gods that only women should ever populate the village. A community couldn't continue without children, however, so some women left to lie with men, and returned with a girl—or empty-handed, if the baby had been a boy that they left with his father. Some of the women remained away, choosing to stay with their sons. Others, like Annika's mother, took in a child stolen from Horde territories or the New World.

It had been Hanna's idea to use the old legends of the hidden folk to keep outsiders away. Through the years, Hannasvik had remained secret—and all the while, they'd prepared for discovery and to defend themselves. Some, like Källa, were called shield-maidens, armed and trained to fight, and on whose shoulders the safety of their village rested most heavily. Annika had been taught to drive and maintain one of the trolls that they used to travel long distances and to haul back surturbrand, the brown coal used in their furnaces.

The day Annika had built the fire, she'd only recently returned from one of those exhausting trips. Leaving her troll at the village, she'd hiked down the rocky hills that shielded Hannasvik from view of the sea, and across the barren flats to a beach not far from the terns' nesting fields. She'd spent the early afternoon collecting feathers to fill in her troll's ragged ruff, and when her stomach had begun to growl, kindled a small fire in the shelter of a wind-scraped boulder to cook the fish she'd netted in one of the tidal pools. Belly full, she'd stared out over the sea and begun to daydream. She hadn't noticed the ship in the distance or twilight falling, turning her small fire into a beacon, until Källa had rushed up and stamped out the flames. Together, they'd hidden as four men rowed to shore and trampled around the beach, discovering the remains. Annika and Källa waited through the night as the men made camp on the rocky flats, not daring to flee lest they lead the strangers back to their village—and not daring to kill them, lest their deaths brought more outsiders to investigate. Annika lived the next day in an agony of unrelenting dread as the men walked near the cliffs of the same hills that concealed Hannasvik; they would only have to climb the peaks to discover it. Källa's sword had been at ready, and Annika had been preparing to race back to the village to retrieve her troll when the men had decided to abandon their search and return to their ship.

Annika hadn't immediately known that Källa had taken responsibility for the fire. Such matters were handled among the elders and in privacy. That Källa was a shieldmaiden, whose duty it was to protect, made the punishment more severe—as had Källa's temper. A terrible argument had erupted between her and the elders, Källa calling them all stupid hags for dreaming that they could continue to hide. The result had been exile.

Källa hadn't come to Annika after the judgment had been passed; she'd simply gone. By the time Annika had confronted the elders with the truth, Källa had already disappeared.

The entire village had supported Annika's decision to follow her, bring her back. It wouldn't have mattered if they hadn't. Annika would have gone after her sister anyway.

A sister in heart—but closer to David Kentewess in blood. Though Inga Helgasdottor had left their village before Annika had been born, she could easily picture her. The only twins in Hannasvik, Inga and Källa's mother had looked exactly alike.

For as long as Annika had known her, Hildegard had worried and wondered about Inga's fate. Those who lay with men didn't always come back. Some fell to danger, some to love, others bore male children whom they couldn't bear to leave. The news would hurt, but she knew that Hildegard would be pleased to finally know that her sister's son had grown into such a fine man, that she'd died protecting him.

And that was the crux of it: Inga was dead. Annika couldn't help her now, couldn't help David—and *wouldn't* risk the lives of everyone in her village.

Not again.

David had said that he'd asked about her schedule, and Annika quickly discovered that he intended to use that information. She managed to avoid him at breakfast by coming into the wardroom late and taking a seat far away from him, then leaving immediately after eating. She did the same for lunch, but when she dutifully sat for her supper before the second dog watch began, he entered the wardroom—though he was due shortly for dinner in the captain's cabin.

The seats around the table were almost empty; most of the crew wouldn't eat until the current watch was over. Elena wasn't there to help her. The first mate's "So you've got a suitor, eh?" left her stumbling for something to say.

Of course the answer was "no," but despite everything, she wished that wasn't so. Annika preferred to think of David Kentewess as a suitor. She still liked him so well, still felt that flush of attraction when he took the seat next to her.

And if he were a suitor, she wouldn't be feeling so stupid.

With heated cheeks, she stared at her plate. Her instincts when she'd left him on the docks had been right. Why hadn't she listened to them? He *had* wanted something from her, something other than time in her bed, and she'd been foolish enough to let herself believe otherwise. And then she'd been foolish enough to ask him whether that was his intention, so he *knew* how she'd mistaken his interest for desire.

Perhaps that was why New Worlders were always so damn proper. It saved them from playing the idiot in front of strangers.

From the corner of her eye, she saw him edge closer. He dipped his head toward her. Annika forced herself to remain still. She wouldn't run.

"You asked why I noticed you at the gates." He pitched his voice low enough that they wouldn't be overheard. "Your accent is the same as hers—and you spoke Norse."

God. Who would have thought a plea for help would have led her to this?

And if her accent had been so easily recognizable, perhaps he'd have known how to find her anyway. She recalled Lucia's request that Annika make her nephew's acquaintance. "I suppose your aunt told you I was aboard."

"No. But she wondered, too."

And that knowledge now colored every conversation she'd had with the woman. Annika had always thought the physician's attempts to probe into her past were the same as every other New Worlder's obsession with a person's origins, as if an opinion of worth couldn't be formed without knowing which soil she'd first walked on.

Her throat tightened into a painful lump. She'd have to leave *Phatéon* for certain now. She'd always been careful, had always adhered to the tale she'd constructed about growing up in Norway. But she also hadn't realized that she had been speaking to a woman

who'd already known someone from Hannasvik. She hadn't realized that Lucia didn't just have questions, as everybody did; Lucia
knew which questions to ask, which answers might have matched
Inga's. How much had Annika inadvertently given away over the
years?

How much had she given away *last night*?

"You hail from Iceland, I think," he said softly, and she closed
her eyes. "And you've never mentioned any males in your past,
only women. My aunt confirmed the same. You called me a daughter, not a son. So I believe Mr. James stumbled close to the truth
when he said that the stories of trolls and witches were spread for
a reason. But you're not from Heimaey. What is the secret? Do they
steal children? Seduce men?"

He was too clever by far. Annika shook her head.

"Please don't pursue this."

"I must."

"Didn't we get along well before this?" In four years, she'd never
been so immediately comfortable with a person. Now Annika could
hardly bear to look at him, but she did, her chest aching. "Please
let it be."

"I can't." The resolve in his tone echoed his statement, but his
expression said that he didn't take any pleasure in forcing the issue.
"I won't hurt you or them, Annika. I swear it."

Just as he'd promised not to expose her secret—but it wasn't
Annika's secret to keep.

Telling him the truth would be far more dangerous than lighting a fire. The women of Hannasvik weren't just stealing babies.
They weren't just seducing men. They no longer worried about the
prince's son they'd killed. They didn't worry about the children
they'd taken, because those children had already been abandoned.

But Annika had seen what would happen to her people if the
New World descended on them. She'd seen men hanged for less

than what the women had done for years. She would never expose them to the ugliest part of the New World, the part that transformed love into sickness and sin.

Not everyone in the New World believed the same; perhaps David Kentewess wouldn't, either. If she told him about the love shared between her mother and his aunt, about so many of the others who'd made their lives together in her village, maybe he wouldn't show the same disgust. But Annika couldn't know how he would react. She couldn't even risk *asking* him without endangering her own position, her own life.

She couldn't manage more than a whisper. "Please don't."

"Annika—"

"I will *hate* you if you pursue this!"

"Fulfilling this promise is more important to me than your good opinion." As if pained, he closed his eye. His gloved fist tightened. "So you will hate me."

And so that was it. Annika pushed away her plate, stood. She couldn't swallow any more, anyway.

David followed her out. "Annika."

She didn't answer, increasing her pace. He moved faster. His large frame stopped in front of her. Annika sidestepped. His arm shot up, hand flat against the bulkhead, barring her way.

She could feel him staring down at her. She refused to look up. "Let me pass."

If he didn't, she'd kick him. Given the circumstances, Vashon would forgive her for it. The captain never tolerated men who used their strength against women.

"When I was a boy, my mother told me stories about Brunhild. How she was canny to Sigurd's deception and took her revenge, even though it meant her own death. I imagine you've heard the same stories, but I'm not him. I don't want to deceive you in any way—and I never meant to. I didn't want you to run from me."

"I'm not running." She'd been walking until he blocked her way. "Let me through now."

He didn't. "She used to sing to me at night, a lullaby in Norse. I never knew the words, though she told me what they meant—the song was about a girl who held a bird in her hands as it died, and then flew away to the heavens with it. Do you know it?"

Yes. Her mother had sung that lullaby to her, too. Annika would sing it to her daughter, one day. Eyes stinging, she shook her head.

"We were in our home when the explosions started at the mountain. I could see it through the window in my bedroom, lighting up the sky with orange. But I couldn't hear it. Only her, as she screamed for me to stand away." He faltered before continuing, the words hoarse. "The shock blast shattered the glass. She caught me, held her hand over my eye and my face, tried to stop the bleeding. And when she saw the mountain fall down on top of us, she covered my body with hers. The beam that crushed my legs cut her in half."

God. Annika couldn't bear the raw pain in his voice, the images he painted. Some words were even stronger than a man's arm, and he used them without mercy. Closing her eyes, she tried to hold back the tears.

"With her last breaths, she told me to be a good man, a strong one, and that she loved me and my father. She asked me to put my blood on her beads and bury them, so she could sit with her mother and sisters in heaven."

The softness of his tone was more destructive than anger could have been. Annika covered her face. Tears leaked through her fingers, her breath shuddering. She heard someone approach down the passageway. David angled his body as if to shield her from view.

He waited until they were alone again. "Tell me again not to pursue this, Annika."

"I can't." How could she? She'd have done the same as he was. Lifting her head, she swiped at her cheeks. "But I can't tell you what you want to know, either. I'm sorry."

His jaw clenched. "I'll find them, you realize. I'll search every inch of that island, and everything we find will be documented, published. But if you tell me, I'll go alone. I'll keep everyone else away, help you protect them."

Anger exploded in her, hot and fierce. Annika welcomed it, fed it, let it push away the pain. "You'll stoop to blackmail? What will you do next, hit me until I tell you? Rape me if I don't? Surely you won't stop at threatening the people I love—and the people your mother loved, too. Her sister. Her mothers. Her friends. How easily you toss away their lives. I doubt that's what she meant by being a good man."

He recoiled as if struck. He shook his head, opened his mouth to respond. Not caring what he had to say, Annika beat him to it.

"Go on, then. Hunt them down." She could threaten as well as he. "I'll let them know you're coming, and how you intend to expose them. You might find them, yes. But you'll be dead before you write a word."

She ducked under his arm and walked away.

"David!" Lucia's smile quickly changed to concern when she saw his face. She stepped back into her cabin, pulling him in. "Are you all right?"

No. And David didn't know when he would be again. "Do you have anything stronger than wine?"

Strong enough to dull this ache. *I doubt that's what she meant by being a good man.* God, that was true. He'd never been so ashamed.

Lucia opened a cupboard as he sat. Glasses rattled. "What happened?"

"I spoke with Annika Fridasdottor. She knows my mother's people."

"I knew it!" With a brown bottle in hand, she joined him at the table. "And what did she say?"

"Nothing." He downed a short glass of the clear liquid, the alcohol scorching the length of his throat. "I threatened her."

Lucia froze. "What?"

He couldn't believe it, either. He had no excuse. Desperation wasn't a good enough reason to threaten a woman—not if his life wasn't in danger. Frustration was no excuse at all. His mother wouldn't have just said that; his father would have been ashamed of him, too.

He'd seen how Annika protected them, and had thought a threat would give her an excuse to tell him—to continue protecting them. He'd never have actually followed through. But she couldn't have known that.

Now, she'd never have a reason to believe otherwise.

God. It had been hard enough to decide between his promise and her goodwill. Yet he'd chosen, knowing he'd lose her new-found friendship—and douse the fire that had sparked between them, too. They *had* been getting along, so well. When was the last time he'd felt anything like this toward a woman? He couldn't even remember one. Tossing that away, choosing her hate, had been one of the most difficult choices he'd ever made.

David hadn't realized he'd bring that hate down on his head so quickly.

"You'll apologize, and it'll be all right." Lucia patted his hand. "She's not unreasonable, David. Odd, certainly. But surely she won't hold words spoken in haste against you."

Remembering her fury, David wasn't so sure. She'd understood the promise driving him; after he'd told her how his mother had died, she hadn't been angry with him for that. Not until he'd threatened her people.

She might not forgive him. David wasn't certain he could blame her. He tipped the bottle, took another swallow.

His aunt watched him, her eyes dark with concern. "Does she know of the vow you made to your mother?"

"Yes."

"Oh." The soft disappointment said Lucia believed that knowledge should have won Annika over. Hell, David had thought it would, too. "She's *not* unreasonable. So I suppose that means she has a reason to deny you?"

"She's protecting those she loves." He pushed his fingers into his hair, held his head in his hands. Despair spread through him with the burning in his gut. "What could I say to convince her to risk them? Nothing. There is no hope."

And he'd ruined everything else between them as well.

"You're a stranger to her, David. When she knows you better, she'll know you won't hurt them. You've waited all these years; a bit more won't matter. Give her time to trust you."

"I'll only be a week on this ship."

"Yes, my dear, but she isn't going anywhere. Next year, when this survey is over, you can try again—and in the meantime, write to her. I'll pass on your letters. Give her a chance to know you."

His body suddenly feeling as heavy as his heart, David nodded. First, he'd apologize—not to win her good opinion again, but because it was the right thing to do. Then he'd beg for a chance to prove himself. His mother wouldn't have asked this of him if she hadn't trusted that he wouldn't expose her people, whatever the danger was.

He'd seek her out . . . as soon as his tongue didn't feel so thick, and his head stopped throbbing. Jesus Christ. What had he just drunk?

The pounding in his brain was soon echoed by a pounding from outside. David looked toward the door. The noise was coming from the passageway, and seemed overly loud—even for an airship.

"It's nothing." Lucia was shaking her head. "Chief Leroux refuses to use the ear horn that I gave to him, which means that he hears nothing and we hear everything."

He smiled with her, then stilled at the first shout. Lucia's lips parted, and they both looked to the door again.

"*Fridasdottor! Come in here, girl!*"

Annika answered, too low for David to make out—and apparently too low for the chief to make out, too.

"*Eh?*"

Her voice rose to match his. "*I will be leaving Phatéon, monsieur, as soon as we return to Port-au-Prince!*"

No. David stood, staggered. Bracing his fist on the table and holding on to the back of his chair, he waited for the dizziness to pass. Lucia caught his arm, looked up at him with dismay.

Walls and the passageway couldn't muffle the chief's irritation. "*Why would you do that?*"

"*I've been looking for my sister. She's not on this route, so I'll be seeking a position on another ship!*"

"*So now I'll have to find two new men?*"

"*Or women, monsieur!*"

"*You smile at that, girl? Go on, then. It'll be a waste teaching you about the generator now, but I suppose a stamp on your license will make it easier to get rid of you.*"

"*Thank you, Chief!*"

He made a sound of dismissal. Lucia released David's arm and moved quickly to the door, opening it.

"Annika!"

She stopped in the passageway just outside the cabin, her expression tightening. Her flat gaze met David's for an instant before she looked to his aunt. Her voice was a thin layer of civility over steel.

"Doctor?"

"I'm sorry, Annika, but we heard—You're leaving *Phatéon*?"

"Yes. It's been four years, and I've been to every American port and around the North Sea several times over. I should have done this before, but I kept making excuses not to."

"I see," Lucia said, and so did David. *He* had spurred her into finally making this decision. "What route will you take now?"

"To the Ivory Market, or to Australia."

"*No.*" David's rough reply brought her gaze to his again. She stared at him for a long second, then dismissed him. His fingers tightened on the back of the chair.

What could he do? Tie her here? Force her to stay?

Threaten her again?

He might. God help him, he might.

Lucia wrung her hands. "Those routes are so dangerous for airships."

With a shrug, Annika said, "I cannot return home until Källa does."

"Will you send us word, letting us know where you are? How you are?"

"No."

Clearly taken aback by Annika's blunt response, Lucia tried again. "If your sister finally answers the advertisement, she will be looking for *Phatéon*—"

"I'll change the advertisements and tell her to go home instead." Her expression softened as she regarded his aunt, but David didn't see any fondness there. Only the same terrible sadness that he recognized from the wardroom, in the moment after he'd chosen to let her hate him. Only the same terrible hurt. "I've been thinking back to the conversations that we've had—and in almost all of them, you pried into my past. Why didn't you just say that I reminded you of Inga Helgasdottor?"

His aunt seemed at a loss. "I didn't want to intrude on your privacy," she finally said.

"Yes, you did. You just didn't want to be caught at it. I thought we'd built a friendship. But when created through an agenda, friendship and trust is nothing. It does you no credit." Annika's mouth trembled before she shook her head, firmed her lips. "And it does me even less, that I could not see what you wanted. I've learned well, though. I won't be so eager for company and conversation, next time."

She walked away, out of David's sight. As if in a daze, Lucia closed the door and returned to the table, pouring herself a drink.

"I cannot even refute it," she said softly. "With every conversation, I attempted to discover more about her—but I remembered your mother's secrecy, and didn't want to make her wary. So I tried to be clever about it, instead. But I like her so well; that was never a lie." She sipped the clear liquor, looked up at him with watering eyes. "What did I say about having time?"

Only a week. And David didn't see a way to have more. He would be leaving *Phatéon* to begin his survey. Annika wouldn't be here when his expedition was finished, and she refused to receive any letters from his aunt—and likely from him, too.

"I'll talk with her," he said. Though he didn't know what good it would do.

If nothing else, he would apologize. At least then his threat wouldn't weigh on him, in addition to the knowledge that he'd lost the chance to fulfill his promise.

But David felt as if he'd lost more than that.

Chapter Five

Bound by the confines of the airship, there were few places to escape someone determined to find her. With assistance from her cabin mates, however, Annika managed to avoid David for the remainder of the journey. When he waited in the passageway on the engine deck, Mary warned her to leave through the boiler room. Elena turned him away at their cabin door and sat beside Annika at the wardroom table; when their watch rotations didn't match, Marguerite brought Annika's meals to their cabin.

Annika knew they all thought that a budding romance had turned sour, and she didn't correct the misperception. She was simply grateful for her friends' help.

Despite what she'd told Lucia Kentewess, Annika didn't intend to lose touch with everyone aboard *Phatéon* when she left the airship—Elena in particular. The second mate had already offered to check on her advertisements, but Annika would have corresponded with her regardless. And despite her angry response to David's threat, she didn't want him to be killed. As soon as they reached Smoke Bay, Annika planned to send word to Hannasvik, letting them know Inga's fate—and that her son sought to bury her beads on the nearby volcano.

As soon as Hildegard heard about Inga, the woman would probably seek out David herself. Annika couldn't guess what resolution they might reach, but one way or another, Inga's runes would find their way back to Hannasvik.

They'd probably reach home before Annika did. Flying another route on a different airship, years might pass before she saw Iceland again.

The realization drove her up to the main deck soon after the lookout spotted the island. Though early in the afternoon, the sun was already low in the sky, piercing the clouds with thin gray light. Bitter-cold wind sneaked around the edges of her woolen scarf, carefully wrapped to protect the skin below her aviation goggles. Heart in her throat, Annika stood at *Phatéon*'s bow, watching the western shoreline and snow-blanketed mountains come ever closer, seeming to increase in height and breadth as they flew in.

The fishing town of Smoke Cove lay on the inland edge of a bay that stretched a hundred miles north; on the peninsula to the south, steam rose like smoke from numerous heated springs. Hannasvik lay hidden among the hills of the peninsula that formed the bay's upper boundary, and on a clear day, the mountain that David Kentewess sought was visible from Smoke Cove.

Today, though Annika stared north, hoping for a glimpse of land closer to home, clouds obscured both the peninsula and the volcano. Only the smaller mountains closer to Smoke Cove were visible across the water, a long ridge of gently rounded peaks, like a handful of children huddled beneath a blanket of snow.

As they neared the settlement, Vashon ordered the engines stopped and the sails unfurled. With engines silenced, the noise from the decks seemed that much louder—the wind whistling through the lines, every voice a shout, the canvas flapping with sharp snaps. Overwhelmed, Annika covered her ears with mittened hands, focused on the town ahead. Built up on the flats that surrounded a natural harbor, the settlement had once been a trading port until the island had been abandoned. Afterward, only a small fishing community remained.

It wasn't so small now. Since *Phatéon* had last come this way four months ago, the number of houses and buildings had doubled— the majority of them concentrated near the lake a mile from the harbor. Unease curled through Annika's stomach. Were so many people coming already?

She stiffened as someone joined her at the rail. No, not *some-one*—without looking, she knew who he was. For a week, she'd avoided David Kentewess, but even as she'd ignored him, she'd been aware of him. Every time she'd turned her face away, every time she'd left a room, every passageway she'd walked—she'd known when he was near.

He was here now. She stood frozen, palms over her ears. Walking away would be best. It would be. But he'd be leaving the ship tomorrow; the danger was almost past. Heart pounding, she lowered her hands and clenched her mittened fingers on the edge of the rail.

If he wanted to talk, she would listen. Oh, but she *wanted* to listen. She'd liked his voice so well, the deep warmth of it, the duh-*dum* rhythm of his speech.

A gust hit the airship, rocking the deck. David gripped the gun-wale, his gloved hand next to her left, his steel hand bare. As the ship settled, he said, "Komlan tells us that Fiore has brought in almost five hundred laborers, not including those in the hold."

Five hundred? She'd known that *Phatéon* carried fifty men in her cargo hold, but five hundred others had already arrived? That awful sense of inevitability weighed on her chest again. How long before they moved outward and north? "It was just a fishing com-munity a few years ago. Some sheep farmers. Why is he bringing in so many men?"

"To build a locomotive railway from Smoke Cove to Höfn."

That route followed the southern rim of the island—and would take them away from Hannasvik. Knowing that didn't ease her worry. Despite Smoke Cove's sudden growth, the population didn't compare to any of the New World towns, and couldn't justify the expense of a locomotive. "Why is he building one?"

"According to Komlan, they'll mine sulphur to supply the spark lighter manufactories."

"And the locomotive will provide transport from the mines to the ports?"

"Yes."

That meant miners—and that likely meant families would be moving in, and the merchants and farmers to support them. Perhaps they'd all stay south for a while. Hannasvik might have a few more years yet. But not long.

Annika expected David to say something similar, to use it as an argument. Why not tell him of her people's location when exposure was so certain? Closing her eyes, she waited. She didn't want to fight him now. She didn't want to run from him again.

"Annika."

Low and solemn, he spoke her name. Compelled, Annika looked up. He didn't wear goggles, and the darkness beneath his eyes and the grooves at the sides of his mouth made him appear tense and worn, as if he'd been the one run ragged by a week of four-hour shifts followed by four hours of tossing in his bunk.

Except for the way he looked at her. There was no weariness in his gaze, only intense gravity, pure focus.

"I'm sorry," he said. "I shouldn't have threatened you or your people. I'd never have carried it out. It was said in frustration, and I've regretted it from that moment."

Recalling his horror when she'd thrown his mother's words back at him, Annika believed him. "Thank you."

He nodded, holding her gaze. "I won't ask again. I understand that you have your reasons to protect them, and no reason to trust me. But I hope . . . I hope for another chance."

Annika wanted to give him one. But her secret would stand between them, and revealing it would never be her decision to make. "A friendship created on the hope that I might eventually tell you wouldn't be much of a friendship."

"There'd be no conditions." He lowered his head slightly, seemed to erase the distance between them. "Would I like to know? Yes, of course. But that isn't why I ask. We *did* get along well. I'd like to try again."

To go on as they'd begun. Oh, she wanted to. But could she trust him? "Let me think on it."

"I leave *Phatéon* tomorrow."

Her gut twisted at the reminder. He was leaving *Phatéon*—and so was she. Their paths would likely never cross again. Extending a friendship was all well and good, but Annika knew that her attraction to him could easily deepen, she *knew* that a part of her longed for more . . . and he didn't. Continuing their acquaintance would only serve as fodder for her silly daydreams. For her own sake, she should end this now.

She couldn't find the words to do it. Each one seemed to catch in the ache beneath her breast and refuse to surface. Perhaps they didn't have to. David seemed to take her silence as a response and looked away from her with a weary nod.

Her throat tightened. This wasn't what she wanted, either.

But the opportunity to give another answer passed when Dooley joined them. Taking the open spot on her right, he rested his elbows on the rail and cast his gaze over them, grinning.

"You two have made up, then?"

"No," Annika said.

He must have thought she was joking. "I'll say, never have I seen him mope as he did this week."

"You don't see it now," David said quietly.

The older man's smile froze in place. He glanced from David's face to hers, and seemed to realize that she'd been speaking the truth. Smoothly, he grinned again and tilted his bearded chin back toward the deck. "Well, I should have said it of Goltzius, of course. Awake until the single hours last night he was, composing a poem to Miss Neves. It's apparently not gone over well, because now he's all in a tiff—though he'll tell you it's because there's no flag flying over the harbor. It's still Dutch land, he says."

Annika didn't agree with Goltzius or Dooley's assessment of him. The younger man didn't look upset; he looked thoughtful, standing at the starboard rail and staring out over the southern peninsula.

Dooley sighed. "At least there's no doubt where his loyalties lie."

"Or yours," David told him.

"It's truth. Many an Irishman stood by on these freezing shores, waiting for the Horde. We've as much reason to fly our colors here—though by current count, I'd say the Castilians outnumber us all." His good humor dimmed a bit, and he looked past Annika to David. "Komlan asked us to supper in town, and offered to give us a copy of the survey they made of the lower rim. Shall we join him?"

"That depends on Miss Fridasdottor's plans." David looked to Annika. "I owe you a meal."

"Oh." No, he didn't—the obligation had been hers. Turning that obligation around must be part of his apology. She'd have liked to accept. "I can't go with you."

"You're welcome to come along with all of us." Dooley angled his head toward hers. "Kentewess isn't familiar with ladies, you understand. He doesn't realize they can't be running off alone with a gentleman."

"I can," Annika told him. Never would she be accused of proper behavior. She met David's gaze and explained, "I have only two hours before my watch begins. I must attend to my personal business while I can."

"Tomorrow, then." His last day aboard. "I'll give you time to think. You'll tell me what you decide."

The determination in his expression said that even if she didn't go to him, he'd seek her out. That even if she avoided him, he'd track her down.

He needn't worry. Annika would let him find her.

She just didn't know what her answer would be.

David didn't often fall into a foul mood. He'd learned long ago to focus on that which pleased him, not let himself be eaten up by doubt or anger. Now and again, however, everything irritated him. He sure as hell didn't want company or dinner. He should have remained on the ship—or walked through Smoke Cove, contemplating how best to persuade Annika not to cut all ties with him. The dread that she might was a dull knife twisting through his gut.

That pain was enough to rouse the sleeping bear of his choler. He shouldn't have tried to ignore it, and remained alone with his dour thoughts until the mood left him. Instead he watched the town pass outside a steamcoach window, brooding while Komlan and Dooley held a conversation around him. The lorries carrying laborers and supplies rumbled on ahead to di Fiore's section camp near the lake, where a stately residence overlooked the laborers' bunkhouses.

Goltzius had remained behind in town. David was already wishing he had, too, if only to ask why no one was patronizing the shops. It didn't make any damn sense. After years of watching his father sweat over a ledger, he was acutely aware of how many customers a shop needed to get by. His father had barely survived on velocipedal sales and repairs, plus the odd tinkering commissions unrelated to pedaling. The number of laborers di Fiore had brought in should have been a boon to shop owners. Instead the locals looked tired, worn—resentful.

Dooley must have thought so, too. "I'd have wagered that we'd see more activity, given that there're five hundred laborers with money in their pockets just come to town."

"Only two hundred and fifty men in Smoke Cove," Komlan said. "Di Fiore insisted that we don't make any problems for the town. Our men eat at the station and they can order anything else they need through our stores so that we don't put a hardship on the town, eating through their supplies and leaving them nothing."

So all the money spent went back into company pockets. That wasn't how David remembered Paolo di Fiore. He'd been a generous man. David's father had said so, too, until the day of his death. Paolo di Fiore had given everything he'd earned back to the people of Inoka Mountain—until he'd accidentally destroyed it.

Though Dooley frowned, he nodded. "I suppose it's no simple thing to restock."

"That's truth. Months might pass before an order arrives—and this has been a hard winter for trading." Komlan grinned suddenly. "But if you're looking for activity, you'll only have to wait a few hours and visit the public houses. There's enough to keep a man entertained."

David knew that Dooley wouldn't be looking for entertainment, but rather for stories from local fishermen. What would they say of the railroad men who'd moved in? "Is di Fiore in town?"

"He is." Komlan gripped the carriage strap as the steamcoach turned onto a narrow drive and stopped. Unlike the houses in town, which were small buildings constructed from dark wood siding and peaked tin roofs, or the weathered stone church, the station house was a three-storied, whitewashed block of a building. "The younger di Fiore, at least—Lorenzo. That was his ferry cruiser floating over the harbor. The elder has his head up in the æther, and is usually at the camp on the southern rim. Smoke Cove is as far as I go. I oversee the work here, while Lorenzo takes his pick of men inland, where the going is rougher. You all right getting down, Kentewess?"

David frowned. Why *wouldn't* he be all right? Rutted snow and chopped ice wouldn't trip him up. But he bit back his irritated response. The man had probably been trying to be courteous, not condescending.

Though cold, the wind wasn't nearly so bitter as it was aboard the airship. Dooley caught his gaze as he stepped out of the steam-coach. The older man wore a tight smile. David hadn't spent much time with Komlan on this journey, but his friend had often visited with the man the first few days. Midweek, David had noticed Dooley begging off from further visits, pleading work that had to be finished before they arrived in Iceland. Obviously he wanted to like the other Irishman, but was having a hard time of it.

Hopefully the survey they'd receive would be worth the time spent at this dinner. Of course, if not for this supper, he'd likely be haunting the airship's main decks, hoping to see Annika.

Moping. Brooding.

Any supper had to be better than hours of that.

David stomped the snow off his boots and followed the others inside. Whatever money di Fiore had made back from the laborers, not much of it had gone into furnishing this house. Though well-appointed, nothing in the front parlor seemed overly grand or osten-tatious, but could have come from Dooley's own house—though his house could have also fit into this one several times over.

The man who rose from the sofa and greeted them wasn't much older than David, with finely tailored clothes and a neatly trimmed beard. Well kept, but not soft. He looked the sort who might traipse alongside them on a jungle expedition, hacking away at undergrowth. His gaze rested an extra second on David's hand

and eyepiece, then came back for another look when Komlan made introductions.

"Lorenzo di Fiore, and here I've brought Patrick Dooley and David Kentewess from the Scientific Society in New Leiden."

A shaggy wolfhound sleeping in front of a fire trotted across the parlor to greet Komlan and immediately stole Dooley's attention. Di Fiore's gaze sharpened on David.

"Kentewess? Are you acquainted with Stone Kentewess?"

"My father," David said.

"And so you are the one who lost his legs." He looked David over again. "You seem to have done well enough despite that. It's incredible how technology aids us."

He'd done well enough? Undoubtedly. But his legs weren't the only thing he'd lost, and technology sure as hell hadn't helped his mother.

Courtesy, David reminded himself. Di Fiore likely had no idea. As his father had often reminded him, every man had a choice: feed that which makes you happy, or feed that which makes you rage. David wasn't certain what Lorenzo di Fiore had chosen, but he seemed to have done well enough, too.

David always chose that which pleased him—and his life *did* please him. Still, it was an effort to say, "Yes."

Di Fiore must have realized his misstep. "Not that it was easy, of course. You must still feel the effects of that disaster. I do, too. It seems we are forever visited by the sins of our fathers, however good their intentions. And how is your father?"

"Dead."

"I'm sorry to hear that. My father said he was a clever machinist."

"He was."

"Your father once sent mine a letter, forgiving him and praising him for attempting to create good in this world, because so few men ever did. That letter meant very much to my father, so much that it was one of the few things he took with him from the insanitarium. Have you ever been inside one?"

An insanitarium? "No."

"Pray that you never are. I read that letter during one of my few visits. I'd spent many years wishing that I was someone else's son—my mother changed her name to escape the stares and the hateful accusations—but your father's words made me understand, for the first time, what a great mind my father had, the importance of what he'd tried to do, and the tragedy of locking him away in that place. I vowed that I'd get him out, and dedicated the next decade to seeing him freed."

A tragedy to lock him away? Thanks to di Fiore, thousands of others had suffered a different sort of tragedy. But there were few things David despised more than conversations where the participants tried to outdo each other by comparing woes and suffering. Perhaps the man had paid enough for it. That wasn't for David to say.

But he perfectly understood being driven by a promise. "It appears you succeeded."

"Too late, perhaps." Di Fiore was silent for a moment, then clapped his hands together. The effort he made to lighten the mood made his smile appear as if fishhooks had been caught in the corners of his mouth and given a tug. "Let us go on up and eat, shall we? The dining room is on the second floor. Can you manage the stairs, Kentewess?"

Goddamn it. He knew the man only meant to be thoughtful, but if David needed help, he'd bludging well ask for it. His gritted teeth prevented every response but a nod.

Dooley clapped him on the shoulder before preceding him up. Yes, his friend had seen this before. Too often, after someone learned of his legs, it was all that they saw in him, all that they thought about, and took a full pendulum swing away from ignoring the prosthetics' existence. Instead, they became overly concerned, coddling him before every move. All well intended, but by God, even good intentions could rub a man raw and threaten to emasculate him.

At least it gave him a good account of Lorenzo di Fiore's sincerity. The man had just said that David had done well despite losing his limbs, and had gone on about the wonders of technology. Now he was asking whether David could climb stairs. Apparently, di Fiore's "done well" had been little more than stroking David on, a bit of flattery and condescension toward a man he thought not truly capable.

David took his time climbing the stairs—why not, at this point?—breathing deep, pushing away his resentment. His father had possessed a talent for saying exactly what a man needed to hear, and David thought of that now. More than once, he'd reminded David that a man wasn't made by what happened to him, but how he responded to those events.

Anger wouldn't serve him now. Explaining rarely did, either; he knew that too well.

David had once broken an engagement over a flight of stairs. Emily had been so sweet, so pretty, one of the most sought-after girls in their town—and she'd told him that she didn't mind his injuries. David, barely past eighteen, and who'd lived for years on the outside of society, always outside, had fallen quickly in love. Though he'd been embarrassed by some of the unnecessary help she'd given him, her concern, he'd ached for it, too—the attention she bestowed so willingly. He'd longed for every gentle kiss she gave to his scars, the tears she'd wept while she wished for each drop to heal him.

Everyone said that she was an angel, loving him despite his mangled face. They didn't talk so loudly about the sacrifice she was making, but everyone knew what had been left unspoken.

David's father had warned him. She'd confused loving him with loving her role as a savior. He'd confused loving her with being grateful that someone would touch him without disgust, like a starving man who falls upon the first ear of corn he finds, though it is withered, without looking farther into the field to see if there are any better to have.

His father had spoken the truth. But hunger was also a fine seasoning, making even the driest food seem succulent. David had been determinedly happy, willing to make the best of every shortcoming . . . until they'd begun talking about moving into her family home, and she'd refused to change the stairs to a ramp for his cart to climb. Her family was wealthy, she'd reminded him; it would be nothing to hire someone to carry him up the stairs. Why change it to accommodate his cart? It was only one flight, and he used his rolling chair inside the house. What difference did it make whether he got into the chair himself or someone placed him there? She wanted to make his life as easy as possible; after all, he'd already suffered so much.

David discovered that he wasn't so hungry, then.

Emily had accused him of letting his pride stand in the way. She wasn't wrong. He'd seen the decades stretching ahead of him— every day that she would tell him not to tire himself. That she would say there was no reason to get out of bed. She would do everything for him, take care of him. He'd understood then that she'd loved him for what he *couldn't* do, not what he could.

David would have rather given her up than his pride. So he had.

There would always be the Emilys who kissed him out of pity, the women who flinched away in disgust. There would always be those with good intentions. It made David more grateful for rare men like Dooley, who took him as he was—and for women like Annika, who seemed to.

No wonder the thought of losing all contact with her cut him so deeply. No wonder the thought of discovering that she might pity him or flinch away frightened him so much.

Di Fiore's opinion, however, didn't matter a bit.

Though not shed of his foul mood, David had calmed by the time he reached the dining room. Landscapes adorned the painted blue walls, but they couldn't compete with the view. Large windows overlooked the frozen lake, the snow pinkened by the setting sun. Mountains rose in the distance, basalt peaks created by an endless tumult beneath the surface, and endlessly worn down by the elements above. Incredible. David lingered at the window before taking his chair.

The table could seat a party twice their size, but was simply made. David had expected fancier decorations, given Komlan's fashionable clothing and expensive jewelry. If this was all di Fiore's doing, however, the man apparently had modest tastes.

Sitting, di Fiore loosened his neckcloth, removed his jacket, and withdrew a pipe from his pocket. He regarded David across the table. "Komlan tells me you're a vulcanologist?"

"Yes."

"And does that pay you well?"

The humor in his tone said that he knew it didn't. Dooley's laugh confirmed it. "We're paid well enough to go on expeditions, but not quite enough to live on at home. Which is why we keep going. Wouldn't you say so, Kentewess?"

That wasn't David's only reason, but he saw no reason to share it here. "Yes."

Di Fiore nodded and gave him a shrewd look. "The company could use a vulcanologist. I'm not the mind my father is, but I'm determined to help him see his hopes for this island come to fruition. The potential here is . . ."

He trailed off, shaking his head.

"Astonishing," Komlan supplied.

"Yes. Everyone in the New World is using coal to heat their boilers, but the *earth itself* can do the same here—but without the smoke, without breathing in air that turns a man's lungs black. Imagine, providing heat and hot water to every home in Smoke

Cove. With enough steam, with the proper turbines, we could electrify the town. Lights in every home, without needing to burn oil. I can hardly imagine it, but my father has already drawn up the schematics. He knows the mechanics of it . . . but I also need a man familiar with volcanic forces, who understands how that all works."

"Oh, and I see why you've brought us here, Komlan. You'll be stealing my partner away from me?"

Di Fiore smiled faintly in response to Dooley's good-natured grumble, but remained focused on David. "I'd offer any amount of money, but since you became a man of science, you obviously aren't driven by the hope of making a fortune. But we could create something great here. We could wipe clean the dirt from our fathers' names."

Dooley frowned. "Your father, Kentewess?"

"He was the head machinist on Inoka Mountain." And he'd never forgiven himself for helping to build that device, even though he'd forgiven Paolo di Fiore for inventing it.

"Think on it," di Fiore said. "I need a man like you."

The work did sound fascinating. More than that, it would allow David to remain on the island after the survey had been completed.

He'd be employed by Paolo di Fiore, though. David felt no anger toward the man but couldn't see himself working for him—and he'd never believed that Stone Kentewess's name needed to be cleaned.

"Thank you for the offer, but I can't. We have a survey to complete."

"I'm sure the society can find another vulcanologist."

"True," David said. "As can you."

Di Fiore conceded that with a nod. "Yes, I could. But I put great stock in destiny, Mr. Kentewess. It can be no accident you're here at the very moment I need you."

It was no accident that David was here, but not for this. He was here for his mother—and he preferred to make his own destiny. But he could see that di Fiore wouldn't take "no" as an answer now.

"I'll think on it," he said.

Di Fiore's lips tugged back in that fishhook smile again. "That's all I ask."

Despite the increase in population, there weren't many more boats in the harbor than usual—and only one other airship, a small ferry cruiser. As soon as the men were out of the cargo hold and their supplies unloaded, the docks quieted.

Annika waited until the steamcoach carrying David was out of sight before loading a hired sled with her own goods and trudging to the general store, swearing all the way. Unlike the port cities in the New World, there weren't any carts to run her down, but the streets were frozen into ruts of mud and snow. In Hannasvik, this would never be allowed. She'd have taken out her troll and smashed them flat.

After fifty yards of straining against the sled harness, the inside of her heavy coat steamed like a swamp. She hoped everyone at home appreciated this.

Captain Ylvasdottor wasn't the only one who supplied their village with goods from outside. Annika often picked up items on request, or things that she believed her people could use or enjoy.

She also bought far too much fabric to keep aboard *Phatéon*. Though Vashon allowed her some space in the cargo hold, it was hardly enough for four years' worth of purchases. Annika regularly sent the extra bolts of material home, where the women could use it—or put it aside until she returned.

All of it would be put aside in the general store until spring, anyway, when someone from Hannasvik would come to collect it; until then, Valdís Annasdottor would keep it for her.

Much like Captain Ylvasdottor, Valdís hadn't thought Hannasvik was big enough for her, and had struck out for the New World fifty years ago. When the ship she'd left on was captured by pirates, she'd taken a decade-long detour around the world before finally reaching the American shores—captain of her own ship, mother to two boys, and with a cargo hold full of silks and gold. Ten years later, she'd returned to Iceland, this time with a cargo hold full of dry goods. She'd set up the general store in Smoke Cove—the first in the community—and lived in the quarters above the shop ever since.

As a girl, Annika had grown up with tales of Valdís's adventures . . . and had been as terrified of the woman as she had been fascinated. One look into the woman's steely eyes, and it had been all too easy to imagine her striding across the deck of a storm-tossed ship, dagger clenched between her teeth and blood staining her sword. It had been easy to imagine her hunting down the marauders who'd murdered the father of her sons, ripping their tongues from their mouths while they pled for their lives. It was easy to imagine her seducing a Horde governor, and laughing as she sailed away with the treasures he'd bestowed upon her.

It wouldn't have surprised anyone who knew Annika that whenever she and Källa had reenacted those adventures as children, Källa had been Valdís, and Annika the cowardly foe.

After four years away and meeting with Valdís on every visit to Smoke Cove, however, Annika was more terrified by the woman's thinning frame, and by the cough that had settled into her chest the previous winter and never completely left. Valdís still had fire in her, and plenty of it—but Annika wished that she had more than two hours to spend.

She left her cart at the door and entered the store. The warm, familiar odor of surturbrand squeezed at her heart. The fibrous brown coal produced more smoke than the black, but the woody scent reminded her of home.

Smiling, Annika unbuckled her jacket. Two women examined the case of books on the back wall. Like the harbor and the streets, the general store wasn't as busy as Annika expected—and to her surprise, the shelves were almost empty, too. Valdís stood behind her counter, her iron-gray braid dangling over her shoulder, wearing the bright green tunic and trousers that Annika had sewn for her.

Annika opened her mouth to call out a greeting when the identity of those two women struck her. Long blond braids. Homespun trousers. A lavender blue tunic that she'd sent to Hannasvik last spring, because it had matched her friend's eyes.

"*Lisbet?*"

Lisbet whipped around, her blue eyes widening. Orange freckles dotted her pale cheeks, and had once been scattered across her nose until she'd lost it in a wild dog attack. Now a silver nose covered the cavity, finely shaped by Lisbet's blacksmith mother.

Laughing, Annika raced across the store and jumped into Lisbet's arms. Her best friend, the closest she'd ever come to having a lover—until they'd both realized that they'd drifted into a pair because it was easy rather than because they wanted each other. Still, the kissing had been nice while it lasted.

In any case, Lisbet had fallen in love with someone else. She drew back, happiness lighting her entire face. "Any news of Källa?"

"No. I'm sorry." Annika couldn't bear the way her expression fell. She looked to Lisbet's mother, Camille—the elder whom Källa had fought with before her exile. In appearance, she was a softer, shorter version of her daughter. "Greetings, Aunt."

Camille enfolded Annika in a hug that brought a lump to her throat. Unlike Lisbet's wild embrace, which had squeezed the breath out of her, Camille's was strong and comforting.

God, but Annika missed her mother.

Camille held her face between her hands. "Annika. It is *so* wonderful to see you here. How are you?"

"Well." She pulled off her scarf and hat, still grinning. "Very well!"

"Your hair!" Lisbet exclaimed, aghast. "That wasn't a joke? Those children stole it?"

"They did." But Annika couldn't laugh at herself for long. The implications of their presence here intruded. "Why are you in Smoke Cove during the winter? Is everything all right at home?"

"Yes," Camille said, then glanced at the door when a fisherman came in.

Valdís joined them, spoke in Norse. "Up to the table, set it for supper. I'll join you after graybeard has gone."

Annika followed the others up the narrow stairs, then sat huddled near the stove in the chilly hearth room. These tin-roofed buildings didn't retain heat nearly as well as the earth-covered homes in Hannasvik. Even the colorful, thick fabrics Valdís had hung around the walls did little to insulate it from the cold outside.

Camille and Lisbet must have been staying here a while. They moved about the room with ease, retrieving a pot, stoking the fire. The visit was obviously soon coming to an end, though: their packs leaned against the far wall, stuffed full.

"We were supposed to meet *Freya's Cloak*," Lisbet said. "Mother and I were leaving for England to find a daughter for me."

Such wonderful news. So why hadn't they gone? Why did Lisbet appear so disappointed? "Were you late arriving?"

"No. Ursula is," Camille said.

"The people who come into the shop tell Valdís that many ships are missing—including those that supply her store. The whalers say it is the megalodons, but airships haven't come, either."

"*Phatéon* did," Annika said. "And we haven't heard any rumors of this sort."

"You came from the New World?" When Annika nodded, Lisbet said, "Most of the others have come from the North Sea or Ireland. We think that perhaps the icebergs or megalodons have many of them worried, so they are waiting until it is safer."

"We have waited for Ursula almost two months now," Camille said with a sigh. "So we're leaving for home tonight, and will try again in the spring."

In the snow? Annika frowned. "How will you go?"

"By boat along the shore, north to the Winding Rock. We've hidden Rutger Fatbottom there."

Annika's troll. She grinned, picturing the trusty old machine. "Give him a kiss for me."

"I will," Lisbet promised.

This meant that her letter regarding David could reach home much faster than she'd expected. "I have news for Hildegard, too."

Lisbet exchanged a glance with her mother. The younger woman's mouth spread into a wide smile. "And we have news for you."

"What?" Annika saw that Camille was smiling, too. "What is it?"

"Your mother was missing you so terribly this summer after your letter arrived," Camille said. "Weeping every night into that crimson shawl you made for her."

That was news to smile about? Annika's heart twisted. "Oh."

"No, no," Lisbet assured her. "It is good. One evening—we don't know what happened to start it, but we heard Hildegard shouting at her in the street. 'You don't *have* to be lonely, you stubborn ewe!' and 'You are not the *only* woman missing a daughter!' Then your mother began shouting back at her. 'You faithless rabbitchaser! If I took you in, I'd find you riding the butter churn by morning!' On and on. Oh, Annika, you should have heard it. Everyone came out of their houses."

"I've never witnessed anything of the like." Camille was wiping tears of laughter. "Never."

"I never knew there were so many ways to insult a person," Lisbet said. "They shouted until Frida's voice gave out, then she stormed off into her home—"

"Probably to find something to write on," Camille broke in. "Your mother never has given up easily."

"And Hildegard followed her. She didn't come out until the next afternoon . . . and we will be delivering her letter to your mother's home, Annika Fridasdottor, because it is also Hilde-gard's own."

Oh. Annika couldn't respond. Her chest was full and tight, her eyes hot.

Lisbet's voice softened. "It was time, yes?"

Yes. Long past time. Annika buried her face in her hands, feel-ing the joyous laughter within but her eyes only crying, crying, as if a huge weight had suddenly vanished, and her relief and happi-ness was bursting out with tears.

"Weeping already?" Valdís came in and stopped, shaking her head. "I shouldn't have left you two alone with her."

Now Annika was able to laugh. She mopped her face, let out a shuddering sigh. "I'm afraid that my news isn't so wonderful. I've heard word of Inga."

"Does she live?" Camille's expression was carefully hopeful. She had been friends with Inga, Annika remembered—the twins, Frida, and Camille, all of the same age, growing up together.

"No," Annika told her.

Lisbet put her arm around Camille's shoulders. The older woman closed her eyes, nodded. "It was too much to expect. If she'd been well, she'd have sent word to us by now. How did you discover it?"

"I met her son, David. He wears her runes."

"Hildegard will want them."

Annika doubted that he would hand them over. "He's here in Smoke Cove, and he's searching for the mountain." At their looks of alarm, she rushed on, "I didn't tell him; he heard me speak Norse, saw my runes, and understood that we were from the same village. Inga asked him to bring her beads here, but he doesn't know where to go. He's determined to fulfill his promise, though."

Camille sat back, her expression thoughtful. "Källa spoke the truth the night before she left."

During their argument? "No."

"Not when she called me a stupid hag. But when she spoke of

the likelihood that Hannasvik would be found. Oh, Annika, your face hides nothing. Do you agree with her?"

She couldn't deny it. "Yes."

Camille sighed. "After two months in this village, seeing how many men have come, I agree with it, too."

"And I've always thought the same, though it's taken longer than I expected." Valdís slapped two frozen cod onto the wooden table and hefted a cleaver. "Tell us, Fridasdottor, what sort of man is her son?"

"A good man." Annika couldn't have said it so quickly of other people. "When I met him, he rescued me from danger in one of the ports, at some risk to himself. We got along well—though we did argue after I learned he was searching for Hannasvik, and he threatened to expose us all if I didn't tell him where it was—but he apologized for his threat, and I don't think he would have carried it through. And I don't think he would hurt anyone, if he could help it."

"Annika." Lisbet regarded her with a look of wonder. "You like him *very* much, don't you?"

"Yes. But I don't know if he holds the same beliefs as many others in the New World, about women taking each other as lovers."

Lisbet frowned. "Is it truly so bad?"

"Yes." Valdís hacked off a fish tail, tossed it to a large orange cat stretching its way from her bed and into the hearth room. "They'll hold you down and try to cure you of it."

"Forgive me, Aunt, but that was many years ago."

"No," Annika said. "I've seen two men hanged for it. I've heard of others sent to insanitariums. A man who is suspected might be beaten bloody by a crowd, and I've seen men come to blows, simply because one suggested that the other lay with a man. It's the worst sort of insult."

"You only speak of men," Camille said.

"Because no one speaks of the women. I only hear faint rumor and speculation—and most of that, too, is couched in insult, such as when they talk of the women who live together in England." She sighed. "Perhaps it is not so bad there, but it's difficult to find out. Simply by asking, I open myself to rumor and risk."

"The Englishwomen thought nothing of it until Hanna told them they should be wary of exposing themselves," Valdís reminded them. "They'd never learned any differently under the Horde—and it has only been ten years since the tower came down. There must be many others who think the same."

"Yes, but there are also many Brits from Manhattan City who are returning to England. We can't know what influence the New Worlders will have—whether they will be told not to expose themselves, too."

A second tail flew across the room. "We cannot know until we confront it, Annika."

"I hope to have a little more time before we must," Camille said, then looked to Annika. "What does Inga's son know?"

"He has guessed some of it—that we are a village only of women, that we have spread the stories of the trolls and witches. I've tried to tell him nothing, but he's clever, and has gleaned what he knows from our conversations."

"If he's clever, why hasn't he guessed the rest?" Valdís frowned at her. "What does he expect a community of women will do—live alone for a hundred years?"

"I suppose that he hasn't guessed because no one speaks of such things, and so he doesn't assume it of us." She flicked the frozen tail back to the cat when he batted it toward her boot. He pounced. "But it cannot be long until he realizes the truth."

"He needs to know before he meets Hildegard."

"Yes." Annika couldn't bear the thought of Hildegard's new-found happiness with her mother marred by cruelty or thought-lessness. She hoped David would be neither. But for her family, she would take the risk to find out whether he recoiled or was disgusted. "I will talk with him of it, and see his response."

And try not to think about how much his response might hurt *her*.

Camille took Annika's hands between hers, regarding her with a worried expression. "You've taken so much upon yourself. It's been four years now. If you can't find Källa, you ought to come home."

Behind her mother, Lisbet bit her lip and looked away. Annika could easily imagine Hildegard's face, too, if she returned without her daughter.

Hildegard would forgive her. Annika would never forgive herself.

"I can't," she said. "I won't, unless Hannasvik is discovered. Unless you need me."

"To fight?"

"Yes." That might be inevitable, too.

"Let us hope it does not come to that." Camille squeezed her hands. "And I will tell Hildegard of Inga's son as quickly as possible."

"He's in Smoke Cove?" Valdís frowned, as if trying to remember seeing him. "Describe his appearance."

"He only arrived today—and he looks much like Källa. He has the same black hair, the same coloring, and he's taller than most men. He doesn't wear a beard. He will be in a dark blue overcoat, which fastens crosswise over his chest with brass buckles. His shoulders are broad, and he is lean rather than fat, though you wouldn't know it from his clothes. His trousers aren't so bad, though the seams are roughly sewn and the fit over his ass isn't as snug as I would like, but his jacket looks to be made for an unshorn sheep, and his waistcoat is loose even when buckled. You will likely not notice, however, because if you see him outside, that overcoat covers it all."

"I wouldn't notice, anyway," Valdís said.

"You will notice him. He looks very serious, at first, but he has three smiles. One is for anyone who reacts to his appearance with fear—though that is not even a smile, I think, but something he does because there is no other response to give. One is for when he is uncertain, and that is only half his mouth, on the side without scars. And there is one that he saves for friends, which moves all of his face, and makes you want to smile, too."

A smile that she hadn't seen since he'd revealed his mother's runes. The realization started a dull ache beneath her breast. She wanted to see that smile again before he left *Phatéon*.

The others were quiet—waiting for more, perhaps. There was too much more. She could go on and on, but Annika remembered one thing that would interest her blacksmith aunt in particular. "Oh! And he has the most marvelous hand. You would be amazed by it, Camille."

The others stared at her. Then Valdís laughed. "May the gods be merciful to you, girl."

Heat rose in her cheeks. Perhaps she had gone on a bit long.

"Annika, the way you speak of him . . ." Camille shook her head. "Should I tell Hildegard more? Should I say something to your mother as well?"

"No." Though it hurt to say so. "I won't see him again after tomorrow."

"Can you be so certain? He has family amongst our people. After Hildegard seeks him out, you may see him again."

Annika hadn't thought of that. Though David couldn't come to Hannasvik, Hildegard might travel to visit with him—and Annika's mother would probably go with her. If she'd found Källa by then, Annika would be free to accompany them as well.

"Does he know about Hildegard? About Källa?"

"Only that I search for her. I've said nothing of their relationship."

"There can be no harm if he already knows everything but the location," Camille said.

Lisbet leaned forward, added with a wry smile, "And if you don't find Källa, return to Hannasvik in twenty years and we'll be old maids together."

Is that what their choice would be? If it was, Annika couldn't think of anyone else she'd rather be stuck with—but she wouldn't give up so soon. "I'll find her."

"You will," Camille said, then gave her daughter's bottom a slap. "And you will not be *old* in twenty years."

"I'm old now, and in twenty years I'll be dead." Valdís scooped the fish into the stew pot, gave a pointed look to Annika. "And house elves aren't coming to unload that sled. I'll open the storeroom. No, Lisbet, you stay and help your old mother finish putting out this supper."

Which meant that Annika was about to get a talking-to. She followed Valdís down the stairs, preparing herself for whatever the woman had to say.

In the darkened shop below, Valdís stopped and gave her a shrewd look before asking, "Why don't you go home now?"

Aside from every reason that Valdís already knew? Aside from Hildegard's disappointment, aside from Lisbet's hopes? Aside from her own need to take the blame of her mistake instead of allowing Källa to pay in her stead?

"Can you imagine the stories they'd tell about me? I don't know that I could lift my head up again. I am already Annika the Wool-gatherer, Annika the Rabbit." All said in fond jest, but they wouldn't be jesting if she failed. "If I went home now, I'd be Annika the Promise-Breaker."

Valdís nodded, lifting the latch to the storeroom. Swords glinted on the walls. Three cannons sat in a neat row, covered by canvas, the balls stacked into pyramids. All of the weapons had come from Valdís's ship, and she kept them in good repair—and Annika had never been certain whether Valdís held on to them because of the memories or in preparation for some other threat. Considering what she'd said about expecting trouble to come to Hannasvik, however, it was probably the latter.

Valdís held open the door while Annika brought in the first armload of silks and velvet. "What makes you believe you'll ever be able to go back?"

It hurt that Valdís had to ask. Did she think Annika would fail? "I *will* find her."

"No." The older woman's bony hand caught Annika's arm as she passed back through the door. "Even if you find her, what makes you believe you'll be satisfied with going back?"

Why wouldn't she be? "It's all I've dreamed of. I've never thought of doing anything else."

"You should."

She was speaking to the wrong person. "I'm not like you, Aunt."

"I know. You remind me of someone else."

"A cowardly foe?"

Valdís thinned her lips and let her go. Annika carried the next two loads in silence—and damn that old woman, her head was filled now, trying to think of something she could do, somewhere else to go. But she loved her troll. She loved Hannasvik. Of course, she'd loved seeing more of the world, too—but Annika couldn't think of anywhere else that she'd like to stop, to settle. Iceland was her home.

Frustration boiled up in her. Dumping the last load on top of the pile, she faced the old woman and threw up her hands. "*You* came back."

"To Smoke Cove."

"Which is close enough to Hannasvik." Annika could imagine herself here, too. It wasn't so different. "And you've done more than I ever will, have more reason not to be satisfied."

"Yes." Her steely eyes narrowed. "Be thankful for that."

But Annika wasn't. She stared at the other woman, realizing. *She wasn't thankful for it.*

Valdís cackled suddenly, watching her face. "So you see."

No, Annika didn't. It was true, she wanted to do more. *What,* exactly, she still had no idea. And she couldn't do it now, anyway. "Finding Källa comes before everything."

"So it does." The older woman sniffed. "The fish ought to be done by now."

And Annika was starving. But she wanted to know first, "Why *did* you come back?"

Valdís turned toward the stair, waving for her to follow. "For the same reason everyone runs back home: lost love."

"The father of your sons?"

"No, though I loved him in my way. This was a widow I met after my sons had grown."

Annika slowed. "From the New World?"

"Yes."

"No one ever said anything of her."

"Some stories you don't share with an entire village."

Oh. Annika wouldn't either, then. "She didn't return your feelings?"

"She did." Valdís paused at the bottom of the stair, looked back. The steel in her gaze had softened. "But she was afraid to act on them. I called her a coward and left, thinking that she would realize how much she needed me and decide that I was worth the risk. It was the most foolish thing I ever did."

"She decided you weren't?" Annika didn't know how anybody could. Valdís would have tripped anyone's heart.

"I don't know. When I returned a year later, she was dead." At Annika's gasp of denial, she nodded. "A wasting of her lungs."

A mist seemed to pass over Valdís's eyes, but with a single blink, there was steel again.

"I came back to die, Annika. Why not? I lived a full life. So I set up my store and planned to while away the years until I could join her." A sharp smile pulled at her mouth, and she started up the stairs. "That's taken longer than I expected it would, too."

David had never been courted before. All through dinner, Lorenzo di Fiore spoke of the geological activity to the south and the schemes his father had envisioned to exploit it. More than once, David caught Dooley's gaze on him, his friend's amusement at the situation as blatant as the attempt to entice him. The work did sound fascinating, and di Fiore's determination was flattering, but David wasn't so hungry now that he couldn't see the withered husks.

Despite di Fiore's claim that this was an opportunity for the sons to wipe clean the sins of their fathers, David didn't believe the man cared about Stone Kentewess's reputation. He only wanted David because his help would please Paolo.

David couldn't blame Lorenzo di Fiore for it, but he had no intention of working for him.

When dinner ended, he had some thoughts of escape. Di Fiore suggested a walk to the nearby public house, and Dooley immediately took him up on it—hoping to speak with locals about the legends, David knew. The older man didn't need him for that.

The temperature had dropped, snow falling in tiny flakes that the wind blew across the rough surface of the street like sand. The public house was a five-minute walk back toward the heart of Smoke Cove, and most of it spent in silence, with their heavy scarves covering their mouths and noses. David walked with his face angled into the wind, so his breath didn't fog his eyepiece.

The warm glow in the pub's windows was a welcome sight—and *Phatéon* hovering over the harbor even more welcome—but David's intention to say his farewells in the street and keep on going waned when he heard the noise coming from inside.

Men shouting—for a pub, nothing unusual. Louder than their

raised voices, though, the repeated strike of metal against metal. CLANG. CLANG. *CLANG!*

Curiosity drew him closer. The building had been recently enlarged. New birch planks adjoined weathered boards, clearly marking a tall addition on the side.

The shouts erupted into cheers and groans, the unmistakable sound of a competition's end, with more losers than winners. The clanging stopped. Dooley glanced back at Komlan.

"Are they hammering rail spikes?"

"A race?" Di Fiore answered with a shake of his head. "We'd rather they expend their energy on the line. This is a different sort of entertainment—an old invention of my father's, put to new use."

Hell. David couldn't walk away now. Inside, the noise and heat were almost unbearable. His eyepiece immediately fogged. He wiped it clear with the end of his scarf, then shed his hat and unbuckled his coat. The main tap room held tables and stools at the bar, most of them full. Di Fiore glanced at Komlan, who nodded and spoke to Dooley. The two men headed into the tap room. Di Fiore gestured for David to join him.

Men crowded the addition, standing shoulder to shoulder. A pair of barkers stood at the entrance, collecting money for cards. The laborers pushed for position around them, most of them shouting in Spanish, but fell back as di Fiore approached. Looking harassed and sweating, one of the barkers managed a smile for di Fiore and handed over two cards.

A stair took them to a second level, open in the center and looking down over the main floor. Two pulleys hung from the peaked ceiling, their cables taut. Though as crowded as the lower level, an empty table stood near the rail. Di Fiore's regular table, apparently.

David took a seat, got his first look over the rail—and into a battered steel face. Twice as tall as a man, an automaton stood off-center in the main floor. An identical opponent was squared off against it, broken in half. The thick torso had folded over backward at the waist, still attached to the legs by thin cables. From above, the clockworks inside the abdominal cavity were visible, a complicated arrangement of gears and rods.

A slow chant began building on the first level. A group of men, four to each side, pushed against a long capstan bar, winching cable around a cylinder. David's gaze followed the length of the cable up to the pulley on the ceiling, and down to where a heavy hook attached it to the defeated automaton's skull.

With a shriek of steel, the automaton lifted its head. Metal groaned as the torso followed. Like a puppet pulled by one string, the upper half rose disjointedly, arms dangling, its head at an angle no human could survive. Finally upright, the abdomen settled onto the legs. A thin man pushed a ladder forward and climbed—apparently locking it into place. A moment later, the laborers at the winch backed up. The cable loosened and the hook slipped out.

The automaton remained standing. Both machines had obviously been through the routine before. Dents and gashes covered the steel housings. Their fists had been pounded into blunt hammers.

Di Fiore slid a paper clamp and a card marked with a grid of circles across the table. "Push out a sequence!" he called over the noise. "It gives the fighter an instruction—the type of punch to throw. Right, left, uppercut, roundhouse, and so on. If the fighter knocks over the other on your card, you win. You can also bet on the time it'll take before one falls."

There were no descriptions of what each sequence would do, no guides. Perhaps that was part of the game—figuring out what each pattern did. David clamped it three times at random.

"Just the card, I think."

The other man nodded. "The odds don't favor anyone."

Di Fiore glanced over the rail, gestured to someone below. Only seconds passed before a boy arrived at the table to collect the cards.

The crowd quieted. Anticipation rose through the noise that

remained. The two barkers approached the fighters. Each carried a stack of cards and inserted them into a slot cut out of the automatons' right legs. A bell rang. The barkers each pulled a lever on the knees and raced out of the arena.

The first right hook landed with a deafening crack. The floor shuddered beneath David's chair, his feet. The second machine flew backward, the cables at its waist exposed. Its roundhouse missed the other automaton completely. Laughter and jeers rose from the crowd. A sharp winding click rose over the noise, and the automaton snapped back into place. The impact of the blow it smashed into the first machine reverberated through David's own chest.

Di Fiore leaned back in his chair, lighting his pipe and studying David through the curl of smoke. "Impressive, yes?"

David had never seen anything like it. His prosthetics were more sophisticated, the sentinels that guarded the American coastline were bigger, more powerful, and he'd seen clockwork machines that were just as intricate—but those clockworks all operated in a predetermined sequence. Even those with variant sequences, such as playing different songs or performing different tricks, operated in a predictable pattern.

It was incredibly impressive. Not as astonishing as nanoagents, perhaps, but well worth the praise. "Are these the only two?"

Di Fiore nodded. "For now, at least. I'll manufacture more soon, but the cards are a sticking point. Everyone is willing to pay for the machines, but no one wants to keep paying for cards after they've used up their first shipment—and of course, we'll make most of our profit on the cards."

Given the number of cards used up in one fight, David believed it. "You said this was an old invention? This card system was developed then, too?"

"Yes. And buried for almost forty years."

"By your father? Why?"

"They were never designed for entertainment—the machines

were supposed to fight the Horde's metal men that they'd heard rumors about. Then the Lusitanians discovered that the metal men were actually soldiers in steam-powered suits, not automatons, and so they asked inventors to create similar technology instead." He smiled faintly. "My father was in the business of war long before he tried to stop it. Do you know what changed his mind?"

David didn't. He shook his head.

"He visited Horde territory."

A thunderous cheer erupted around them. David glanced over, saw the first automaton had taken a blow that tipped it backward . . . and slowly over. Its shoulders *thunk*ed against its legs, guts exposed. Di Fiore tugged out his pocket watch.

"Good time." He tucked his watch away. "Listen to them. Even those men who don't win are always more satisfied when the fight lasts a while."

Long enough to get their money's worth, anyway. The boy brought two more cards. David punched out five circles. "What did your father find?"

From his own travels, David had an idea. The Horde-occupied territories he'd passed through hadn't been anything like he'd expected, considering the tales of terror he'd heard growing up. Some of the stories were true—the Horde did possess giant war machines. The Great Khan did have an iron fist that would crush anyone who stood against him.

But people were crushed in the New World, too. In many ways, the Horde citizens he'd encountered were no different than people anywhere else—and the differences that did exist were seemed no greater than the differences between the people of Manhattan City and Lusitania, or the Liberé and the Arabic tribes of the Far Maghreb.

"He found nothing," Di Fiore confirmed. "And this was twenty years before the tower fell in London. The Horde had no navy— only merchant ships and barges. All these years, we'd been terrified that they'd arrive on our shores, and the Horde had never been interested in coming. They weren't breeding animals to women." He frowned and tilted his head, as if in concession to a point David hadn't made. "The frenzies were real enough, it's true. The infected were forced to breed when the tower sent out the right signal. The zombies are real. The laborers' augmentations were real—though you, of all people, can see the good of that, too."

No, David couldn't. There was nothing decent about forcibly amputating a person's limbs and replacing them with tools, simply to create a more efficient work force. David couldn't argue that he hadn't benefited from the technology, but he'd never call the original application *good*.

"I don't think my situation is comparable."

"Perhaps not. My point is, my father realized that everyone's fear of the Horde was all a fear of nothing. No one bothered to look beneath the stories—but at the same time, that fear united all those kingdoms and countries for centuries, gave everyone a common purpose." His voice rose with the fervor of a man at a pulpit. "My father wanted to give everyone something to hope for instead. You saw the mountain builder region before he arrived at Inoka. The hills stripped, the plains lying fallow, all of it barren as a result of their endless disputes. What did your people call it? A locust war?"

They hadn't been his father's people, but David didn't think pointing that out would make any difference. Many people lumped all natives into a single group. "A grasshopper war."

"Over a small bit of land that they ruined while they fought over it. Coal smoke choking everything, the rivers black. But my father gave them something else to fight for: He brought to them a mountain that reached up to the heavens, and at its heart a machine to clear the air, clean the water." He paused and drew on his pipe before adding, "And he did stop the disputes. Not the way he planned, of course."

Not the way he planned? The disputes ceased because thousands of people were dead, and no one wanted to continue a war while they picked up pieces of their children and wives.

A deafening screech from the fallen automaton prevented immediate reply—perhaps for the best. The metallic groan continued as men hoisted the machine. With a mix of fascination and revulsion, David watched di Fiore observe the proceedings.

Was this what it meant to be Paolo di Fiore's son? To admire his father, he had to reinterpret and justify his failings, his mistakes?

He turned to David again. "What do you believe is stronger—fear or hope?"

Where the hell would a question like that lead? Almost afraid of the answer, but curious despite himself, David responded honestly. "I want it to be hope. I don't know if it is."

"Neither do I. But I want to find out." He looked over the rail as a new fight began—not watching the automatons, but the men shouting below. "I'm not a naturalist like you, or an inventor like my father. I'm an observationist. I put things together to see what will happen."

"Things?" That wasn't what di Fiore was looking at now. "Or people?"

"People, this time. Those crushed beneath the boot of the Castilian court. Those ruled by fear of torture, of hunger, of death." He glanced over as Komlan joined them, a drink in hand. "We'll feed them, let them grow strong, tell them they can win—teach them to fight. And we'll see what happens when the work is done."

The meaning of that sank in. "You're sending back an army?"

"We're sending back *men*," Komlan said, obviously familiar with di Fiore's plan. "Men who've been taught to get back up when they're knocked down, to try again."

David had no love for Castilian royalty, but it seemed a cold-blooded way to send men to their death—especially as di Fiore had no investment in their victory or loss, except to observe an outcome.

"We also need men on that floor, instead of machines." Komlan gestured toward the fighters. "It would be more of a victory when they see one of their own struck down, then get back up."

"No," di Fiore said. "Someone has to be defeated. We don't want anyone to see himself as the person who loses."

Komlan nodded thoughtfully, sipping his drink. "Well, what of bringing in augmented buggers from England? We could put a man with a hammer against a man with spring legs, or a meat cleaver against a gaff-man. They'll heal quickly, too. A man watching won't see himself in them, won't think of his pain and defeat the same way."

David unclenched his jaw. "I assure you, we do."

Both looked to him—di Fiore *observing*, Komlan frowning. "No need to be overly sensitive about it, son," Komlan said. "Those Englishmen raised under the Horde think differently than you or I do. If they agree to fight, there's no harm done."

Except that they would be asked to fight because they weren't considered men. Because that difference made it easier to watch them draw each other's blood.

"Kentewess is right," di Fiore said. "Men like him have had to fight harder than all of us, every day; so did those under the Horde. They've already felt enough pain, so why add more? It should be a lesson to the rest of us, to remember how our lives could be much more difficult. We need to be thankful for what we have—and we have these fighters."

Bludgeon all of that to hell. David didn't want to be a hero, or a lesson. Just a goddamn man. People treating him like less or more than one made his life more difficult than losing his legs ever had.

Cheers sounded again as the automaton fell. Beaten, broken in half, but easily repaired. David suspected that the two men at the table didn't see him much differently.

Annika did. And he would rather see her.

He rose abruptly, gathered his coat. "I must take my leave. Thank you for the meal, and the conversation."

Di Fiore stood. "I hope we didn't upset you? We didn't mean to run you off."

"I'm not running." But he didn't see the sense of staying where he was. David fed that which made him happy, not angry. "I have plans to see a woman."

"Ah." That fishhook smile appeared again. "I hope you have an answer for me."

David was waiting for an answer, too. Though he hoped to see Annika tonight, however, he wouldn't ask her for it yet. "I must refuse. Your offer is generous, but I'm satisfied with my current situation."

"I urge you to reconsider. My father could use your help."

"I won't change my mind."

Di Fiore nodded, held out his hand. "Until next time, then— when I'll try harder to persuade you."

He could try all he liked. David took his leave, found Dooley drinking with a fisherman in the tap room. The older man took a single glance at his face. "So they got to you at the end?"

"I'm done with it," David said.

"Go on, then. Svenson and I are trotting up to the next pub, where it's a bit easier on the ears. I'll see you when."

With a nod, David made his way outside. God, he could breathe again. A heavy clang sounded behind him. A mild tremor ran up his legs . . . and continued.

That wasn't the automatons.

He rode through the minor quake, watching the houses, listening. Sheep bleated behind tall fences, but everything else remained quiet. Not strong enough to damage any of the buildings, the

quake had either centered miles away, or hadn't been that powerful to begin. Many of the townspeople likely hadn't noticed it
at all.

David started off again. Two inches of snow had covered the
street, making the going more treacherous now that he couldn't
spot the icy ruts as easily. Lamplight glowed in the windows of
the houses, casting patches of gold over the white. Two women
approached, each wearing thick coats with furred hoods, tapping
through the snow ahead of their feet with wooden staffs, testing the
ground. Heavy packs burdened their shoulders. He edged toward
the right side of the street to give them more room.

The first woman paused, staring at him through the dark. Damn
it all. The last time he'd passed a woman on a darkened street, she'd
screamed and run, and he'd spent the rest of the evening wavering
between pissed off and guilty, in turns.

His foul mood had just left him. Why this?

"David Ingasson!"

He stopped, shock rooting him in place. *That accent.* But she
wasn't Annika. His light-enhancing lens clicked into place, showed
him a pale face and a silver nose beneath the shadow of a hood,
and the softer version of that face a few steps ahead.

Heart pounding, he found his voice. "Yes?"

The older woman spoke. "You seek to bury your mother's beads.
If you give them to me, I will see that it is done."

She would? He could hardly comprehend how she even *knew.*
"Annika told you?"

"Yes."

Annika had told them. Yet they weren't hostile. Whatever she'd
said must have put him in a better light than his threat deserved.

"What say you, Ingasson? The blood of her sister will do as well
as yours, and will guide Inga to her own mother's side."

Surprise struck him again. *"Her sister?"*

"Yes."

He had another aunt? "What is her name?"

"Hildegard." The woman smiled slightly, as if amused by his astonishment. "Will you give them over?"

Torn, David considered it. The task would be completed . . . but his mother hadn't only asked for her beads to be buried. She'd asked *him* to do it. "I promised that I would bury them myself."

She nodded. "So I will tell the others. Where do you travel to next, Ingasson?"

"Vik, for the next month." With forays north to the glaciers. "Then we head to Höfn. What is your name?"

"I am Camille. She is Lisbet, my daughter." The girl hadn't taken her eyes off David during the conversation, but he hadn't seen any wariness there. Instead she wore a smile with her lips pressed tight together, as if suppressing laughter. "Can I trust you not to follow us?"

He wouldn't have, anyway. But David sensed that if he broke that trust, she'd see that he never fulfilled his promise. "Yes."

"Safe journey, Ingasson."

They started off again. David watched them go, still disbelieving that they'd ever been there—and soon, he realized, there wouldn't be evidence that they had been. The snow fell steadily. Their tracks would be filled in by morning.

In a daze, David returned to the airship. *He had another aunt.* The cargo lift carried him up to the main deck, where he paused. Annika stood at the starboard rail, immediately recognizable by the brightness of her scarf. She wore the blue wool mantle that covered her from shoulder to thigh—the balloon warmers radiated heat the length of the deck, making a coat unnecessary.

She didn't look up at his approach, but leaned against the side with her elbows resting on the gunwale and her chin propped on mittened hands, her gaze fixed north. David stopped, taking her in, feeling the painful twist in his chest as he studied her face. Her faraway expression held longing, sadness—as if whatever she wanted wasn't here.

Almost everything that he wanted was. He cleared his throat. Annika glanced up. Her smile of greeting eased the pain near his heart.

And he was beginning to realize just how much he owed her. Despite her insistence that she couldn't help him, she *had*. He didn't know what would come of the discussion Camille had with the others, and he didn't know whether she'd done it for his sake or for his mother's, but he'd always be grateful for it.

"Thank you," he said.

Her brows came together and she straightened, turning to lean back against the rail. "For what?"

"I met Camille and Lisbet."

"Oh." Her eyes widened, lit by surprise. "What did they say?"

"Camille said she would see my mother's runes buried for me."

"And?"

"I refused. I promised my mother I would do it, and so I will." The heat from the warmers was painful against his back now. When they'd been under way, the constant wind had kept them from becoming too hot, but the wind from the bay wasn't doing the same job. He turned, feeling like a piece of a meat on a spit. "Now I wonder if I was mistaken. If she only wanted to have them buried, does it matter who buries them? But if she meant for me to do exactly as she asked, then I'm the only one who can. What if I fail, however? What if I refused my only opportunity to see the task done? I'm not sure what serves her best."

Annika pursed her lips as if considering the dilemma. Her mouth plumped, and for an endless moment, David wasn't torn with indecision at all. He wanted to taste her mouth beneath his, to feel the heat inside, to know the sweetness of her kiss.

Desire stirred up an ache that had become all too familiar since he'd met her. David turned against the rail again and let the cold breeze hit his face. It didn't help.

Finally, she shook her head. "Who can know what she intended? But everyone will think well of you for adhering to your promise."

He wanted them to. He wanted *her* to. After years of not caring what others thought of him, here he was worrying about it again. "She said I had an aunt. Hildegard."

"Yes. She is Källa's mother."

"Your sister, Källa?" He searched her face, couldn't find the slightest resemblance to his mother. "We are cousins?"

"No." Annika studied him in return, her expression suddenly guarded. "Källa and I have different mothers."

"And fathers?"

She shrugged, as if to say it hardly mattered. He couldn't imagine. David's father had meant everything to him.

But if Annika and Källa had different mothers and fathers, he must have misunderstood what she'd meant by the term "sister." Very likely, she used it as some religions did, referring to all other women as sisters. Källa must have been close to Annika, however, if she'd spent four years looking for her.

She was still watching him in that careful way. Still unsure. Or just so accustomed to concealing her origin that sharing made her wary.

"You're searching for my cousin." At her nod, that sense of wonder came over him again. He had another aunt. He had a cousin. "Let me help."

Her eyebrows arched. "How will you?"

"I'll do what you do. I'll buy advertisements—but with a wider range. I'm not limited to an airship route. I correspond with scientists around the world; I know they will help."

"Why? You don't know her."

"I'd like to."

She narrowed her eyes. Not certain of him yet.

"Think on that, too," he said. "Give me your answer tomorrow."

"All right."

The airship's bell rang four times as she spoke. The middle of a watch, he realized.

"You aren't on duty?"

"I am, but we're in port, and there's little to do that I haven't already done." She turned toward the bay again, her face flushed with heat. "I only have to stoke the furnace and check the warmers. They were running a bit hot."

"Only a bit?"

Suddenly laughing at him, she said, "Yes."

"How long before you have to go?"

"About half an hour before I need to stoke again—and I'm waiting to see that the warmers cool."

"So you have a little time."

"Time to talk about something else." Her eyes still alight with humor, she asked, "Shall we finally talk about you?"

They'd never gotten to him the first night. This was long overdue. "All right."

"Do you chase volcanoes because of the promise to your mother? Have you been hoping to find the mountain?"

"That's how it began. I read as much as I could, searching for any mention of a burial site. I became fascinated along the way." That search had led him to her, too—and he'd become just as fascinated again. "Even after I bury her runes, I'll continue to study them."

She looked at him as if he were mad. "Why?"

He grinned. "We have to live with them, don't we? It's better to understand them than to just fear them."

"There's good reason to fear them."

"Yes," he agreed.

She studied him, brows lowering, her lips pursing again. He only had to lean over and press his mouth to hers. Would she soften against him? A gasp of surprise against his lips, then a deeper taste . . . or she'd push him away.

God, he was a fool. She was still debating whether they could even be *friends*, and yet he was dreaming of kissing her? He was aroused at the thought of her melting against him? He'd obviously lost his mind. David turned again, made himself focus on her eyes.

That didn't help much, either.

She looked out over the bay again, her gaze lost in the distance, her expression pensive. "I suppose you want to make certain that what happened to your mother doesn't happen again."

"It will happen again," he said. Not the same sort of disaster, but a disaster all the same. "And again and again."

"Then why?"

"Because we might make a difference. If we predict an eruption, we can move a population to safety."

She glanced back at him. "You can predict one?"

"Not yet." He grinned when she laughed. "But there's more than that. A century ago, the year after the fissure eruptions, temperatures dropped—not just in winter, and not just in the northern regions. It was among the worst famine years worldwide, even among the Horde. Many of us think that it was caused by the ash in the air, blocking the sun."

"Truly?"

He nodded. "It also happened after the eruption at Krakatoa. So if we study the volcanoes, if we know how much ash they eject, how high it goes, where the wind takes it, we can help people prepare for long winters, low harvests."

She looked up at him, a new light in her eyes, as if seeing him now in a different manner. "That's . . . admirable. I thought you might be seeking glory."

That startled a laugh from him. "No. There's not much glory to be had. Most of the work is tedious and dirty, the weather always too hot or too cold, and in the middle of an expedition I often have to remind myself why the hell I'm risking my life for it."

"Yet you still make something good out of it."

"Volcanoes do that, too." He was determined to make a believer of her before the night was through. She listened so closely, rapt— no doubt she'd soon be fascinated, too. "For all of their destruction, they create even more. New islands, new lands. All of Iceland."

She slanted him a disbelieving glance.

"I swear it," he said.

With a nod, she looked out over the water, her gaze sweeping the mountains in the distance, the shoreline nearby. Seeing them differently, he thought.

"That's a much better answer than glory," she said softly.

"Don't think too much of it. I wouldn't reject glory if it came to me." He loved her quick laugh, her wry nod. Though in truth, he *had* rejected it—or at least the greatness that di Fiore had offered. David glanced toward the bow, where the ferry cruiser was tethered twenty yards away. "That's Lorenzo di Fiore's ship."

"The man building the rail?"

The rail. She must have been one of the few people who didn't hear the di Fiore name and immediately think of Inoka Mountain. "Yes. Dooley and I had dinner with him."

"What was he like?"

Broken, he thought. Broken long ago by his father's disgrace, and put back together in the wrong way. David couldn't pity him for that—but perhaps that was his own failing, the effect of his own past.

And what was di Fiore like now? "He's the sort of man who never seems to listen during a conversation. He only waits for his turn to speak."

Annika wrinkled her nose and made a strangled noise in the back of her throat.

David laughed, nodded. "Yes. Exactly like that."

"So you didn't like him."

"Not particularly, no. But I never expect to get along with anyone quickly."

Her gaze lifted to his, her humor softening into a wistful sigh. "Neither do I."

He wanted to see her smile again. "I had an advantage, if you recall—my odor wasn't offensive."

He was rewarded by the curve of her lips, a flash of her teeth.

"Oh, yes," she said, and leaned closer, her face nearing his throat. David froze. He felt the warmth of her breath, caught the scent of her hair—like rosemary, or the heated pine of a forest in the summer. She inhaled and drew back, turning toward the warmers with her hands pressed to her cheeks. "You're still all right."

"Good." David could barely manage that. He turned again, hiding his body's response.

She glanced at his face before looking away. Her eyes closed briefly, then she peeked at him again. "Was that a soap? It was nice."

"Shaving soap."

He heard the roughness of his voice. God. She could come close again, if she wanted to, smell it for as long she liked.

"Oh." She bit her lip, seemed to hesitate before saying, "Mary Chandler is the worst person to learn anything from. She said that native men don't have to shave, and that is why they never wear a beard."

"Perhaps some don't. I do, but I don't have to shave often—yet I know others who shave every day. Others pluck out the hairs as they grow in, starting when they are young men."

"So it is a fashion."

"For some. I know others who've grown out a beard—and most have been living in the cities for some time."

"Trying to fit in?"

Or because they already did. "Yes."

A heavy sigh escaped her. "I don't think I ever will fit in. Only at home—and even there, not in every way that I would like to." She glanced up at him. "Sometimes I think it would be nice to be normal somewhere."

He knew that feeling—though he wasn't feeling it now. "I think that place is here."

Her gaze followed the path of his hand as he indicated the space around them. She glanced up with a smile and a curious look.

"Did you ever try to fit in?"

"Not with the whites." David thought of stopping there, but knew they weren't just talking about him because he was in the conversation queue. At different moments, he could feel her weighing his words, as if she needed to make a judgment or come to a decision. And he supposed she did—tomorrow.

If he wanted her to trust him, evading or lying would do him no good.

He looked out over the water. "Many of my father's people were among those who converted when the Europeans first came. My name—Kentewess—identifies me as one. When I was a boy living in the east, the reclaiming of the old ways had just begun, so I didn't think of it much. But when we moved to the mountain builders' city with di Fiore, many of those around us took great pride in never having converted, never having lost history to Europeans. And when I was with the other boys, I would do everything I could to avoid mentioning my name, and gave them instead the name of an ancestor. I'd ask my father for legends, for tales—not even to truly honor them, but because knowing them made it easier to not feel . . . European."

"Did it work?"

She was watching him, angling her head slightly as if to better see his expression. He turned again, suddenly conscious of his good side.

"In truth, I don't know that it ever mattered to the other boys as much as it mattered to me. I never felt as if I fit in, but I was never excluded, either." He shook his head. "Now, I think about my father more than I ever do them. I remember the anger I felt toward him for converting—even though he hadn't; our ancestors had— and I remember the guilt for feeling that anger. He never went by any name but Kentewess. And even though I turned my back on that, he was never angry in return. He said I would find my way." He glanced at Annika, gave a wry smile. "Then the mountain came down, and I was never likely going to fit in anywhere, no matter what I called myself."

Especially after his nanoagent infection finished off any chance of ever being accepted. After the Europeans had come, disease had devastated many of the native tribes in the east. Now, though some infected men bribed their way past the port gates and into the cities, they were summarily rejected from native enclaves—including the town where David and his father had retreated to after the Inoka Mountain disaster. The town hadn't been much different than many European communities of similar size, but descendants of converts had begun to reject the European influence, reclaiming the past. Giving children the old names . . . *christening* them with the old names, and either not seeing the irony or ignoring it.

The Americas would never be as they'd been before the Europeans arrived. It would be true of Iceland, too, whether the Dutch returned or only miners came. Her village, once found, would be irrevocably changed.

No wonder Annika was terrified that they'd be discovered.

"You call yourself Kentewess now," she said.

So he did. "But not as a statement—unless it's the pride of being my father's son. I can't imagine carrying any other name."

Her eyebrows arched. "Not even Ingasson?"

He'd never considered it before. "Perhaps I'll add it."

She smiled, but it froze when her gaze fixed on something behind him. David looked over his shoulder. Maria Madalena Neves had come up to the main deck, wearing a red cloak trimmed in white fur. Her nurse accompanied her—not the older, stern woman that David had imagined, but as young as her charge, and pink in her cheeks.

Annika sighed. "She's beautiful, isn't she?"

"Yes." He couldn't deny it.

"She doesn't fit in, either. You've heard where she's going?"

"Heimaey." When she didn't respond, David glanced over. She was watching him again, her expression uncertain . . . then slowly hardening with resolve. He frowned. "What is it?"

"Do you know *why* she's going there?"

The heat in his face wasn't just from the warmers. "I've heard that it's to keep young women . . . intact."

And that was about as awkward a thing a man could say, but Annika didn't seem to notice. "My first year aboard, we took a different girl there and I overheard a few of the aviators discussing the island. They thought the Church spread the story about them all being virgins to protect them."

"From what?"

Annika glanced across the deck again. "*Look* at them. When she thinks no one is watching."

He did, and Maria Madalena appeared just as haughty and regal as when she'd slammed the door in David's face. But not at every moment, he realized. The nurse spoke to her, and he saw the softness there, the warmth—the tight smile that seemed to suppress laughter. Then she caught the eye of an aviator and tossed her head, every inch the arrogant, rich woman again.

What would the Church be protecting them from? David wasn't Catholic, but he'd read some of the more contentious historical debates while at the university. Remembering the wake of terror following the first reports of the Horde's frenzies, and the Church's call for leniency toward sodomites at the same time several king-doms had been writing severe punishments into law, one possibil-ity seemed more probable than others.

Carefully, because even the suggestion could harm the young woman, David said, "You think they're Sapphists?"

"I don't know what that means."

"They share a bed."

"Yes." Her gaze didn't waver from his. "I also heard the aviators say that it's a sickness, and the cure is a man between their legs. Do you think so?"

He frowned. "Forcing any woman is indefensible."

"No," she said. "Do you think it is a *sickness*?"

The directness of her query demanded honesty. "I haven't thought about the reasons for it."

"You need to. Before you pledge yourself to helping Källa, before Hildegard comes for you. If you think it's a sickness, you need to give those runes over and let them be."

Understanding slipped in, and in the space of a breath, tore apart every assumption he'd made. Reeling, David shook his head, trying to reorder everything he'd learned about his mother's peo-ple, to see through this new lens.

Why hadn't he seen it before? Good Christ, it was so obvious. She and Källa had two mothers, yet they were sisters. They were a community of only women . . . and both Annika and his mother had kept them secret, protecting them.

They were right to protect them. God knew what would hap-pen if the women were discovered.

Her gaze was still on him. Her stiff expression gave little away, but she held herself tight, her mittened hands shaking. "Will you think on it, David Ingasson?"

David nodded, hoping the response would reassure her—and realized that he *had* thought on it before, though not regarding women. He knew of several male colleagues who were rumored to have shared more than tents during their expeditions, though the rumors were quiet, for fear that the men would be hurt by them. David wasn't interested in that sort of companionship for himself, but he didn't care that others did. He didn't care that his mother's people did the same.

Except for one.

Was this why Annika had told him she wouldn't share his bed without love? It would be a simple claim that could keep men at arm's length without risking herself.

David had no right to ask. He knew it. There was small hope of anything ever coming of his attraction to her . . . but he needed to know if that little hope was actually no hope at all. "You?"

She bit her lip, clearly uncertain, and David felt like an ass. "You don't have to—"

"I don't know," she said. A worried line formed between her brows. She glanced back at the deck, and her voice lowered to a whisper. "I don't know. There was a girl, a friend. I hoped it would become more, but it never did. Then I thought perhaps there weren't enough women in Hannasvik, and so I couldn't meet the right one."

Then she'd begun searching for Källa. "But it would be difficult to find someone in the New World," he realized. She'd be taking a tremendous risk.

"Yes." She exhaled a shaky breath. "But I also wondered if I was like some of the other women who preferred men, even though they'd never seen one. I thought that when I left, I would know for certain. But I didn't. Four years, and there was no one that I . . . no one . . ."

Her lips pressed together and she stared out over the water. Tension held David still. She seemed on the verge of bolting, and he feared that a word or a movement might startle her away. He couldn't imagine the terror that must be coursing through her now in sharing this with him. He'd have done anything to ease that for her, but he knew there was little to do—only clench his fists and wait, his chest aching for her, his mind filled with slowly building anger.

This *shouldn't* be so terrifying to confess. She shouldn't have to fear anything.

"I *have* felt attraction to a man, but only—" She cut herself off, hesitated before starting again. "In general, I think women are more appealing in appearance."

"So do I," David said, and was gratified to see her quick smile. Her expression lost some of its petrified rigidity.

She looked up, met his gaze. "What I told you is true—I want to love someone first. Man or woman, I don't care. I want to feel as if my guts are riveted together, to feel as if I would do anything just for a kiss, or a touch, or to see them. I want to feel as if I can't live without them, and if I have to . . . if I *have* to live without them, I want to feel as if every moment I had with them was worth a lifetime of love. And I want to be loved that way in return."

Her words gripped his heart, twisted it hard. That was what he wanted, too.

Annika caught her lip between her teeth again, watching him—uncertain again, he thought. "Does that sound like a foolish dream?"

"If it is, then I'm a fool, too."

This time her smile came more easily, appeared less brittle. The ring of the ship's bell sounded. She startled, glancing back at the deck and blinking.

"I'm due below again." She backed away from the rail, her eyes still on his. "So will you think on it?"

He didn't need to. But he doubted that she would believe an answer given so quickly. "I will," he said. "And you'll give me your answer tomorrow, too?"

She nodded, her gaze holding his for another long second before she turned. David watched her go, then looked out over the bay. Movement near the shoreline caught his eye. Two figures in a boat, rowing north.

Camille and Lisbet.

His heart gave a heavy thud. He studied the mountains across the water again, then the conical peak that rose even farther in the distance, and remembered Annika's faraway expression as she'd gazed in the same direction.

David would have wagered anything that the burial site he sought lay up there, somewhere. But he would wait. Camille had asked him not to follow them, so he wouldn't take advantage of the path he saw them travel now. And to tell him all that she had, Annika must have begun to trust him—or discovering his reaction before he met with Hildegard had been worth the risk she'd taken. So he would wait for his aunt. If she didn't come, then he would look to the northern peninsula again.

And he would wait for Annika's answer tomorrow. It was incredible, but despite the satisfaction of his work, the imminent fulfillment of his promise to his mother, any future happiness seemed to be riding on the thin hope of continuing their friendship.

David thought his heart was riding on it, too.

Chapter Six

Annika had told David to think on it, but throughout the night and the next morning, it was she who thought of nothing else. Whether stoking the engine or lying in bed, she recalled the stunned incredulity in his expression when he'd realized the truth. No revulsion had followed, but that might come as his shock receded.

Anxiety kept her company through the hours. If he felt disgust, that would be the end of their acquaintance. She would send word to Hildegard, and try to forget that she'd ever thought well of him.

And try not to feel devastated, wondering how she could have been so *wrong*.

If he didn't believe they were all suffering from a foul sickness, however . . . she simply didn't know what her own answer would be. Continuing to correspond with him would imperil her heart, and Annika wasn't adventurous. She'd always known what her life would be—and though the search for Källa had thrown a spanner into the works, as soon as that was over, Annika planned to continue as she'd started.

Her attraction to him threatened to disrupt everything. She'd have been content in Hannasvik. Even if she'd never fallen in love, she'd have found a daughter and raised her alone as her mother had done. She'd have been satisfied.

But it was true that when she'd left her village, she'd hoped to find a woman who stirred her passion. None had—and she hadn't met any men to do it, either.

Until David. Annika still didn't know if she was attracted because of his sex, or if it was just *him*. But he had been the only one to affect her so deeply—and she believed it could easily become more. If she turned away his offer of friendship, however, Annika would lose this opportunity forever.

If he didn't desire her in return, the opportunity wouldn't matter—and she'd never seen any indication that he did. He'd *told* her that wasn't what he wanted. And the night before, when she'd moved in close to sniff his neck, he'd only stood rigidly, then turned away from her.

She didn't want to spend her life hoping, longing, waiting for his feelings to change. She didn't want to end up heartbroken as her mother had, the person she loved within reach, yet still alone.

Then again, her mother wasn't alone any longer—and Annika imagined that her happiness now patched over the years of hurt.

She didn't want to return home and wait to die.

She didn't know what to do. Each option rolled itself over again and again, hope and dread filling her in turns. Her mind roiled about, refusing to rest, and she was exhausted when the forenoon watch ended. David wasn't waiting for her outside the engine room, as she'd half expected; Annika tried not to feel disappointment. He was probably allowing her to come to him in her own time rather than pushing her to make a decision. She could appreciate that.

She also wanted her decision to be important enough to him that he couldn't help but push.

Hearts were silly things.

She couldn't seek him out yet, however. The first engineer's endless duties called, and the warmers needed to be checked again now that the sun was up and heating the surface of the balloon. She climbed the ladder to the main deck, wishing that the engine wasn't so loud. He could be nearby, and she wouldn't hear him.

Oh, but she didn't need to.

He stood so tall. And next to the first mate, his shoulders appeared twice as broad. How could she possibly not see him?

Like the aviators on deck, he wore a knitted wool cap lined with fur and with flaps to protect his ears. His gaze caught hers as she came out of the companionway, and her breath seemed to stop. Annika wondered if he heard anything that Mr. James was saying to him. She couldn't hear anything at all—not the thrum of the engine or the rush of icy wind. Only the pounding of her own heart.

She made her way across the deck. Before she could say a word of greeting, Mr. James asked, "So you're awake, eh?"

"I—" Annika stopped, utterly confused. Was she not supposed to be awake? Had someone said she wasn't? "Yes. I'm just coming off watch."

Standing beside James, David averted his face, seemed to stifle a laugh.

"As am I," James said. "Are you taking lunch, Mr. Kentewess?"

"When Miss Fridasdottor does."

"So it's like that?" James nodded, smiling. "I'll leave you to it, then."

Annika waited until he was out of earshot, then turned to David. "Do you see? Why would he ask that? What am I supposed to say?"

David grinned. "Yes. Though I'll ask something else he did: Are you taking lunch soon?"

"I have to check the balloon pressure first." She reached into her belt for two of the candies she'd found at Valdís's store and started for the warmers. "This will hold you until we eat."

He took the candy, and she popped one into her mouth, relishing the smooth, creamy texture. He only looked down at his with an odd expression. Not longing, exactly, but a degree of wistful sadness.

"You don't like butters?"

"I do, but don't eat them." His thumbs rubbed over the twisted ends of the paper. "My father designed the machine that wraps these."

"He did?"

"A commissioned job, shortly before we moved to the mountain builders' city. We visited the manufactory one day, and I ate dozens. My mother laughed at me and told me to stop, that I'd make myself sick. I didn't." He looked up, and she realized that expression hadn't been sadness, but the sweetness of a memory held painfully tight. "I don't want to eat one and discover they weren't as good as I remember."

"They are."

His gaze fell to her mouth. "Perhaps I'll try again."

Sudden need screwed deep, a coiling ache that tightened her skin. He could taste her. Lips open, tongue seeking the sweet flavor . . . and she would discover if his kiss would be as good as she hoped.

But he apparently didn't mean to taste anything now. He looked away and tucked the butter candy into his pocket. Turning to hide her distress, Annika stared at the balloon's gauge. The pressure was within limits. She fiddled with a valve. Anything to delay speaking with him again while her throat felt as if a sharp rock had been shoved down it.

Was this what the future would be? Always hoping . . . always disappointed?

The engine slowed to half speed. A great huff of steam released from the stern. Annika looked beyond the bow. Heimaey wasn't far, the black cliffs of the island rising up out of the sea.

She swallowed the ache, faced him again. "We'll be there soon."

"And Vik not long after."

"Yes."

Where he'd depart the ship. She might never see him again. Now she felt sick. She led him to the side, where they wouldn't be overheard. The butter candy tasted cloyingly sweet now. Her tongue found sharp edges that had formed in the smooth surface. She spit it over the rail and braced herself for his reply. "Have you thought on what I said?"

"Yes." His strong gaze held hers, unwavering. "It doesn't matter who they lie with."

"No. It *does* matter. It matters to my mother and your aunt, it matters to me because I love them, it matters to all the women of Hannasvik, whether they lie with other women or not—and it must matter to many New Worlders, because they'd done their damnedest to stop women from loving each other."

He nodded, as if to show that he understood the distinction. "I don't think badly of them for it. I don't think it's a sickness."

Relief slipped through her, unwinding the knot in her stomach. "Thank you." She drew a deep breath. "And you still want to help look for Källa?"

"Yes." He seemed to relax as well, his shoulders no longer so stiff. "So you will stay in touch with me?"

Would she write him, tell him of all the people she met, the things she saw?—and did she want to receive his letters in return? Oh, she *did*.

But how long would it be before she lived for those letters? Upon a week's acquaintance, she'd already come this far. How long until she was all in? And if he wasn't . . . would he ever be?

If she stopped this now, Annika could save herself. She could return to Hannasvik after finding Källa and be content.

"Annika?"

His ease was gone, shoulders stiff again. Why did this even matter to him?

She had to know. "What would be the purpose? The only reason you sought me out was because I might help you fulfill your promise. Well, Hildegard will come for you now; your promise will be fulfilled. Why continue this?"

"*Why?*" His jaw hardened. His gaze burned into hers. "For two people who don't fit anywhere, we get along well. The purpose is . . . friendship."

Friendship. That *was* worth a lot. All that Annika had of value were friends—and family that she didn't see often enough. Without them, she had nothing.

But she wanted more. Her eyes stung. She looked down as her vision blurred, and her body stilled.

His hands had clenched on the gunwale—his steel fingers had splintered the wood. This mattered more than he was saying. Perhaps all he had were friends, too. Family that he didn't see often enough.

Annika wasn't adventurous. She didn't take risks. But she would now.

And whatever came of it . . . would be what came of it.

She glanced up into his rigid features. "All right. Friendship."

His sudden smile washed away the tension. "Thank you."

Thank you. Just as a friend would say. Already, she wanted more. Already, it was hurting. She wasn't just a coward—she was greedy, too. Hopefully, this need would soon dull.

He must have been watching her face and misinterpreted her reaction. Softly, he assured her, "I won't betray your trust."

"I know," she said.

It was one of the reasons she liked him so well. Her life *was* richer for having him as a friend, so she couldn't pity herself for long.

And friends and family weren't all they had. Annika had her engines, her clothes—and he had his volcanoes. *Phatéon* flew past one of the smaller islands, a giant snow-covered rock jutting out of the water. In the summer, it would be green with moss and grasses, with puffins nesting on the cliffs and the women from Heimaey waiting at the edges, trying to catch the birds in their spring-launched nets.

But the island didn't smoke or steam. "Will you tell me that this was made by a volcano, too?"

He didn't immediately answer. Annika glanced at him, but he was looking past her, beyond the ship. His brows had furrowed, and a tight frown flattened his wide mouth. She followed the direction of his gaze to the main island, at the small town nestled behind a cragged cliff. Rows of cottages formed two neat streets that led to the stone abbey. Annika had always liked the look of Heimaey when flying in. Unlike every other settlement in Iceland, there was no need for high fences to keep the wild dogs away from the livestock. It made the town appear more inviting, open.

David glanced at the quarterdeck. "The lookout needs to put eyes on that island."

Elena stood near the helm. With a wave, Annika flagged her down. Her friend came forward with the spyglass and studied the island.

"I don't see anything," she said.

"I don't either," David said. "No smoke from the chimneys. No one walking in the streets. And look at that field."

Elena's mouth parted. She sent a horrified glance at David, then Annika. "I'll call for the captain."

She set off at a brisk pace, her lips tight with worry. Annika looked at the island again. To her eyes, the field was nothing but a blanket of white.

"What are you seeing?"

"Dead sheep covered by snow." David's voice was grim. "I'm afraid the people might be, too."

No tracks marred the pristine surface of the snow. It lay untouched, with only the shape of the lumps to tell them what lay beneath—and had for a few days, at least. One snowfall likely hadn't covered the sheep so well. Sleds stood abandoned with their runners buried. Drifts piled up against the cottage doors.

Except for one door, which stood open. In the street, another lump lay beneath the snow.

Annika stood with David on the foredeck, looking over the desolate scene. Dread filled her chest, making it impossible to speak. Vashon ordered *Phatéon* to circle the island, searching for any indication of life. Almost every crew member not on duty had come up to see, but despite the numbers crowded along the rails, the only sound came from the huffing engines. Finally, Vashon ordered the engines to a stop. The sails came up, slowing them until *Phatéon* hovered over the main street.

The captain joined them on the foredeck. "Anything?"

"There's no heat," David said. "If there were any fires burning, I'd be able to see some indication of it. But everything is stone cold."

"Perhaps everyone has left the island, Captain," Elena suggested.

Annika hoped so, too.

"Perhaps. We'll go and see." Vashon strapped on her pistols. "Fridasdottir, Pickart, you're with me."

Annika glanced at Elena. They were both joining her. "Yes, ma'am."

"I'll accompany you, as well," David said.

"I'm sorry, Mr. Kentewess, but you can't. Dr. Kentewess?"

Though Vashon's voice softened slightly, there was no give in it. "You will join us, too."

But she hadn't been off of the airship in years. Eyes widening, Annika looked to the doctor. Her face pale as milk beneath her mink hat, Lucia nodded and stepped forward. David opened his mouth; his aunt quelled him with a glance. His jaw clenched, but he nodded.

"Mr. James, you have the deck," Vashon told the first mate. "No man steps foot on this island. Cover us from above."

They followed her onto the cargo lift where Lucia stood, trembling as the clacking chains broke the unnatural silence. The woman's anxiety increased as they descended, her breath coming in quick bursts. Annika took her hand, held her gaze. She couldn't promise that Lucia would be all right.

Only this. "If you need me, I'll be here for you."

Lucia nodded, her fingers tightening on Annika's.

They stepped off the platform into knee-deep snow. Vashon waded to the buried form in the street. There was no need to say what needed to be done. Annika let go of Lucia's hand and began scooping away snow, with Elena working on the other side. Light and powdery, it brushed away easily until they hit a crystalized layer below, and the brushing became scraping. Slowly, the snow revealed a pair of unlaced boots, legs frozen a pale blue, a white linen nightgown.

"Damn it." Vashon's breath huffed out. "Uncover all of her."

They did, working over her head first, carefully brushing her face clear. Her dark hair had been loosely braided, and her expression was peaceful—as if she'd passed in her sleep instead of lying in a street.

Lucia examined her, and as the seconds passed, her breathing slowed and her hands steadied. By the time she looked up, frowning, her earlier anxiety had all but gone. "I don't see any injuries."

"How long has she been here?"

"Frozen as she is, Captain, it's impossible to be certain. I don't think it has been long."

"It's only two or three days' worth of snow," Annika said. "The first layer of powder fell last night, but the rest warmed in the sun during the day before freezing again, and below her it's packed hard from use. It was probably the prior evening, or the evening before that, depending on how much time passed between the two snowfalls."

"And she was in bed, or preparing for bed." Vashon nodded and looked to the nearby cottage. "She left the door open and came out to see . . . what?"

Annika couldn't imagine. She shook her head, saw Elena do the same. Sorrow lined her friend's face as she gazed down at the woman.

"Should we cover her, Captain?"

Vashon gave Elena a pistol. "You and Fridasdottor go into the cottage, find a blanket."

Annika hoped they wouldn't need a lot of them. Snow had spilled through the open door, sloping down across the floorboards and over the edge of a rag rug. The cottage only boasted one room, and it was small, tidy. Annika dragged a colorful quilt from the bed, trudged back out to the snow. Above, crew and passengers lined *Phatéon*'s side, looking down. Annika saw David's worried expression before a splash of crimson caught her eye. Maria Madalena Neves stood with her nurse, her beautiful features cast into sharp lines of despair.

Annika couldn't bear to look up again. If this had been a place for her and her lover to go and live without fear . . . it wasn't anymore.

Elena reached the captain, shook her head. "No one else was inside, ma'am."

"All right. The doctor and I will check the next cottage. You two take that one."

Annika plowed through the snow with Elena. This cottage was larger, with a separate sleeping chamber. In the hearth room, a cat lay curled up in front of stove. Annika bent to slide her fingers through its fur. "Frozen stiff."

"And killed in its sleep," Elena said, covering her mouth. "It got the better of a *cat*. What could do this?"

Annika shook her head, battling her own terror. Whatever had done this, could it still be here?

They found two women in the bedchamber. Elena pulled the blanket away. They lay back to back in nightgowns as if asleep. Swallowing past the ache in her throat, Annika examined their necks and faces.

No blood, no bruising. "Do you see any injuries?"

"No." Elena dragged the blanket back up, carefully covered their heads. Her voice was thin with fear. "Annika."

"I know." She was scared, too. Heart pounding, she studied the room. A writing desk sat beneath a window. "There's a diary."

Elena picked it up, flipped through the pages. "It's in Spanish. The last date was three days ago—and there's an entry every day. So it must have happened that night. Should we take this?"

"Yes. Is there any mention of what happened?"

"I'll look." She read as she walked, only glancing up as they came out into the sun. "Do we keep checking each house?"

Annika didn't want to, afraid that they'd only find more of the same—but knew they would, in the hope that they might find someone alive. Across the street, Vashon and Lucia emerged from their cottage. Judging by the tight set of their features, they hadn't seen anything different than she and Elena had.

They met in the middle of the street. "We have a diary," Elena said. "There's no mention of what caused it yet, but I'll keep reading to see if there's anything odd in the weeks before. Two more women were inside."

"We found one more in bed." Vashon closed her eyes, rubbed her forehead. "All right. Dr. Kentewess, return to the ship and send down every female crew member. We'll bring one of the bodies to sick bay. Try to figure out what killed them. The rest of us will search every cottage, every building."

"Shouldn't we bury them, ma'am?" Elena asked.

"We can't. The ground is frozen."

Which was why the women of Hannasvik only buried their beads. "We could build a pyre."

"These are Christian women, Fridasdottor." Vashon's voice had a razor's edge.

"Yes, ma'am." Though leaving them to rot didn't seem right, no matter what they were.

The captain must have agreed with that, at least. "Anyone we find out in the snow, we'll take into one of the cottages. The cold will keep them until we can notify the Church. Once we've finished, we'll fly on to Vik. There's a priest there, if I remember. So let's get started. Pickart, you and Fridasdottor search the cottages in this row."

They started off with Elena's nose in the diary. Halfway there, she shut it with a gasp.

"What is it?"

"Nothing," Elena said. But her face colored, and Annika didn't think the blush came from the cold and the effort of walking through the snow. "I'm not sure they were all Christian women, though."

"Neither am I," Annika said wryly.

Though maybe she was, a little. Sunday services included versions of stories that Annika had heard many times, passed down from Hanna. How many did Annika have to hear before she was one or the other?

"The captain knows you didn't mean anything by it." Elena

kicked away the snow piled against the cottage door, pushed it open. "You're different, Annika, but you're not unnatural."

This was unnatural. Another woman sat frozen in her bed, this one older, her hair white, the tight curls cut as short as Annika's. Her shoulders propped by pillows, she'd been knitting a hat when she'd died. Her chin rested against her chest, as if she'd fallen asleep as she'd worked.

Annika's vision blurred as she pulled the blanket up. How many women lived on this island? She didn't know how to bear doing this over and over again.

Elena was managing better. Eyes clear, she said, "Let's go on."

They searched five more cottages, found more women, all in bed and sleeping—some single, some together. Elena abruptly stopped in the sixth doorway.

"Go on back. Not these."

What was different? Frowning, Annika pushed past her. Oh. Her heart constricted. They hadn't been sleeping. Unclothed, they lay in each other's arms. "I didn't know you were so modest, Elena."

"Annika, don't." Elena's frustrated sigh followed her inside, and her silence held until Annika covered them. "You waste your pity. They brought this on themselves."

Annika stilled, certain she hadn't heard that correctly. "What?"

"Don't you see? All of these women are like this—committing unnatural acts that led to an unnatural death."

Disbelieving, Annika stared at her. Elena was the kindest person she knew. To hear her speak so cruelly was shocking. "You don't believe that."

"Oh, you're so innocent. Soft-hearted. Come on."

Elena took her hand. Feeling brittle inside, as if that touch might break her, Annika yanked it away.

"God, Annika, you belong on Hymen Island more than they do. Do you understand what these women were doing?"

"I understand perfectly."

"I doubt it. You have no idea what it's like to grow up knowing that the Horde might land on your shores at any moment."

No. She'd been afraid people like Elena might. "What does the Horde have to do with it?"

"You know what they did to the people they controlled, those frenzies? Those bugs in their blood drove them to pure lust—not caring whether the person they were with was a woman or a man. It's horrifying."

Annika knew all about the frenzies. Some of the Englishwomen had lived through them, had passed the stories down. They'd described a terrifying loss of control, forced to rut with anyone nearby whether they wanted that person or not.

These women had been making love. "You'd compare being raped to this?"

That was horrifying.

"Thanks to the Horde and their frenzies, the infected in England don't know what family is. They never married, never raised their own children, never learned the natural order of life. These women aren't controlled by bugs, but they're still giving in to that urge. Something is wrong in them, Annika, and what you see isn't love. It's just lust. And if it continues unchecked, the New World will be the same as any Horde territory." She glanced over at the bed. "That's probably why they are all sent here—so they can't corrupt the rest of us."

"No." Annika wanted to slap her. "They're brought here for protection from people who think like you."

"Damn it. Can't you see—" Elena broke off with a long-suffering sigh. "You have a good heart, Annika, but you're too sensitive. You'll understand, one day. Come on."

Annika already understood. Elena thought they were all sick. Only this morning, she'd been terrified that David would have this very response. Now, she was glad to have taken a risk.

This wasn't the friend she'd expected to lose today.

* * *

It was impossible to remain still. David paced the deck, frustration and worry dogging every step. On the street below, Lucia directed three aviators carrying a blanket-wrapped form onto the cargo lift. He couldn't help his aunt. He couldn't help Annika. He could only watch her go from house to house, her expression when she emerged telling him that she'd found more death inside.

He stopped pacing, clenched his hands on the gunwale when Annika came out of the next cottage. Something had changed. Instead of the sorrow that had seemed to weigh on her shoulders and the unsettled fear that kept her gaze darting around, as if she expected a threat to jump out from beneath the snow, now her posture was stiff, her expression devastated. The second mate walked ahead, a faint scowl darkening her face.

An argument?

Look up, Annika. He wanted to see her face better, to offer whatever support he could. Her eyes remained downcast. She disappeared into the next cottage.

Christ.

The cargo lift clanked into place. The other men gathered at the gangway, their heads bare, their faces reflecting his own frustration. David joined them, removing his hat as the aviators carried the dead woman past. Lucia followed, her mouth set and eyes dark with worry. She caught his gaze, paused.

"What happened to them?"

"We don't know." She tugged at the fingers of her gloves, gestured for him to walk with her. "Most of them were sleeping—even the animals. I couldn't find a mark on them. Have you ever heard of such a thing?"

"Not outside a cave."

Lucia's gaze sharpened. "You refer to the miner's death?"

"Yes." Concentrations of toxic gas suffocated the men. When

the bodies were found, the miners appeared as if they'd fallen asleep.

"At least one woman was out in the open. Do you know of anything else that is similar?"

An entire town dead? "I've heard of one village smothered when gas erupted from a volcanic lake. But the people were burned, had lesions on their skin." He looked out at the cliffs, the small cone on the west side of Heimaey, the nearby islands. "This is an active region. This island might be, too. Perhaps a chamber of gas lay below the water, and a tremor broke it open." David had to admit he was grasping. "I don't know."

And he wasn't the best man to ask. He waved Dooley and Goltzius over, told them what Lucia had found.

She looked to Goltzius. "Could it be a plant? Something they've eaten?"

"Not at this scale. And the animals were affected, too—so it would have to be something everyone ate, yet there are no visible signs." The Dutchman shook his head. "It doesn't seem likely."

"No, it doesn't." Lucia sighed. "Mr. Dooley?"

"It's a terrible thing, but we've all heard of the weapon that could have killed every bugger in England last year. I'm wondering if these women were infected."

David sure as hell hoped not. "And some signal killed them— like from the Horde towers?"

"I wouldn't be knowing that. But aside from the miner's death, it's the only instance I've ever heard of a man dropping dead all at once, without a mark on him."

The concern on Lucia's face deepened. She looked up at David. "I can't test for infection after they're dead. Those nanoagents are too small for me to see, even with a microscope. Can you?"

"No." Eyes made from mechanical flesh could, but he only had lenses. "But we don't want to know if they're infected; we want to know if they *aren't*. If even one woman isn't, she wouldn't have died from a signal or a weapon that destroyed the bugs. You could exclude it as a cause, at least."

"But, David—I can't test for *no* infection, either."

"The women searching the cottages can. Tell them to look for any evidence that the women suffered a winter cold." David hadn't been sick even once since he'd been infected. If ever badly injured, he might contract a fever as the bugs worked to heal him, but he was immune to the diseases that threatened many other explorers— or aviators. A man blowing his nose aboard an airship was so common as to be unremarkable. "A handkerchief, for instance."

Lucia nodded. "I'll tell them."

She started down the companionway. David returned to the ship's side to look for Annika. Dooley and Goltzius joined him.

On his left, Goltzius said, "No matter what caused it, the news-sheets will spread the sensational story of beautiful, untouchable virgins taken to Heaven."

God. That was true enough. Would such a story inspire girls to keep their virginity, or rush to lose it?

"Only in Manhattan City," Dooley said, and not to be out-done, gave his own spin. "In Johannesland, they'll say the fissure spirits from Iceland stole their souls."

"They'll *all* say it was a Horde plot," David said.

Dooley nodded. "That'll be the way of it, though using that as your prediction is akin to cheating. They're always saying it's a Horde plot. Is all right with your girl, Kentewess?"

Annika had emerged from another cottage. The weight of sorrow had returned, slumping her shoulders. Despite the bulk of her heavy clothing, she appeared small and fragile. Brittle.

His voice roughened. "I don't know."

"It's awful work. I wouldn't want to be in her place for any-thing," Goltzius said quietly.

David would give anything to take her place, but he could only watch and wait.

Hours passed. Several soiled handkerchiefs found in the cottages showed evidence of winter colds and put paid to suspicions that the women had been infected. His aunt finished her examination—and due to the concentrations of blue-burning gas in her lungs, she believed the woman had died of asphyxiation, but she couldn't be certain.

The afternoon light had faded by the time Annika and the others returned to the ship. David waited on the deck. The devastation and sorrow had passed. In their place he saw utter exhaustion.

Should he go to her? Annika took the decision out of his hands. She came toward him, dragging off her hat. Her arm fell back to her side as if the motion had been a momentous effort. Even her black curls lay flat, hours under the wool plastering them to her head.

He frowned at her. "You should rest."

"We have to be ready to fly in thirty minutes, so I have to be in the engine room in five." She glanced over as Mary Chandler stopped at her side. Puffy red skin surrounded the woman's eyes. "Go on to your bunk. I'll take the first watch."

The older woman patted her shoulder. "You're a good one, Annika. Don't you let Elena tell you you're wrong."

Sudden tears shone in Annika's eyes. She nodded and waved the older woman on. "Thank you."

David waited until she'd gone. "What happened?"

"The rumors about the island are true. Elena thought the women deserved it—and that it was the Horde's fault. I told her that was all guff, and she said I was naïve and stupid. Then she said the same about the women to Mary later, and Mary laid into her."

Good for Chandler. She couldn't have known how much Annika would have needed to hear that.

Perhaps she needed to hear it now. Her tears spilled over. She bent her head, turning away from the deck to hide her face.

"Is there anything I can do?" His chest ached. God, he wanted to hold her. "Anything at all?"

"Yes." She looked up with a watery smile. "Pretend that I'm brave."

"I don't have to pretend."

A quick laugh escaped her. She wiped her cheeks. "You're good at this."

He'd persuade her. "You're brave to trust me."

"No."

"Yes." He lowered his head toward hers. "I could use what you've told me of my mother's people—and your own history. I could trade my silence for Hannasvik's location."

Her smile returned again. "That doesn't require trust. I'd never reveal it."

"Never?" He might not have helped, but at least he'd distracted her. "Is that secret worth dying for?"

"Yes."

"You say it so quickly."

"So you don't trust that it's true? But it's an easy answer. It must be the easiest way to die: protecting someone you love. Your mother did."

"Yes." Without hesitation.

A long breath shuddered from her. Her smile faded. "For some-one, it's easy. For something, though . . . I think it's harder to die for something you believe in. To stand up and to say that something else is wrong. I said it to my friend, but would I shout it aboard this ship? I don't know. I'd be too afraid of what would happen to me, because so many think as she does. I hate myself for this."

"When you're surrounded by stupidity, self-preservation isn't a sin."

"Refusing to challenge that stupidity and letting it continue might end up hurting someone you love, later. I'd die to protect them, but not to tell people that I've kissed a woman, too?"

Alarmed, David shook his head. Though he agreed with her in

principle, he'd be the first to knock her off the pulpit if she intended
to shout it from the deck. If she intended to risk herself, to stand
for her people, he'd be there with her—but there had to be better
ways of going about it.

"And would your mother want you to die for someone else's
stupidity?"

"No. But I don't know that what she wants would matter, because
she'd risk herself for me, too." Her expression slowly deflated on a
sigh. She looked exhausted and miserable again. "Excuse me. I'm
going to hide in the engine room and cry."

She returned to the deck earlier than he anticipated. The
sun still shone in the southwestern sky, casting golden light across
the water. Behind her aviator goggles, her eyes were red.

"The chief sent me up to eat until the engine needs stoking
again. I can't take a bite."

After the day she'd had on Heimaey, he wasn't surprised.
"You're brave to defy his orders."

"Oh, you *are* good at that." She laughed a little, shaking her
head. "I'll be stupid if I'm caught. But I realized that it's less than
an hour's flight to Vik."

And she'd wanted to spend that time with him. Pleasure swelled
in his chest—and was joined by tearing pain.

They had less than an hour.

Her gaze met his. "And I wanted to tell you how much I
admire you."

Sudden dread weighed heavy in his gut. He'd heard that before.
If she admired him for losing his legs, he wouldn't be able to bear
it. "Why?"

"Because you intervened at the port gate in Navarra. No matter
your reason, you risked yourself to help me. I'd just passed a line of

people waiting for food. I thought, *I could give them the few coins I have.* But I didn't dare. I could have probably done it without being seen, but I didn't take that risk."

So this still ate at her. "A few coins isn't worth dying for, Annika," he said. "They wouldn't buy more food than the Church gave them. And if you *had* been caught, the people you tried to help would have been arrested, too."

"Perhaps." Her forehead creased as she considered it. "I'm not even certain if it would be about helping a person, or just making a statement of how stupid it is that I wasn't allowed to help them."

"So you're a troublemaker at heart? Ah, well—I suppose I am, too. I want to walk through the gates simply because I'm not supposed to. The restrictions against the infected are idiotic." The result of fear cultivated over centuries. Eventually, they'd all pull their heads out of their asses. "If you broke every stupid rule in the New World simply because it was stupid, you'd never have time for anything else."

"I should choose one or two that matter, then." Though she wore a faint smile, her gaze remained serious. "If I had been caught, died for it—perhaps someone would realize how stupid it is to die for a few coins. If enough people recognized it, they could make a change. But I didn't risk anything. And when I was stopped by the port officer, I thought, *Who would come help me?* I wouldn't even risk giving money to the hungry. You risked it, though. You came to help me."

She gave him far too much credit. "Because I heard your voice."

"Would you have helped me anyway?"

"Yes. But it wasn't the risk you imagine. I knew the port officer's attention would shift to me, and that he'd feel threatened by either my hand or the infection."

"He could have clubbed you."

"I heal quickly."

"But you can be hurt just as easily as I can, and I'd fear a club even if I was infected. Stop arguing, David. You risked your life to save me." Her eyes narrowed behind the goggle lenses. "Would you have killed me to fulfill your promise?"

"*What?* No." He'd die to protect her.

"I'm glad." For the first time since arriving at Heimaey, real humor lit her face. "You'd be a bad friend if you did."

"Yes. But I'd be a good son."

Her laugh lifted through him. He loved her mouth, her teeth, the flush of cold on her cheeks.

A bell rang on the quarterdeck. Annika glanced over her shoulder, then south, out over the sea. "We're hailing a ship."

A wooden ship, wide at the bottom and narrowing as it rose to the main deck, with a high stern. Under full sail, her white canvas bowed in the wind.

"A fluyt, I think," Annika said, squinting against the sun. "A cargo ship—usually Norwegian or Dutch."

"They're flying Norwegian colors."

She nodded and looked toward the quarterdeck, where Vashon issued orders. "We'll hail them and ask their captain if they've heard of anything similar to Heimaey. Since they're sailing around the rim, they might be headed there—or to Smoke Cove."

"So we can warn them, spread the news."

"Yes."

Phatéon slowly banked south—taking them farther away from Iceland's shore. "This will delay our arrival in Vik."

"Yes." She held his gaze for a long second. Then her smile faded, and she looked west. Heimaey rose in the distance. "Do you think the women were killed because of what they did?"

"An act of God?"

"No. Someone else."

"Someone who hated them enough to kill them all?"

"Or feared them."

It would probably be a combination. He hesitated, but there

was no delicate way to say it. "If someone hated them *that* much, I don't think he'd kill them so painlessly."

" 'He?' "

"Or she." Though David couldn't imagine that.

Annika nodded. "I've seen that before—a crowd cheering as two men were hanged."

Jesus Christ. She'd seen that? David never had, but he'd heard of the mob executions. "Yes."

"So you believe it was a natural death?"

He nodded. "Probably a toxic gas that formed naturally."

"Like the fissure eruptions? The gases poisoned some—and others were smothered by ash."

"Yes. That's not what happened here, but it could be similar."

She seemed to take comfort in that. He wished to hell that it was appropriate to do more. Hold her, perhaps—or touch her hand.

In all this time, he hadn't touched her. Not her skin, not her clothes. He wanted to, before leaving *Phatéon*. He would hold the memory close until he saw her again.

Her mittened fingers rested lightly on the rail. He could slide his gloved right hand against her left—or cover it with his. Maybe she wouldn't pull away.

His heart raced as he screwed up his courage. Damn it, he should just kiss her. She'd admired him for taking a risk. But he'd never feared the port officer's reaction—and he'd never longed for anything as much as this.

He'd wait until she closed her eyes.

They widened, instead, at the same time a commotion on the deck alerted him. Aviators shouted to each other, while Vashon trained her spyglass to the south.

David looked out toward the ship. "What happened?"

"The fluyt ran up a flag," Annika told him. "They're asking for help."

A puff of smoke appeared at the fluyt's side. Another. Behind the ship, two geysers of water erupted.

Annika's mouth dropped. "Did they fire their cannons?"

"Yes," David said, watching.

Men scrambled on the decks. The cannons blasted again. What were they shooting at? He searched the rolling waves behind the ship. No other vessels . . . just an enormous shadow on the water.

He glanced up. Aside from *Phatéon*, the skies were clear of airships. Not a shadow, then. Something under the water. Something huge—four times the length of the cargo ship.

Impossible.

David shook his head, looked again. His estimate had to be wrong, or his perception of the depth and distance was. The shadow followed directly behind the ship's tail. "How long is a fluyt?"

"Sixty feet or so. What are you seeing? What are they firing at?"

A megalodon? But he'd never heard of those giant sharks approaching this size. Only krakens, yet they were all south of the equator.

"I don't know, but—"

A *whale*. The massive squared head burst up out of the water, dwarfing the fluyt. Heavy jaws yawned open. Masts snapped, sails crumpling. The monster engulfed the cargo ship in a single bite.

Annika shrieked, clapped her hands over her mouth. The shouts from *Phatéon*'s deck echoed David's own disbelief. *Impossible.* The jaws clamped shut. The head submerged, followed by the sleek back of the long body as it dove.

The fluyt was gone. A thick swell rolled out from the site, the edges of the water churning.

Annika's breath came in gasps. "Was that a whale?"

"A machine," David said, then repeated it as Vashon appeared at the side, looking over with a stunned expression. "It was a machine, Captain. A steel submersible."

The biggest one he'd ever seen or heard of.

"The megalodons have steel armor," Vashon said.

"Not armor made of square plates."

"A submersible, then. Pirates?"

"I didn't see any people." But what other reason to come up from beneath to snatch a ship? "It's a good strategy, if so."

"Like a whale attacking a seal," Annika said.

Vashon nodded. "Do you see any survivors?"

"Only crates, a few timbers." His telescopic lens showed little else. His thermal lens revealed less. If a sailor had dropped into the water, he might not appear much warmer than his surroundings. "A man could be clinging to the other side of one."

"Thank you. If you ever give up vulcanology, Mr. Kentewess, I will take you on as a lookout." Vashon clapped him on the shoulder, and called as she walked away, "Forward and on! We'll fish out any survivors. Fire up the generator! I want a rail cannon on that water."

Aviators ran to carry out her orders. The quartermaster shouted into the bank of pipes, alerting the rest of the ship. Dooley joined them moments later, shaking his head.

"We've just heard. Is it true? A whale swallowed a ship?"

"A submersible did." He glanced at Annika, who still stood wide-eyed and dumbstruck, her fingers gripping the gunwale as she searched the water for survivors—or another glimpse of the whale. "We're almost over the site now."

They all looked over. Floatsam bobbed in the water. No men clung to any of the crates.

A shadow rose beneath the water. A trail of bubbles preceded it, collecting at the surface and washed away by the rolling sea. Beneath the huff of the engine, the deck had gone deathly quiet. Aviators lined the rail, waiting.

Annika's mittened hand covered his. David froze. She folded her fingers over the back of his gloved hand, their tips curling round to his palm—holding on as anticipation mounted. Heart pounding, he stared at her profile, watched her full lips part on a gasp. Her fingers tightened, and he felt the impression of each one through the thick wool, the strong clasp of her middle fingers, the soft pressure of her smallest.

Almost dizzy with the unexpected pleasure of it, he followed her gaze down. The top of the whale's head surfaced, revealing steel sheets riveted like an old ironship hull, so broad that an airship twice *Phatéon*'s length could have landed on the head without wetting its keel. The rest of the body floated beneath the water, the water churning above the tail.

With a hiss, a circular plate near the front opened like a blowhole. Steam billowed out.

Astonished murmurs rose around them. A tremor shook Annika's fingers.

"Ships and airships." She looked up at him suddenly, eyes wide with alarm. "Lisbet said that ships *and* airships had been disappearing. Captain Vashon!"

Pulling away, she ran for the quarterdeck. The whine of the electrical generator sounded. The deck crew mounted the rail cannon.

Too late. In a burst of steam, a harpoon launched from the blowhole. Aviators shouted, ducked. David forced himself to wait, to see what happened.

Tipped by a barbed steel head and trailed by a long chain, the massive spear hurtled past the cruiser, ripping through the metal fabric of the envelope and piercing the side of the balloon.

"Dear God in Heaven protect us," Dooley breathed.

Chaos erupted on the deck. David glanced back, searching for Annika, and saw her racing toward the warmers. Vashon shouted for everyone to toss over their lamps, their cigarillos, to stop all fires on the ship.

With a winding *clack*, the chain drew tight. David braced his hands against the rail, prepared for the jolt as it dragged them down. It didn't come. The spear slipped out, fell onto the submersible's head with a loud clatter. The winding continued, pulling the harpoon back into the blowhole. David glanced up. A narrow hole remained in the metal fabric, the ragged edges fluttering as the hydrogen escaped.

He hoped to God all of the flames were out.

For a breathless instant, he waited, but they didn't explode. The balloon would slowly deflate, instead, the ship sinking onto the water. Below *Phatéon*, the whale submerged again—to wait, David realized, like a predator that lamed its prey and waited for it to fall.

Vashon strode to the side of the ship, looked up. For a long moment she stared at the balloon, her jaw clenched. Grief passed through her expression, her face closing in on itself; then she opened her eyes and issued orders in a voice like iron. Aviators scattered.

Annika raced toward him, fear and determination tightening her features. She glanced at Dooley, indicated them both. "Get your things ready, but don't carry much. We'll try to make it to shore, but if we can't, we'll take the gliders."

They wouldn't risk the lifeboats with the whale in the water. "Are you coming directly back?"

"Not yet. I have to stoke her as high as possible—we'll let the engine take us as far as she can back to shore before they ring the bell to abandon ship. I must go." She backed away, holding his gaze. "Safe journey, David. Mr. Dooley."

She turned and ran for the ladder. David glanced at Dooley.

"They'll put the passengers off before the crew. When they evacuate, you take the first round of jumps. I'll stay back until Annika goes."

Dismay filled his friend's face. "I'm not thinking that's—"

"I'll help her shovel. I need you to look over my aunt, take her with you. Please."

"It's an arseways time for you to fall in love." Dooley clasped his hand, gave a firm shake. "All right. So long as you're off when the crew goes."

"I will be."

Because he'd be making damn sure that Annika made it off, too.

Chapter Seven

Though Annika wished David had stayed above, she was glad to see him—and she couldn't afford to reject his help. She gave him two pieces of cotton for his ears and a shovel, then steered him toward the furnace. She climbed up to the engine room and saw Mary coming in. With the engine already at full steam and David helping below, there was nothing for Mary to do here but wring her hands. Annika shoved her out to collect their things and to wait for evacuation.

Down to the boiler room again. David had stripped off his coat and jacket, tossed them over her blue mantle. In his shirtsleeves, he rhythmically scooped shovelfuls from the rolling bin to the furnace. Annika dumped the bin onto the boards, left him a small hill of coal. She pushed the bin to the coal bunker and refilled it before jettisoning the rest through the emergency chute.

She felt faintly sick. Fifty tons of coal, straight into the drink—but it would lighten the ship, give them more of a chance. Digging her boots in, she hauled the full bin back to the furnace, grabbed another shovel.

Scoop and toss. Scoop and toss.

Her world narrowed to that single motion, repeated over and over again. Her back ached. Her face itched with sweat. How far had they been from shore when the harpoon had struck the balloon? Ten miles, perhaps. At full steam, a little over fifteen minutes. They had to be close. She hadn't yet heard the bell signaling the order to abandon ship. Perhaps they would make it to shore? If so, she needed to close all of the hatches, stop the engine before they landed or risk their own propellers tearing *Phatéon* apart.

She glanced at David. The white-hot glow from the furnace glinted off his beads and eyepiece, glistening over the sheen of perspiration. Unlike Annika, his pace hadn't slowed. He looked as if he could keep this up for hours—and with the nanoagents, perhaps he could. "I'm going to see where we are!" she shouted.

He nodded without breaking the rhythm: scoop and toss. Annika's sweaty hands almost slipped on the ladder rungs. She hauled herself up into the engine room and stopped, her heart thumping.

She could see Iceland's shoreline through the portholes. Oh, that couldn't be right. They were at the tail of the ship, the portholes on the sides, and *Phatéon* was supposed to be flying toward the island; she should have only been able to see the ocean. And the ship was low, low—only a few yards above the surface. Was Vashon hoping to settle into the water and let the propellers drive them in, like the engine of an old ironship?

It wouldn't work. *Phatéon* would float for a short time, but the weight of the engine made her draft on the stern too deep. The engine room would flood, water pouring in through the hull along the propeller shafts and vents. She'd drown within minutes.

Annika yanked the cotton from her ears and shouted into the pipes. "Captain!" No answer. But someone *had* to be on the bridge. *"Captain!"*

What the devil was going on?

Her stomach sank, and she knew. Panic followed her to the

porthole again. She pressed shaking hands against the thick glass, stared toward the shoreline. There, the winged figures in the air. Gliders.

They'd already abandoned ship . . . and she hadn't heard the bell.

Terror exploded within her. They had to go *now*. She hauled the engine lever back to STOP, blew the vents open wide, and raced to the hatch. "*David!*"

He looked up at her scream, dropped his shovel.

"They've abandoned ship! Take your coat. Run, run!"

He did, scooping up her mantle and his coat. His boots rang against the ladder rungs as he climbed. Though slowing, the engine still huffed, but it was nothing to the pounding of her heart in her ears.

She took the mantle, dragged it on as they raced down the passageways, up the stairs. She burst up onto the main deck, chest heaving.

"Oh, sweet heavens."

The balloon was sinking in on itself like a swaybacked pony. *Phatéon* barely skimmed above the waves.

David gestured to the shore, where black sands stretched back to a low plain, then rose abruptly into cliffs. "It's not far. Are there any more gliders?"

"We can't jump from this height." They'd just fall into the ocean. Annika pushed her hands into her hair, mind racing. "A lifeboat. The moment *Phatéon* settles into the water, we'll swing it over and row to shore."

"And the whale?" He looked behind them. "They're likely waiting."

"We'll row fast. If they're after cargo, they shouldn't bother with us." Annika hoped so, anyway. She studied the familiar shoreline. They'd still be twenty miles from Vik, walking all the way. "We need clothes. As fast as you can, as warm as you can find, only what you can carry. And a weapon, if you have one."

She worried more about the dogs than the pirates.

"How long until we land?"

"Three minutes, perhaps."

"Christ."

She hurried with him down to the second deck; she continued to the next. The pack that she'd carried from Hannasvik still lay in the trunk beneath her bunk. She dragged it out, stuffed the sack full of old clothes. Her new outfits would be lost—but she could make more. She grabbed her spark lighter, wrapped it in oilcloth to keep out the wet. The spanners still tucked in her belt would have to serve as weapons.

David met her at the companionway, a pistol holstered at his thigh and a similar pack slung over his shoulder. Taking her hand, he raced with her to the main deck, then amidships, where the boat was cabled against a mast.

She stopped, out of breath. "I thought you didn't run?"

"Metaphorically." His quick smile drew a laugh from her. "How do we free this boat?"

"We have to wait until *Phatéon*'s belly is in the water and she's stopped." It would be a rough ride until then. She pointed to the pulley and the long arm. "As soon as we do, you heft that rope, I'll swing her to the side. We'll get in and drop down by pulling that release."

He tossed his pack into the boat, then hers. The engine gave a final huff. The sound of the ocean rushed in, the wind sharp against her face. Annika looked over the bow. Even with the propellers stopped, they still flew quickly over the waves. So quickly.

She faced David again. "There's going to be a jolt when we hit those swells! We'll skip along before—"

The deck reared, knocking her to the deck. Icy spray crashed over the bow. Annika sat up, wrapped her arms around the mast. David crouched beside her, gripped the timber with his steel hand.

His gaze searched hers. A fine mist covered his lens, matted his lashes. "Are you all right?"

She nodded. Another jolt bucked her forward, then backward as the ship bounced off another wave like a stone skipping across the water. Around them, *Phatéon* shuddered, creaked.

Another jolt. Pain tore across her shoulder as the force of the impact ripped her away from the mast—threw her toward the bow. A crate skidded beside her and smashed into the bulwark. A heavy wave crashed over the side in a thick wall, pounded onto her back like fists. Salty, freezing water surrounded her, burned her eyes and nose. She couldn't breathe. The wave receded over the bow, dragging her with it. Her hands scrabbled against the boards, searching for anything solid. A rope slid through her mittens and slithered away too quickly to grasp.

Her collar pulled tight. David hauled her back onto the deck, features harsh, the edges of his lips white. "Annika!"

"I'm all right." She struggled to her feet, coughing. *Phatéon* rocked beneath her feet, water lapping at her sides. The last crash into the wave had stopped them. "Get the boat."

And quickly. She was scared now. She'd have to change clothes as fast as she could while he rowed, and exchange her soaked mantle for the coat in her pack. In this cold, wet meant dead. Her muscles were already shaking, her fingers aching.

David grabbed the pulley line, hoisted the boat—and froze. Annika barely had a second to look around, to see the giant waterfall passing over the bow, the enormous cavern behind it. David leapt for her. His arm caught her waist and dragged her to the deck. His body covered hers. Heavy drops of water rained onto the boards, the balloon.

Falling from the whale's mouth as it swallowed them, Annika realized numbly.

Everything went dark. David's lean form tensed above her. "Hold on to me."

While he held on to something else, she guessed. She wrapped her arms around his chest, her legs around his waist.

The deck tilted violently, throwing them against the wooden bulwark. David's low grunt of pain was lost in the screech of metal, the splinter of wood. *Phatéon* was moving—sliding, her bottom scraping along a metal surface, gaining speed. David gathered her closer, his body straining as he held her against the ship's side. Terrified, Annika squeezed her eyes shut, gripped him tighter.

The crash almost tore her away. She screamed, held on. A deafening crack echoed through the dark. The airship shuddered.

His hand stroked down her back, his voice a soothing murmur. "Shhh, Annika. We're all right."

Annika realized she was shaking, whimpering pitifully against his neck. A few deep breaths helped her to stop. She opened her eyes.

Utter darkness, but there were noises. The thrum of an engine. The rhythmic, gasping thrust of a pump. The insistent drip of water. The hiss of the warmers. David's ragged breath.

Men shouted in Norwegian. The sailors from the fluyt . . . or the pirates?

Gingerly, Annika unwound her arms, sat up. The deck sloped to port, as if *Phatéon* had come to rest on that side. Not steep, but enough to be disorienting.

"Are you all right?" His voice was rough.

"Yes." She reached for the rail, pulled herself up to her knees. "Can you see anything?"

He apparently could. "We're in a hold—a big one. The walls are steel, but there's a stair on the side that leads up to a hatch door. The floor is flooded, but it's not deep. Only a few feet. The fluyt is here. *Phatéon*'s stern rammed into her side."

"I hear pumps," she said. "Air pumps, I hope."

The balloon was still deflating. Even if the hydrogen didn't explode, a leaking balloon in an enclosed space could make the air too dangerous to breathe.

Oh, and she would *not* think of the women on Heimaey. Terror already had her trembling enough. At least it wasn't the cold—though that was seeping in, too. She needed to change her clothes before long. Hopefully, her pack was still in the boat.

She got her feet beneath her. David caught her hand.

"Stay down."

She crouched again, staring into the dark. "Why?"

He whispered now. "Men are coming into the hold."

"With no lights?"

"They're wearing goggles—and carrying weapons."

Thankfully no lanterns, not with the balloon still deflating. "Guns?"

They'd be stupid to fire one.

"Swords and crossbows."

Dread joined the terror. "Pirates?"

"Probably." His hand tightened on hers. "I think they have light-enhancing lenses."

Weapons, darkness, and lenses that allowed them to see. The only reason to combine them was horrifying. "How many of them?"

"A dozen. Oh, Christ." David flattened her onto the wet deck. "Down. All the way down. We'll crawl to the ladder and stay hidden behind the bulwark as long as we can. Are there any more weapons aboard? I only have a pistol."

"No. They all fire. Maybe a knife in the galley."

"Bludging hell." He drew a sharp breath. "Go."

She scooted ahead on her elbows and knees, driven by panic, guided by memory. A scream ripped through the dark—and was cut short. Her teeth clenched against a terrified whimper. Another scream. Men shouted in confusion, pled for mercy. Someone was running, splashing through water. She flinched as another cry sounded, closer, thinning into a gurgling moan.

David came up beside her, urged her on. "There's the ladder. As quickly as you can."

She found the edge, grasped the rails, and slid down to the second deck. Moving to the side, she stood shivering in wet, heavy wool. She discarded her mittens, heard the wet plop against the boards.

The thud of David's boots followed. "They're searching that boat and killing the crew," he said. "They'll search *Phatéon* next. There're too many to fight, and God knows how many are manning this damn whale, but if they don't find anyone, they'll assume we all abandoned ship. Do you know a place to hide?"

Annika the Rabbit always knew a place to hide. "The engine room. There's a smuggle hole there."

He took her hand again, tugged her forward. Water splashed under their feet, the remnants of the wave that had washed over the upper deck—but the lower levels wouldn't be wet. Annika stopped, pulled her hand free. She stripped the mantle and her tunic over her head, toed off her boots.

"Annika?"

"I'll lead them straight to us, dripping a trail."

Her trousers were next, leaving her clad in a chemise, drawers, and her wool stockings. All damp, but not soaked.

His voice was strained. "You'll freeze."

Not in the engine room. Not for a while, at least. She collected her clothes and belt, keeping her largest, heaviest spanner. Her palm against the bulkhead, she felt her way to the nearest cabin and tossed them in. A wet flop told her David had removed his overcoat. She held out her hand. He threaded his fingers through hers, led her on.

The heat of the engine room had never been so welcome. The warmth seemed to embrace her, reassure her with its familiarity.

"Where's the smuggle hole?"

"In the floor, around the starboard side." She followed him across the boards, picturing the layout in her mind. "In line with the third piston. There's a spring-lock in one of the boards, disguised as a knot. Press it down with your thumb, and when it's all the way in, twist it clockwise a full turn."

He let her go. The scrape of metal sounded, then clicking as the locking mechanism disengaged.

"Now count three . . . four boards to port. The hatch is there. You'll have to slide the regulator on the desk between the planks to pry up the door."

A minute later, hinges squeaked. "Will we both fit?"

She heard his doubt—he must have looked inside. "A French count and his wife did, and they were both well fed."

Though it had been a squeeze. The space was no wider than her bunk, and not much deeper. The hole had been built between the decks, but couldn't be so large as to arouse suspicion. From the boiler room, it looked like a pipe conduit.

"Will we be able to breathe?"

"Those pipes have open ends."

"All right. Even if they have thermal lenses instead of light enhancers, the heat from the boilers and engine will overwhelm them—and they shouldn't be able to detect us through the floor." He took her hand again, but hesitated before moving again. "The way this floor is tilted, you'll be sliding up on top of me."

"I'll try not to squash you."

"That's not what I—" He stopped abruptly, made a choked sound that might have been a laugh or a groan. "All right. I'll get in. You come after."

She waited until he settled. Feet first, she felt her way in. David lay on his back, stiff as the boards around them. The hole wasn't wide enough to lie shoulder-to-shoulder. She tried to hold herself up, scrunching her back against the wall. She only managed to overbalance and fall against his arm.

Struggling to brace herself, Annika pushed against his solid chest. "I can't seem to—"

"Roll up against me."

"But if I can—"

"Annika."

With a sigh, she did, rolling onto her hip and half lying against him with his arm trapped between her stomach and his left side. Her neck bent awkwardly when she tried to rest her head on the boards. "Can I put my head on your shoulder?"

He slid his arm from between them, giving her room. "Yes."

She moved in closer. The cotton of his shirt was damp, but his shoulder was broad and warm beneath her cheek. His arm came around her, metal fingers resting lightly at her waist. She could feel the structure of his prosthetic through her thin chemise and his shirt sleeve, the hard muscle of his biceps narrowing to the hinge of his elbow, the steel of his forearm across her back.

All strength. She wouldn't have felt as safe with anyone else.

"All right?" His whisper sounded lower, rougher.

"Yes."

He moved against her, reaching up. Hinges squeaked again as he lowered the lid over them. A click sounded—the locking mechanism. Unless the pirates already knew where this smuggle hole was and how to open it, they'd remain undiscovered.

Where were the pirates now? She listened, but only heard their own breaths and the faint ticking of David's pocket watch. Were men still screaming outside? It was worse to imagine that they weren't, that all the screams had been silenced. Perhaps some of the sailors had realized what was happening. Perhaps they hid now, too. Waiting, while someone hunted them in the dark.

A tremble wracked her body. Again. Her teeth chattered.

His arm tightened. "Are you cold?"

"No." Just shivering—reaction finally settling in. She clamped her jaw tight, then opened it again to ask, "Are you afraid, too?"

"Yes."

"You don't show it."

"Because you can't see me."

She lifted her head and pressed her ear against his chest. His heart beat slowly, evenly. Unlike hers, racing as she recalled the whale's gaping maw, the petrifying collision with the fluyt, and the screams afterward. David lay unafraid, but she could only think that she didn't want to die now, didn't want to end here—and how close they'd come to it.

Her eyes burned. *Oh, not now.* She squeezed them shut. Whether terror or relief, she didn't know, but she couldn't stop the pressure welling in her chest.

No sound. She would *not* expose them to the pirates with her sobs.

Her breath shuddered. She felt David's fingers in her hair, brushing the curls back as if to reveal her face. "Annika. Are you all right?"

Yes. But only because he was here.

She broke, curling against him, burying her face in her hands. He held her until the storm of silent weeping passed, until she used the hem of her chemise to wipe her face, feeling utterly stupid.

"I'm sorry," she whispered. "I've never been the brave one."

"Who was?"

"Källa." She settled her head against his shoulder again, rested her hand over his heart. "She was the one who would explore the New World. The one who'd leave and bring back tales that our children would repeat. She always wanted to have adventures, to face danger."

"Has Källa ever been swallowed by a giant mechanical whale that shoots a harpoon out of its blowhole?"

She had to smile. "Probably not."

"You'll have that story, then." His thumb brushed over her cheek in a light caress, as if wiping away a tear. "You've had a hell of a day, Annika. Heimaey, Elena, now this. Crying over it is no reflection on your courage."

Annika buried her face again. Oh, he was the most wonderful person—and his words the most wonderful thing anyone had ever said to her. It *had* been an awful day.

And he was very good at pretending she was brave.

"Thank you." It was muffled against his chest. She lifted her head when another thought occurred to her. "Do you think these pirates are responsible for the death in Heimaey?"

"I don't know. They weren't killed the same way."

"No." She bit her lip, realizing that their situation now might be disturbingly familiar to him. Darkness. No room to move. A woman on top of him. "Being in here doesn't remind you of the mountain crushing your house?"

"Not until you mentioned it." His voice was dry. "But, no—it doesn't. This doesn't compare in any way."

No, she supposed it couldn't. They were both alive, both unhurt.

His muscles tightened as a faint thud came from one of the upper decks. "They're aboard."

His whisper was hardly more than a breath of sound. She nodded against his shoulder, reached for her spanner. If the pirates found the smuggle hole, there wasn't much she could do but whack at their hands. Still, broken fingers couldn't hold a sword.

Judging by the noise they were making, the pirates searched every cabin, every storeroom. She waited in an agony of tension. Finally, steps approached the engine room. Someone walked across the boards above—looking around the sides of the engine.

A male voice called down the passageway; the man above them answered. Spanish, she thought, but it might have been Portuguese. The planks creaked as he moved about, stopping frequently. Annika stared into the darkness, unblinking. Though she couldn't see a thing, she didn't dare close her eyes. She imagined him crouching, searching beneath the machines, glancing behind the banks of pipes. Taking his time, making a thorough examination.

He climbed down into the boiler room, and she waited, certain he'd realize the pipe conduit was a fake, that they'd be discovered. She heard him dig through the pile of coal, as if making sure that no one hid within. He opened the bunker, his steps echoing hollowly inside.

The steps retreated. The sound of male voices came again, farther away now. David's fingers squeezed lightly at her waist, as if to reassure her that they'd made it. Long minutes passed, then there was only quiet again—except for the distant thrum of a powerful engine. *Phatéon* moved around them, an almost imperceptible swaying.

"We're under way," she breathed, and felt his nod. "How long should we wait in here?"

"They wouldn't take two ships just to kill the crew. They must be after the cargo."

And they'd have to unload it. What would they do with the ships then—spit them out and let them sink? If so, David and she needed to escape before they emptied the hold. But where to hide then? They'd be stuck in the submersible whale, without a boat in the middle of the ocean.

But, no. That distant thrum told her more than that, the distinctive thrust of so many pistons. "That engine is enormous. They can't possibly supply their furnace with enough coal if they only take it from stolen ships. They must have a port somewhere—and probably not too far away."

"So we'll hide on this ship until we reach it?"

"Yes." They had to anyway. There was nowhere else to go. "Were they speaking Spanish?"

"Yes. They're Castilian." He sounded suddenly tired. "You should sleep now. You might not have the opportunity later."

She'd have loved to sleep. Her shivering had eased, but now she was aching, exhausted. "I don't think I can. Not while we're trapped here, waiting."

But between his warmth, the gently rocking ship, and the soothing thrum of the engine, she did.

* * *

The sudden quiet of an engine at dead slow woke her. Annika opened her eyes to darkness again, David's arm still around her, his body tense. He hadn't slept then—or had been unable to. The gentle swaying of the ship had sharpened, become more pronounced. Each swell rocked her into his side. She lay like softened butter against him, savoring the unfamiliar pleasure.

"Awake?" he murmured.

She hadn't made any noise. "What gave me away?"

"You opened your eyes."

Oh. She'd forgotten he could see. Thankfully she hadn't drooled—not that it would have mattered. His shirt was still damp, as were her drawers and stockings. "I think the whale might have surfaced. It feels like we're pitching against the waves."

"Swallowing another ship?"

If so, they needed to brace themselves for another collision. But, no. Silence fell as the engine stopped. Then a distant bump, a faint shudder. "I think she's being tethered—or docked, like a sailing ship."

"So they'll come for the cargo soon."

"I don't know." She paused, listening, but heard nothing else. "If she was an airship, she would sit until the officials came aboard and inspected her papers, and then a full day might pass before she was unloaded. But I have no idea what pirates do—except that they usually leave the crew alive so they can be ransomed."

"Yes, they do. They also don't swallow ships using a giant mechanical whale."

"Perhaps they stole that, too." But the ironic edge in his voice made her wonder, "You don't think they're pirates?"

He didn't answer, his fingers tightening at her waist. She heard it, too—footsteps, voices. Her heart clattered against her ribs. They came directly to the engine room.

Had she and David been discovered after all?

She barely dared to breathe. Beside her, she heard the quiet click of a pistol cocking. The rigidity of his muscles changed the firm pillow of his shoulder into stone.

Two men entered the room and stopped after taking a few steps. They spoke, their conversation brisk. Annika didn't understand a word of it. Within minutes, they left again.

Though she longed to ask David, she didn't dare speak yet. She waited. When enough time had passed without hearing anyone, she wondered, "What did they say?"

"That *Phatéon*'s engine is in better repair than the fluyt's."

"Of course it is."

His chest rose on a quick, silent laugh. "Of course. That's why they'll begin dismantling it tomorrow and send it north for the drill."

North? On the southern rim, all of Iceland was north. And moreover, "Why would pirates be *drilling*?"

"They're not pirates. They're di Fiore's men."

The railroad man? "Did they say so?"

"No. But Paolo di Fiore is one of the few men in the world who could imagine a submersible like this *and* build one that works. And they've been hiring hundreds of Castilians and bringing them to Iceland."

Who also spoke Spanish, and who were now in possession of a whale that only di Fiore could create. David's conclusions made sense, but she still couldn't understand *why*. "You think di Fiore is paying them to destroy ships and kill their crews? And the only reason is to steal engines? Why would they agree to that?"

And why wouldn't di Fiore just buy the engine instead?

"Not every man would do something like this, for any amount of money. But di Fiore's son might have picked out the ones who wanted blood. He likes to put people in particular situations, just to see what they do."

Horrifying. "And the drill?"

"He has some idea of exploiting the volcanic activity on the peninsula south of Smoke Cove. Perhaps it's for that."

Had they traveled all the way back to the west side of the island? "How long did I sleep?"

"Only half an hour."

Not that far, then, unless the whale's tail propelled the submersible faster than any vessel she'd ever heard of. "Should we continue to wait? It's dark outside by now."

"We'll wait. Komlan said di Fiore had a camp on the southern rim; we're probably there now. If so, this submersible might not be manned overnight. Most of the camp should be asleep by midnight. We'll go then."

"On foot?" They could be a hundred miles from nowhere. "Not in winter."

"Perhaps we'll find a boat or a balloon."

And perhaps they'd have to run for their lives. Best to rest until then.

Finding sleep again was difficult, however, despite her exhaustion. Her fatigue wasn't so deep and her fear wasn't so sharp, and they couldn't overwhelm the awareness of his long body against hers. The right leg of her drawers had ridden up, and with every small movement they made, the wool of his trousers rasped a tantalizing prickle over her bare skin. He no longer smelled of soap, but smoke and coal dust. She wanted to taste his skin, his lips, to run her hands over his broad chest.

But daydreaming never did her any good.

She put such imaginings away for now; she had more important matters to consider, such as not dying. They wouldn't be in a rush at midnight, and could spend more time collecting the items needed for a trek through the snow. Food from the galley kitchen—and knives, too. More spark lighters and kindling. If her pack had been soaked, she would need another coat. Her wet boots posed a serious problem; she couldn't walk on frozen feet. Most of the crew would have been wearing theirs when they'd abandoned ship, and few would have an extra pair lying about. They were simply too expensive.

Thinking of boots, Annika drifted to sleep. She woke up slowly, comfortable and warm, sprawled atop David Kentewess. Straddling him almost, with her thighs alongside his and her face buried in his warm neck.

She didn't open her eyes. His body was rigid beneath hers, his breathing shallow. She felt a faint pressure on the backs of her thighs, just below her bottom—his fingers, lightly holding on.

A little shock ran through her at the realization, a quiver of heat that shot from his fingers to the intimate flesh between her legs. She stifled her moan, the instinctive rock of her hips, aware of the tightening of her nipples against the hardness of his chest. Planed with taut muscles, his torso was solid, angular . . . and a thick ridge dug into her lower belly.

Oh. Was she squishing it?

Annika lifted her head. His shallow breaths stopped, as if he braced himself against pain. "Am I too heavy?"

"No." His voice was hoarse.

It sounded like she was. She shifted her weight onto her knees, raised her body a little. His fingers curled against her thighs before he let go. His body seemed to arch up against her before he groaned and lay flat again.

Was it that sensitive?

Curious, she reached between them. Her hand found the hardened tip through his trousers, and followed the thick length to the root.

Astonishment dropped her mouth open. She'd seen drawings. She'd glimpsed aviators' penises. They'd all dangled a few inches, soft and limp. She'd known a man's member stiffened during the sexual act, but she'd imagined it would be the size of one or two fingers—and had never suspected a man's organ could be this big, this rigid. She measured the length again, stroking her cupped palm over rough wool, testing the width with her fingers. Incredible.

David shook beneath her. "Stop. Annika, stop."

She froze. Was she hurting him? "I'm sorry. It's just . . . not what I thought it would be."

"You thought it was the pistol?"

Absurd. "No. You'd have to be an idiot to tuck one there. I meant that your penis wasn't."

He gave a strangled laugh. "Of course. A village of all women. But you know what it is?"

"I've seen rams mount ewes. But it wasn't anything like this." Hot and hard, filling her palm. She tried to imagine him inside, not like a finger at all, but so much thicker, longer.

Oh, she desperately wanted to know.

"The sheep?" He spoke evenly now, but each word seemed flat, lacking the duh*dum* rhythm she liked so well. "No, it's not like that. Forgive me, Annika. I wouldn't have . . . If I could help it, I wouldn't have let it happen."

But it *had* happened. Because he'd desired her, too? The needy ache between her thighs deepened.

"You said that you didn't want to bed me." Even now, she remembered the disappointment of that. How stupid she'd felt for revealing her own attraction.

He didn't reply for a long second, a hesitation that seemed to last forever. "With you over me like this, it happens whether I want you or not."

Oh. This thickness beneath her hand wasn't for her?

Her lungs seemed to squeeze in around her heart. He was the only person who'd ever made her ache like this—and he'd have been aroused no matter who she was.

"Annika?" Concern filled his voice.

He could see her, she remembered. He could watch her reactions.

She pasted on a smile. "Like a ram to any ewe, yes?"

"Do you fondle the sheep, too?"

She yanked her hand from between them. "No. I'm sorry." Embarrassment boiled up. She'd groped him like an animal. Cheeks hot, she cast about for any other topic. "What time is it? How much longer do we have to wait in here?"

"Another hour." Frustration roughened his voice—or anger.

An hour, and she could still feel the phantom touch of his fingers on her thighs. When she slid off of him, her hip brushed over his erection. He stiffened again.

But not for her. She lay in the dark, her throat aching with humiliation and disappointment. The boards were hard beneath her, and colder now. Though the air in that small space remained warm, a chill sank into her side, her back.

"Is it all men?"

"All men, what?"

"Do you all harden for anyone?"

A long silence, followed by an abrupt, "Some do."

"But not every man does?"

"No."

"So some will harden for anyone, but others only desire one person. They only want to be with the one they love."

"Yes. As you do."

Yes. Though she had been aroused before—never as much as she felt with him, but she understood how the body could respond in such a way, even without love. Perhaps he waited, too.

"Have you bedded a woman before?"

She knew it was improper to ask; she didn't care. He exhaled sharply, as if through gritted teeth.

"Yes," he said. "Two."

Pain slipped like a knife through her ribs. Oh, she hadn't truly expected that—and she cared now. She wished she hadn't asked. And she should stop herself from asking more. This was like rolling down a mountain: knowing the danger, but still unable to slow down.

She jumped anyway. "Did you love them?"

"No." His voice was harsh, no longer a whisper. "And that's enough of this."

Annika nodded and laid her head on his shoulder, but the pain continued swelling up in her. Strange, awful pain that throbbed like a physical wound, pulsing open wider with each beat of her heart. Oh, but it needed to stop. There were so many different things she should be thinking about—her list of items that she'd fallen asleep on. The boots she needed to find. They were in a mechanical whale and murderers waited outside somewhere. But all of that seemed so far away. Eyes closed or staring into the dark, she could only see him kissing another woman. She could only imagine someone else finding him hard in her hands. He'd desired them enough to bed them, even without love. Had he kissed her breasts? Licked between her thighs?

Yet he didn't want any of that with her. Annika thought she could have loved him—she was well on her way. But he wasn't even interested.

He'd only asked for friendship. It had been so stupid to hope for more.

The lump in her throat grew excruciatingly thick. How could she be crying again? She tucked her chin down, hiding her face. She couldn't bear for him to know.

"Annika?"

"Yes?" Despite her efforts, her voice hitched.

"You're crying?"

Humiliation surfaced, caught in a net of anger and pain. Couldn't he stop watching her for a second? His damned eyepiece. Wildly, she reached up, covered the lens. "Stop spying on me!"

Metal fingers caught her wrist. His body heaved, and he all but threw her off him. She hit the wall, not hard enough to knock out her breath, but stunned out of her tears. He held her there, stiff-armed.

"*Don't.*" Hard, furious, as if ground out beneath clenched teeth. "Don't *ever* blind me."

Was that what she'd done? Horrified, she realized it was true. She'd blinded him. Unthinking. As horrible as ripping away Lisbet's nose, or kicking away Chief Leroux's cane. So caught up in her pain, she'd lashed out in the worst way.

She had no excuse. Annika nodded, her lips trembling. "I won't." And because it wasn't enough, "I'm so sorry."

Harsh breathing filled the silence, then a tortured denial.

He let her go suddenly, pulled away from her in the small space. Annika held herself against the wall, shame joining humiliation and misery. A rough curse filled the air. The crank of the lever followed, the clicking of the gear locks—abandoning the smuggle hole, though it was earlier than they'd planned.

Getting away from her.

Cold air rushed in as he left. She felt her way out, wishing he could take her hand again and guide her, knowing he wouldn't. Crossing her arms over her chest, she shivered in the darkened room.

He stood closer than she expected, his voice sounding oddly hollow after the intimacy of the hole. "Did I hurt you?"

Her wrist? "No."

Every other pain was her own stupid fault.

"I'm sorry for that." A ragged draw of breath. "And I won't touch you again."

She closed her eyes. No crying. *No crying.* "I know."

"Annika, I can't promise . . . I don't—" He broke off. Silence filled the room until he spoke again, each word low and urgent. "I don't know what we'll find when we leave *Phatéon.* You have good reason to doubt my friendship now, but I beg you to trust me until we're safe again. Whatever happens, I'll protect you. I understand if you refuse to continue our acquaintance, after."

Disbelieving, Annika stared through the darkness. New Worlders made absolutely no sense.

"David, I attacked you." And that wasn't all. "Before that, I groped you. That's not what a friend would have done. If you'd done the same to me without an invitation, I'd have thought you an animal. That's not propriety, but decency—and I flung it over the side. *You* have reason to doubt my friendship, fondling you even though I knew you didn't want me, simply because I hoped that the hardness meant you did. So I'm thoroughly ashamed of myself in addition to my other humiliations, because we're in considerable danger and yet I'm thinking only of bedding you when I should be thinking about where to find a dry pair of boots."

He didn't immediately reply. Then, "Look in the stateroom."

Because Maria Madalena was rich and moving to an island off Iceland. Yes, she'd have brought several pairs—and she was tall, unlike Annika. Her feet would probably be bigger, and too-large boots were always better than too small.

She waited, but he didn't respond to the rest of her outburst. Mortified by it, perhaps—or simply kind enough to let it go without adding to her humiliation.

All right, then. She held out her hand. "Will you lead me there?"

The warm clasp of his fingers over hers served as his answer. He drew her toward the door. "Do you have dry clothes?"

"In my cabin." And more in her pack, hopefully still in the lifeboat. "How wet was your coat?"

"To hell with my coat."

David suddenly stopped, dropped her hand. Annika bumped into him—not into his back, as she'd assumed, but his front. The hands she automatically raised to brace herself flattened against his chest. He faced her, but she couldn't see anything of his expression. Her eyes searched the darkness anyway.

He bent his head. She felt his inhalation against her hair, the warmth of his breath against her temple. "I lied to you."

Lied? She could barely think. "How?"

"I let fear rule me." Fingers traced down her cheek. Lips parting, she turned her face toward his caress. A large palm cupped her jaw. "Fear that I'd frighten you away. Fear that you'd push me away. I'd like to be ruled by hope instead."

"What hope?"

Firm, warm pressure against her lips. Annika had barely a moment to realize—*he'd kissed her*—before that touch was gone. She stared up through the darkness, blinking.

His breath shuddered. "Forgive me. I should—"

"Do it again," she finished for him.

She didn't wait, bunching her fists in his shirt and lifting onto her toes, searching for his mouth. She found his chin, overshot to his cheek. David stilled against her, then the hand cupping her jaw slid into her hair. Angling his head, he guided her lips to his. Lightly, so lightly, his mouth slightly open and a whisper of breath mingling with hers. Annika's pulse raced. Oh, this was wonderful. So sweet, almost chaste, and yet her pulse was *racing*.

Marveling at the sensation, she trailed soft kisses along the seam of his lips, gently tasting their firm width. Perfect. She could do this forever, but he lifted his head when she reached the corner of his mouth.

His lips pressed to her brow. "It wouldn't have been anyone," he said, his voice rough. "It was hard because of you."

Oh. He made her hope now, too. "But you said—"

"I lied."

"Not words. You gave no indication. You never touched me, or flirted, those little things that show interest."

"Neither did you."

"I told you I wasn't bold."

"And every conversation put lie to it. You say things no else would dare."

"Only words. I'm not bold when I need to *do*."

"Yet I was supposed to do?" His chest rose sharply beneath her palms. She thought he might have been laughing. "I was in agony today, wishing that I could touch your hand. Then agony again when I had all of you against me."

Truly? That was marvelous. "Because it isn't proper?"

"Because I thought you didn't want it. You said you wouldn't bed me without love."

"Yes. But that is only the bed. I want to kiss and do all of the rest while falling. That's the fun of it, don't you think?"

"I hope so." He wasn't laughing now. "You believe it takes years for love."

"Yes." Torture. A sweet one. "Everyone I know has taken years—but that might be because everyone in my village has known each other all their lives. I wouldn't mind being wrong."

"Even if you're right, I'll wait."

He might have to anyway, if Annika didn't find Källa. But she wouldn't think of that now. The pain that had been tearing at her chest eased. She smiled into the dark, a stupid silly smile full of daydreams, all so visible to him. "Are you smiling, too?"

"Yes." He lifted her fingers to his mouth, and she could feel it, the one he used that engaged all of his features, not the half smile, not the one weary with the world.

His smile faded beneath her fingertips. "I don't know what we'll face, Annika."

"I know."

He met her halfway, his mouth covering hers, hungrier now, harder. His arm wrapped around her waist, lifted her against his chest. Her lips parted under his. Annika moaned as he deepened the kiss, tasted her. Longing twisted beneath her heart, a delicious, welcome ache. She wanted this so much. This was what she'd *always* wanted. Capturing his face between her hands, she kissed him with every bit of need and hope coiling within her.

Chest heaving, he lifted his head. Slowly, he let her slide down his body, as if he couldn't bear to let her go yet. "I'll do all that I can to protect you, Annika. But you *will* abandon me if I can't. You will save yourself."

"No—"

He stopped her protest with another kiss. Then softly, "Yes."

Arguing would do no good, she realized. "We need our packs."

They weren't going to get them. The balloon had deflated, covering the access to the main deck like ice over a lake. In the forecastle companionway, she shoved against the taut metal fabric over her head. The envelope hadn't completely flattened; at least a few feet of air still remained inside. Pushing with all her might, she couldn't move it an inch.

David had no better luck. "Can we cut through?"

"No." A steel-tipped harpoon launched from a whale could, but nothing they had was sharp or strong enough. "Even if we could, the balloon covers the lifeboat, too. We'd never be able to find the packs before we suffocated."

"Dooley and Goltzius wouldn't have taken their packs on the gliders. They'd be too heavy. We'll use theirs."

"I need clothes from my cabin, first."

He led her down the passageway. The darkness had become oppressive, pressing down on her like the balloon on the deck— made worse by knowing that because the balloon was there, they didn't dare light a lamp.

In her cabin, he helped her find woolen stockings. Her heart pounded as she rolled them up her calves, wondering if he watched her. She wrapped more stockings up in a tunic to take with her. The two pairs of homespun trousers in her trunk were of a lighter weight than she wanted, best for summer, but her winter trousers were wet, and she could layer one pair over the other. She had mittens, scarves, and hats aplenty, bought with her eventual return to home in mind.

Next to the stateroom, where she waited as he searched for

boots. Relief rushed through her when he located a pair, and she vowed eternal gratitude to Maria Madalena when he returned a moment later with a heavy, hooded coat lined with mink. She put on another pair of stockings to fill out the larger boot size, then followed him to his cabin as he collected the packs, removing some of Dooley's and Goltzius's belongings, replacing them with their clothes.

They ventured down to the galley kitchen, and Annika realized how starved she was when he pushed a piece of flatbread into her hand. She ripped into it, listened to him rummage through the stores. "Nothing with a strong scent," she warned. "No blood or juices at all. The wild dogs will be on us."

He expelled a short breath. "It would be damned easier if we could take our own dogs."

"The clockwork ones?"

"Yes. But I don't know how we'd get them out of the cargo hold and through this whale. And they make a hell of a lot of noise—it's likely better to sneak away."

Annika wasn't so certain. The clockwork dogs and the sled might expose them to di Fiore's men, but they'd be facing more danger than that beyond the camp. She didn't see another option now, however. "We need something flat and light to use as snow-shoes, something narrow enough to walk on—and rope to tie them to our feet."

"I have rope." The rummaging quieted, as if he'd stopped to look. "The drawer faces?"

That would do it. "Yes. We need four. I have a pry bar in the—"

A screech sounded, the spine-cringing shriek of iron nails torn from wood.

Or he could just use his hand. Three more times, then she heard the rasp of canvas as he arranged everything in their packs.

A few minutes later, he helped her strap it onto her back. "All right?"

It was lighter than many she'd carried. "Yes. Are they even?"

"No. I'm infected by nanoagents. You're not."

And much stronger because of it, less likely to tire. Fair enough. "We can leave through the cargo hold, but we'll make noise," she said. "It might be better to climb out of the vents in the engine room. We can find more rope in the bosun's locker."

Annika's heart thundered as they descended to the engine deck again. This was it, then. *Phatéon* had been her home for four years; she'd have liked to see her off in a better way.

She'd have liked to *see* her off at all.

The engine room was still slightly warmer than the rest of the ship, and the air through the vents cold, but not freezing. By touch, she tied the rope off on a pipe and waited for David to climb down from the vent's opening, where he was studying the hold outside. Slowly, she realized that there must have been a light in the whale's hold. Though still dark, she could just make out David's shape against the vent, like a shadow on a black wall.

He returned to her side, took the coiled rope from her hands. "They've pumped out most of the water."

But not all of it? She hadn't relished the idea of wading through the icy water in her bare feet, then taking the time to put her boots back on, yet that was exactly what she'd have to do. Bending, she started to untie the laces.

"What are you doing?"

"There's no point in having dry boots if I just soak them again."

"Leave them on." His voice stopped her. "I'll carry you."

"And then *your* feet will—" Freeze. "Oh."

Her cheeks heated. His quiet laugh was followed by a brief kiss to her lips.

She savored that as he left her side, tossed the rope through the vent, and went through. Annika climbed up to the opening, her eyes adjusting to the faint glow coming from the opposite end of the hold. *Phatéon*'s hull was a dark curve, the hold beyond a darker shadow—but not an endless one. She had the faint impression of cavernous walls, a tall ceiling.

She heard David's boots scrape the hull, then the quiet sweep of water as he waded around the ship to study the rest of the hold. A minute later, he tugged on the line, signaling her to join him. Annika clung to the rope, arms aching with strain. The engine room was on one of the lower decks, but the tilt of the ship had raised this side. Her muscles were trembling by the time she neared the floor. His hands gripped her waist, drew her in until she was cradled against his chest.

"All right?"

She nodded, the back of her neck stiff with tension. "Where's that light coming from?"

"It's a lantern hung up at the top of the stair. I don't see anyone."

With water splashing at his ankles, he carried her around *Phatéon*'s side. Once past her bulk, the light showed more shadows, clearly delineated shapes. The fluyt had capsized, her deep keel jutting toward the ceiling, her broken masts a tangle of timbers and canvas that lay drunkenly against the aft wall. Enormous hydraulic pistons stood at the port and starboard sides—to open the whale's mouth, Annika realized.

She'd have marveled if she hadn't been so terrified.

Half-submerged bodies strewed the floor. David's arms tightened around her. Annika held on, stricken. She'd seen death before, natural and accidental—and worse. The neglect of a body in the streets. The terrible glee of the hanging. The quiet horror on Heimaey.

Nothing this cold. The crew had gotten no chance to fight back. They'd been slaughtered.

David set her down at the bottom of the stairs, the steel grating slippery beneath her boots. They climbed to the landing, her heart jumping with every small sound. She wanted to protest when David extinguished the lantern hanging near the door, but knew he was right to. After a second's thought, she caught up the lantern's handle and tied it to her pack.

She pulled her spanner from her belt. His hand gripping hers, he led her out of the hold and along another metal-grated passageway. After twenty yards, he paused.

"We're at a junction. A large source of heat lies somewhere ahead of us," he whispered.

"The furnace?"

"Probably. This passage leads there. Another leads left. And there's a ladder to a round hatch over our heads. It might be a way out."

Or it might open up to a bridge, or some other cabin filled with men ready to shoot them. "Which way does it swing open?"

"Out."

A good sign. An outer hatch of a submersible would never open in. "What does the ceiling look like?"

"A slight curve."

Like the top of a whale's head? She took a deep breath. "Try it."

His boots rang softly on metal rungs. She heard a clank, then the distinctive sound of a turning wheel opening a bolt-and-lock mechanism. They both quieted, waiting and listening. No one came to investigate the noise.

"I'll open it now," he said softly. "Pray there's not a lookout."

She did.

Chapter Eight

The gods didn't shit in her eye. A fat snowflake drifted through the open hatch, instead. Cloud-filtered moonlight shone like a beacon after the darkness, flooding the passageway.

Heart in her throat, Annika watched David climb through the hatch. He paused with his head and shoulders exposed, scanning the submersible's hull. No one shouted an alert.

David glanced down. "It's clear."

She emerged amidships atop the whale's back. Half an inch of snow had accumulated on the riveted hull, thinning toward the tail, where the lingering warmth from the furnace melted the falling flakes. Bolted against the port side, a ladder led down to a wooden dock. Like David, she sank into a crouch, trying to make her silhouette as small as possible. Their position offered no concealment.

But it offered them a view. The whale had docked in a small cove. At the cove's head, cliffs rose against the clouded sky, with ice sheeting down their jagged sides. Behind the whale lay the sea, the crashing waves a dull roar. The rail camp had been constructed alongside the water, a collection of a dozen clapboard buildings built up on three sides of a small clearing, its perimeter lit by lanterns hanging near each door. Not a large camp, but the long buildings could have been bunkhouses, each holding twenty or thirty men. A ferry cruiser hovered over the clearing.

Annika recognized it. "That's the airship we saw in Smoke Cove yesterday."

Mouth set in a thin line, David nodded. "Di Fiore's."

Best not to return to Smoke Cove, then, even if they were closer to that settlement than they were to Vik. Though they could find safety with Valdís, di Fiore had several hundred laborers at the nearby rail camp. The man had already destroyed their airship, ordered his men to kill the fluyt's crew. She doubted that he'd hesitate to kill them, too.

They'd try to make it to Vik, then. Everyone from the airship would have headed in that direction, too—and Captain Vashon didn't know di Fiore had been responsible for *Phatéon*'s fall. They could regroup, figure out what to do.

First, she and David had to get there.

They couldn't climb the icy cliffs. They didn't dare try to cross the cove without a boat. They'd have to make their way through that camp.

"There's a watchman," David said softly.

Annika saw him, standing between two of the bunkhouses. He faced the clearing, his back to the cove. Her heart sank. The buildings didn't form a circle around the clearing, but three sides, and the fourth side open. Though shadowed, the moonlight on the snow would reveal their movements. Even if they skirted around the camp, using the buildings for cover, he'd see them as soon as they ventured beyond the last bunkhouse.

Was there anything to hide behind? She studied the open edge of the clearing, and her lips parted as she recognized one of the shadowed shapes. "Is that a two-seater balloon?"

"Yes. With an open cart and a steam engine."

Blast. The cart would offer no protection and the sound of the engine would expose them long before it built up enough speed to fly away.

David frowned. "What the hell is behind them?"

In the dark, she couldn't quite make them out. Three ambulatory machines, of some sort. Their shapes seemed familiar, but . . .

Annika's heart leapt. Astonishment stole her breath. "Trolls."

"What?"

"Trolls. But with no skins, no disguise. That's what's underneath." Her astonishment faded into dread. "Why do they have them?"

David stared at her. "The trolls are *real*?"

"I told you."

"I thought it was just a story."

"Mostly. But stories are more frightening when there's some truth to them." And the terror was hers, now. "David, they must know about Hannasvik. They must have stolen these, killed everyone the same way as the sailors—"

Annika had to stop herself. Whatever had happened, she couldn't think of it now. She thought instead of the sailors on the fluyt. She thought of what would happen to David if they were discovered. Fear wouldn't help her now. She needed anger. Resolve.

She built up both. "We'll take a troll. I can drive it."

"That's not leaving quietly."

"If I'm in one of those, we won't need to." She caught his hand. "Listen."

His gaze on hers, he angled his head. She saw the moment he heard it—over the roar of the ocean, a distant barking. Dogs.

"If we don't take it, we're not going to make it far."

He nodded. "How long will you need?"

"After I'm inside, fifteen minutes to stoke the furnace and build up enough pressure."

"All right."

She hesitated. "If the watchman sees us—"

"I know." His face was grim. "I'll do it."

Sick at heart, she nodded. They climbed down to the dock—out in the open but shadowed by the bulk of the whale. The angle of a nearby building concealed them from the watchman as they traversed the small rise between the water and the camp. Staying low, they crept quietly to the rear of a bunkhouse, Annika wincing at every faint crunch of snow. David crouched against the clapboard siding, shrugged out of his pack, and glanced down at the pistol holstered at his thigh.

He couldn't use it. The report would wake them all. He closed his eye, then looked to Annika. Wordlessly, he gave over the gun. Her throat tight, Annika took it.

His chest rose on a deep breath, and for a long moment, he stared at his steel hand as if the contraption were alien to him. His mouth firmed as he stood. He stalked around the side of the building, out of sight.

Waiting was agony. She clutched the weapon, listening desperately for any sound. Only the ocean, and the faint snoring from inside the bunkhouse, the whisper of the breeze and falling snow.

Then the soft crunch of footsteps. David appeared, carrying the watchman's body, the man's rifle slung over his shoulder. His neck had been twisted at an unnatural angle. A terrible ache built in her throat. They'd had little choice, but she'd never killed anyone before. She couldn't imagine what David must be feeling. Except for the tight clamp of his jaw, his expression revealed nothing.

He laid the watchman in the snow, covered his face with his hat. Silently, he holstered the pistol and took her hand. Together they skirted around the edge of the camp to the trolls.

It was a relief to see that they weren't any of the machines from home. These were new and identical, whereas each troll from Hannasvik had been constructed with different salvaged pieces. Perhaps these men had come across one that had been hidden and copied it. The mystery of how they'd built these remained, and it could still mean that a driver from Hannasvik had been killed in the same way as the fluyt's crew, but Annika wasn't so afraid that her home had been raided.

She felt the belly of each. Two were already warm. She chose the one farthest away from the camp, quietly opening the hatch in the chest. She'd slept in her troll many times, but not when at home. Hopefully whoever drove these slept in the bunkhouses.

They did. The hearth chamber in the chest was empty. The furnace burned low. She stoked it, glad to see the coal bunker was full. After closing the vents, she lit a lamp and searched the driver's locker, found the tool she needed. She climbed back through the chest hatch; David waited outside, watching the bunkhouses and the hovering airship.

Gas grip in hand, she crept to the second troll, and clamped the tool over the hinge bolt on the hind leg. She couldn't budge it, until the hard strength of David's body pressed against her back, his hands gripping the handle below hers. The bolt squeaked as it turned. They both froze, listening. No movement in the camp. She continued loosening it until the bolt barely held the leg joint together.

Her chest hurt when they finished. Oh, this was horrible. Though only a machine, what she'd just done would have destroyed a century's worth of painstaking work and maintenance in Hannasvik. These weren't hers, they weren't old, but a lifetime of caring for a troll made it difficult to see them any other way.

But she had to. With David's help, she loosened the bolts on the other three legs, and saw that her troll's nose had begun to steam. Snow fell steadily as they worked, heavy flakes that stuck to their clothes. By the time they finished with the third machine, the boilers were ready.

Inside the troll's hearth chamber, he had to stoop over slightly. Except for the floor, there was nowhere to sit—and unlike Annika's troll, no bunk, no stove, and not much storage aside from the coal. The men at the camp must not use it to travel long distances, just to work—or perhaps to carry laborers to wherever the drill was.

Annika slipped out of her coat. The chamber was already warm; soon it would be hot. David tossed his pack into the corner, brushed the snow from his shoulders before unbuckling his overcoat.

"What do you need me to do?"

"Stoke, after a bit, but we'll be all right for a while." Annika threw the engine lever to full steam, and grinned as the troll gave a satisfying huff and shudder. "For now, just hold on to something."

She climbed up the short ladder to the troll's head and eased into the driver's seat. Her boots fit snugly into the stompers that drove the back legs. A sweet sense of belonging slipped through her. Four years had passed since she'd driven a troll, but each movement remained wonderfully familiar. Reaching up, she opened the eye louvers. The steel flaps lifted, showing her a view of the camp through multiple narrow strips. Cold air slipped in, faint light from the lanterns.

"Good Christ." David stood on the ladder, looking over her shoulder at the jungle of levers and pulleys. "You can drive this?"

"Yes." She had only a second to familiarize herself with the differences. The controls were the same, the gauges new—and a welcome addition. She wouldn't have to stop to check the pressure of the steam, the temperature of the furnace.

"They're coming," David said.

No alarm yet, but the engine had woken someone. A man strode across the clearing.

Annika hauled back the lift lever. The troll rose smoothly, still on all fours. So beautiful. The right foreleg grip didn't perfectly fit her fingers, the leather worn down by a century of women, but the pulley wheel didn't squeak.

The troll jolted forward a step. A *thunk* sounded on the floor behind her. David swore.

"Sorry." But she'd told him to hold on. "She's strong. Stronger than mine. It might take me a few seconds to adjust."

Laughing now, he climbed onto the ladder again. His fingers wrapped securely around the top rung. "I'm ready this time."

Annika eased her forward with small steps. The man in the clearing stopped, waving his arms and shouting at them—probably thinking that someone had taken a few drinks before crawling inside. That was usually why the trolls at home went on unexpected walks.

The troll's nose touched the flank of the second machine. "We need to name her," Annika said, slowly pushing down on the stomper.

Silence was David's only response. She glanced back. He wore a stunned expression, watching through the eye louvers as the giant machine toppled over. Steel shrieked. Even over the huffing of their engine, the crash was deafening.

"Jesus," he breathed.

Annika turned toward the second troll. In the clearing, the man raced forward, probably hoping to reach her before she pushed it over. A toppled troll was almost impossible to lift to its feet again without another to pull it up.

"I'm so sorry," she said, setting her nose against the machine's hip.

"For what? This is incredible!"

"I was saying it to the troll." Perhaps it did seem odd. "I grew up with them. They all have quirks, personalities—or they seem to. Some don't like to work in the cold. Some are terrible in the heat, or after crossing a river. Some will quit for no reason, then you've got to coax them and oil every inch until they start again, or there's some setting that has to be perfect, and that setting is never the same on another troll. What I'm doing now is awful."

Absolutely nothing like killing the watchman must have been, but still difficult. She winced as the leg buckled, then headed for the two-seaters. She didn't need to tip the balloons. One step crushed the frame.

More men surrounded them now, all shouting, waving their arms, then racing out of the way as she turned to crush the next two-seater.

"Go now, Annika," David said.

Yes. The tenor of the men's shouts had abruptly changed. Perhaps they'd thought the driver was drunk, but not now. They must have found the watchman's body. "The airship?"

"Leave it. Go before they get their rail cannon up."

God. Had they fired their engines? Annika yanked the head pulley, rocked back to look. The vents were still open. They'd need at least ten minutes before the engines were ready, and several more before an electrical generator could power the cannon.

"That's di Fiore at the rail," David said, and she saw the man looking over, silhouetted by the lamps on deck. "Observing it all."

They wouldn't give him any more to see. Annika hauled the troll around, pumped her legs. Men leapt out of her way. The troll moved easily, working up to a smooth gallop by the time she turned her toward the shoreline.

"Do you know where we're going?"

No idea. "To the ocean, and along the beach as far as we can. We can go faster on the sand, and if the snow keeps up, they won't be able to see us or follow us as well."

"Can *you* see?"

Through the dark and snow?

"I'll need . . . a bit . . . of help." She huffed as hard as the engine, arms and legs pulling and pushing in time with the troll's. Oh, she felt those four years now. She'd become soft. Stoking an engine was nothing compared to this. "Look . . . for boulders."

"Like watching for icebergs?"

"Yes." A stitch formed in her side. The flatbread she'd wolfed down felt like a rock in her stomach. She just had to push past it.

Down to the beach, to the edge of the waves, where the tide erased the snow as quickly as it fell—and would erase their tracks, too. Chunks of ice littered the black sand. Which way to go? They needed to head toward Vik, but she didn't know whether the camp lay east or west of that town. They were headed east now; every step might be taking them in the opposite direction they wanted to go.

She slowed to catch her breath, turned the troll to face the water. "Can you see Heimaey?"

David scanned the horizon. "Yes." He pointed southwest. "There."

So they were going the right direction, but how far away were they? Closing her eyes, she forced every other thought out of her mind. *Phatéon* had flown this way several times, and when she'd been younger, Annika had ridden along this route as a driver's apprentice. Had she seen the cove?

She *had*. During the summer. Ducks had been nesting along the banks of the cove, and had flown up when the troll disturbed them. They'd taken one for supper, but hadn't eaten it until they'd stopped for the evening, after they'd turned north, heading for the pass between two glaciers.

She opened her eyes. "We're thirty miles west of Vik."

Even on foot, not an impossible distance. A full day's journey in the summer, and only three hours of walking by troll—but she had to assume the airship was behind them. Annika turned the troll east again, slowly gaining speed.

"Can we make it to Vik tonight?"

"Yes. But we need to stop and hide. We're too easy to spot." And they should stay hidden during the day, too. "We can start again tomorrow night, when they likely aren't looking for us."

"You know of a place to hide *this*?"

"I know one." Ten miles away. Given the time it would take for the ferry cruiser to start after them, she could stay ahead of any pursuers if she moved at a quick trot.

Forty-five minutes at a fast clip. She'd done this before; she could do this again.

Forty-five minutes of endless pushing, pulling. Beyond a burn in her thighs, her arms. Tortured breaths squeezed her lungs, but after ten minutes, it was all the same pain.

Relief took the edge off when she finally saw a small river that fed into the ocean. She turned north. The troll followed the winding bank, forced to go slower now, Annika carefully picking her way across the moonlit snow. Her arms and legs trembled. Finally, cliffs rose ahead, with a wide bowl carved out of their face. A tall waterfall cascaded down, thundering as they drew closer. Mist drifted through the eye louvers, welcome on her heated, sweaty face.

Annika drove the troll into the shadows on the inward curve of the bowl. During the day, the depth of the cliffs and the mist would prevent anyone spotting them from above. She backed as far as she could against the rocks and settled the troll down, wincing as she unclenched her hands from the pulley grips. Blisters had already formed and broke.

So soft and weak. She was ashamed of it. She'd never let herself become like this at home.

David sucked in a breath. "Annika."

He reached for her hand. She shook her head, pulled it away. Her arms didn't feel like her own. "Will you stop the engine?"

When the huffing slowed, she realized he'd done it. Legs shaking, she pushed out of the seat, and David was there again, holding her waist as she trembled her way down the ladder. Humiliating. She should have been able to just jump down.

Her face was hot, throat parched. The engine puffed its last, surrounding them with sudden quiet—only the hissing of the boiler, the muffled roar of water. David's hands steadied her. In the soft glow of the lamp, the angles of his face seemed sharper, the shadows deeper.

She wet her lips. "Is there a cup in the pack?"

"Yes. Stay put." He dug through the canvas, moved to the hatch.

"Take the furnace poker," she said, and added when he glanced back at her, "for the dogs."

He smiled slightly, lifted his steel hand. "They're welcome to take a bite of this."

She had to smile, too. He returned a few seconds later, mist clinging to his clothes like diamond chips. Her fingers trembled violently, sloshing the water. He folded his hand over hers, watched as she drank. "Sit. Rest."

"I can't." She stretched her arms over her head. "I need to get out and walk."

She wouldn't go anywhere fast, but she couldn't sit yet. She'd ache worse afterward if she did.

He reached for their coats. She groaned, pushing her arms into the sleeves.

Face dark, he slung the rifle over his shoulder. "You'll show me how to drive this tomorrow."

"No." She appreciated the offer, but it was impossible. "If she tips over on a wrong step, we won't get her back up—and everyone tips theirs the first few times."

She followed him through the chest hatch, waited as he closed her up. The mist on her face was freezing, not quite as pleasant now. She tugged her hat down over sweaty curls.

Snow crunched under their feet. No dog tracks marked the fresh fall, but a few hare trails told her they wouldn't be far away. The bottom of the bowl carved by the waterfall spread south into a rolling plain. The troll's tracks along the riverbanks had almost filled. She glanced up into the cloudy sky.

Annika couldn't see anything through the dark and the heavy flakes. "Do you see the airship?"

He pointed to the southeast. If they'd still been on the beach, they'd have been overtaken at any minute. "You were right to stop."

"It's just habit—it's what you do when driving a troll. They're useful, but as soon as you're seen by an outsider, you run away and hide as quickly as possible."

"Like a rabbit."

"A big, powerful one." She smiled with him. "We should name her after one."

He nodded. "Rabbits are supposed to bring good fortune."

"Truly?" She liked that.

"Yes. According to my father's people, at least."

Perhaps they were right. This one had been lucky so far. "Austra Longears."

His brows rose. "Longears?"

"Do you think 'Tastylegs' is better? She's a rabbit."

He grinned. "Longears, it is. What did you call the troll you drove before?"

"Rutger Fatbottom." She laughed at his expression. "I didn't name him! He was passed down to me. But he *does* have a hefty engine back there."

Unlike David, who faced away from her to study the slope of the cliffs. "Tomorrow, I'll climb up and make certain there's nothing else we need to avoid ahead of us."

Annika nodded, looked back at the waterfall. Inside the bowl, ice from the mist covered the bottom half of the cliffs. "When I was here last, it was a cloudless night and the moon was full. There was a rainbow."

"At night?"

"Yes. During the day, too, with the sun shining down on the mosses against the rocks, catching all of those drops like sequins.

Beautiful. But the rainbow at night was so unexpected, so incredible. Do they know what does it?"

"No. We know water acts like a prism, but we don't know why the light is made of different colors—though there are several theories."

He knew so much. Annika felt as if she'd been constantly learning since leaving Hannasvik, whether she put any effort into it or not, and there was still so much more to know. So many things it never occurred to her to ask about. She tilted her head back.

"Sometimes on clear nights, lights dance across the sky. Have you seen them?"

"In Norway, and in Far Maghreb."

Far north and south. "When I was a girl, I used to stay up on clear nights, waiting. They always came on the nights I didn't wait, so I was never ready, rushing out in my nightclothes—and then shivering while watching." Perhaps they were up there tonight, above the clouds. "Do they know what makes them?"

"No. A few think that the world moving in orbit forces the æther to compress near the poles, and that the greater density creates a prism. Others think that the æther is already denser in some spots than others, and the lights come and go as we move through the different densities."

"You don't think so?"

"Not just me—many others don't. The pattern isn't regular enough. If we're orbiting at the same speed, through the same space every year, we should be able to predict the lights. But we can't. So the rest of us just admit we don't know."

She was surprised. "I've noticed that's difficult for New Worlders: admitting you don't know."

His laugh burst out on a frozen puff of air. "Perhaps. But for my mother, too, I remember."

Ah, well. She grinned. "My mother, too."

"So it is not just a New World affliction?"

"I suppose not. But at least we don't always try to take the brown out of bread. Why do you do that?"

Still laughing, David shook his head. "God knows."

"It's like eating raw dough."

"I wouldn't know—but at least I've never eaten raw dough."

She wrinkled her nose at him, then sighed. "I stole it. My mother wouldn't let me try a piece. I should have listened to her."

"That bad?" His laughter quieted as she nodded. "Do you miss home?"

"Yes. My mother more than anything. I'd have gone back long ago, if not for Källa." Now she was desperate to know how and why di Fiore's men had trolls. "I want to go back now."

David looked away from her, toward the roaring falls. "There are no males at all?"

"No."

"What about the boy children?"

"There are fewer than you might believe. Many of us are abandoned children from the New World or England. The old stories of seducing men were true. The first women thought they'd been blessed by the gods to bear only girls. *That* wasn't true. Bearing a girl was a blessing—not because of the girl, but because the mother didn't have to make such a terrible choice. Many of the women who bore male children stayed away rather than abandon him. So in the more recent generations, it's understood that if a woman chooses to lie with a man, to make certain he is a good man who will raise the boy well . . . but not many of those women ever return, anyway."

She paused. That was part of the reason why her mother had been so angry when Hildegard left. Not just because she'd been unfaithful, though that had hurt; the terror that she wouldn't come back was even greater. And when Hildegard *had* come back, her mother clung to the reason of infidelity to keep her anger alive . . . and the fear of being hurt so deeply again.

Annika loved Hildegard, and understood what had driven her. Her twin sister, Inga, had left; no one knew what had become of her. Their mother had recently died. She'd been desperate for a child, and in Hanna's family line they'd always borne children of their blood. But Annika also understood her mother's anger. Hildegard had put her through hell then refused to apologize for causing that pain, believing that any apology would suggest she'd also been sorry for having Källa.

It wasn't the same.

Annika was sorry, so sorry that she'd put her village in danger. She wasn't sorry that stupidity had led her here, to be with David now.

She glanced up at his profile. "Your mother must have thought your father was a good man."

"He was. And she wouldn't have left him—but later he told me that she'd missed her home, too . . . and that he'd always been afraid that she would leave us." He looked away from the waterfall, offered a bleak smile. "Perhaps he should have let her go. She wouldn't have been there when the mountain came down."

But she wouldn't have been there to save David, either. "If Inga stayed, it's because she wanted to."

He closed his eye, nodded. "It was difficult for him, knowing she might leave. *Not* knowing where to find her if she did."

"But if she left, she wouldn't want to be found." When he looked at her, the pain in his gaze made her rush to reassure him, "Obviously that wasn't the choice she made. He ought to have trusted in that instead of fearing it."

That bleak smile again. "That's not easy."

"I suppose not."

She couldn't imagine never seeing David again, and she'd only known him a week. But she was more aware of her own vulnerability now, too—how easily those fears could hurt, the desperate need to avoid any pain.

A distant bark. She glanced in that direction, her hand falling to the spanner at her belt. "Should we go back inside?"

Because she didn't want to see him hurt, either.

David seemed to have drawn into himself. Annika quietly watched him as she put potatoes on the furnace to roast, as he pulled a leather-bound notebook and a bottle of ink from Goltzius's pack. He rolled blankets out into a pallet on the floor, sat with his back against the hull and his legs extended. Like her, he was in his shirtsleeves and trousers; it was too warm inside the troll for anything else. He still wore his boots, however, while she'd removed her stockings and hung them up to dry. She busied herself for a while, laying out the rest of their wet clothes, checking the gauges, poking at the potatoes. Finally she joined him on the pallet, sinking down beside him with her legs crossed.

"What is that?" She could have answered her own question: a poor excuse to sit close.

He didn't look up. "My journal was in the lifeboat. So I'm using Goltzius's specimen book instead."

Curious, she glanced at the page. He'd already filled it—and he wrote incredibly fast. "What language is that?"

"French."

"No, it's not."

A smile tugged at the corner of his mouth. "It's shorthand."

"Do you write this a lot?"

"Every day." He paused at the end of a page, finally looked up. "On an expedition, keeping a journal is more important than all else—we learn that from the very first."

"In scientist school?"

"That's different—that's the university. But everyone who applies for expedition funds is required to take courses teaching them to survive. That is where they stress the journal. Partially, because we don't have to rely on memory when we record our data, but it also leaves a record of the steps we've taken. Everything we learn about exploring, about surviving—one of the most critical is making certain the journal survives, even if we don't."

"It's more important than a life?"

"No. I left mine behind, after all." His gaze fell to the page again. The ink had almost dried. "Death isn't uncommon among naturalists. There's tremendous value in knowing where they went . . . where they might have stepped wrongly."

"So someone else doesn't do the same thing?"

"Or so that someone can try it again, but in a different way." His thumb brushed over the page. "Perhaps my work is all I'll leave behind. Perhaps I'll never be able to report what I've found here or what I might discover in the future. Perhaps I'll never come to any grand conclusions or make any great discoveries. But if it adds to something, if someone else can use my work to reach another goal, to make another discovery, my journey won't be in vain."

Her heart caught. Once, when wondering why he chased volcanoes, she'd hoped that he wasn't like Sigurd the Deceiver, but what he spoke of resembled those old stories very much—not in an old way, but a new one.

"So these journals are like epics of scientific study."

He grinned with her, but nodded. "I have my heroes."

"You make me want to be a naturalist."

"The pay isn't as much as a stoker's."

Gold was fine, undoubtedly. "But it must be quite something to matter. To be a part of something bigger, despite the risk. I think you all must be very brave."

"Or lucky." A flush rose on his neck. "You matter, Annika."

"Oh, certainly. Nobody else can shovel coal."

"Anyone can chase volcanoes, too. I don't know anyone else who can drive a troll."

"We were both lucky tonight, then." She smiled at him, then

looked down at his notes. She wished he had his journal—she'd have learned shorthand just to read about what he'd done and where he'd been. "Do you write everything?"

"Almost."

And if they found his journal, the men at the camp could read it now. Sudden alarm made her glance up. "Did you write about Hannasvik?"

His gaze locked with hers. "No."

"Why leave it out? It wasn't your secret."

"But it's personal—not for the world."

"Will you write of di Fiore?"

"I already have."

"And the troll?"

"I only said that it was a machine we used to escape."

"And the watchman?"

"Yes."

His expression didn't change, but she remembered how he'd gathered his breath before, the hardness of his jaw afterward.

"Have you ever killed anyone before?" she wondered.

"No."

"I'm sorry."

She should have been bolder, offered to do it. Maybe with the troll.

No. If they'd been in the troll, they wouldn't have had to kill anyone. They would already have been safe.

"I'm sorry, too." He opened his steel fingers, looked at them. "I never think of it as a weapon. I know others do when they see me. They think about how easily I could snap a neck—how easily I could snap *their* necks. They're right. I wish it had been more difficult," he said softly. "More like what it felt."

Her throat ached. "If it had been, he could have raised an alarm. We'd be dead."

"I know. I don't regret it. I'd do it again." He closed his fist. "I'm just sorry that I had to."

She nodded, glanced down at the page. "Is that what you wrote?"

"Not the part about how people see me."

All of them idiots. "It's too personal?"

"Yes. And I wrote that I'm not the same man. I recognized the threat, I knew what had to be done . . . yet I hoped to think of any other way to get us both across that clearing without raising any alarm. Knowing that I couldn't find another way takes something from me. Almost everything I've read or heard said that I'm supposed to feel powerful now: I killed a man. I defeated him, I was stronger." He shook his head. "But it felt the opposite. I think the power must be in the choice, because when I realized I had none, I felt completely powerless—and if I ever have a choice, if our lives aren't at risk, I won't do it again. I can't imagine what must be in men who kill when there is no threat."

Neither could Annika. "That sounds personal, too. Not scientific."

His brows drew together. "But it is, in its way. A man is dead. I've written the effect it had on me. Perhaps that will matter one day, too."

"So these journals are not just tales of scientific heroics. They are also the study of men." She would love to know the conclusion. "What will happen to your expedition now?"

"We'll suspend the survey." He tipped his head back against the steel hull, stared up at the ceiling. "We lost all of our supplies. So we'll have to wait until we've reported what happened, return to New Leiden, and procure new equipment—if the Society decides to pay for it again. Depending on what happens here, they might not send another expedition to Iceland for a while."

So he'd leave. A steady burn of pain started in her chest. And she could never ask him to stay, because that work was too important.

He fought to change the world for the better, to make it safer, to do good. He mattered.

She glanced down, picked at a stray thread on the hem of her trouser. "What will happen to di Fiore?"

"I don't know. Because Goltzius was onboard, the Dutch will probably send men to retaliate, then keep a physical presence in Iceland to reestablish their claim on the island." He sighed, lowered his head to meet her gaze again. "*Phatéon* is gone. What will you do?"

Try not to be miserable. Try to focus on the excitement of the new, instead of feeling alone again. "The Vashons will send for us. Then I'll find work aboard another airship and continue looking for Källa."

"And after you find her, you'll return home."

"Yes." To Iceland, at least. Valdís might have been right; she might not be able to return home. And she didn't want to live anywhere that David couldn't go.

He nodded, as if he hadn't expected anything else. "Will you still write to me?"

"Yes." And hopefully meet with him. "I'd like to visit, too—whenever your expeditions allow it."

"Whenever you want." His dark gaze held hers. "I also wrote that I kissed Annika Fridasdottor. I wanted the world to know. I would shout it now, but there is only you to hear it."

She smiled, her heart tripping over the ache. "Would you like to do it again?"

"I wouldn't like anything more."

"Well, *I* would like to do more than kissing."

"God, yes. I would, too."

He hurriedly put the journal aside, capped the ink. Remembering the delicious sensation of straddling him, Annika slid over his muscled thighs, her face even with his. With a soft groan, he reached for the lamp.

"Leave it on," she said, and pressed her mouth to his jaw.

He pulled away—not far, tilting his head back against the hull. His voice was rough. "You don't want to see me while we do this."

She frowned. Perhaps he had reason to assume that was true, some experience that told him it was, but it wasn't. "You're wrong. I do."

He was a man of science. She'd figure out a way to prove it, if she had to.

His chest rose on a shuddering breath. "I don't want you to remember me like this."

Well, then. There was nothing to prove. She capped the flame.

So dark. She wanted to see his expression when she kissed her way across the width of his mouth, but Annika didn't need it to tell her what he felt. The stillness of his chest said the same breathless anticipation held him in its grip. By the tightening of his hand on her hip, she knew he kept the same desire barely reined in. She coaxed open his lips for a long, slow taste.

Oh, this need. It twisted in her gut, painful, wonderful. Hungry. She buried her hands in his hair, pulling him closer. Wanting him all.

With a soft growl, he pushed her over, laying her back on the blankets. Still kissing her, his hands braced beside her—his hips between her legs. Oh, *yes*. Her hands fell away from his shoulders to the pallet. She arched up beneath him, moaning into his mouth at the sudden, delicious pressure against her heated flesh. His erection rose behind the confines of his trousers, thick and hard.

All for her.

"Annika." He groaned her name. "May I touch you?"

She would die if he didn't. "Hurry."

His head lifted as his hand slid up her side beneath her hem. He didn't hurry. He was watching, she realized. Watching as her tunic rode up over his wrist, as he bared her to his gaze. His fingertips lightly stroked her waist, her ribs. She didn't need to see his expression now, either. He touched her with reverence, as if she were the most incredible thing he'd ever beheld.

And despite his wish, she would *always* remember him this way.

"My God, Annika. You're so beautiful." He sounded almost drunk, as if each inch of skin he'd revealed had been a sip of wine. "Touching you is the sweetest pleasure I've ever known."

Oh, how she wanted to please him. "Then touch me everywhere."

He pulled the tunic over her head in a whisper of cotton. A shiver raced over her skin when his warm palm cupped her breast. Her nipples tightened, aching for his caress. A riot of desire tore through her. She wanted to slow down and she wanted to rush. Her fingers twisted in the blankets; her breath came in pants.

His callused thumb swept over the sensitive peak. An exquisite jolt of pleasure stiffened her body, and slowly released her on a moan.

His mouth found hers again, hovered over her lips. "All right?"

Perfect. Her hands slid back up over his shoulders. The heavy weight between her legs kindled a deep, ravenous fire that burned through her veins.

"Yes. But I want more."

He gave a strangled laugh. "I can't stand much more. I'll be all over you."

That confession excited her more than any touch. *All over her.* She wanted that so much. On a surge of need, she drew him down. "Then we'll go until we can't stand it anymore."

His lips opened over hers, hotter, harder. Annika met him with a thrust of her tongue that seemed to roll through him, a wave that ended with a rock of his hips into hers. His fingers plucked at her nipple, making her gasp, then his mouth was suddenly there instead, scorching, sucking. Mindless with the pleasure of it, Annika cried out. Her legs wrapped around his lean waist, her back bowing. Her hands grasped for his, to hold on, to entwine herself around him in every possible way.

He stilled, shuddered. His cheek turned against her breast, his voice hoarse. "Not there. I can't bear it."

Steel, she realized. Her fingers had intertwined with his steel ones, and he didn't like his prosthetics touched or encumbered. "I'm sorry. I forgot."

She felt his nod, and the ragged breath against the moist tip of her breast. His tongue flicked over her nipple, a teasing taste.

"Tell me what pleases you most, Annika."

This. Everything. Oh, she didn't know. She couldn't guess if everything she wanted to do would please her . . . but she always enjoyed one thing.

"I make myself spend with my hand. I'd like yours there, instead."

He didn't move. He didn't respond.

Annika bit her lip. "Too bold?"

"No." A rough denial, followed by a hesitation. "I . . . Here?"

His hips rolled. Her inner muscles clenched in response, a tight, insistent ache. Annika closed her eyes in the dark, her lips parting.

"Yes," she breathed.

The heavy weight between her thighs lifted. His palm smoothed down her belly, fingers splayed. "Beneath your trousers?"

"Yes." But she stilled when a tremor shook his hand. Was he uncertain? "Don't you pleasure yourself?"

"Yes," he said ruefully, and she could easily imagine his grin. "But never with a woman. I've never done any of this."

But . . . ? "There were two."

"It didn't work out well. I want this to." His mouth found hers, lingered until her breathing quickened again. His hand slid lower. "Tell me what to do."

"You just have to rub." And not very much. Just thinking of his touch was already bringing her toward the edge.

Her fingers clenched on his shoulders as he backed away, lifting himself over her. He tugged the ties at her waist, unbuckled the side. His harsh breaths filled the air.

"Off or on?"

He wouldn't need them off; she never did. But she didn't just want the touch of his hand. She loved the way he looked at her. "Do you want to see me?"

"God, yes."

"Off."

She helped him, lifting her hips and shoving them over her thighs, then lay back. Silence. Sudden trepidation tightened her skin. How *did* she look to him? He'd liked her up top, but now she felt awkward and exposed, with her legs parted and knees bent—nothing at all like the poised and elegant women in New World fashion plates and advertisements. Should she twist onto her side, look over her shoulder?

Unable to bear the quiet, she whispered, "Should I put them back on?"

"No," he said, and that single hoarse word erased her fear. His mouth eased over her lips, parted them with a penetrating sweep of his tongue. His fingers trailed up the inside of her thigh. Anticipation trembled through her. He paused, as if waiting for a protest.

She could only offer encouragement. "Let me touch you, too."

"No." He kissed her again, said roughly, "I'll make a mess all over you."

When he came? "I want that."

He shuddered. His hand slid higher. His head lifted. Watching, as his fingers brushed her curls. Desperate for a stronger touch, she raised her hips, bumped up into the flat of his palm. He pressed down, the heel of his hand against her clitoris. Oh, like that. Just like that.

"Right there, David."

He rubbed a small circle. Her back arched on a ragged moan.

He groaned against her mouth. "Let me hear that again."

She couldn't have stopped herself if she'd wanted to. She cried out again, her hands clenching on his shoulders, her hips pumping against his hand. Need tore a hole through sense, awareness. She only knew the stroke of his hand, the heated thrust of his tongue. He pressed harder, faster. Her body bowed, head falling back, and his arm slid beneath her shoulders, lifting her, capturing her nipple in his mouth. Delicious suction joined the quickening movement of his hand, leaving her writhing.

David's pleasured moan reverberated against her breast. Her excitement seemed to feed his, hand rubbing more urgently over her clitoris, drawing out her helpless cries. No finesse, only hunger. She was almost there. Almost there.

"Inside me," she gasped. "Your fingers. Please."

His hand slowed. "Do you have any women's oil?"

Any what? She couldn't think. "Women's oil?"

"To make it easier. My hands are big. I don't want to hurt you."

She finally understood. "I'm wet enough. Feel."

His muscles stiff with tension, his middle finger slid between her slick folds. His tortured groan matched hers. "You are. God, you are."

How could she not be? Never had she been this aroused, this desperate for release. Her body shook with anticipation, with need. The thick glide of his finger paused for an eternity at her opening. Annika whimpered in frustration, raised her hips, trying to urge him in.

Gently, he penetrated her. She cried out as her body clamped around him, as a shock wave of pleasure rode outward, rocking her against his hand, drawing him deeper.

"Christ." He cursed through gritted teeth. "Good Christ."

His mouth came down on her breast again, sucking her nipple to a burning point, the thrust of his hand and the rubbing of his thumb sending her flying, flying. Her body locked, shuddered. Her scream caught in her throat, emerging in short, breathless bursts that echoed the clench of her flesh around him. He continued thrusting, rubbing, until she had to push his hand away—it was too much. Too much.

But so wonderful.

His chest heaving, David sat up, drew her over him. Her hands cupping his jaw, Annika kissed him hard, delirious with pleasure, her body warm and liquid. The rivets loosened, for a short time. She wondered how long it would be until they tightened again.

She hoped not long. "You, now. Let me touch you."

He became utterly still. What was he thinking? She couldn't tell—and she'd have given anything to see his expression now. After a long moment, he nodded stiffly against her hands.

She was still unsure. Was he only agreeing to please her? "Do *you* want me to?"

"God, Annika. So much. But not out of obligation."

Spoken harshly, there was no mistaking the longing, the need. She smiled against his lips and reached between them. "This isn't a trade. I'd want this even if you never touched me. But after you did, I was greedy and wanted to go first."

He tensed again as she deftly unbuckled his trousers. "And now?"

"Still greedy."

She wanted to see his face as she gripped his heavy length with both hands, but his short, shuddering breath gave her enough. His head fell back. She kissed her way down his throat, longing for his mouth, but greedy to hear the sounds he made, too.

He was hot against her palms, silky skin over steely flesh. What to do now? She squeezed gently. His hips bucked, thrusting his erection through her grip. His hand covered hers for a brief instant before his fingers clenched on her hip, as if to stop himself from guiding her, to hold himself still. His breathing was quick and rough.

She licked the base of his throat, felt him shudder. "How do I do this, David?"

"Any way you like." He gave a short laugh. "It won't take long."

Then she'd like to please him as much as possible in that short time. "How would *you* do this?"

"Up and down."

Oh. Like a piston. And now it was easy, so easy to imagine his thick shaft working into her as his finger had. Breathless, she pumped her fists. He made a strangled noise, hips jerking, fingers clenching.

The rivets inside her were tightening again. "Are you watching?"

"Yes."

So he could see the sway of her breasts, the spread of her thighs over his. He could see her slick flesh, so close to her hands, stroking his length as he would stroke into her body. But not as wet as he would be inside her.

Her mouth could make him wetter—she'd heard the women of Hannasvik talk about how best to lick. The same would likely work for men, too, though everyone in the New World was too proper to talk about using a mouth in that way, except as an insult. What would he think of it?

She would find out. Slowly, Annika scooted back until she knelt between his legs, kissing the hard muscles of his chest through his shirt as she descended.

"Annika." His body stiffened, his voice hoarse. "Annika, no, you don't have to—"

She did. She wanted to know his reaction, his response—and she prayed he wouldn't think less of her for it. Gripping his shaft, she opened her mouth, licked the thick head. A shout, quickly muffled by the clench of his teeth. His erection pulsed beneath her fingers. Oh, his response was even more than she'd hoped. She licked the broad tip again, slower this time, absorbing the salty taste, the unexpected smoothness of his taut skin. His hands came onto her shoulders before falling away. Her flattened tongue swept over him again, and his tortured moan was the most wonderful sound she'd ever heard. She licked, licked, then remembered to pump her hands. A memory of the exquisite sensation of his mouth on her breast led her to suck on the head.

With a hoarse cry, his body bowed, pushing him deeper past her lips. Reflexively, she jerked her head up. Before she could lower her mouth again, he caught her face in his hands.

"That's enough, now. That's enough." Panting, he covered her hands with his, squeezing. A vicious shudder wracked his frame, and he called out her name. His shaft throbbed against her palms. Wetness slid over her fingers.

His seed. When she loved him, this would be inside her, too.

The thought of it warmed her. He'd make a good father. And she wanted this with him every night, every day.

While he regained his breath, she crawled up over him again, straddling his thighs, kissing his lips. For the first time, she understood perfectly why some women remained with the men they'd chosen to lie with. It simply hurt too much to go separate ways.

But neither of them had much of a choice.

Chapter Nine

Annika had been right about the dogs. By mid-morning, David had seen almost two dozen slinking around the troll—thin, mangy curs that snapped and snarled when another dog came close. Not a pack, he thought. Just drawn by anything that moved, that might smell like food.

Fortunately, they also scared easily. An icicle hurled their way sent them scattering, tails between their legs. Not for long, though, and even a man with a steel arm and legs felt bludging vulnerable when he had to expose softer bits and relieve himself.

He finished just as a few of the curs stole into throwing distance again. A tossed handful of powdered snow held them off until he reached the chest hatch. His eyepiece immediately fogged in the warmth of the troll's hearth chamber. Annika still lay sleeping on the pallet they'd made on the floor, clad only in her underclothes, her head pillowed in her arms. Her thin gray chemise rode up around her waist, exposing the dip of her spine. Pink bows marched down the side her cream linen drawers; a lace ruffle emphasized the swell of her bottom.

And *this* was vulnerability. David's lungs seemed to squeeze in around his heart at the sight of her. God, she had him wrecked.

He stripped off his coat and glove. Mindful of his wet boots, he carefully lay down on his side next to her. Propping himself up on his steel elbow was awkward, but it kept his right hand free to touch her. For now, he didn't. He merely watched her instead.

He'd never slept with a woman before. He hadn't slept much the night before, either—he'd remained awake, savoring the feel of her against him.

His breath stirred the curls at her nape. She lay with her face turned toward him, her profile soft in sleep, her lips parted. Her beaded necklace had twisted around, the inscribed bones nestled in the hollow between her shoulder and neck. He read the runes again, the name of each woman who had led to this one. Annika, daughter of Frida.

Annika, who spoke an entirely different language than he did—no matter that she called it English. Her definitions of "brave" and "bold" were much different than his.

Last night, she'd touched him without fear. Already skating on the sharp edge of need and love, he'd almost broken when her hand had found his, had all but shattered when her fingers entwined around steel as if there were no difference. As if to her, he was just a man—no more and no less.

David didn't know how he'd ever let her go.

But he would have to; that much was clear. He'd known the very thing that had brought Annika to him—her search for Källa— would take her away, but for a brief time he'd hoped to eventually follow her. When his obligation to his mother was fulfilled, he could help her search.

Now he realized that the search for Källa wouldn't take her away; finding her sister would. Annika would return home . . . and he couldn't follow her there.

His gaze traced the fullness of her bottom lip, the hole in his chest stretching like the next year, two—his life, without her in it. Empty, except for her brief visits. When the sun set, they'd be on their way. Closer to Vik. Closer to going separate ways.

David had never been good at feeling sorry for himself, but he was putting in an effort today.

Her thick lashes flickered. She met his gaze for a moment. Her lips curved faintly before her eyelids drifted shut again. "Just two more minutes."

They weren't going anywhere yet. "You can have more than—"

"Shh."

He grinned. After a moment, the corners of her mouth tilted upward again, though she didn't open her eyes.

"I'm having a good dream. I don't want it to end."

Neither did he. "About?"

"You."

Her spreading smile told him what that dream consisted of. His body instantly stiffened, recalling the astonishing pleasure of her mouth.

"I intend to rename you Annika the Bold."

Her smile faded. She looked up. "Annika the Improper?"

She knew she had been. So she must be asking whether it bothered him. "Everyone should be as improper. And as surprising."

Even knowing she cared nothing of propriety, he'd never expected to feel her mouth on him. He'd never have asked it from her—and wouldn't have imagined that she would even know to pleasure a man in that way.

She answered his unspoken question. "I've heard it mentioned."

"By the crew?"

"Yes. But anyone who licks someone's penis . . . is not thought well of."

So that was why she was uncertain now. Though if it offered

someone even a fraction of the ecstasy she'd given him, men should be begging for it and worshipping anyone willing to. "But you did anyway, despite that risk?"

"Some women I know like it very much. I thought a man might, too. I wanted to please you as much as I'd been, despite what you might think of me afterward."

"I think well of you. I couldn't think any better of you." And his mind was painting images of her again, her body bowed, her desperate cries as she came, the sweet clench around his fingers. He could have used his mouth, instead. He could have known her taste. God, he wanted that. "Would you like it?"

"Yes." But she grimaced. "Not now."

Still sore from the previous day. Gently, he rubbed the back of her shoulder. She groaned, closing her eyes. He froze. Was he hurting or helping? After a motionless second, she sent him a deathly glare.

"Don't stop."

With a smile, he obediently continued. "So everyone is improper in Hannasvik."

"No." With another groan, she turned her face into the cradle of her arms, straightening her neck. "We're all perfectly proper there. Everyone in the New World is rigid and absurdly frightened about the most natural things."

Perhaps they were. "Were you one of the abandoned children?"

"Yes."

"From where?"

"Manhattan City." Her voice was muffled against her forearms. "Why do you ask?"

"I'm curious." He wanted to know everything about her.

She pushed up onto her elbows, looking back at him with a slight frown. "What does it tell you about me?"

"It tells me where they found you." And let him picture her better.

"But about *me*?"

"Nothing." But she was irritated, clearly. David was fascinated. He hadn't expected this reaction. "Why?"

"I've never understood it. That is always the first thing someone asks: Where are you from. Not 'What do you like?' or 'What do you believe?' or even 'What is your mother like?' which all have more bearing on the person I am. And if I don't tell them where I'm from, they try to guess. Even though there are other people with my color spread all over the New World, they always assume that I'm Liberé—until they hear me speak. They know by my accent that I'm not Black Irish, and not from Manhattan City—though that is partially correct—and not from Lusitania or Castile or the disputed territories. It drives them mad, as if to know me they need to know where I am from."

"I'd like to know where you're from." He grinned when she snorted. "You only notice it because no one needs to ask in your village. You all grow up knowing each other."

"Yes, but what does my coming from Hannasvik tell you? Nothing at all. What have you found out now? That I want you to lick between my legs. But it wouldn't hold true for everyone from Hannasvik. Some women don't like to be licked. Some think it should only be discussed privately, and others think such things are better discussed frankly. Some do not want to lie with women, some do not want to lie with men. Some want to leave, some don't, some dare to leave, some don't. Some are brave, some are vain, some are pious, and some of us just speak of the gods and know in our hearts that they only exist in Hanna's stories. Manhattan City is not the reason I love to sew clothes, and neither is Hannasvik. It is not the reason I love smoked fish. It is not the reason for anything about the way I am."

He'd have to remember to rile her up more often. God, she was incredible—her color high, her eyes all but sparking.

"Having smoked fish available in your village might be why you like it," he pointed out.

"But that's not why I love butter candies or maize bread, which I never had before I left Iceland." She narrowed her gaze at him. "Are you poking at me?"

"Yes." And enjoying the hell out of it.

Her expression softened. "Then tell me why it's so discomfiting not to know, when a few conversations would tell someone far more about *me*? Why is everyone in the New World so obsessed with where everyone else came from?"

"You're obsessed with concealing it."

"For good reason. What is their good reason? What is it about being born in a certain place that somehow allows people to immediately sum me up? As if I can only believe one thing, support one idea."

David had no answer to that. "It's polite. A quick way to discover common ground. It's well intentioned."

"But ultimately false. Everything they think they know is based on assumptions that will be overturned the longer the acquaintance lasts."

Their acquaintance had lasted long enough that he could guess why this roughed her nerves so much. She loved her people and missed her home yet had had to disavow them. The common ground was as false as the assumptions she disliked.

"And every time someone asks, you're forced to pretend Hannasvik doesn't exist again."

"Don't try to be clever."

"I can't help it."

"Pfft." She wrinkled her nose at him. "Everything I said is still true. People always ask, and they think it means something. Don't tell me you've never noticed it?"

"I suppose I do it all the time," he said. "I have noticed this: You are irritable after you wake."

She grinned suddenly. "My mother called me Annika the Sleeping Dragon because I was such a danger in the mornings. But I never feel as if I get enough."

And she truly hadn't in the past week, David knew. A heavy shift rotation, without the nanoagents to help her along as they did him. It was no surprise she'd dropped off so easily inside the whale, then again the previous night. "And what is your mother like?"

A laugh rolled through her, and she dropped her head back into her arms with a groan. David resumed rubbing the tense muscles along her spine. He didn't know which pleased him more: that she welcomed his touch, or her blissful sigh as she did.

"Stubborn," she said. "The only argument I ever won was when I told her I was leaving to look for Källa. She eventually agreed that I had to, or I'd never be able to hold my head up at home—and the guilt would crush me. How could I be happy like that? I would be as miserable as she was." Her lips pursed, her expression pensive. "I think she might be happy now."

David frowned. "Because you're gone?"

"Oh, no. I think she's much like your aunt—often sad. There are pieces of her life that gave her joy, however, and I am one of those." Annika bit her lip. "That's probably why I liked Lucia so well."

Who'd begun a friendship under a false pretense. "She's sorry."

"I know. I knew it then. But I needed to be angry first." Annika looked up at him. David wanted to turn his face, present his good side. He didn't. "I'll miss you so much. I wish we had more time. There are so many things I want to know about you."

There were many other things he wanted to know, too. He suspected that a lifetime wouldn't be long enough.

At this moment, he wanted to know her taste. He wanted to feel her wet and trembling beneath his mouth, to give her even a fraction of the pleasure she'd offered him.

Not yet. Not until these knots beneath his fingers had loosened. He bent, kissed her nape. "I'll be improper later."

* * *

David never got the chance. The distant thrum of an airship engine alerted him after noon. It flew south of them—heading west. Returning to the rail camp, and hopefully abandoning the search.

He looked for the airship again as the sun set. The sky was clear. Annika stoked the furnace, and soon the troll's nose steamed, the engines huffed. He watched her ease into the driver's seat, still stiff. God, David hated that he couldn't help her.

. She must have caught his look. "It's not far," she reassured him. "Only an hour and a half."

He nodded, took his place on the ladder behind the head to serve as her eyes—though she wouldn't need him as much tonight. Few clouds scudded across the sky. The moon shone bright over the snow, illuminating a clear path along the river.

David remained on the ladder, anyway, watching over her shoulder. She started off at an easy pace. Only an hour and a half. There was too much to ask, too much that he wanted to know. She must have thought so, too. Every breath not spent driving the troll was answering his questions or asking her own.

The low plains rolled out ahead. Too soon, they reached the shoreline again, the black sand strewn with rounded stones. They spoke less now as Annika had to navigate around basalt flows, to head away from the beach and behind high cliffs, waves crashing at their base. The dogs were everywhere. Not the same ones as at the waterfall, trotting alongside for a while before slinking off into the dark.

"It used to be hares." Without a break in the rhythm of her pumping feet and pulling arms, Annika wiped the sweat from her face. "A hundred years ago, when Hanna and the Englishwomen first came, they couldn't keep a garden because the hares would eat the greens as soon as they shot up out of the ground. It hardly mattered, though; the women got fat on rabbit."

A hundred years ago. "After the fissure eruptions?"

"Not long after."

A grimace of dismay suddenly pulled her lips tight. She'd realized what she was revealing, he thought.

"I still don't know where it is," he reminded her. "Everything else hardly matters."

She nodded. "About two generations ago, they started speaking of the dogs, instead—how many there were."

A few dogs left by the early settlers, and a bounty of hares. It was no surprise that their population had exploded, but that couldn't last forever. "They'll likely die off, too, after they eat all of the hares."

"They already have. That's why the dogs have been so bad, we think—why they began attacking us and the flocks eight or nine years ago. They never used to be such a problem."

"So the women of Hannasvik aren't eating hares now?"

"Sheep, now and again. Mostly fish."

"So you're on the coast."

Her jaw clenched. After a moment, she said, "Lake fish."

He kissed the side of her neck. "Trust me."

"I do. But I shouldn't be stupid—so careless. That was why Källa left in the first place."

Then he was glad that Annika had been careless. He wouldn't voice that, though.

She slowed the troll, looking ahead to another cliff, its face jutting into the sea. "We have to go up around those, then Vik should be in the hills beyond it. Do we drive in?"

Her instinct was to hide the machine, he knew. But as another cur darted in front of the troll's feet, he shook his head. "We don't have much choice."

She nodded. Only a few minutes more, then. He fell silent, saying as much as he could with kisses to her shoulders, her neck, breathing in the scent of her hair. He would let her go. He *would* let her go. It wasn't forever. Just for now.

God, he was terrified that it would be forever.

Annika stopped on a snowy rise overlooking the small town. Her breath hitched. She reached back, brought his hand to her mouth. His throat closed when she pressed a warm kiss to the center of his palm, when she vowed, "I *will* write. And visit, as soon as I'm free."

And he would try to make that day come more quickly. "I'll help you search."

"Yes."

For a brief moment, her lips trembled against his fingers. Then her shoulders straightened, and she reached for the foreleg pulley again.

Composed of a handful of houses and shops nestled on the rolling lowlands, Vik was a stone's throw from the ocean, overshadowed by the rise of the cliffs to the west and the highlands to the north. The town didn't possess a harbor, but David expected to see more flat-bottomed boats drawn up to the edge of the beach. Only a few were tied upside-down, their keels buried in snow.

The town lay quiet. Not the deathly stillness of Heimaey, but it still struck David as strange. Though it was early, warm lamplight only glowed in a few windows.

"No sheep. No ponies," Annika said. "Though they have fences to keep the dogs out."

But not a troll. Slowly, they passed an outlying farmhouse, and followed sled tracks onto the main street through the town. A long rectangle of light suddenly spilled from an open door. Annika stopped the troll. They both recognized the woman coming out into the street, a pistol in hand, and the man behind her. Vashon and Dooley.

Relief rushed through him. So at least some of the passengers and crew from *Phatéon* had arrived safely. Now, where was his aunt? The captain appeared to be shouting. He couldn't hear a word over the huff of the engine.

Annika pushed up out of the driver's seat. He helped her down the ladder, opened the chest hatch, and dropped down. Snow crunched under his feet. Vashon stared at him over the barrel of her gun, astonishment widening her eyes. Dooley let out a shout and came forward, clapping David on his back, laughing. More people emerged from the house—some crew he recognized, others he didn't know. Finally, there was Lucia, rushing to him with tears standing in her eyes.

She caught him in a fierce hug. Annika disappeared into the troll again, Vashon behind her. His chest tightened. Already out of his sight. He'd known it would happen. He'd hoped it wouldn't happen so quickly.

Lucia stepped back, wiping her face. Beside her, Dooley was shaking his head.

"We were thinking that we'd lost you. A few of the aviators didn't make it to shore."

His gaze swept the gathered men. "Where is Goltzius?"

"His glider brought him in, then he got himself chewed up by dogs." Heavy concern lined the older man's face. "He saved that Lusitanian girl's nurse when they chased after her, then went down under a tangle of them. It took four of us to beat them off."

And Dooley's own hand was bandaged, David saw. "Was it bad?"

"He'll be all right, especially as Miss Neves hasn't left his side. I'll tell you, she's a formidable woman. Goltzius will heal or perish by her wrath." He looked up at the troll. "Where'd you get this?"

"We stole it from di Fiore's camp."

Neither Dooley nor Lucia appeared surprised when he said the name. Behind him, Vashon emerged from the troll. Annika came next, her mouth set, her eyes wide and shining. She looked to David.

"Some more has happened," Lucia said quietly. "Come on in where it's warm. We've got a decision to make."

The small house wasn't much warmer than outside, and David thought most of that heat was due to the number of people in it—aviators, and a few women and children who must have been local to Vik. He recognized the ship's senior staff from the wardroom. Elena caught Annika up in a tight embrace, laughing. Annika returned it, though she only smiled and her posture was stiff.

He was steered toward a wooden table in the hearth room. Annika sat across from him a moment later, with Vashon at the head, her uniform still pressed, her posture regal. Lucia took the chair beside him, and everyone who didn't sit crowded around.

It didn't take long for Annika to recount everything that had happened after the whale took *Phatéon*. When she was done, Dooley introduced the owner of the house—a thin Norwegian woman who appeared on the edge of exhaustion.

"They've been almost starved out here. No supply ships have reached them in four months—and most of the men in town are dead. The whale swallows up their boats when they take them out fishing." He looked to the pale woman again. "They've lost others, too. Her husband, then her son. He and five others struck out for Smoke Cove and Höfn, seeking help. That was a month ago. They've been getting by on rationed stores, but those are about to go dry."

And they'd go faster with an airship crew and passengers here. Vashon sat forward. "The coal is about to run out, too. So we put as many people as possible into each house—fewer houses to heat, fewer stoves to fire. And today, Vik received a visit from Lorenzo di Fiore."

Around noon, David wagered. He'd seen the airship returning to the rail camp. "Is he coming back with supplies?"

"No." Vashon's gaze held his. "Unless we give you up."

Annika drew a sharp breath. "Because we took the troll?"

"He mentioned nothing of that machine—and I don't think he knew who was in it. Di Fiore wants Kentewess alone," Vashon said, before looking to David again. "He said that you shouldn't have turned him down. He thought that Mr. Dooley lied to him when he said you were lost."

Jesus Christ. Stunned, David could only shake his head. He'd known di Fiore had been upset when he'd rejected the man's offer. But these were the demands of a madman.

Lucia took his hand. Her face was pale, her jaw set. Red stained Dooley's cheeks—still angered by di Fiore's visit, no doubt.

"If we produce you, we'll receive all of the cargo in *Phatéon*'s hold," Vashon said. "Di Fiore will keep the engine and the ship, but all of the food stores bound for Heimaey will be delivered here."

Before coming into the house, his aunt had said they had a decision to make. It was clear that *David* had a decision to make . . . but it wasn't one at all. Should he refuse and let everyone starve around him? That was no choice.

And di Fiore, that damned observationist, was probably only forcing the choice on them to see what they would do. To see what David would do. It shouldn't have been difficult to guess. Leaving with di Fiore would be a small sacrifice. The man didn't even ask for his life—just to work with his father. Of course David would accept. Only a monster needed to test it.

"He's returning tomorrow?"

"Yes."

David nodded. "I'll go."

A chorus of denials rose around him, the fiercest one from Annika. Her chair skidded back. Hands braced on the table, she leaned over and stared him down, her jaw set. "You *won't.*"

God, he loved her. "He doesn't plan to kill me."

"Not now, maybe."

"I won't watch you starve, Annika."

A dangerous glint lit her eyes. "There are a lot of dogs."

"It's true," Vashon said. Her voice rose as she spoke, clipped and furious. "And I'll be damned if I let him take my ship and hold my food hostage until I beg for mercy, then force me to trade over a passenger under my protection." On a deep breath, her tone evened out again. "At any rate, once we've eaten through those stores, what then? It will be easier to leave on foot in the spring, but there's still a risk. Di Fiore could have Smoke Cove in his pocket the moment he sees a threat."

Annika sank into her seat again. "What of Höfn?"

"And hope di Fiore hasn't bought that, too?" Vashon shook her head. "He has five hundred and fifty men in Iceland. Perhaps two hundred in Smoke Cove. You estimated fifty more at the camp. That is too many left unaccounted for. Maybe some are working on the drill that Fridasdottor mentioned to me, but perhaps more are in Höfn. He's locked up half this island; I have to assume that he's tried to take the other half, too."

Annika nodded, her eyes shadowed as she met David's gaze. Resolve set her expression. "My people can help."

Everyone looked to her. Heart pounding, David reached for her clenched fist. "Let me do this, Annika."

"No."

Vashon frowned. "Where are they?"

She evaded. "We have more trolls. More machines like the one outside."

The room had become deathly quiet. Without expression, Vashon studied Annika's face. David could all but see the captain thinking of witches and trolls, and reconciling those stories with the odd stoker who'd boarded her ship four years ago.

Finally, the captain nodded. "How long will it take?"

"Usually only three or four days, but I've never crossed during the winter. It might be slower, take twice as long. Add another day if I have to backtrack. After I've reached them, we'll need a few days to prepare, then the same amount of time coming back. At most three weeks, if I have trouble traveling over the highlands. If I'm gone more than a month . . . I'm not coming back."

"In a month, I'll be taking the few boats left and raiding that rail camp myself," Vashon said. "What will you need?"

"The coal bunker is almost full. We'll leave half here for heating—I know a few places to restock on the way. The surtur-brand doesn't run as hot, but it'll push her. There are a few pota-toes and pieces of bread left in our packs from *Phatéon*'s galley, enough to last those three or four days, so we won't have to take any from the stores." She met David's gaze again. "I need someone to help me see during the nights, so that I'm not bound by the short daylight hours."

"Also, so that he can't give himself up," Lucia said, her fingers tightening on his.

"Yes," Annika said. "And so di Fiore can't take him."

So it wasn't his decision, then. That was all right. David liked their choice better.

"All right," Vashon said, and her gaze found the first mate standing behind Lucia. "James, please help Fridasdottor secure everything that she needs. Quickly, now. Mr. Kentewess, I hate to push you out the door, but I expect di Fiore to return tomorrow, and we'll need to erase the tracks from the machine."

David stood. Just arrived, and quickly leaving again. "Of course."

He met Annika's eyes for a brief moment, then she was away with James, half of the aviators following her. Wearing an expres-sion of deep satisfaction, Dooley rose to his feet.

"And that'll do for me. I'll be looking forward to seeing di Fio-re's face when a few more of those machines walk through his camp."

David would look forward to it, too. He had to completely grasp that it would happen, first. He and Annika were traveling to Hannasvik.

Lucia touched his arm. "If you can spare a moment, David, Mr. Goltzius wants to have a word with you and Mr. Dooley together."

He'd spare it. A narrow wooden stair led to a small bedchamber. An oil lamp burned low, casting golden light across the bed. Goltzius lay with blankets tucked under his arms. Bandages swathed his neck and forearms, the back of his hands. Maria Madalena Neves sat on the high-backed chair beside him. Whatever care she'd been providing, it didn't appear to be the gentle sort. The look she gave Dooley could have cut through ice, and thinned to a razor when David followed him in.

"We won't tire him, senhorita," Dooley said. "Or upset him."

She exhaled sharply through her nose—exasperation, disdain, and a warning all in one breath. David was impressed. With a sweep of her skirts, she left. He glanced back at the Dutchman, who was laughing.

"I would tell you that she's not at all like that, but it's only half true. She is when we're not alone, but when we are, she's really quite something."

Remembering the softness he'd seen while she'd walked the deck with her nurse, David believed it. Maria Madalena might let her guard down for brief moments, or when she was with the man who'd rescued the woman she loved, but the rest of the time, David suspected that the haughtiness was as much a part of her as the gentleness was.

David nodded, looking Goltzius over again. Despite the bandages, the man looked well enough. No sickly color, no fever. "How are you, then?"

"Just torn up. Worse on the legs, but aside from the scars, I'm assured I'll walk easily enough again. Your aunt has taken fine care of me."

"And she's not the only one, I see."

"An unexpected reward for rushing headlong into danger without the sense to first grab a club." Goltzius's smile seemed flat now, his humor strained. "But I did not ask you up here to wag on about my heart. I must confess a deception to you both."

Dooley's bushy brows rose. "Oh?"

"Yes." He met David's gaze squarely. "I was sent here by my cousin to determine whether rebuilding Dutch settlements would be a viable effort. We knew that di Fiore was bringing Castilian laborers in, and we didn't want to lose the island through our inaction if it was worth having."

David exchanged a glance with Dooley, saw the same lack of surprise.

"We know," he said.

Goltzius blinked. "You know?"

With a laugh, Dooley claimed the chair beside the bed. "Kentewess and I have been out on expeditions too many times for such news to set us back on our heels now. There's never been any place we've ever been that didn't profit or benefit some Society patron. Sometimes, that purpose is well hidden, and we have to look sideways to see it. The moment you came on in place of our first botanist, though, we only had to look at you straight on."

"Ah, well." A flush rose over the young man's cheeks. He cleared his throat. "When we're in New Leiden again, I'll do what I can to see that the survey continues. I won't be able to return, however."

"Well, we'll still need a botanist, won't we?" Dooley frowned. "Is it the dogs? You'll heal up, get back on your feet. With our equipment, we'll be prepared for them."

"Not the dogs." Beneath the curling red mustache, his mouth firmed. "I have another interest now. I will soon be married."

There could be no question as to whom. Torn, David clenched his jaw. With Heimaey gone, Maria Madalena and her lover had almost no protection. A husband could provide it, and no one would think anything of her nurse accompanying her, remaining by her side.

But did Goltzius know? Even if her attitude changed with him, even if she showed affection, that couldn't be the love Goltzius hoped to have. Perhaps that would be enough for them both—and if Goltzius loved her, surely he wanted to protect her.

David didn't know what choice either one of them had.

"Senhorita Neves?" A troubled expression tightened Dooley's face. "You have spent a bit of time with her."

"Yes."

The older man made an obvious effort at humor. "And now you're in love? You and Kentewess both. They must have been serving quite the dish at the captain's table. Lucky for me, my heart's already taken, or I'd be weeping over Vashon."

Goltzius managed a smile, but it didn't last. "Yes, well. I believe it was something she ate after Heimaey. There was some talk about the women there, if you remember. We thought it best to put those notions to rest before she and her friend were hurt by them."

So he *did* know—and planned to sacrifice his own happiness to protect her. "You're a good man."

"No doubt of it," Dooley said.

"And she's a forceful woman." Goltzius laughed a bit. "This wasn't the adventure I expected, but I will see where it takes me."

Not far, if David didn't start off soon and bring help. With a warm wish for Goltzius's recovery, he took his leave, walking with Dooley out into the snow.

A frown had etched itself across the other man's forehead. "He's a stronger man than many," he said. "It would be easier to hurt her, I'd think. To force her into the role he wants her in."

Uncertain, David simply looked at him.

"What, you were thinking that I don't have eyes to see or ears to hear? My mother didn't push me out squalling yesterday."

"Or even the century before," David said dryly.

"That's a fact, and accounts for all the wisdom I've gained and you refuse to heed. So are you all right to go?"

Aviators surrounded the troll. None of them seemed to be carrying anything, so whatever supplies they were taking must have already been loaded.

"I think so."

The older man glanced up. "Not much snow to cover you."

"We'll have a good start tonight."

Knowing Annika, she'd go until she simply couldn't anymore. Then David would take care of her as best he could, wishing every second that he could do more.

"I'll also want to be hearing about these trolls when you return," Dooley said.

David couldn't do that, either. "Not from me."

"Fair enough. I'd rather hear it from the driver's mouth."

"If she wants to."

The other man nodded. "Then I'll see you when."

This time, they were better prepared to spend time inside a troll. A feather tick mattress was brought in, a pot for cooking, extra oil for the lamps. Many of it came from the houses of those already dead; it felt a bit like raiding, but Annika swallowed that guilt. There was nothing to be done for them now—she could only focus on helping those left.

Supplies stowed, she checked Austra Longears over again, tightening bolts and oiling joints—then covering some of her nakedness by tying a red ribbon in a bow beneath her nose. She said her goodbyes to Elena and Mary. Both looked at her differently now that they knew she'd come from a village full of witches and trolls; Elena's hug felt stiff. Annika didn't let herself dwell on that, either. If four years of friendship hadn't taught Elena the sort of woman that Annika truly was, then the rest hardly mattered.

But she had to laugh when, in the middle of her embrace, Mary said, "I *knew* you weren't from Norway."

The last bin of extra coal was scooped from the bunker and carried away. Mr. James came out of the hatch, his thin face red from the heat. Annika waited for a question she couldn't answer, and was surprised when he said, "I suppose you've seen that I don't always know what to say to you."

Well, she *could* answer that. "No."

Nodding, he took off his hat, awkwardly scratched his head. "You've always seemed to be somewhere else. Somewhere better, I thought, and I hated to intrude on that by asking about it, so I always said the first thing that came into my head instead of just saying what I was thinking. But this is easy to say, and I'm thinking it, too: Good luck to you."

Oh. That was truly wonderful of him. "Thank you."

She shook his hand, then straightened as Vashon approached. "Come with me inside, Fridasdottir."

Annika climbed through the hatch after the captain, saw the other woman's attention fall to the bedding on the floor. Her direct gaze rose to meet Annika's.

"Tell me truly, stoker: Is this arrangement acceptable to you? Mr. Kentewess seems to be a well-mannered young man, but the fact is, you are an unmarried woman and vulnerable."

What could David do to her that he couldn't do to a married woman? "He won't hurt me."

"But this will affect you in other ways."

Understanding finally dawned. "Pregnancy? I've never considered that a vulnerability—and it won't happen, at any rate, because I haven't taken his seed. I hope to, though. Some day."

"I was thinking of your reputation, not of babies," Vashon said dryly. "Though now I wonder if this would only solidify the reputation you've already gained."

For being improper? Annika knew it best not to smile, but could not stop the twitch of her lips. "I believe that my reputation is safe, Captain. I have never thought less of any woman who lies with a man."

"Yes, but it is not usually what we think of ourselves that makes our lives harder or easier; too often, it is what others think of you."

"I will take that risk."

"Godspeed to you, then." Vashon paused at the hatch, straightened again. "*Trolls*, Fridasdottor?"

Annika shrugged. "They're big and frightening. You have sentinels."

"So we do." Humor lifted the corners of her mouth. "I suddenly feel as if I might have been concerned for the wrong person. You will let Mr. Kentewess know that you hope to take his seed?"

"I won't do it while he's asleep, I assure you. He'll know."

"I suppose he will."

With a short laugh, Vashon dropped through the hatch. Annika started the engine, then glanced out. David was embracing his aunt, who was looking up at him with teary eyes and a determined set of her chin. Oh, Lucia. What must she be feeling now? After years aboard *Phatéon*, she'd been forced off twice: first into a town full of the dead, and now into a town full of people who might be, if they didn't soon receive food and help.

Whatever she was feeling, Lucia managed to step back, give him a pat on the chest as if to send him off. After a quick word to Dooley, he strode to the troll, holding Annika's gaze. She backed up as he came inside, closed the hatch.

He unbuckled his coat. "Are we ready, then?"

"I am." She watched him take in the changes she'd made, as his gaze lingered over the mattress. "You're not upset that we overruled you?"

"You had a better option. A real choice."

"Yes, but I'd have been angry anyway."

He grinned. "On principle?"

"Yes." She climbed into the seat, opened the eye louvers, and sighed at the sight of everyone gathered in the street—their expressions hopeful, worried. Some afraid. "I wanted more time with you. I didn't mean to get it this way."

"No. But I won't waste the opportunity," David said. He waited until she hauled the troll around before adding, "Go as far as you can. When you stop, I'll lick you."

Her feet almost missed the step. Heat flared through her belly, her heart speeding up. "Be careful," she warned. "With incentive like that, I might quit early."

"No, you won't."

"You know me that well?"

"Yes."

So he did. Too many people were depending on her to push as hard as she could. Rest would become a physical necessity at some point, and she could be with him then. But if she stopped early, the guilt wouldn't let her enjoy it.

She didn't think David would enjoy anything that came at the expense of their friends, either.

The troll ambled past the last farmhouse, started up into the hills. Pushing the stompers took more effort, but she wasn't yet out of breath. "Is it cruel to make you wait for me?"

If he ached even half as much, Annika thought she must be.

"In bed?"

"Yes."

"No. I would be cruel to pressure you before you're ready."

She *was* ready. And hoped for so much. But did she love? How could she know?

She knew this: "I want to scream from wanting you."

"God." Warm lips opened against the side of her neck. "I do, too. I would love to be inside you, tasting your mouth, listening to every moan."

"David—"

His teeth closed over her earlobe, a tiny erotic pinch. Goose-flesh erupted over her skin. Annika's hips rocked in the seat. She slowed the troll before she tipped it, her breath coming in desperate pants.

"I can't, David. I can't drive when you do that."

"Then I'll wait." His voice was husky, low, sending another delicious shiver through her. "I'll always wait, Annika. I'd rather take the time to learn what you like, what you don't—so that by the time you love me, *if* you come to love me, I can make certain it's good for you."

A little bite had pushed her near to climax. She didn't see how the rest wouldn't be good, too. "Do you truly think it might not be?"

"I don't know. You asked me about others once. I had to pay both of them. They didn't enjoy it, I didn't enjoy it . . . but each time was nothing like it has been with you." He was quiet for a long moment. "I wish that I'd waited to fall in love, too."

Her throat ached. "You can wait for it now."

She felt his laugh against her hair, the shake of his head. This time, the kiss he pressed to her neck wasn't openmouthed and hot, but soft and sweet.

"I'll just wait for you," he said.

It couldn't be long. But if she began to dream of loving him, they'd probably find themselves tumbling over a cliff. She pushed harder, concentrating on the ground ahead.

When they reached the river and turned north, David asked, "Are we heading in the same direction?"

"Yes." Though her lungs ached, her breath had evened out enough to speak. "That waterfall marks the route to the pass between the glaciers. We won't stop there tonight, though."

And it was slower going past the falls. The ground became rougher, a near-constant incline. Abrupt ridges threatened a wrong step, boulders lurked under the snow to trip and roll. Twice, she backtracked to find gentler slopes to climb.

Hours passed. The ground evened out when they reached the valley that served as the pass, but Annika couldn't go on any longer. She found a sheltered spot and sat the troll down. David pushed the engine to stop. Annika remembered his promise to lick her now, but lovemaking seemed to be the last thing on his mind.

It was the last on hers, too. While he opened the hatch, she picked up a spanner. None of the mangy curs had been in sight for the past hour or so, but she hoped the dogs didn't surprise her with an attack while her ass was bare. She hurried through the necessary, used snow melted against the troll's belly to wash. Covered again, she lingered for a few more seconds, looking up.

David joined her. Though the sky was clear, no lights danced across the heavens tonight. She studied the man beside her, instead—the strong line of his jaw, the slight bump in his throat that so many men seemed to have, and that became more apparent when they tilted their heads back. Was their throat more sensitive than a woman's? She would kiss him there, and find out . . . though not now. The top of her head only reached his chin; she'd have to leap up to put her mouth on that spot. He was so very tall. Never had she been more aware of the breadth of him, his height.

He glanced down at her, and she saw the change in him as his gaze slowly fell to her mouth. He hadn't been thinking of licking her when they'd stopped, but he was now.

"Do you want to go in?" His voice had deepened. Her belly suddenly seemed to hollow, then fill with heated anticipation.

"Yes."

Heart pounding, she climbed through the hatch. David followed, caught her against him, his hard chest against her back, his arm around her waist. With his long body pressing against hers, he slowly unbuckled her coat, unwrapped her scarf.

His lips found the side of her neck. "This has become my favorite spot while you drive."

Hers, too. With a soft moan, Annika's head fell back against his shoulder. David nipped at her exposed throat. Need rushed through her, sensitizing her skin, bringing every touch into sharp awareness. His strong body behind her, the rigid length against her back. His arm at her waist, and his other hand sliding up her side beneath her chemise.

His large palm cupped her breast, his thumb sweeping over the hardened peak. Her knees went weak, her nipples achingly tight. His mouth opened over the skin below her ear. Light suction joined the gentle tease of his fingers, a line of fire that raced from his mouth to her breast. How could he do this so easily? And yet she still wanted, needed, so much more.

Panting, Annika arched into his hand. "David—"

"I know. God, I need to taste you."

She tried to turn and find his mouth but he lifted her, instead—carrying her not to the mattress, but toward the troll's head.

"Tell me if you don't want this." His voice was rough as he set her feet onto the third ladder rung, halfway up to the driver's chamber. "I've thought of nothing else this entire way."

"Thought of what?"

"I watched you climb in earlier. You have the most incredible bottom."

He pressed gently against her back, as if urging her to bend over. *Oh.* Realization struck, followed a wicked stab of need. Suddenly trembling, she leaned forward, gripping the back of the driver's seat. Though she could only see the driver's chamber, Annika could too easily imagine the picture she made, bending over the top of the ladder, her backside at a height with his mouth. She wore trousers now, but soon she wouldn't. This might be improper even by Hannasvik's standards.

She didn't care. David's groan echoed through the hearth chamber, as if the sight of her tested his control. Strong hands smoothed down over her wool-covered bottom, his thumbs sliding closer together as they delved lightly into the crevice between her thighs. Annika shook, her fingers clamping on the seat.

He paused. "All right?"

"Yes."

So very much all right.

His left hand found the buckle at her waist. Breathless, Annika stared blindly into the forest of pistons and levers. She would never see them again without remembering the tug against her side when her trousers loosened. Without remembering his fingers hooking beneath wool and linen, the gentle rasp of steel and the graze of his nails against her skin as he slowly drew them down to her knees. Without remembering the warm air of the hearth chamber slipping over her bared cheeks, and his humid breath.

Firm lips pressed to the sensitive crease at the top of her thigh. Annika groaned and closed her eyes, waiting in a torment of anticipation and need.

His hands gripped her hips, adjusted her angle. His tongue swathed a sudden path up her inner thigh. Annika cried out, her body clenching, an unbearable ache filling her heated sex.

"God. And you're already so wet. You can't know how much that means to me."

He palmed the back of her trembling thighs, to hold her still or to support her, she didn't know. Kisses trailed up her inner thigh, ever closer to her center. Desperate whimpers rose unbidden from her throat, became a needy gasp when she felt the brush of his fingers over her clitoris.

"This is where I rubbed you."

"Yes." It was more moan than word.

"This is where to lick?"

Please. "Everywhere."

His mouth covered her. Annika cried out, her body stiffening, surprise pushing her onto her toes. He followed her up, his tongue rubbing, rubbing, until acute pleasure bordered on pain. She gripped the seat harder, fighting the need to writhe against his mouth, to push away. Then he released her, but that was a new torture, a slow lick up through her slick folds.

Rough palms smoothed over her bottom again, as if reassuringly, and she realized that her breaths were coming in keening sobs.

"Those sounds you make—God, Annika. That's exactly how I felt with your mouth on me. I want to do this to you forever. And so much more."

Inside her? Oh, but she wanted that, too. She'd always thought to wait for love, but this act had to be just as intimate—and she'd be devastated if he did this with someone else.

Was that love? Or just desperate need? Did she want him so badly because she was falling in love, or because she was already there?

Another lick chased that question from her mind. His hands caught her hips, held her still for his tongue, and for the longest time there was only that, only that, until he eased back, as if realizing that even though the sound of her moans bordered on agony each lick was the sweetest torment, and he meant to draw it out.

Then his mouth covered her again and she came in a rush, screaming and crying his name, the gentle suction against her clitoris the most painfully intense, incredible bliss. He held her upright when she drifted down from it, her body limp.

He carried her to the bed, laid her down. When she reached for his trouser buckles, he caught her hand.

"I want to give you the same pleasure, David."

He tucked her against his chest, her head pillowed on his arm. "You already did."

Perhaps it was for the best. A yawn overtook her, a heavy

lethargy. She turned her face into his neck, inhaled his smoky scent. So wonderful. "I want to do this every night."

A laugh rumbled from his chest. "I'd be glad to oblige."

She could so easily imagine being with him. No good came of such dreams—but for tonight, the rest of the world could go to hell.

The troll suddenly seemed to sway, then settled into a gentle rocking. Annika tensed. "Do you feel that?"

"Yes." He pulled out his watch—not just to note the time, she realized when he didn't immediately put it away. He was seeing how long the quake lasted. "How stable is the troll?"

"I've been through rougher earthquakes inside one. We've never tipped." And even if they did tip, it was better to be inside than to have the enormous machine fall on top of them while escaping.

After almost a full minute, the rocking ceased. David tucked away his watch, settled against her again.

"Do you have to write that in your journal?"

"I will after you've fallen asleep." He pressed a kiss into her hair. "You've a long way to drive tomorrow."

They were away long before dawn, roasted potatoes for breakfast leaving him pleasantly full, and Annika the best company that he could imagine. The sun rose midway through the morning into a brilliant sky, the reflection on the snow almost blinding. His smoked lens only helped a little; before long, his head ached from the brightness and constant squinting. Annika repeatedly wiped her eyes, lowering the louvers as far as she could without closing them. The head of the pass stretched before the troll, almost flat here but rising toward the rougher highlands. Chunks of ice and boulders dotted the ground. From the valley floor, the glaciers to the east and west appeared like mountains, the edges of the ice standing in jagged, black cliffs.

"I don't think I've yet seen a single tree," David said. Or any dogs today, either.

"There are some." Annika steadily stomped and pulled. "We'll see birch groves in the highlands—though not many."

"The sagas speak of forests."

"What sagas?"

"Older stories—from before the Horde. Some of the great families still have manuscripts in Norse." And he'd read copies of them while searching for his mother's people, hoping to find similarities. "Many of the stories are the same as those she told me, but there are differences."

"How so?"

"Brunhild's story, for one. How she took her revenge on Sigurd, though she died carrying it out."

"Yes. That's one of my favorites."

He grinned. Her favorite was incredibly bloodthirsty. "But that's not the end. There's another story with Brunhild in the Underworld, where she and Sigurd are lovers—and Brunhild claims that all of the pain and betrayal no longer mattered, that it was what she'd had to bear before they could be together."

"And Sigurd was some kind of *reward*? That's horrible," she said, and glanced back when he laughed. "Isn't it?"

"I believe it's supposed to be the happy ending she deserves."

"But he deceived her—and doesn't deserve her."

"Is deceit so unforgiveable?"

"That sort of deceit is. It is one thing to lie and deceive for good reason, but it is quite another to hurt someone with those lies and to expect no consequences." A frown had creased her brow when she looked back at him again. "He pretended to be someone else in bed. Imagine if Dooley came to my bed and said that he was you. Should I ever forgive him?"

David would kill him. "No."

"I agree. So I will pretend that I never heard such nonsense. Hanna's version is much better."

Hanna . . . and Hannasvik. "Your village is named after her? Is she the same Hanna from my mother's runes?"

"Yes. She was from a noble family in Norway, in fact." She rolled her shoulders, as if to loosen them. "And she married a relation of your friend Goltzius. Hanna's line is all blood, and you're directly descended. So I suppose you might be a prince of some sort."

David laughed, until he realized that she was serious. "Truly?"

"Oh, yes. Källa, too . . . Prince David."

He laughed again at the absurdity of it. "The royal line doesn't follow the women."

"Why is that? It's seems foolish. A baby could be any man's. You can only know for certain who the mother is."

"So they marry virgins—or hope that she is."

She was quiet for a long moment. "I suspect that explains quite a lot about the New World. Why do the women allow it?"

Allow it? David had never thought of it in such a way. Marriage had always been a matter of protecting a woman, loving her, carrying on the family name . . . because without that protection, without a man's name behind hers, a woman had very little. Even many of the female scientists he knew had to secure the approval of their husbands or fathers before pursuing their chosen field, and were sometimes forced to abandon that pursuit when other demands were made of them. There were exceptions, of course—there were always exceptions—but it was a sobering realization.

"They don't allow it," he said quietly. "They don't have the choice."

"Oh." Her chest rose on a soft, drooping sigh. "That's terribly sad. In Hannasvik, we always have choice. To go or to stay. To return or to continue on outside the village. The choice is never easy, but at least we have one."

"Is that why there are no men in Hannasvik? The women are afraid the choices will be taken away?"

"No. Men are thought well of, for the most part. That was just how it began—the will of the gods, or so Hanna said—and became set in stone."

"And no one has broken that rule?"

"Not in my lifetime. And if others have broken it—bringing their sons back, perhaps—I have never heard of it. But I imagine it must have happened at least a few times over the past century."

"What would they have done to her?"

"She would be exiled, most likely. But they would have helped her. There are always others who have left. They'd have made sure she found them, that she wouldn't be alone. They'd have done the same for Källa, but she left before they could."

Did Annika risk the same? "Yet you plan to take me there?"

"To Hannasvik? Oh, no. I know of a safe place a few hours away from the village. I'll leave you there." She paused, bit her lip. "I hope you know . . . it's not a lack of trust. I just won't break that rule when I have another choice. It wouldn't be fair to them to bring you in, unless everyone in the village agrees on it first."

"I know."

In truth, he was relieved. David didn't want to be the reason for her exile—not when it would hurt her. He was just afraid that if he let her out of his sight, he wouldn't see her again.

The quiet between them extended—comfortable, until he became aware of her sudden tension. The troll slowed.

"David." She opened the louvers wide. "Do you see that shadow?"

Slightly to the left—an oval with crisp edges. No cloud cast a shadow like that.

Dread weighed heavy in his chest. "An airship?"

And they hadn't heard the engines over their own.

"Yes." Her breath was coming fast. "Blast it all. There's nowhere to hide here."

"Stop, then, and let me out." Throat aching, he pressed a kiss to the back of her neck. "Di Fiore only wants me."

"I won't leave you."

"You have to—and bring back your army of trolls to rescue me."

A geyser of snow exploded directly ahead. White powder blasted through the louvers. Annika cried out, stopping the troll. Heart pounding, David hauled her out of the seat and into the hearth chamber.

He brushed the snow from her hair, her face. "Are you all right?"

"Yes." Her fingers gripped his shoulders tight. "That was his rail cannon."

God. "Can a troll take a hit from one?"

Her eyes squeezed shut. She shook her head.

"All right." Desperately, he kissed her forehead, her trembling lips. How could he protect her now? "Stay with me. He won't get a damned minute of my help if you're not safe. And we'll play along until we can escape. All right?"

Her mouth firming, she nodded. He helped her into her coat, opened the hatch. Taking her hand, they walked out from beneath the troll.

The ferry cruiser hovered overhead, chains rattling as the cargo lift descended. Di Fiore stood on the platform, backed by three men armed with rifles.

Di Fiore's mouth opened when he saw David. As if stunned and doubting his sight, he blinked quickly. An instant later, his lips pulled back into his fishhook grin.

"Mr. Kentewess!" Above his beard, his skin was red from the cold. "This is astonishing! *You* stole our walker? When my men found your pack in the lifeboat yesterday, we thought you'd been swept overboard. But you must have been on the airship when Jonah swallowed you?"

The *whale* was Jonah? Di Fiore must have heard a different version of that story than David had. "We were."

"How fortunate for both of us, then, as this gives me an opportunity to return your journal. It was fascinating reading, I must say."

David's jaw clenched. "Return *Phatéon*'s cargo to her captain, too."

"All right." He laughed at David's expression. "You thought I might object? I have no reason to. And you must be Annika Fridasdottir. I've read about you, too."

Oh, God. David knew exactly what he'd read—and no, di Fiore didn't need to hold the food hostage. The bastard had the means to make David do whatever he wanted right here.

Though her fingers tightened on his, Annika didn't respond. Di Fiore's gaze slid over her, assessing, lingering on their linked hands.

"And so which one of you drove the walker?" Though he asked, di Fiore must have already known. His focus remained on Annika, as if watching for her reaction. "Miss Fridasdottir, I think. That's so very interesting—and useful to me."

That was enough. "You'll leave her alone. I'll come with you."

"Of course you will." Di Fiore's gaze met his again. "But you don't have to worry that I'll threaten her. Now, another man might do so—but there's no surprise in that scenario. You will be heroic, make any sacrifice to save her. I know this. So threatening her is of no interest to me."

"Then what is?" David preferred not to be surprised.

"You have friends in Vik. I've already promised to return the cargo—and I will. You will come with me for that. But what will make you stay?" His expression cooled. "I think that this will do it: If you or Miss Fridasdottir try to escape, then the town of Vik will have the same fate as Heimaey. I won't hesitate, of course. The results of any test are never certain until they've been repeated."

He'd created the disaster at Heimaey? David stared at the man, staggered. Good God. Perhaps di Fiore was lying . . . but they wouldn't be able to take the risk of finding out.

"Come along. They're expecting me at the glacier camp, and

following your tracks has already caused enough of a delay." Di Fiore stepped aboard the lift platform. "Leave the walker. My men will gather your things from inside and drive it back to the rail camp—where it is sorely needed to clean up the destruction you wrought."

David glanced down at Annika. Her gaze had narrowed on di Fiore's back. David squeezed her hand, and she looked up.

"All right?" he asked softly.

She nodded—not trembling now, but her face set and a blood-thirsty glint in her eyes. David thought that his expression probably appeared the same.

"We'll wait until the right time."

Her fingers tightened on his in response. Together, they boarded the lift.

Di Fiore smiled. "I told you this was destiny, Mr. Kentewess. You can't fight it."

Not at this moment, perhaps. Di Fiore had landed a heavy blow—but David would be damned before he stayed down. He'd wait for his opportunity, the right moment to strike back.

And he wouldn't hesitate to use a steel fist.

Chapter Ten

Annika stood silently with David, clinging to his hand and looking over the side of the ferry cruiser to the glacier below. She could feel the anger boiling off him, but he didn't express it, didn't show it. Annika doubted that she was as successful hiding her feelings. She didn't speak of them, though. She didn't want to give di Fiore the satisfaction of knowing how angry she was . . . and how helpless she felt.

She glanced back at the quarterdeck, where di Fiore chatted with the pilot. He looked no different than any other man aboard. A dark beard covered pleasant features, his expression mild and open.

The face of a monster.

He'd been responsible for that cold, calculated death on Heimaey. She couldn't imagine how it had been done—or why. Some experiment or project. Annika wasn't certain that she wanted to understand. She only knew that they had to get away.

There was no place to hide on the glacier. Unlike the pass, it wasn't flat—the surface of the ice buckled, creating peaks and valleys; crevasses yawned open, a sheer drop into darkness. But all of it was barren, white. If they escaped from a camp, di Fiore would only have to look through a spyglass from the deck of the ferry cruiser to see them in the distance. The glacier wasn't large, though. From the center, a half-day's hike east or west would take them to the edge. So their best hope of escape would be to leave at night, to get off the glacier as quickly as possible, and return to Vik before di Fiore managed to find them. Once there, she and David could warn the town.

It would be dangerous, terribly dangerous, especially if they were hurrying. A tumble into a crevasse would be deadly, whether they were in a troll or not.

But they *had* to escape. They had to hide. Annika didn't believe for one moment that di Fiore would let them go when David finished the project his father was working on.

She angled her head closer to David's. "I thought he wanted you on the peninsula south of Smoke Cove."

"That's what he said. Perhaps that was the lure."

"What could he want on a glacier?"

"A glacier with a volcano beneath." His gaze narrowed—looking at something she couldn't yet see. "I read about it during my preliminary research on the island. They called the volcano Katla, the witch."

A witch? "That's not one of our stories."

"No. This was from before the fissure eruptions. Legend is that someone stole the trousers that let Katla run endlessly without tiring, and she killed the thief. But the thief's ghost returned for her. So she ran from him and threw herself into the volcano. The eruption created a flood that destroyed the nearby villages."

Annika frowned. "But the volcano is covered by ice. How could she throw herself in?"

He grinned, shook his head. "I don't think you're supposed to interpret the story so literally. But looking at it now, I *do* think there's some truth to it." His humor faded. "Look at the surface, how often the ice has broken apart and shifted. Those depressions, as if the rocks beneath are sinking. There's likely water trapped beneath, melted but unable to escape until the ice breaks and shifts again. And if there's an eruption, the lava melts the ice from above or below and floods the surrounding land."

"Oh." She could have told him that. "Quite often, in fact. We rarely come this way, particularly across the plains to the south. The floods are unpredictable."

"And we should have hired the women of Hannasvik as guides."

She might have enjoyed that. "You meant to come up here for your survey."

"Yes. And it would have been more difficult than we realized. The terrain is rougher. We would have had to hire a balloon or an airship."

She couldn't mistake the irony in his tone. Here they were, on an airship—and he had his journal again. Di Fiore had carried it up from his cabin shortly after they'd started out, and gave it over to David with a smile for him and a wink for her.

Though David hadn't said a word, Annika had been surprised that he hadn't strangled the man there and then.

"This doesn't have to be a lost opportunity," she said. "Perhaps you can conduct part of your survey while you're here."

"No. The only thing I care about is getting you away from here." He met her eyes again, his expression focused, intense. "I will do anything to keep you safe. *Anything*. For now, he wants me to help his father, and he was smart enough not to threaten you. But if you feel threatened for even a second, it's over. I'll rip his head off, and face whatever comes next."

Which would probably be di Fiore's guards. Annika glanced back, saw his cold, assessing gaze fixed on them. A shiver raced over her skin. She quickly looked ahead again.

The airship gained altitude, giving her a better view of the glacier ahead. Beyond the next rise, an enormous balloon sat on the glacier, as if a giant's airship had been trapped beneath the ice. Annika stared at the long envelope, mouth open. The balloon couldn't be as large as it appeared . . . but the whale shouldn't have been, either.

It was oddly shaped, flatter toward the bottom. The gas inside the metal fabric must have been cold, but the shape of the balloon appeared heavier than it should have if filled with hydrogen—or even with natural air. Pipes led to the bottom of the balloon.

David pushed his scarf down, inhaled. "Do you smell that?"

A familiar pungent odor. "Like the mudpots, or the hot springs."

"Sulphur."

On *Phatéon*, Komlan had said that di Fiore's men were mining for that mineral. "Are they drilling through the ice, then?"

They were obviously doing something. Annika's gaze followed the pipes south, where a tall structure rose. The steel framework resembled a tower of scaffolding. The tower supported a large steel capsule, long and smooth, rounded on each end.

Annika squinted across the distance, but couldn't make sense of the object at the top. "Is that a submersible?"

The capsule resembled one, though it stood vertically rather than lengthwise. Annika couldn't imagine why they'd need a submersible on the ice . . . though David had said that water was trapped below.

He shook his head. "I don't see any propellers—but there's a borehole in the ice beneath the tower."

So they *had* drilled through the ice. Steam drifted around the base of the tower, rising from the hole. "How deep does it go?"

"God knows. Look there, Annika."

To the north. A troll was crossing the ice—not Austra Longears, but an identical machine. "Where is it going?"

"There." David pointed directly ahead. "A camp."

Annika could see men moving about and another troll, but expecting buildings similar to the rail camp's, she didn't immediately spot them—only mounds of snow that formed long, regular shapes, but weren't tall enough for bunkhouses. Yet they were, she realized. Instead of building on top of the ice, they'd cut down into it. She was looking at peaked roofs with eaves almost flush with the ground.

Though the three-sided layout was similar to the rail camp's, now she saw that it was much more extensive. Smaller buildings with roofs that were hardly more than a bump sat behind longer ones. Steam rose from one small building, and the snow over its roof appeared thinner, the surface icier. A furnace chamber, perhaps, that heated the other buildings. Good. If she ever needed a distraction, a furnace could usually provide a deadly one.

And even better, in the clearing sat a means of escape—several means, in fact, in the form of two-seater balloons. Several of them possessed engines. Those would be too loud, and they would take too long to rise into the air. But at least one was pedal-powered— that would be quiet. She and David could climb into the seats and be on their way within seconds. Flying, they could hurry to Vik without worrying about crevasses and dogs. With a few hours' head start, a two-seater could reach the town before the airship.

She quickly forced her gaze away from it. No need to alert di Fiore to her interest in the machine. She and David would need to figure out a way past the guards, first.

Di Fiore must already expect that *someone* might want to escape. Four guards stood at the corners of the snowy clearing. Dogs wouldn't attack them here, and no one could approach the camp without being noticed, so those guards must have been appointed to protect di Fiore and the equipment from people who were working here.

David must have been thinking the same. "The guards," he said quietly, and she nodded.

"We'll have to wait." But at least there was hope.

The ferry cruiser's engine quieted. Momentum carried them over the camp, where the guards below secured the tether line.

Di Fiore met them at the cargo lift. "Mr. Kentewess, I know that I have acted in a high-handed manner. Please understand, this is for my father. What the world took away from a brilliant man, I will give back. My father spent years in that insanitarium, with his hands restrained—but his mind wasn't. His dreams were the only freedom he had. Now I will be his hands, and I will fulfill those dreams at any cost. Do you understand?"

"We understand. We've already seen the cost that people pay for it," David said.

Di Fiore nodded, and continued on as if David's only response had been agreement. "My father has suffered from doubt. You *will not* doubt him, no matter how outlandish you believe his ideas might be. I will not see him hurt in any way. You will never say a word of your injuries, or the loss of your mother, except in how you are grateful for what happened to her, and how the pain you suffered after her death made you a better man."

David's jaw turned to stone, the edges of his lips white. She'd never seen him truly angry before. He was now. Her hand tightened on his. Annika couldn't hold him back, but she could remind him that he wasn't alone in this.

"Then I'll say nothing at all." It emerged through gritted teeth.

"That is acceptable, too. He can see for himself that you're healthy, strong. The scars can't be helped, but you have a woman with you, so not everyone is repulsed by them. He'll believe that you live a full life."

Annika would kill him herself. This time, David's hand tightened on hers. The cargo lift jolted into motion.

His voice rising over the clattering chains, Di Fiore continued, "And if any of those topics arise, whether you've said anything or not, the primary message will be: You've forgiven him. In that, I will tolerate no deviation."

"I can forgive Inoka Mountain," David said. "That was an accident. But I can't forgive Heimaey or the whale. Those women and sailors were deliberately murdered."

The other man nodded. "And my father isn't responsible. As I said, I am his hands—and he doesn't have to know how I've procured everything he needs. Nor will you tell him. Such knowledge would place a great burden on him, and he already carries enough."

But di Fiore obviously bore them well. He spoke of murder as if discussing the weather, with barely a change in his mild expressions. No doubt he would kill them as easily if they upset his father.

The platform reached the clearing. They stepped off onto well-packed snow. A small dark-haired boy raced away from one of the houses, laughing and with his arms extended. Di Fiore's face changed, lit by sudden delight and a warm smile. He swept the boy up, swung him in a quick circle. Wild giggles followed.

Di Fiore set the boy on his feet again, crouched. "Well, now. Did you miss me? I see that you've escaped without your coat again."

He tugged on the hem of the boy's small wool pullover. Annika narrowed her eyes, looked closer. His blue pullover had been woven in a familiar pattern, much like the ganseys that the women in Hannasvik wore on their fishing boats. The pullovers were common among fishermen, but she wouldn't expect to see one here—and every pattern was distinctive. Perhaps this one had been made by someone who hailed from the same location as one of the original Englishwomen.

Perhaps. But she doubted it.

Dread filled her again. She'd managed to convince herself that di Fiore hadn't found her people, but obviously someone in his camp had stumbled across more than trolls.

Di Fiore pushed the hair from the boy's flushed face. "Now, Olaf, come and meet the man who is going to help your father."

Olaf looked over at David. His dark eyes widened and he cringed back, hiding his round face against di Fiore's chest.

Di Fiore firmly turned the boy around. "No, Olaf. Those are only scars, and you mustn't be frightened of them. Say, 'I am very pleased to meet you, Mr. Kentewess.'"

The boy obediently mumbled the words, his gaze fixed on his boots. Oh, but it was excruciating, standing through this. Beside her, David wore his weary smile. A flush darkened his jaw. He let go of her hand.

Annika didn't know whether to take it again, or whether to let him be. But she'd rather be wrong than make him suffer through this exercise alone. She threaded her fingers through his.

He glanced down at her, and his smile changed, warmed.

"And now say, 'I am pleased to meet you, Miss Fridas—'"

"Annika!"

The shout came from across the clearing. Heart pounding, Annika looked up. Källa stood in front of a snow-covered roof, staring at her, holding a boy's coat, her sword strapped across her back. Disbelief had widened her dark eyes. Her mouth hung open, but now it widened into a smile, then a whoop of laughter.

"Do you see?" di Fiore said. "That *is* interesting."

On long legs, Källa crossed the snow at a run and engulfed Annika in a hug, lifting her off the ground, then swinging her around as di Fiore had done with the boy. She threw her head back as she laughed, her long braid winding into the basket of her fur-lined hood.

"Oh, Annika." Källa finally set her down, nearly squeezed the guts from her with another hug. "What are you doing here?"

Uncertain how to answer that in front of di Fiore, she shook her head. "I would ask the same of you."

"For the same reason, I imagine. Paolo's work is so amazing, isn't it?"

"Yes. Though I'm not sure what it is yet. I've only seen a giant whale."

"A whale?" Källa shook her head, laughing. "You have not changed a bit. Though I—" She broke off suddenly, turned and scooped up the boy. She faced Annika again, spoke formally in Norse. "My son, Olaf. Olaf, this is your aunt, Annika."

Some part of her had already put those pieces together—but Annika hadn't wanted to, knowing who the father must be. But she forced that away. "We are well met, Olaf Källasdottor."

"Källasson," her sister corrected with a grin. Her eyes narrowed slightly when Lorenzo said softly behind her, "Di Fiore."

Olaf hid his face in Källa's neck. His mother's smile returned. "He's very shy. He's much like you in many ways, Annika."

"How old is he?"

"Two years."

And Lorenzo di Fiore was the father. This time, she couldn't push that realization away. Annika stepped back, found David's hand again, welcomed the warm support. She'd never felt so off-kilter. Källa looked to David, then to Annika's face again.

Källa's feet shifted—preparing to attack, to defend. Her voice remained pleasant. "Are you with this man?"

"Yes."

Di Fiore came to Källa's side. "Mr. Kentewess is a vulcanologist with the Scientific Society of New Leiden. He'll be assisting my father."

"Mr. Kentewess." Källa nodded a greeting to him, then met Annika's gaze again with a question in her eyes. "I can't believe you stepped a foot away from home."

That was not what she meant. Källa knew that Annika had traveled all over Iceland in her troll. Her sister wondered how she'd come to be with David.

"I left home, searching for you."

"What for?" Puzzlement creased her brow, then she looked up as the cargo lift rattled, began to rise. "You are not waiting for your things? Well, let us go inside, then. You can tell me there."

She started back across the clearing. Annika followed, holding David's hand. His fingers tightened on hers. She glanced up, saw his concerned gaze on her.

"All right?" he whispered.

Annika lifted her shoulders. What should she feel? Happy that she'd found her sister, yes. But to find her here with Lorenzo? Everything was turned about. Did he keep Källa here under some threat? Annika hadn't missed the wariness in her posture, the hint of temper when Lorenzo had given Olaf his name. But that was Källa the Shieldmaiden, always watchful, possessive—and easy to anger.

Annika didn't know what to tell him—and then she lost the opportunity. Her mouth closed as di Fiore fell into step beside David.

"Where is my father, Källa?"

"In his laboratory." She glanced over her shoulder. "He has been testing the suit since last night. I finally got him to sleep a few hours this morning."

She led them down steps made from steel grating, much like the stairs in the whale's hold. They entered a tunnel made from snow bricks that arched over their heads in a smooth curve. The passageway opened into a hearth chamber with a wooden floor, and walls made from blocks of blue glacial ice. Steel struts supported a peaked tin ceiling that must have been strong enough to bear the weight of the snow Annika had seen from above. Despite being surrounded by ice and snow, the chamber was cool, not cold. A pullover like the boy's would keep anyone inside warm and comfortable.

A wooden table claimed the center of the chamber. A cast-iron stove stood away from the ice walls, a ventilation pipe rising through the ceiling. The opposite end of the chamber opened to another snow tunnel.

Di Fiore started toward it. "I'll take Kentewess to meet my father while you and your sister reacquaint yourselves."

Annika glanced up at David. With a gentle squeeze of his fingers, he let her go and followed di Fiore. Heart thumping, feeling suddenly overwhelmed by the sense that this must all be a terrible dream, Annika watched him disappear into the tunnel.

"All of these living quarters are linked—and there's another system of living chambers and tunnels for the laborers." Källa sat Olaf on the table and took the chair in front of him, rubbing her face into his belly before starting a game of clapping his hands. She spoke over his giggles. "Why are you here, Annika?"

"Lorenzo forced David to come. I was with him, so I came, too."

"And why are you with him? Has something happened at home?" Worry tightened her face. "Are our mothers all right? And by Brunhild's bloody hands, Annika, *sit*. You look ready to bolt. But you must know I would never let anything hurt you here."

Annika knew that Källa would try to protect her; she just didn't know if Källa *could*. Still, she took the chair beside her. "Our mothers are fine. They've made up."

Källa paused in the middle of a clap, glanced over. "No."

"Yes. They share the same home now."

Joy suffused her expression. With a laugh, she kissed her son. "Oh, that is very good news. And Lisbet?"

"She's fine. She misses you."

"I miss her." With a wistful sigh, she skimmed her forefinger down Olaf's nose. "Is that man yours? You held his hand."

Hers. "Yes. And he is also Inga's son."

"Inga? My mother's Inga?"

"Yes. He came to bury her beads."

Worry creased her brow again. "He found Hannasvik?"

"No. I met him on an airship."

"And *why* were you on an airship?" Humor and frustration laced her voice now.

"Looking for you. When I found out you took the blame for my fire, I told the elders. They revoked your exile."

Källa closed her eyes. "Annika, I did that for you."

She already knew that. "But I didn't ask you to sacrifice yourself for me."

"So I should let my sister be punished for a silly mistake? Annika the Rabbit, who hides the moment trouble comes?"

That stung. "I only hide to protect everyone. I've *never* run from my responsibilities."

"Not with your legs, Rabbit. Here." She pointed to her head. "Always running off to somewhere safe. You're only brave when you're inside a troll, Annika. If you'd been sent out of Hannasvik and into the New World, you'd have found the nearest hole and never climbed out."

But Annika wouldn't have been exiled as she had been—only after Källa's temper had erupted had she been sent away. That didn't matter now. Obviously, Källa thought that she'd saved Annika from exile.

And even if that were true, Annika wouldn't have found the nearest hole. *Phatéon* had been a safe haven of sorts, yes—but she'd left it often to visit the port cities. She'd been planning to leave the airship permanently for a more dangerous route.

A route that Källa wouldn't have been anywhere near. Annika had never expected to find her here in Iceland. Four years of searching, and she'd been a few days' journey from home. Annika didn't know whether to laugh or cry.

Cry, most likely. Had her sister truly believed that she wouldn't survive outside of Hannasvik?

"Källa." It was a struggle to keep the hurt out of her voice. "I have been in the New World for *four years*."

"Well, now you can run back home, and I will continue protecting you all."

"Protecting us?" Annika shook her head in disbelief. The resentment in Källa's voice didn't surprise her. She'd been tossed out of Hannasvik, after all. She'd made a sacrifice that Annika had thrown back at her. But she was also with the man who posed the most danger to everyone in Iceland. "Do you know what Lorenzo di Fiore has done?"

"Yes. Perhaps not all of it, but enough." Her eyes hardened. "Who do you think that I'm protecting you all from?"

Annika didn't know. She didn't understand any of this. "How is being here protecting Hannasvik?"

"I met Paolo only a day after I left, Annika. He and Lorenzo were on the peninsula—he needed a volcano, and he'd chosen ours. So I convinced him to go south, away from Hannasvik, where the volcanoes are more active."

"And then you stayed with him?"

"Lorenzo is ready to take all of Iceland over to help his father. I had to make certain that Lorenzo never looked in that direction."

Stunned, Annika stared at her. "You knew all of this about him and still had a son with him? You lay with him?"

"With Lorenzo?" Disgust curled Källa's mouth. "I lay with Paolo. I would as soon bed an orca as I would his son. There's something wrong in him, Annika."

It wasn't Lorenzo? Relief swept through her, lightening some of the weight around her heart. "Is he forcing you to stay here?"

"No. I'm protecting you all, as I said. And Paolo, too. As I understand it, there are many men in the New World who would be glad to hurt him. Lorenzo worries that one of them might come for Paolo, if they knew he was here."

Because of the disaster that had killed Inga. "Why not kill Lorenzo?"

"I promised that I wouldn't until his father passed on." Källa held her gaze. "I don't want to see Paolo hurt, either."

And if she'd bedded him, she must believe that Paolo was a good man. "But Lorenzo knows you will kill him?"

"Yes."

"Then why keep you on?"

"I make Paolo happy. And because I know the island, and told him how to build the trolls. I was hoping to hurry all of this up. Until it is over, I'll protect Paolo, watch over him."

"Why?"

"Because Paolo is not always here to look after himself." With a soft smile, she glanced down at her son. "Paolo is much like you, too, Annika—a dreamer. But his dreams are much bigger."

Though he and Lorenzo walked alone through the tunnels, David chose not to beat the man bloody, drag him up to the airship, and demand they return to Vik. David might have risked the guards. He wouldn't risk Annika.

In relation to the rest of the camp, these living quarters made up the southern leg of the three-sided layout. The snow tunnels led through several ice-walled chambers of the same size as the hearth chamber, with more tunnels leading offside to smaller, individual chambers. The sides of each chamber were only waist high but with the peaked center of the ceiling rising to a comfortable height. Most were empty, and though David didn't remark on it, Lorenzo offered that he preferred not to be disturbed while sleeping—and which David took to mean that he didn't trust anyone to be near him during that time.

Paolo's laboratory formed the corner between the southern and eastern sides of the camp, where the laborers and guards resided. The laboratory could have fit two of the hearth chambers inside, and another stacked on top. They'd dug deeper into the ice before laying the floor, and the blue ice walls rose twice as high. The effect was strangely beautiful—though the laboratory itself could have come directly from the New World. Slate boards had been nailed into the ice walls, with diagrams and calculations scrawled in chalk. Long tables held an array of equipment and glass tubing. Machine parts lay scattered beneath a drafting desk. Chickens clucked in a wire pen.

A tray of half-eaten food teetered on the corner of one table, as if abruptly forgotten. Deeper into the laboratory, a man sat on the wooden floor, bent over the domed helmet in his lap. No shirt covered his upper body, revealing age-softened muscles. He wore no proper trousers, only a pair of woven short pants and boots.

In the twenty years since David had last seen him, Paolo di Fiore had lost most of his dark hair. A faint brown tattoo wound from the top of his head to the nape of his neck, resembling the twisting figure of a branching tree.

"Father!"

Though he frowned, Paolo didn't look up. He lifted the helmet to look inside the steel dome. Much like a diving helmet, David thought, except that it wasn't brass. Lorenzo had mentioned a suit, too. David glanced up, saw it hanging on a metal frame that stood beside a glass chamber in the corner. Unlike a canvas diving suit, it appeared to be made from the same metal fabric used to make airtight envelopes for balloons and airships.

He glanced back at Paolo as the man set the helmet into his lap again. Oh, good God. Pity roiled heavy and sick in his gut. Two short metal posts protruded from the top of his skull. At first glance, David had thought the posts belonged to something behind the man, but when Paolo had moved, he saw that they had been attached to his head. Screwed into the bone.

Jesus. And so that wasn't a tattoo, either, but a scar. He'd heard of such things—the electric shocks applied to the residents of insanitariums. But they'd always seemed too cruel to believe, more like the fear-driven rumors that often spread about the Horde.

Lorenzo placed a coat over his father's shoulders. Paolo gave an irritated shrug, looked up. "Eh? What is it?"

"Your clothes, Father."

Paolo glanced down. His irritation smoothed into a laugh. "Ah, yes. I put on the æther suit, but I was so eager to make the adjustments, I forgot to dress again. Thank you, son."

Concern creased Lorenzo's brow. "Where did you wear the suit?"

Paolo pointed to the corner of the laboratory. The glass chamber, David realized. Sealed at the edges and taller than a man, it possessed a single small door. A pipe led into the back wall, originating from somewhere outside the laboratory. Dead mice lay on the floor.

"I already tested the suit, Father."

"Yes, but until there is something else in that chamber to prove that the gas is inside, we can't be certain it works. We can't smell the gas. We can't see it. We can't know if it's there unless something else perishes. It will be the same when the gas is æther, instead. And that is why I went in."

Lorenzo shook his head. "I made certain, Father. With better examples than mice."

Heimaey, David realized. He'd tested the suit on Heimaey.

Hot rage pushed through his chest. Lorenzo met David's gaze, a cold warning. David clenched his jaw.

"Dogs are not better than mice," Paolo muttered, buckling his coat.

"They're larger and they were out in the open, just as you will be. I wouldn't risk your life, Father, by only testing on mice in that chamber. The gas is cold when it comes in from the balloon outside; it's heavier. You could be breathing good air up top while the mice die below."

"That is why I lay on the floor while I was inside." The older man stood, spotted David. His body stilled like a startled deer's. He offered a faint, hesitant smile, then an uncertain glance at his son.

"This is David Kentewess. Stone Kentewess's son."

"Oh." Friendly curiosity suffused his expression, but he walked almost sideways as he approached, as if keeping open the option to race the other way. "I see the scars. But Kentewess's boy wouldn't walk again."

"Show him your hand, Kentewess."

Pity competed with anger—but David had no interest in hurting this man. He held up his hand, spreading his fingers. "My legs, too."

But he'd be damned before putting the rest of himself on display.

Paolo's mouth opened on an O of wonder. "How marvelous it is," he breathed softly. His gaze rose to David's again. Deep lines settled in his face. "But I'm so very sorry for it."

"He has no hard feelings, Father."

"It's true," David confirmed. He felt them for the son instead. "We are well met."

"And he's a vulcanologist. He has come to help."

Paolo's eyes rounded, delight pushing his face into a smile. He suddenly started toward the drafting table, gesturing for him to follow. "Oh, come then! Has Lorenzo told you? I've calculated the amount of ice necessary to propel the capsule, the rate of melting and conversion to steam after it reaches the magma. But how do I trigger the eruption? I've thought to collapse the magma chamber"—he slapped his hands together with a loud *crack!*—"and those explosive charges are being laid in the ice tunnels. But what am I not accounting for?"

David tried to catch up. "You want to *cause* an eruption?"

"Yes! The pressure required, the amount of ice, it's all calculated. We just need to make certain it will blow at the right time. If it goes without me in the capsule, it's all for nothing."

"The capsule on the tower?" Resembling a vertical submersible, David recalled. A borehole had been drilled beneath it.

"Yes, yes. It will drop in!"

With Paolo inside the capsule. Inside a suit. David shook his head. Did the man intend to pilot the capsule through molten rock, propelled along by steam? Even surrounded by steel, he'd be dead within moments. Or did he believe the quacker scientists who claimed that a magical Underworld lay below the earth's crust? Or even more absurd—that a primeval world existed at the center of Earth?

He looked to Lorenzo, who was staring at him with bullet-hard eyes. *Don't express any doubt*, he remembered.

David couldn't doubt anything yet. First he had to understand what Paolo wanted to do. "For what purpose do you intend to use the capsule?"

Paolo's brows lowered. He frowned at his son. "Did you not tell him?"

"I haven't had the opportunity," Lorenzo said mildly.

"We will take that opportunity now. Where's my coat?" With his hands in his pockets, he looked around for it. "We'll go out and show him."

"Show me?"

"The tower, the capsule. Look." Paolo waved to the slate board, then turned to Lorenzo, who held out a pair of trousers.

Crossing to the wall, David studied the chalk drawing. Two circles each took up one half of the board, one smaller than the other. On the larger circle, a small tower had been drawn on the upper arc. A line spiraled outward from the tower and around the larger circle, until the spiral reached a distance halfway across the board. The trajectory changed, and the spiral continued inward around the smaller circle, drawing closer with each revolution until it finally met the circle's edge. With disbelief, David read the labels beneath the two circles:

EARTH. MOON.

"I'll ride in the capsule across the æther, and build a new home on the lunar surface." Beside him, Paolo was looking up at the board with a brilliant smile. "Isn't it marvelous?"

Chapter Eleven

Annika spent most of the afternoon wandering through the chambers and tunnels. Källa had informed her that she could move through the camp as she liked, and Annika took full advantage of it. Still, she found little in the way of weapons or to use as a means of escape. The furnace could create a possible distraction, as could piercing the pipes that carried heated water through the chambers, warming the air—a safer method of heating in the enclosed spaces than multiple stoves would be, unless the water flooded everything.

She paused once, frozen as a small tremor shook the ground. A muffled cracking sounded from deep below. Annika was accustomed to quakes, but not while walking through tunnels of snow. She hurried outside.

In the clearing, she was relieved to see that none of the tunnels had collapsed. The sky was clear overhead; the airship had already gone. She hoped that Lorenzo kept his promise and sent *Phatéon*'s cargo to Vik, but didn't trust that he would. Why give them food then threaten to kill them all? He could just as easily lie, say the cargo had been delivered, and she and David would have no way to know.

Escape was still their best option. Of course, now she had to wonder whether Källa would go, too. Annika couldn't imagine leaving her. But if her sister was determined to stay, she might have to.

She circled the clearing, aware of the watchful eyes of the guards. The balloons were tethered, she saw, but not locked. Good. She paused at the entrance to the laborer's quarters, then moved on when a guard approached her, frowning.

Källa soon joined her with a fussy Olaf in tow, tugging at her hand and trying to get away. She let the boy go and they watched him run for the nearest mound of snow. Within seconds, his coat was on the ground.

Her sister sighed. "I don't know how he opens the buckles so quickly."

Especially while wearing mittens. Annika could only shake her head. Of all the roles she'd imagined Källa in when she'd found her—adventurer, shieldmaiden, perhaps even a mercenary or pirate—Annika had never imagined that her sister might also be a mother.

And she was still a shieldmaiden. Annika glanced to one of the guards standing at the edge of the clearing. "Why do you protect Paolo when Lorenzo has all of these men to do it?"

"Because he doesn't trust them to do it properly." A wry smile twisted her sister's lips. "He doesn't trust me, either. But at least he knows I will protect Paolo and wait to kill him."

"Then who are the guards for?"

"The workers." They both paused as Olaf tumbled down the snow mound. Laughing, Källa called encouragement to him. When the boy regained his feet, she continued, "Lorenzo pushes the laborers as far as he can. He hires the guards to have protection near in the event he pushes them too far."

Annika hadn't seen any of the laborers since she'd come back out to the clearing. Why weren't they outside? Surely they didn't like to be cooped inside throughout the day. "Are they not allowed to come out?"

"They are." Källa gave her a sideways glance. "But they are like boilerworms."

The giant mechanical worms that bored their way beneath the Australian deserts. Valdís had brought back tales of the dangerous creatures, and the hunters who'd died trying to capture the worms as trophies.

The laborers were like *those*? "How so?"

"They lie in wait. They play dead. Lorenzo thinks that the men are beaten, their spirits broken, but . . ." She trailed off, shaking her head. "I don't believe the same. I think they merely bide their time."

"Until what?"

"Until they are done waiting." Källa met her eyes, suddenly serious. "If that happens, Annika, do what you do best: hide. Find me if you can, but if not, find a hole and wait for the fighting to end."

Annika stared at her. "Do you think it will be so dangerous?"

"I don't know. I have seen how they look at the guards, Annika, when they think no one sees. Just a glance now and then, as if they forget to hold it in . . . or can't any longer."

But di Fiore was an observationist. "Lorenzo doesn't see?"

"He does. But he has made up his mind that they will never act upon it."

That couldn't be true. "Then why the guards?"

Källa laughed a little. "Because he isn't a fool, Annika. Even he knows that he might be wrong—Oh, Olaf! You silly flounder."

She strode forward to pick up the boy, who'd landed on his face in the snow. He opened his small mouth and a horrid wail split the quiet in the clearing. Källa cooed and brushed away tears while Annika watched, trying not to laugh too loudly. The sobs didn't stop. With a sigh, Källa gave Annika a long-suffering look and headed back toward the living quarters.

Not long afterward, a troll ambled into the clearing. A new driver, she thought, watching each stiff step. It stopped, settled with a huff of steam. The chest hatch opened, and men emerged one at a time, their eyes downcast and walking in a line. Each one carried a mask of leather and glass, with two circular protrusions on each side of the mouth. If they were on the verge of rebelling against di Fiore, Annika couldn't see a sign of it. Without speaking or looking up, they trudged across the clearing and into their quarters. A few minutes later, a new line of men—twenty-five in all, Annika counted—climbed into the troll. It rose and ambled off to the south.

Disturbed, she returned to Källa's hearth chamber. Her sister sat at the table, looking harried and with her braid in disarray, rocking a sleeping Olaf against her chest. She held her finger to her lips when Annika entered.

Annika stifled her laugh. Källa responded with a deathly glare and a wrinkle of her nose, then pointed to the snow tunnel.

"I've had them put your packs in the last chamber," she whispered. "You'll have more privacy there."

The individual chamber was smaller, the roof lower. A bed stood in the center of the floor, a trunk at its foot. An oil lamp with its sconce embedded in the ice wall provided a dim light.

Annika searched through their packs. Her spanner and his pistol had been taken. She pressed her lips together in frustration, then smoothed her expression when she heard the crunch of approaching footsteps.

A moment later, David ducked through the low entrance. Her heart gave a wild leap, and her body followed. She threw herself into his arms, loving the strength and the warmth as he caught her against him, surrounded her.

"All right?" His voice was gruff.

"Yes." Everything had been awful. But not now. "You?"

She felt his nod against her hair. His arms tightened, and he held her, held her. Finally, he stepped back, cupped her face in his hands.

"We need to leave here," he said.

"I know how. We just have to find the right time. We can wait until then."

"Yes." He glanced at the bed. "We're sharing?"

"I told Källa that you will be the father of my children. I didn't want to be separated."

"Good. To both, if you'll have me. I'd like to make babies with you."

She grinned. "You're thinking of that now?"

"It's a better thought than any other I've had today." He dropped a quick kiss to her mouth, stepped back to unbuckle his coat. "So that was my cousin?"

His question held a note of wonder. He only had a little family left, she remembered. What did it feel like to suddenly gain more?

"Yes," she said.

"And the boy, too."

Judging by the flatness of his voice, Annika guessed that he'd assumed the same about Olaf that she initially had. "Yes. He is Paolo's son."

His brows rose. "Paolo's?"

"Yes." She watched him shake his head, as if he were trying to reconcile that information—or perhaps trying not to imagine the act that had led to it. "What is Paolo like?"

"Confused," he said. "Not childlike, though he possesses an innocent sense of wonder at times. I remember him differently—as forthright, focused, and thoughtful. Gentle and kind. Now, he only focuses for short times."

"Is he still kind?"

"Yes." He withdrew his journal from the pack, then slanted her an unreadable glance. "Did Källa tell you what he intends to do?"

"Send a capsule to the moon—along with plants and soil—so that he can build a farm." And she'd laughed wildly until she'd realized Källa had been serious. "I didn't believe it."

"It's all true." He looked around again. "No desk?"

Nowhere to sit at all, except for the trunk and bed. "Only at the table. We'll sit there soon for supper."

"All right." He tossed the journal onto his pack. "Will you lie with me until then? I need to gather my thoughts before I write, anyway."

She'd gladly lie with him. For the first time since she'd seen the airship's shadow on the snow, the thin, sour coating of dread and panic receded from the back of her throat. She pillowed her head on his shoulder, flattened her hand over his heart.

Perhaps this was love, too. Not just the tearing desire. Just the contentment of being with him, at a time when she shouldn't have been able to find any ease.

"What thoughts are you gathering?" she asked after a moment.

His chest lifted beneath her hand as he drew a long breath, released it slowly. "I'm worried about the glacier's stability."

"The quakes?"

"Not just the quakes. Paolo's plan. They're digging through the rock and ice over the volcano's caldera, placing explosive charges designed to collapse part of the glacier into the magma chamber below."

While they were on it? "Will that work?"

"Honest to God, I don't know. I've never heard of anyone trying to force an eruption—but if that magma chamber collapses, it will sure as hell do something. And I'm not sure the steam pressure will be redirected through the boreholes as they hope it will be." He shook his head. "They've drilled other boreholes that will force the steam into the hole below the tower. The plan is to drop the capsule into that primary borehole, letting it plug. The steam builds up and forces it out—like a cork from a bottle."

"Launching it to the moon." She felt silly even saying it.

"Yes."

"Will *that* work?"

His laugh rumbled against her hand. "I have no idea. He's calculated the necessary pressure needed to produce the proper acceleration, but whether the volcano can produce that sort of pressure . . . It's impossible to know."

"But you can't express any doubt."

His laughter stopped. "No."

"At least he's not hurting anyone." Unlike his last big experiment.

"That he knows of." With another deep breath, he pulled her closer. She felt his inhalation against her hair. His hand stroked the length of her back, before beginning a leisurely massage down her spine. "And Källa is here. Are you glad you've finally found her?"

"Yes." She bit her lip. "And no."

His fingers paused. "No?"

"When she left, it was because she'd taken the blame after I almost exposed Hannasvik to outsiders. She was protecting me."

"You didn't know?"

"I did. But I always thought that the names she called me were a joke. The sort of thing you say when you tease someone that you love. Annika the Woolgatherer, Annika the Rabbit. I didn't know until today that she truly believed them. That she believes I'm too weak to survive the New World."

"And you've spent four years proving her wrong."

Perhaps. But she wasn't wrong about all of it. "She said that I'm only brave when I'm in a troll. That's true, I guess." She sighed. "What do you think of Lorenzo?"

He didn't immediately answer. Annika turned to lie against his side, pushing up on her elbow to look down at him. He wore a troubled expression, his brows drawn.

"That bad?" she wondered.

David nodded. "He's determined to help his father, no matter the cost. I knew that. But I don't know whether he understands right from wrong and does the wrong anyway . . . or if he truly believes that there's nothing wrong with what he's doing, and that the greatness of his father's quest justifies the steps he takes."

To knowingly commit evil, or to commit evil without recognizing that it was. "Which is worse?"

"The second."

Annika didn't completely agree. She supposed it depended on the circumstances. "Which do you think Lorenzo is?"

"The second." He lifted his hand, smoothed back the curls from her forehead. "Everyone makes choices that they know aren't right. And we recognize that they aren't right, so we feel regret or remorse, even if we'd make the same choice again. It's a part of being human, part of what separates us from beasts. But I can't see any regret in him. He killed everyone on Heimaey simply to test his father's æther suit—not even as a necessary evil, but because he could. That giant balloon out there is filled with the gases released during their drilling. They deflated it over the town while he walked through the streets wearing that suit."

Horror settled deep, splinters of ice in her stomach and heart. "He walked through himself?"

She would have guessed that he'd forced one of his men to do it.

"Yes. So he's not just willing to do anything to help his father—he has no remorse, and no fear."

"That's terrifying," she whispered.

"Yes," David said, and held her tighter against him.

Lorenzo was the observationist, but Annika found it almost impossible not to watch him during dinner. She couldn't make herself stop—and she simply couldn't understand him. How could he laugh and play with Olaf, and be so gentle with his father? How could he ask after their comfort, and promise to see that a desk was brought to their chamber the next day? How could he look and act so human when only a few days ago he'd strolled through a town while the women died around him? When he'd been the one to cause their deaths?

The father could not have been any more different from the son. She saw him looking at her several times, shy and hesitant, and offering her a sweet smile when she met his eyes. She didn't know what to think of the posts stuck to his head, but when Källa gave her a warning glance, she understood that it was better not to ask—at least for now.

Paolo seemed genuinely adoring of Källa—who liked him as well, even if not in the same way she'd been with Lisbet. Some of his shyness dropped away when he realized Annika was her sister.

He pushed his stew away, eagerly leaning forward on his forearms. "You are Annika the Rabbit?"

Oh, that had never bothered her before. It stung now. She frowned at Källa. "You told him?"

"There was not much else that I could say about home."

And they couldn't now, either. Aware of Lorenzo watching, she let her irritation go. She didn't want to give him anything, didn't want him to know her in any way.

"She described you as more colorful," Paolo said.

"I usually am, but I lost all of my clothes."

"Oh? What are you wearing, then? It must be the most wonderful illusion ever created."

She had to smile. "I lost all of my colorful ones."

"A whale ate them," David said dryly.

Annika covered her laugh, didn't dare look at Lorenzo. Said like that, it sounded almost as absurd as . . . flying to the moon.

"Ah." A deep, wistful smile softened Paolo's face. "I used to dream that I would be a whale. It seemed a wonderful thing, floating through the ocean, warm with my own blubber—and very far away from people, except for the whalers." Humor replaced the softness of memory. "Of course, if I were a whale, I would shoot a harpoon back at them, and laugh at their surprise. I once considered making such a creature—a submersible, of course, not a true whale. But I thought it would be too silly, in the end."

Annika couldn't stop herself. "So you didn't finish it?"

"Oh, no. Only the schematics. I'm not allowed to buy engines anywhere in the New World. That stipulation was included in my parole." He looked to Lorenzo. "My son has been wonderful, procuring them for me at his own expense. I'm afraid I take terrible advantage of him."

Warmth filled Lorenzo's expression. "Nothing is too much for you, Father."

"Not even the moon," David said. "What made you dream of that?"

The wistful smile came again, but tinged by the memory of sadness, pain. "In the insanitarium, I could see my window from my bed. I would not be feeling well, very often. And they didn't always let me move. But I could see the moon as it passed my window—and it always seemed so very cold. So empty and lonely. I thought it would be an amazing thing to look up and see a man there. And eventually, many men building cities instead of war machines. We could labor together to create the perfect world, where everything would be clean. So clean. It could be a new start."

Paolo's voice was unbearably hopeful. Unbearably sad. Her throat tight, Annika found David's hand beneath the table.

"It *would* be an amazing thing," she said.

Looking charmingly pleased, the older man flushed a little. "Yes, well. Until then, we do what we can here. Every bit helps."

To keep everything clean? "Such as using the pipes for heating instead of many stoves."

"Yes! I would rid our chambers of oil lamps, if I could."

"He truly would," Källa said, laughing. "Please don't encourage him, Annika."

"I won't," she said, then looked to Paolo again with a grin. "Have you seen the electric lights? I visited a fair in Nova Lagos once, and they had one on display. A man pedaled a velocipede, and it illuminated the entire tent."

"I refuse to pedal all night," Källa said.

"That is why the hot springs are—" Paolo stopped, his face lighting. "Have you seen the bath chamber? I just remembered that Källa once said that you enjoyed the springs very much. This is not the same, but quite a lovely feature of this camp."

She had seen the room not very far from her own chamber, filled with steam, pipes, and a tin tub. Annika had never used a tub in her life, and she couldn't help but imagine that it was like sitting in a giant's cooking pot. "I was in the chamber earlier. But I can make do with a pitcher."

"Oh, no, I must insist. It is quite lovely, I promise. Like our own little spring."

"Annika's very modest," Källa said on her behalf.

Beside her, David seemed to choke.

"No one can see you there," Paolo assured her. "It is private."

"I—"

"Would love to, I'm sure," Lorenzo said quietly, and Annika's protests died away. "It must be difficult and sweaty work, driving the walker."

Feeling as if she'd suddenly been caught in a snare, Annika nodded. "Yes."

"But I couldn't help noticing that you do it very well."

"She's better than I am," Källa said.

"In that case, I wonder if you would drive the men to the ice tunnel tomorrow while Mr. Kentewess is with my father. Since you also believe that his goal is an amazing one, I'm certain that you would like to contribute to his project as well."

Annika didn't want to. But she couldn't waste the opportunity to see more of the glacier, and perhaps the means of escape. "What is the ice tunnel?"

"The ice cap is almost a half mile thick in places. We can't drill that far to place the charges, so we've dug a tunnel that allows us to start at a more reasonable depth. We have to carry the workers to thes current location."

"Beneath the ice?" David shook his head. "No."

"Yes."

"There were tremors today. We heard the ice crack," he said.

"So there have been on many days. But there's never been a cave-in or tunnel collapse." Lorenzo offered a strange smile, as if the sides of his lips had been jerked back. "Isn't that right, Father?"

"Yes."

Annika looked to Källa, who nodded.

"I insist," Lorenzo said.

Instead of ice blocks, wooden planks formed the bath chamber's walls. Copper pipes crossed the ceiling, dripping hot water to the boards below. David's eyepiece fogged the moment he entered. Switching to thermal offered him a view of a fuzzy yellow mess. He reached for one of the towels rolled up on the shelf instead.

Annika looked doubtfully at the tin tub sitting beneath a gooseneck faucet. She tested the stream of water with the back of her hand, nodded. "It *is* nice." She glanced back at him. "Do you want to join me? It's big enough for two."

Though David would have liked to, he shook his head. He wasn't prepared to show her that much of himself yet. "You don't have to drive to the tunnel tomorrow. Lorenzo can insist all he likes; I won't have you forced into it."

"I know. But if nothing else, I'll have access to a troll, and permission given by Lorenzo to drive it. If I ever have to use the troll to smash him flat, the guards won't be so quick to shoot at me when I start her up."

If she chose to go, then David would try to push away his worry. "I'm beginning to realize that you're a bit bloodthirsty."

"No." She pulled her tunic over her head, revealing the beautiful curve of her spine. Familiar heat pooled in his groin. "I just like to see people get what they deserve."

"Which includes smashing them flat."

"All right. A bit bloodthirsty, then."

David supposed that he was, too. But he didn't want to think of Lorenzo now. He dragged a chair up to the tub as she peeled away the rest of her clothes.

She kicked away her drawers, glanced over her shoulder. "You plan to watch?"

"I'm hoping that you'll teach me how to be modest."

Her grin matched his, then changed to a quiet *hiss* when she stepped in. David lived and died a thousand happy deaths in the brief second when she bent over to brace herself, rump high and her sleek thigh lifting over the edge. A soft groan filled the chamber as she eased down, and he could only imagine her making the same noise if she eased down over him, hot and wet. God. His cock swelled as he pictured it, and David welcomed the throbbing ache, loved the wholehearted response of his body. Annika didn't deserve anything less.

And by God, when he looked at her, even the painful constriction of his trousers felt good.

She dunked her head, came up dripping and pushing the hair out of her face. Her eyes opened and met his. With a playful smile, she moved toward him and folded her forearms on top of the tub's rolled edge. She crooked her finger, gesturing him closer.

He was happy to oblige. Bracing his hands on the edge of the tub, he leaned forward. "Close your eyes."

She did, her wet eyelashes forming spiky fans against her cheeks. He sipped a warm drop from her jaw before coaxing her lips open, his heart pounding and his eyepiece fogging again as he savored her taste.

When he drew back, she followed him for a few inches, her moist lips parted, her cheeks flushed from the heat and the kiss. Slowly, as if her eyelids were heavy, she looked up at him. He didn't want to wipe his eyepiece clear again when she did. He didn't want to ask her to look away.

Damn it all. He hated having half of his vision obscured.

He rubbed the lens shield clear. She watched—not his eyepiece, but his face. God knew what she saw.

But of course, being Annika, she told him.

"David, I want to tell you . . . I don't know if any of this hesitation is to spare my feelings, but I wanted you to know, the scars, the steel—they don't matter to me." She stopped. Frowning, she pushed the wet flop of curls back from her forehead, tried again. "No, that's not what I mean. They *do* matter, because they are a part of you. But I don't see them in the same way that I think many others do."

From that first night on *Phatéon*, when they'd spoken so easily after Mary Chandler had called him horrid, he'd known that Annika didn't see them in the same way. But he still did, sometimes. "I was almost never this self-conscious with stumps. That was just . . . what happened. And when people reacted or stared, it was easier to push away." He lifted his hand. "But this, I did to myself—and sometimes it's grotesque, even to me. Not always, because I don't think of them much unless I'm aware that someone is looking. And they're damn useful. But I have moments."

"And I've been looking at you a lot."

"Yes." And he didn't want to disappoint her. Sometimes it was easy not to give a damn what people thought. He cared what Annika did.

"I'll confess, I would look. I think they're adroit and amazing, not grotesque. But I wouldn't want you to be uncomfortable. Have you ever thought of going to England? Perhaps no one would stare."

"I *have* gone. But I still have the scars. And since I'm native, as soon as I'm away from the ports people look anyway."

She laughed, nodded. "At me, too. I suppose there is always something to make us different. I wonder if anyone at all ever feels at home."

"I do. With you."

"But not completely comfortable."

"Not even with myself." He dipped his fingers into the water, felt the heat soaking in. "You are home in your skin. I am still trying to get there."

"I'll try not to make it more difficult. There are other equally nice things to stare at." With a small splash, she glided back from the edge, stretched her arms over her head. "And I will think about how your hands make me feel, wondering what magic there is in them."

"I think the magic is in your breasts."

Her head fell back on a laugh. Then, affecting a sultry smile, she cupped them in her palms, her thumbs sweeping over her puckered brown nipples. "They are nice. But this doesn't feel half as good as when you touch me. Do you see the soap?"

His mind had fogged over. Several seconds passed before he realized what she'd asked. Swallowing hard, he glanced down, saw it on the floor. He scooped up the small cake and she took it from him without touching his steel fingers.

Not repulsed. Just careful.

And he felt wonderfully cared for. "You wouldn't mind if I touched you?"

"I'd love it." Without hesitation.

Perhaps she should hesitate, and think about it.

"It's not at all like my skin," he warned her.

"Colder, harder." She nodded. "But it is *you* touching me. I don't care how you do it."

And David wanted to take this risk. "Close your eyes, then. Turn around."

She did, smiling. He stripped off his shirt, scooted the chair as close to the tub as possible. Taking the soap from her hand, he dropped a kiss to her wet shoulder. With a sigh, she leaned forward, wrapping her arms around her bent knees. David soaped her back, loving the ridge of her spine, the tight span of her waist. Her arms were so incredible, strong with sleek muscles. He rinsed the soap from her skin, and she sat back against the side of the tub, her eyes still closed. With agonizing hope tightening his throat, he reached around with both hands. A metal palm wasn't good for lathering, so he only gently cupped her breast. Soft weight, smooth skin, her warmth almost indistinguishable from the heat of the water. The sensations weren't as sharp as in his right hand, but as he flicked his steel thumb across the hardness of her nipple, it didn't matter. She gasped in the same way, let her head fall back against his shoulder with a moan.

His hand didn't feel as much. She did.

And his heart felt full to bursting.

"All right?" His voice was hoarse.

Hers was a breathy whisper. "Yes."

He couldn't reach down any farther, not without overbalancing the chair. He wouldn't get into the tub with her. Perhaps one day.

She touched his fingers. "Are *you* all right?"

"Yes." Perfect. "Slip your hands down now, Annika. Between your legs. And we'll see what we can do together."

* * *

What they managed to do left her limp against him, her head pillowed on his thigh as he sat up in bed, writing his journal. Though she lay quietly, David found himself distracted by the softness of her cheek and the curve of her mouth—and by the fresh drawers she'd pulled from her pack, the blue satin ribbons that gathered the hem at her knees, the bow at her waist that begged to be untied.

God, such fripperies could wreck a man's mind.

She opened her eyes when he closed the journal, put it aside. "Do you think di Fiore read it?"

"Yes. But there's nothing in there to worry about. I'd only written up to the night in Smoke Cove. I mentioned the fighting machines, but I didn't mention my opinion of him."

"I told you about my people that night."

"Yes. But I only included my opinion of you."

With a grin, she rolled onto her back and looked up at him. "What is your opinion of me?"

"Fairly positive." He laughed when she wrinkled her nose at him, shook his head. "That is all I'll say."

She flicked her thumb against his leg, but smiled when he pulled her closer, lay against her side. He drew in the clean scent of her hair, brushed his fingers through the springy curls. With a sigh, she rested her head on his shoulder.

Warmth filled his chest—and a careful hope. "You don't have to find Källa now."

"No."

"What will you do?"

"I don't know." She looked up at him. Flickering lamplight painted a warm glow across her cheek and nose. "We need to get away from here, first."

"Yes."

"What do we do about Lorenzo?"

Stop him, if they could. But di Fiore's fate was second to David's primary concern. "I'm more worried about getting off this glacier before they attempt to launch that capsule."

"Do you think the ice will collapse?"

"I don't know. Lorenzo is concerned about his father's reputation—and destroying this camp might seem like a good way of making certain that no one ever talks about what truly went on here."

"Then killing the people in Vik, too."

"Yes. Di Fiore might play with them for a while, but eventually he'd want to silence them." And they knew he wouldn't hesitate to do it.

"So he'll leave everyone here to die—except he'd take Olaf with him."

"Yes. The boy is a di Fiore."

Annika nodded against his shoulder. Almost absently, her fingers rolled the runes at his throat, clicking the bones together. "He and Källa have an agreement: She won't kill him until after his father is gone. I think he'll leave her behind to die, too."

"Do you think she'll wait?"

"She made the promise, so yes. Unless she believes that he'll take her son—and then may the gods help him. Or not." She lay quiet for a moment, her fingers twisting, clicking. "If we have to stop him—kill him—I'll do it this time."

David frowned. He folded his fingers over hers, stopped the nervous rolling. "We're not taking turns."

"I know. But you shouldn't be the only one to bear that burden."

"And I'd rather not lay it on you simply to spare myself." He never wanted her to wake up, feeling the snap of bone beneath her hand. He never wanted her to lie in bed, wondering whether a man she'd killed had a wife, children, and a name. He never wanted her to spend hours trying, yet again, to think of any other option, to imagine any other choice—and knowing that even if one did present itself to her, that it was already too late. He never wanted her to feel as damned helpless as he had. "If it comes to that, we'll do what we have to. But I'm more interested in protecting you than killing him, and making certain we leave this camp alive."

"Yes." She tilted her face up, pressed her lips to his jaw. "What did you end up writing in your journal?"

"About di Fiore's experiment. I hate everything that Lorenzo is doing . . . but if Paolo's capsule flies at all—even if it fails to reach the edge of the glacier, let alone the moon—I won't be sorry to have seen it."

"I won't, either. It would be a different world if we looked up and knew a man had been up there."

"Yes." They'd see everything in a different way. Nothing would seem impossible. "That is what di Fiore might have read."

"In your journal?"

"Yes—in that last entry. It was after we spoke on *Phatéon*'s deck—when you told me to decide whether everyone in Hannasvik suffered a sickness." He felt her tense against him, reassured her, "I didn't write that. Only that now and again, something comes along to change the way I think. Something that completely changes how the world looks. A few years ago, the Society published a journal written by a man in England during the early years of the Horde occupation. He must have been infected, his emotions dampened, but he still wrote—and even though it is all physics and numbers, there must have been passion behind it. A need to pursue his science, which the Horde's tower hadn't been able to take away from him." In David's experience, there was always passion behind every great discovery and invention. "The journal had been hidden in an attic for over two hundred years, and in them, he describes motion. We already knew many aspects of it—the properties of inertia, the relationship between force and acceleration—but not using the same mathematics, and none of the rules had been unified in the same way before, interrelated in the same way. And then there were his theories of gravity, which didn't overturn Hooke's laws, but refined them, deepened them. One journal absolutely changed how we see so many things, yet now they seem so obvious. Many physicists are still reeling."

Annika pushed up on her elbow as he spoke, her brown eyes widening with wonder. "I have no idea what you're talking about, but I like the way you speak of it. That seems incredible."

She was incredible. "You did the same to me. You completely turned the world about. It is like paddling along in a canoe and suddenly being capsized—except that as soon as the boat upends, you realize that you'd been paddling along upside down and never realized it because you could breathe and see. And until you take a real breath of air, see what everything looks like without the water distorting the view, you believe that the upside-down world is the way things are. But you tipped me over."

Tears glittered in her eyes. "You truly wrote that?"

"Yes." And that he'd fallen in love with her—but it was already so much deeper now. "Don't cry."

"I can't help it. That's the most wonderful thing anyone has said to me."

"We are even, then. You're the most wonderful thing that has happened to me." His breath stopped when she lowered her head, softly kissed him. David held her, savoring every moment, and when she pillowed her cheek on his shoulder again, said roughly, "We *will* make it off this glacier—and make certain that you can go home again."

Chapter Twelve

Annika woke alone, missing David's warmth. She pulled the blanket tighter around her shoulders, sneaked an arm out to light the lamp.

His coat was still draped atop their trunk, so he must not have gone far. Good. Her world had turned upside down, too, though not in such a marvelous way. But with David here, nothing seemed too terrible to bear.

Did *that* mean she loved him?

It seemed that her feelings for him must be love. Not just need and want, and his wonderful ability to ease them. When she thought of never seeing him, of losing him . . . that pain wasn't at all like rivets, but a sword ripping through her gut.

He'd said that he'd make certain she'd reach home again. Annika wasn't sure where that was anymore.

Footsteps from the snow tunnel drew her gaze to the chamber entrance. David ducked through, his hair wet, his damp shirt clinging to his shoulders. His gaze found hers. His mouth widened into a grin. "I can't let you smell better than I do."

Sudden need twisted deep. He bent for his pack and Annika stifled a small moan, watching him. Her gaze slipped over his broad back—so much strength. She wanted to clench her fingers on his shoulders, bite him there. And his hard chest, the tiny nubs of his nipples that she felt through his shirt. She wanted to lick him there. Then his ass, oh, she'd take such a firm grip. He was all muscle beneath those horrid trousers.

She sat up. Cool air slipped through her chemise, teased her tightening nipples. "When we are away from here," she said, "I will make you a new pair of trousers."

"Why?" His head lifted. His voice roughened. "Annika."

No need to ask what he'd seen in her expression. She was starving—and too busy staring at his ass to glance up. "I must tell you something. It might alarm you."

"Alarm me?"

He straightened—already aroused. A bulge formed behind the front of his trousers. Oh, she had not even seen his erection yet. Only felt his thick shaft in her hands, tasted him. Panting now, remembering, she licked her lips.

"There's nothing I enjoy more than being with you. You're an incredible friend, an amazing man. I love the way you talk, what you say—all of it. And when you touch me, it feels as if there's nothing else in the world but us." She managed to lift her gaze a little. His damp shirt clung to his stomach. There was muscle there, too, to explore with her hands, her mouth. "But right now, I am looking at you, and I think nothing of how much I love being with you. I think nothing of love at all. I only think that I want you on this bed, to claim every inch of your body for mine, take you deep inside me where you have no escape."

"Annika."

There was more than a bulge now. She finally looked up. "I don't feel at all like a rabbit, David. I feel like a wolf. Does that frighten you?"

He dropped the pack and strode toward her, his gaze feral. In a swift movement, he caught her wrists in his hand, pushed her back down on the bed. His legs trapped hers. He stretched her arms up over her head, his body rising over her, inhaling her scent up the length of her neck.

His voice was a growl against her ear. "Does this?"

He flipped her over onto her stomach. Annika gasped. Strong hands gripped her hips, hauled her up to her knees then pulled her back, grinding the ridge of his erection against her soft flesh. Need ripped through her, pulsing deep and hot.

"I think of this, Annika. Of simply taking you."

Rough fingers dragged her drawers over her bottom, baring her to his gaze. She heard the buckles of his trousers releasing, then he rocked forward, his thick shaft thrusting into the channel created by her closed thighs. She cried out, her cheek against the mattress, her fingers clenching.

Slowly, he drew back. "I dream of pushing myself deep inside, telling you that you're mine, mine, *mine*."

He pounded against her with each "mine," shattering strokes through her slick folds, his shaft riding against her clitoris—and then stopping, his hips hard against her backside, his erection clamped between her thighs and her need-swollen flesh.

Empty, aching, all but sobbing with desperation, Annika pushed up on her hands, tried to rock back against him. The grip on her hips held her fast. She bowed her head, frustration screaming through her.

"Inside me, David. Please. *Now*."

With a curse, he dropped his forehead against the back of her shoulder. The tiny movement nudged him deeper, settled him more firmly against her sex. His ragged breath shuddered over her skin, and he gave a tortured moan before slowly pulling away. Though she knew he was right, Annika cried her denial, pushed her hand between her thighs, trying to ease the ache.

David turned her onto her back again. A long, lingering kiss only deepened the sense of loss. He lifted his head, and she saw the same agony on his face.

His voice was tight. "You're all right? Not frightened."

"No." Just dying of need. "Only of how much I want you."

He gave a short laugh, nodded. "I know."

Both of them dying. "Can we finish like that? Not inside. Just . . . rubbing against me."

A wry expression lifted the corner of his mouth. "I couldn't for very long. It's difficult to kneel. But I've mastered the crouch." He brushed her hair back from her forehead. "I'll figure out some way. Bending over farther, so that I can put more weight on my hands. Or we'll try it standing. But for now . . ."

Sliding down the bed, David pushed her legs apart, draped her thighs over his shoulders. Oh, yes. Anticipation lifted through Annika, rolling her hips.

He looked up, his gaze locked with hers. Slowly, he lowered his head—and before his mouth took her, he growled a single word.

"Mine."

He'd never be satisfied.

Throughout the morning, the realization distracted David from his study of di Fiore's survey maps. All of his life, he'd made an effort to concentrate on things that pleased him, and to be content with what he had. He wouldn't be able to do both with Annika. At the beginning, he'd thought that he could be happy with anything she gave him.

Now he realized that he'd always want more. That he'd never be content until he had all of her.

Not simply making love, though he wanted that so fiercely it ripped through his guts. But whether she took him to her bed or not, David wouldn't be satisfied until he had her heart.

Even then, he wanted more. He wanted her for the rest of his life. And on his dying breath, he would still want another second with her, another hour, another lifetime.

Falling in love with her had capsized him again, turned another part of him over. Looking at himself, David wasn't certain if he liked the new view. He'd promised himself that if she ever left him, he'd let her go. Now, David didn't know if he could. If she left, he feared that he'd break that promise and chase after her.

He prayed that he'd never have to.

"Shall we play this one again?"

David looked up. The suit lay across Paolo's work table, abandoned. The older man had been sketching the chickens for almost an hour, accompanied by a gramophone. He cranked the device now, and despite his query, they had no choice but to play the same song again. Paolo only owned one wax cylinder recording, a lively arrangement of flutes and drums. David had never heard it before this morning; now he could whistle it in his sleep.

But it didn't distract him from work—he had only himself to blame for his poor performance that morning . . . and his memories of Annika, crying out as he thrust against her.

God. He was doing it again.

"That song is fine, yes," he agreed.

Smiling and cranking, Paolo nodded. A few moments later, he muttered while walking away from the gramophone, without having started the recording.

Easily distracted, too. David was in good company.

He studied the map again, the shape of the topography. What had he been thinking of before he'd lost himself to the luscious memory of Annika's wetness against his bare shaft?

He'd been thinking of Katla, the witch.

"Paolo." He carried the map to the drafting table, where Paolo sat absently eating a biscuit. Källa hadn't brought in any food to him this morning, but David didn't ask where he'd found it. "When Katla erupts, there will likely be a large volume of meltwater as the volcano heats the ice."

"And steam. Which is what we need."

"Yes. But look at the elevation, the probable drainage route— and Vik is here." He pointed. The town hadn't been marked on the map. "It will drain in other directions, too, but the primary flow will probably take this path."

"Yes, I see. What is Vik?"

"A town."

"No, no." He was smiling again. "I specifically asked Lorenzo. There are no settlements on that side."

"I was there, not a few days ago."

"No. There cannot be." Suddenly agitated, he stabbed his finger at the map. "Smoke Cove is here. There is the camp. Why is your Vik not here? If there was a town, there would be a record of it. But it is not here. It is not on any of these maps."

Paper crinkled and ripped as he shoved the map away.

"It is there," David said softly.

"You were turned about. There is nothing there. I would not harm another town."

David would hate for him to harm one, too. "That is why—"

"You're mistaken!" Paolo roared. Face red, tendons standing out on his neck—then suddenly quieting, sitting back again. In a tremulous voice, he repeated, "You're mistaken. It's not there. Lorenzo looked."

And he apparently needed to believe his son as much as Lorenzo needed to push every problem out of Paolo's path—even if that problem might be Vik. *Goddamn it.*

All right. He wouldn't convince Paolo that the town was there. So he'd have to find another way. David returned to his table, refocused on the map, studied the location of the explosive charges.

Could he give Paolo reason to relocate those, alter the pattern of the ice melting? No. That might change how the ice collapsed but couldn't change the surrounding land or the flow of water.

There had to be something else. He had to think of something else.

"Oh, is it over so quickly?"

David glanced up. Paolo was looking toward the gramophone with his brows high—surprised by the silence, but he'd never restarted the music.

Perhaps that would be an option. Maybe they didn't need to stop this project or attempt the impossible task of redirecting a flood. He just needed Paolo to focus in another direction, to make another project more important. Determined to help his father, Lorenzo would follow.

What would interest him? "Lorenzo told me that you had plans to utilize the thermal activity on the peninsula south of Smoke Cove—to provide the town with heat so they didn't have to rely on coal."

"Yes." Paolo didn't look up from the suit. "It was just a fleeting thought I had."

"Lorenzo said that you'd hoped to electrify the town, too."

"I have made many plans, and never made anything of them. It is the way of it."

"It's a pity. My father once mentioned something similar when he heard of the geysers in the Yellow Rock Mountains—or using the natural steam to power the turbines instead of relying upon furnaces." His father would forgive him this lie. "He'd always hoped to see it come to fruition."

"Did he?" Paolo looked up, interest lighting his expression.

"Yes." When in truth, David was making most of this up based on what Lorenzo had told him about the project, and their conversation over dinner the previous night. What had Paolo said to

Annika about using the pipes to heat the living quarters? "He believed that every bit helps."

The other man nodded. "So it does."

For the first time in her life, Annika didn't feel comfortable while driving a troll. It was impossible with Lorenzo standing on the ladder behind her, breathing down her neck, and twenty-five laborers crammed into the hearth chamber.

Barely a word passed between them—not at all like the laborers who'd come from Castile to Smoke Cove in *Phatéon*'s hold. Though Annika hadn't seen much of them, she'd often heard them, the songs they'd sung that she couldn't understand, full of hope and the promise of work. Perhaps Lorenzo's presence stifled any chatter now.

The sun hadn't yet risen when they left the camp. Annika followed a worn path, lit by the lanterns at the troll's nose and shoulders. The route had been well used, but she still stepped carefully. Sharp cracks from the ice had sounded throughout the night. It was impossible to guess when a crevasse might open, creating a gaping death drop where there'd only been ice the day before. They traveled north, away from the tower and capsule. After five miles, she reached the mouth of a rounded tunnel.

"It stretches ten miles south again," Lorenzo said. "The men work around the clock."

Then he'd have done better to build crawlers instead of trolls. The walls of the tunnel were smooth and high enough for the troll to pass through on all fours. The flat, rough floor would provide adequate traction. But it was still better to have tracks or sled runners on ice rather than feet.

She slowly approached the entrance. "Did you drill this tunnel?"

"No. The drill is for the vertical shafts and boreholes. We tried melting through, but the water refroze too quickly, and extraction became a problem. So we've resorted to old-fashioned labor. The men are digging through."

"Through the *ice*?"

"And rock. I've brought in foremen from the Lusitanian mines to oversee the work. Theirs is the nearest in expertise. They've done a fine job so far, don't you agree?"

Expertise? The Lusitanian mines had a terrible reputation—using infected laborers smuggled in from Horde territories because they could work longer and be fed less. If digging these tunnels was anything like laboring in the mines, it was no wonder these men looked downtrodden.

Annika only shook her head, unease lifting the small hairs on her skin as they entered the tunnel shaft. The lanterns threw golden light across the rounded blue walls, and ahead for almost twenty yards. Beyond that, all was darkness.

"There are a few turns where we decided to dig around the rock rather than blast through, but you'll see them before you have to avoid them."

Unnerved by the enclosing ice, the dark ahead, Annika didn't answer.

Lorenzo didn't seem to care. "I must say, though we've had men in that seat for months, they don't drive with half the confidence and skill that you do. Even Källa, when teaching them, didn't drive as well."

Of course not. Källa saw the trolls as a tool or a weapon, something she used. When Annika drove, she saw the engines as a heart and the machinery as muscle and sinew, extensions of her own—and when Annika was in the seat, the troll had more of a brain.

She would not tell Lorenzo that, however.

"I was surprised when I realized that you are the rabbit sister she told us about. I didn't know when I read about Annika Fridas-dottor in Kentewess's journal that you were the same woman.

It's fascinating to know now. It makes me even more curious about you."

Annika didn't intend to satisfy that curiosity.

"I had wondered what sort of woman would be with Kentewess. Either she thought so little of herself that she settled for less than a man, or she was grateful for it—the sort of woman who likes to crush weak men beneath her heel. But when I realized who you were, I wondered if you were like Källa, using him for your own purposes. But you're not any of those things."

The troll's right foreleg slipped. Annika steadied it, said through gritted teeth, "David's not less of a man."

"It also interests me that you know anything about what makes a man, never having seen one. Oh, yes. It was quite simple to figure out what Källa never said. About why she led us away from the upper peninsula."

Annika's heart thumped, her pulse pounding in her ears.

"She was protecting them, I realized."

Then Annika didn't need to confirm it.

"Do you know the lengths she will go to protect them? I didn't either, but I wondered. So I found out."

Horror crawled in Annika's stomach. What had he done? Every horrible story she'd ever heard about the ways that men could hurt women flooded her memory. But, no. He hadn't threatened her yesterday because he already knew what David's response would be.

Knowing she played into his hands by responding, not caring, she asked, "How?"

"I gave her a choice between Heimaey and your village. She chose Heimaey."

By the gods' tears. Lorenzo couldn't be a man. He couldn't be a human. Only a monster could do such a thing. "To kill one village or another? That's no choice."

"Oh, it was. She could have refused to choose between them and leave the burden all on my shoulders. She didn't. She took the burden of responsibility in exchange for certainty. It's admirable, I suppose. Self-sacrificing. All that mattered to me was that the suit worked. The rest was just interesting."

And Källa should have broken her promise and killed him there.

No, Annika realized. Källa *would* have broken her promise and killed him there. Her sister knew that Lorenzo had something wrong in him, and probably suspected worse. But if he'd threatened Hannasvik that directly, she wouldn't have hesitated.

"What choice did you really give her?"

"No choice. I asked her what she would kill, if she could. She told me that she'd kill the dogs."

Yes. That was Källa.

"Now you think, 'He is deranged. He is inhuman.' Will it make killing me easier?"

Annika actually thought it would. But David had said he called himself an observationist. Perhaps that was all that Lorenzo wanted—to see what reaction he could prod from her.

"Do you actually believe anything you said about David?"

"No." There was a smile in his voice. "I have not quite figured you out. Who killed the watchman, I wonder? You or Kentewess?"

Would he retaliate? They'd killed one of his men. "I did," she said.

"See? Now you lie, probably to protect him. I know it was Kentewess. His neck was broken. If you had killed him, you'd have used something to do it with. Källa used to say that you are the rabbit, that you're only brave inside a machine. I think you're braver than she said. I don't think she was all wrong, however. You'll use a tool, but only because you recognize that you're weak."

Källa wasn't wrong—and as she traveled through the tunnel, Annika gave serious thought to killing him with the troll at the first opportunity.

The end of the tunnel appeared, lanterns flooding the tunnel with light. Men with pickaxes chipped away at the wall. Others carried blocks and wheelbarrows full of ice to a train of carts that stood on sled runners rather than wheels.

If Lorenzo left the troll, she would smash him in front of these laborers and face whatever came next.

He must have realized it. After she set the machine down and the men began filing out of the chest hatch, he told her to come out of the seat.

"You must stoke the engine, of course," he said. "Also, once a day, you will drag the carts out of the tunnel to dump them. You will be responsible for securing the train to the walker. I don't trust them to do it properly."

In truth, Annika didn't either. The men appeared exhausted. In their place, Annika didn't know that she could properly secure anything. Her mind never worked well when she was tired.

Why would he push them this far? Was this just cruelty of the same sort as in the Lusitanian mines, or was he hoping to see what they would do?

"A pitiful sight, aren't they?" Lorenzo stood beside her, looking over them. "They are interesting, too. Some men whom we've brought from Castile to Iceland thirst for blood. Some just want to work, take pleasure in earning their wages, in being strong. If you kick them down, they get up and keep going. Very few ever kick back . . . though some are beginning to."

Good. She hoped they eventually kicked him down, too. "And that is the reason you have so many guards."

"You see well." He glanced at her, then back at the men. "But I don't need guards for these men. If you knock them down, they stay down until you tell them to get up again. And they'll stay up until they fall down. I hope to see what it takes to make them get back up on their own, to kick back. I tell the foreman to punish them for the slightest infraction. But no matter how unreasonable it is, these men never fight back."

He gestured toward a laborer who had bent over, the head of his pickaxe braced against the ice floor as if stopping to catch his breath. A giant of a man in a gray fur hat and coat, the foreman approached him, brandishing a club. Annika expected a warning. But the foreman simply struck, a sharp *thwack!* across the top of his head. The laborer staggered, but didn't fall. The other men didn't stop, didn't look around.

The foreman raised his arm again.

Too shocked to believe what she was seeing, Annika could barely speak. "Stop him."

"He's not even in the steel suit that they use in the mines. With their numbers, they could overpower him. They don't even try."

She balled her fists. Did he want a reaction from her? *"Stop him!"*

Lorenzo called out. The foreman looked around. Behind him, the laborer lifted bloody fingers from his head.

"We'd better get him back into the walker with the others and see that he receives proper attention, yes?"

Sick with the horror of it, Annika nodded.

"You're very kind, Annika Fridasdottir."

No. Just human.

She returned to the troll, never hating anyone so fiercely in her life. It shook through her, swelled through her chest and stung her eyes. Lorenzo climbed the ladder behind her. Could she do anything from here? No. But twenty-five men were inside that chamber. Every single one must have reason to hate him.

Why didn't they kill him? Why didn't they revolt as Källa believed they would? What were they waiting for?

Whatever Källa had seen in them, Annika couldn't see it now. Only men who'd been beaten and hurt. Only a monster who'd taken pleasure in hurting them.

She started the troll again, fighting back tears of rage and sickness. Lorenzo wouldn't squeeze a single drop from her. She would never give him that satisfaction.

And yet she must be already. Her breath came short and fast. Her control over the troll was failing, the foreleg sliding, the rhythm off, everything swaying, off balance.

No. That wasn't her. This was a quake.

Sudden terror iced her chest. She dropped the troll into a squat. Violent jolts rocked through them, the lanterns swinging wildly, pure darkness ahead. Sick with fear, Annika gripped the levers, praying that the tunnel didn't collapse.

Her stomach felt on the verge of vomiting when the shaking stopped a minute later. Her limbs were heavy, impossible to lift, to start moving again—fearing that with a single step, the ice would shatter around them.

Behind her, Lorenzo said, "Well. We made it through that."

That was enough to get her going again. Smashing down on the stompers, she drove the troll hard through the tunnel, desperate to be out—and away from the monster behind her and the horror she'd seen.

She almost cried with relief when the faint light appeared through the dark. The sun had risen while they'd been beneath the ice. She didn't care that it all but blinded her as she emerged onto the glacier path.

A two-seater balloon was flying toward them, two figures in the cart. With her heart in her throat, she recognized the second man. David.

"And look at that, now."

Lorenzo sounded surprised, but she wasn't. David would have felt the quake. He'd known she was in the tunnel. Of course he would come.

Or perhaps he was surprised that David had convinced a guard to take him.

"You might as well stop, then. A few minutes of sun would do us well. And we can send our bleeding man back in the balloon. It will be faster, and I'm sure Kentewess will not mind riding with us."

Annika knew that Lorenzo just wanted to see what happened, wanted to observe them together. She didn't care. As soon as the balloon landed, she ran to David. His arms closed around her, and the tears she'd been stopping had to come now. She buried her face in his shoulder.

David didn't let her hide. Gentle fingers tilted her chin up. Dark concern shadowed his face, deep worry. "Are you all right?"

Throat blocked by a sob, she nodded.

"God, Annika." He clutched her to him. "I was terrified. I could only imagine the glacier falling in on you."

She'd been terrified, too. But she wasn't now. Only relieved, so relieved. She was all right. With David, it wasn't just riveting need. The world around them was falling apart, but there was something good here in his arms, something perfect.

And she knew exactly where home was.

She caught his face in her hands. "I love you."

His lips parted. He stared at her, his gaze full of disbelief and hope, as if he thought he'd only imagined the words. So she said them again.

"I love you, David."

Tears glistened in his eye. Then his mouth covered hers, a kiss brimming with hope and joy, and that pushed the rest of the world away.

He lifted his head. His voice was rough with emotion. "I love you, too."

Her heart leapt. "Already? I thought it would take you years."

He laughed, nodding, and suddenly she was smiling, laughing, kissing him again. Even Lorenzo's clearing throat couldn't dim this happiness. She took David's hand, led him back to the troll.

And it was much easier to drive when she wasn't alone.

* * *

With Lorenzo in the troll with them, she had little opportunity to speak to David before lunch, and then his attention was
demanded by Paolo, who had carried in a journal and a survey
map. She could not keep her eyes from him as he bent his head over
Paolo's notes.

He loved her.

She regarded him with a silly grin until she happened to glance
toward Lorenzo. The other man was frowning slightly, which sent
a chill through her bones.

"What are you working on, Father?"

Paolo didn't lift his head. David did, his gaze meeting Lorenzo's, and she'd never before seen his expression so cold. "I asked
your father about the project on the peninsula."

"It is quite something," Paolo said. The eagerness lighting his
face resembled the same eagerness she'd seen the previous night
when he spoke of the moon project. "I'd forgotten how elegant it
was, which is likely why it appealed to Stone Kentewess as well. He
always said in his designs that the elegance is in the simplicity, and
this is, in fact, very simple—though the work might take years."

He laughed as if making a joke. Lorenzo's brow creased.

"Years?"

"Oh, yes. We have been looking through my notes all morning.
The idea is simple, but there will be much to build."

"But you still have to finish the suit."

"The suit is done." Irritation filled his voice. "It has been done."

"Then the project is all but done, Father. We have only the final
charges to lay."

His father suddenly laughed, nodding. "Yes, yes. It will be perfect. It will be ready for me when I've finished with this."

"You want to put it on hold?" An edge of strain appeared in

Lorenzo's voice. "We are fortunate today that the earthquake did not ruin it all, Father. If we delay, it's a certainty that something will."

"Then let it!" Paolo snapped.

Surprised by the sudden vehemence, Annika looked to David. He wore a smile she'd never seen before, hard-edged and satisfied. He met her gaze and it changed, warmed.

"Father." Lorenzo spoke with the measured tones of someone out of patience with a child. "Anyone can imagine this. If Stone Kentewess did, then anyone can build it. You don't need to. It's a small idea."

David's expression didn't even flicker, as if he didn't feel the insult to his father. He remained silent.

Paolo shook his head. "Even small ideas are critical. You cannot calculate the area of a circle without first learning to add two and two. You have only to look at Newton's journal to see that it is true. All those men who were in a race to answer everything missed the simplest answer of all. I did the same with the mountain at Inoka. I meant to do everything at once: to heal the land, to clean the air, to stop a war. This will be a small step, yet it can still mean so much, count for more. Every little bit helps."

"But the *moon*, Father. A legacy like that would overshadow the mountain. It could repair the di Fiore name, make it a worthy name for Olaf."

"Olaf will make his own name. What will you make of it?"

"I will be the man behind you. The man who always supports his father."

"Then support me in this!"

Lorenzo's jaw tightened. Silenced. Annika stared in awe, then looked to David. Somehow, he'd done this—and he'd used the most effective weapon against Lorenzo: his father.

Would he retaliate? Blame David?

Annika couldn't guess—but she didn't think it would be right now. Lorenzo stared at his father as if no other man existed in the world.

Finally, he nodded. "I promised to help you fulfill your dreams, Father. You can count on me for this."

Lorenzo didn't join her on the next trip to the tunnel. A few words passed between the men, though so low she almost couldn't hear them under the engine. As they were in Spanish, she couldn't have understood them, anyway—she was simply glad to hear them.

She was pleased by everything. David loved her. She loved him, too. They might be soon abandoning this project and leaving the glacier. Lorenzo would be more of a danger, she knew. He would likely want to silence everyone in Vik and at this project so that they couldn't smear the di Fiore name. But she and David *would* escape. She had no idea what the future might bring after that. Perhaps she would stay in Smoke Cove while he went on expeditions. It would kill her to be so far apart, but she would wait for his return.

Or perhaps she could convince him that all of his expeditions needed a troll.

She was so full of hope. She couldn't stop dreaming of how it would be with him—not just in bed, though she anticipated that, but beyond the bed, too. Her dreams eased the fear, made the trip to the end of the tunnel pass more quickly.

The men filed out. Annika stoked the engine. The ice cart needed to be disconnected from the troll, so she tucked a spanner in her belt and dropped through the chest hatch, her mind still on David. The bolts loosened with a few sharp twists. The huffing engine above her drowned out every other sound.

Except for a crack and a sharp cry of pain.

Frowning, Annika looked behind her. Near the cart, a man lay on the ground, his arm raised to protect himself. A cube of ice had shattered at his feet. The foreman stood over him, lifting his club again.

"Stop that!" Annika shouted over the engine, stepped forward. "You stop that now!"

The foreman looked to Annika. His eyes narrowed. He started toward her.

Shaking with rage, Annika gripped her spanner as he came closer, all but looming over her. Did he think to intimidate her with his great size? No doubt he meant to make her back down, make her run. He wouldn't dare hit her.

He did.

His arm drew back and struck. Astonishment made her slow. She ducked to the side.

Pain split through the side of her head.

Darkness clouded her vision and suddenly receded. Her stomach was churning, her throat sour. When had she fallen to her knees? Her shaking hand fell away from her temple. Blood dripped to the ice floor and froze in crimson dots.

Giant boots stopped in front of her. Annika looked up, cringed. The foreman was still there, arm raised, poised to strike again.

He punished for any infraction. But if she stayed down here, maybe she wouldn't be hit again. Or she could get into the troll, hit him back.

Or hit him now. Her fingers tightened on the spanner.

She swung hard. The heavy head smashed into his knee, the impact jolting through her arm. A shout of shock and pain tore through the sound of the huffing troll, the pounding in her ears. His arm came down.

But he was tall—his arm had a long way to go. She was a rabbit, small and quick, dodging the strike. The club chipped ice from the floor. With both hands, she slammed the spanner's steel shaft down on his wrist.

A kick knocked her back, stunned. The spanner skidded away. Panicked, she scrambled for it. A hand grabbed her leg.

Screaming, Annika curled up and covered her head, waiting for the blow. There was only a *thunk!* of flesh.

Then only the huffing.

Slowly, she raised her arms. The laborer who'd dropped the cube of ice stood over the foreman, a pickaxe in his hands, the point buried in the foreman's head. With a jerk of his arms, he pulled it out. Blood ran in a river.

She stared up at him in astonishment. He stared back, his chest heaving. Annika wasn't sure who was more surprised.

But at least she knew one word. *"Gracias."*

Eyes still wide, he nodded.

Annika scooted away from running blood. Reaction set in like a punch to her chest, her stomach. She rolled over, heaved up her lunch, and knelt there, coughing and gagging. Everyone stared at her—fifty men, all as speechless as she. Annika pushed to her feet and gestured to the troll—but not everyone would fit. She bent for her spanner, moved to connect the carts again.

Finished, she gestured again. "Get in. I'll take you all back to camp."

A murmur ran through the men. Then the one who'd stopped the foreman stepped forward, shouted, raising his arms and the bloodied pickaxe. The men piled into the troll, the carts.

Work was done for the day.

Chapter Thirteen

Annika had to slow a few times in the tunnel, dizzy with sick nervousness and the cut on her head, but steadied by the time she drove into the sun. The train of carts slid easily behind her troll, crowded with men. She drove straight into the clearing, settled the troll down.

Annika almost wished that she hadn't been so quick to leave the driver's seat when Lorenzo climbed up from the living quarters, frowning at the men in the carts. Some were still looking down. Others met his eyes.

His gaze froze on her forehead. "What happened? A cave-in?"

"No. We killed the foreman."

He blinked, stepping back to look at the men again, then back at Annika, as if trying to decide who had done it. "How?"

Pleasure tinged the question, as if he enjoyed the surprise. She didn't intend to give him any more. "We didn't bring the body. It's probably frozen to the tunnel floor now."

"I'll get it. Go on in, have your head looked at."

Dismissing her, he turned and spoke to the men. There was

nothing more she could do here. She staggered a bit on the steps, but had steadied again by the time she passed through the tunnel and into the hearth room. Paolo and David were still at the table, maps spread across the surface. David glanced up.

"Jesus Christ." His chair crashed back, and then he was at her side, his arm around her waist. He steered her to a seat. "Are you all right?"

"Yes. Mostly bruised."

Paolo appeared beside her with a bowl of steaming water in his hands and a towel. David took the cloth, gently dabbed her forehead.

"What happened? Did the troll tip?"

"The foreman clubbed me."

David froze. She'd seen him kill a man. She'd never seen him murderous. He spoke a single word, lips peeled back from bared teeth.

"Where?"

"He's already dead. He was hitting one of the men. I yelled at him to stop. He came after me, but I didn't think he would hit me."

Still shaking with rage, he dabbed at the blood again. "But he did."

"Yes. I hit him a few times with the spanner. Then one of the men caught him in the head with the pickaxe."

"Which one?"

"I don't know his name."

"I'll find out. I'm forever in his debt."

No need for that. "I already thanked him."

"Annika!" Källa paused at the entrance to the snow tunnel, staring at her. "Are you all right?"

"Yes."

"Did you tip the troll?"

Annika glanced up, met David's gaze. She had to laugh. He still wasn't. "No."

"The foreman clubbed her," Paolo supplied.

Källa sucked in a sharp breath. Her hand clenched, as if around the handle of a sword. "Where is he?"

Annika only shook her head, then rolled her tongue across the roof of her mouth. The taste of sour and sickness still lingered. "I need to wash."

David bent, picked her up, cradling her against his chest.

"I can walk," she said.

"But I need to hold you."

She smiled, laid her head against his shoulder. "All right, then."

In the bath chamber, Annika rinsed out her mouth. While the tub filled, she dunked her head under the stream of running water, gritting her teeth against the sting in her scalp.

"It'll start bleeding again," David said, a clean towel in hand.

She pressed her fingers to the cut, looked. Only a little blood. She accepted the towel and pressed it against her head, using her free hand to remove her boots and stockings. After rolling her trousers, she sat in the chair and draped her legs over the edge of the tub, let her feet soak up the heat.

"We're leaving tomorrow for Smoke Cove," David said. When she glanced up at him, eyes wide, he nodded. "Paolo agreed that we should begin working on the other project."

She leaned against the back of the chair with a happy sigh. "And he wants you with him, so Lorenzo won't do anything to jeopardize that."

"Yes." He crouched beside her. The crinkle of paper sounded. Her gaze dropped to his hands. "I was saving this."

A butter candy. He untwisted the wrapper and slipped it into his mouth. Her breath caught as he rose, moving in for a slow kiss. The candy melted between them, creamy and sweet, and he lingered over her lips long after it had gone. As if reluctant, he finally lifted his head, but remained close, his breath mingling with hers.

"It's still perfect," he said.

And could be more perfect. She wound her arms around his neck. "If you carry me to our bed."

The muscles in his shoulders stiffened. "You're certain?"

"I want to." But still she felt his hesitation. "You don't?"

"Oh, yes. But there's more to consider than that." His palm covered her belly. "Other consequences."

He would be a good father. But he was right. Annika wasn't yet sure what she'd do next, where she'd go when he finished the project in Smoke Cove. It might be best to wait before having a baby. "Then don't spend your seed inside me."

"There's still a risk."

"I'll take it."

"Not alone. I'll take it with you." He lifted her out of the chair, her bare feet dripping. "A father or not, I'll be there for you, give you anything you ever need."

He'd already given her his love. That was all she needed.

Her heart pounded with every step. He carried her through the snow tunnel, ducking into the chamber. She couldn't look away from the bed. The lamp burned low, dancing shadows across the ice walls. He eased down with her, no candy between them now, but the kiss just as sweet.

He paused to look at her, his hand shaking as he caressed her cheek. Then his mouth was on hers again until she was panting, breathless. Her head fell back and his lips trailed the length of her neck, wringing a moan from her throat. Big palms cupped her breasts, fingers teasing the peaks into aching hardness. Oh, he'd learned her body so quickly.

She pulled the hem of her tunic up and over her head. Cool air kissed her nipples, drawing gooseflesh and a shiver over her skin.

His tongue traced the curve of her breast, flicked across her nipple, and she shuddered again.

"Too cold?"

"No." Inside, she was burning.

"Do you want the light on?"

"It makes no difference. I just imagine you over me."

He nodded, kissed the tip of her breast before sitting back. With his gaze on hers, he reached for his collar, dragged his shirt off over his head.

Oh. She hadn't imagined him perfectly, but near to. Her fingers had already traveled the corrugated muscle of his abdomen, the hard planes of his chest. His runes gathered in the hollow of his throat, swinging away from his skin as he leaned forward, tossing the shirt across their trunk. Strong collarbones supported broad shoulders. Muscles bunched in his upper arms, leaving a smooth meld from flesh to steel above his hinged elbow.

Her gaze rose to his again, and she saw the vulnerability there. He'd made this effort. She'd offer honesty in return.

"I knew that prosthetic was well made, and thought I might stare at it in appreciation. But, David, it hardly compares to the rest. I don't know if I'll be able to take my eyes off any of you."

He laughed, shaking his head. "I'm not sure I'm brave enough to show you the rest."

"I wouldn't care if you never did." She bit her lip. "No, that is a lie. I want to see this."

She stroked her hand down the front of his trousers, found him hard and ready. He stiffened and groaned in response.

"May I look now?" She was utterly a wolf.

"Yes."

By touch, she unbuckled the waist, watching his expression. His smile was teasing, his gaze hot.

"You won't see it if you're looking at my face."

"If it keeps growing, it will be tall enough to pop up between us."

His body shook on a laugh. She grinned, glanced down. *Oh.* She'd imagined this, too, but not everything. Fine black hair arrowed down from his navel and thickened at the base of his shaft. His heavy length overfilled her two hands, his testicles a firm weight in her palm. Tight skin stretched over the head—and had been so silky against her tongue, salty and slick. Her fingers closed around him.

David sucked a sharp breath. "No, Annika. I want to last inside you."

This time. She let go, spreading his trousers farther open and back over his rigid buttocks, exposing ridges of muscle than ran in a *V* from his lean hips to his groin. Annika moaned, her body clenching as she realized: all of that strength would be behind his long shaft, driving into her.

Then David was over her again, his lips on her breast a shock of heat after the cool air. Annika cried out, her back arching as he sucked her nipple deep into his mouth. Bracing his weight on one hand, he slipped the other down over her stomach, beneath her waistband. His fingers found her wet.

With a rough groan, he shoved her trousers down. Her drawers went with them. Even as Annika kicked them free of her ankles, his hand slid between her legs. Two long fingers sank deep. Oh, but this time she wanted more. His hand thrust against her. Her hips jerked into a desperate roll.

She gripped his shoulders. "David. Please, David."

His mouth left her breast, found her lips in a hot, rough kiss. "I'll bring you close first. Make sure you're wet. If anything hurts, I'll stop."

It hurt not having him. "I won't stop you."

"Promise me."

His thumb rubbed over her clitoris. Her back suddenly bowed, body trembling. She clung to his shoulders, shaking her head. She wouldn't promise this. She never wanted him to stop.

Desperation made her lie. "It has to hurt the first time."

Because it probably wouldn't. She'd taken his fingers, and there was only pleasure here, maddening desire, a deepening ache. But she would say anything to reassure him. Anything to be certain he was inside her.

"Then stop me if there's more than a little pain."

Relieved, she nodded. Anticipation and need boiled through her as he settled between her thighs—and a sharp coil of nervousness. Why did he fear hurting her so much? Annika hadn't worried about pain before, but now she did. Her body slowly stiffened, tense as she waited for him to tear her apart.

He came over her, resting his weight on his right forearm, his left reaching between them. His face was directly above hers, but he was looking down.

"I'll try to be slow." His voice was tight with strain. "Not rough like this morning."

Those three hard thrusts against her. *Mine.* A jolt of arousal shot through her at the memory, was echoed by a needy throb deep inside. She felt him against her, looked down. Angling his hips, he guided his shaft to her entrance. The wide tip pushed through her slick folds—too far. He slid up over her mound, the head glistening.

He groaned. His chest rose on heavy, rasping breaths. He held himself still, as if regaining control. After a long moment, he asked hoarsely, "Will you spread your legs wider?"

She did, aware of the soft prickle of his wool trousers on the inside of her thighs. Feeling suddenly vulnerable, she glanced up at his face. Tension held his jaw tight. His body shook as he lifted back, guided himself slowly to her again.

Desperate not to hurt her. Taking so much care.

With his steel thumb against the top of his shaft, he angled the head toward her. He slid through her folds again, nudged against her entrance. His back flexed, ever so slightly. Pressure built against her opening. Her breath came in rapid gasps.

"Annika."

She glanced up. His dark gaze locked with hers. Below, the pressure rose almost to pain and then suddenly became a burning sting, a tight stretch. Unbidden, a whimper of uncertainty escaped her lips.

David instantly stilled. "Are you all right?"

"Yes." She looked down. He hadn't gone in very far. Just the wide head, lodged inside her.

A quiver raced through his body. He strained above her, every muscle stiff and his tendons standing in sharp relief. "Am I hurting you?"

No. It just felt bigger than she'd expected. Stranger, too.

Her hands slid down his shoulders, gripped his biceps. "I can take more."

She watched him slide deeper, stretching her to the verge of pain but not over, it was just intrusive, and odd, and all that she could feel as he sank halfway into her was more pressure, pushing outward from her core as if he invaded all of her, not just this space between her thighs. Then he stopped, withdrew slightly, and she saw the slick moisture oiling his shaft, because he'd been inside her, and she was wet, so wet and ready for him to drive deep. Her body tightened, squeezing around him, and she gasped.

He froze. "Stop?"

"No. Oh, no." She raised her hips with a deep, needy moan, pushing herself up and forcing him deeper. "David. More."

Bracing both hands beside her shoulders, he rocked against her, each shallow thrust sinking farther into her, until he was locked against her, deep, so deep, he couldn't go any deeper until her back arched and her thigh dragged up over his hip, and then he was. Annika cried his name on a sobbing breath. Her inner muscles clenched around his thick shaft, unbearably full and tight inside her.

With a tortured moan, he drew back. She writhed as he pressed forward again, trying to ease the pressure, trying to increase it, trying to draw out the exquisite sensation of David sliding deep, then pistoning against her, into her, so slow at first then a quicker, more desperate pace. Then slowing again, his head hanging, the mattress bunched in a fierce grip.

Trying to not spend. An effort for him, torture for her when he stopped. She urged him on, and his head lifted, his gaze burning into hers. Determination set his jaw. His hand found her knee, pushed it higher. Pushed his thick length deeper.

Oh, but she couldn't take more. A keening cry erupted from her with each hard thrust. Then shallow strokes, as he exhaled in bursts through gritted teeth. Hard again, her breasts swaying with the force of it and warm steel pressing her knee higher and rough fabric a soft burn against her thighs. Then only David, so deep, her body tightening around him then shuddering as she cried out, clenching around the heavy shaft still driving back and forth inside her. David groaned and shook. With a final, deep stroke, he suddenly left her empty, his hot seed spilling onto her belly.

His chest heaving, he settled between her legs again, his weight braced on his forearms. Annika wrapped him tight. Sweat glistened over his skin. He stroked hair back from her forehead, kissed her mouth, then rolled over so that she lay atop him.

Utterly replete, she kissed him languidly, then said, "I want you back inside me."

He smiled against her lips. "Give me twenty minutes to recover. And you can be like this, on top."

She wanted to be in every position. "And then we'll figure out a way to bend over like wolves—like we almost did this morning."

"Ten minutes to recover," he said, and then grinned up at her when she laughed. "And I've already figured it out. You will kneel on the edge of the bed, and I will stand on the floor behind you."

She couldn't wait. "Kiss me until then."

"As long as you like."

"Forever," she said, and he got off to a perfect start.

* * *

Annika woke to a soft *whump!* A familiar sound, but not here.

Beside her, David lifted his head. "What was that?"

"The snow tunnel collapsing, I think."

"Was there a quake?"

"I didn't feel one."

She sat up with him. There were different sounds now. Distant shouts, loud cracks.

Not the crack of ice. Gunshots.

He threw back the blanket. "Hurry, into your clothes—"

A loud crash came from nearby, followed by a rumble that shook through the ice walls.

"Hurry," he finished. "That didn't come from beneath us."

She yanked on her trousers, a pair of stockings. Her tunic and coat. She spun in a circle, searching for her boots, then remembered—"I left my boots in the steam room."

"I'll get them. Don't move. Scream if you need help."

She nodded, then pulled on her hat, wrapped a scarf around her face. Blowing out the lamp, she waited in the dark.

David returned too soon. "The tunnel did collapse—it's blocking the way. I'll carry you up and around."

Hating that she would be a burden, even for a short time, she sighed as he swung her up. "You're carrying me everywhere."

"I'll carry you anywhere."

He always knew just what to say. Annika smiled, linked her arms around his shoulders. David left the bedchamber slowly. The tunnel had fallen in on itself halfway through to the next chamber, the sides still standing waist-high, braced by the surrounding ice. Cold air bit her cheeks. The heavy *huff* of a troll's engine joined the shouts, the shots—and above that, the sound of a larger engine and the hum of propellers.

"The airship," Annika whispered.

They reached the end of the tunnel. Broken blocks of snow mounded at his feet. David peered toward the clearing. Annika arched her neck to look, but her view was blocked by the still-standing tunnel wall.

"What do you see?"

"They're killing the guards."

Who? "The laborers?"

He nodded, eased back. Annika stared up at him, trying to grasp what it might mean. The laborers were rebelling against di Fiore. Källa had been right. But if they planned to destroy everything, kill anyone who'd been in authority or part of the capsule project . . . that included her and David, too. Paolo, Källa, and Olaf.

She hoped they would be more determined to escape than bent on revenge.

"We can't wait here," she whispered. "If they come, there's nowhere to hide."

"I know. Hold on."

Carrying her against his chest, David climbed up the fallen side of the tunnel—away from the clearing—and quickly moved behind the standing wall, where he crouched out of sight.

"We'll stay on this side and head around to the laboratory to find your sister," he said softly. "We can use the roofs as cover."

Not all of the roofs, she saw. Someone had driven a troll into the bathing room, where it had crashed through the ice blocks and tipped over into the dugout floor. Another troll lay on its side in the middle of the clearing, engine huffing and nose steaming. Bodies littered the snow, blood crimson against the white. Where were all of the laborers? She could still hear gunshots, shouts, but there was no one alive in the clearing.

A body dropped out of the sky and onto the bath chamber, smashing against the troll's flank with a dull clang.

Slapping her hands over her mouth to stifle a shriek, she looked up. The airship. The rebelling laborers had taken the airship. She flinched as another body fell—an aviator. David's arms tightened around her. Then more bodies, and she buried her face in David's neck as the crew slowly rained down, some of them already dead, some of them screaming until they hit the ground.

Someone above unhooked the ferry cruiser's tether; the cable slithered to the snow. The airship flew slowly south, the propellers turning lazily and steam billowing from the tail, as if they hadn't known to close the vents. The night quieted, except for the huffing of the fallen troll.

Only two of the big machines had been wrecked. "Do you see the third troll? We need it now that the airship is gone."

David shook his head, rose from his crouch. His gaze swept the clearing, the surrounding buildings. "They didn't leave any weapons, either."

"Källa should have something." Her gaze lit on the two-seater balloons. One had deflated—a stray bullet, perhaps—leaving an engine-powered balloon, and the pedal balloon. "Are we going to stay here tonight?"

"I hope to God we don't."

She agreed. They could be in Vik by midnight. "We need to fire up that balloon so it'll be hot enough by the time we're ready to go."

Her heart pounded as they crossed the clearing, and she listened for any sound over the *huff*ing of the troll. Nothing. No one shouted or shot. Either everyone was gone or dead, or there were others hiding, too. She started the balloon's burner, and they crossed the clearing again, down the steel steps. The hearth chamber was dark, cold. Annika could only see faint shadows, but David moved without hesitation to the far snow tunnel, pausing to look in each chamber they passed. He entered the tunnel leading to the laboratory, abruptly stopped.

"It's us, Källa," he said into the darkness. "The others have fled."

A lamp flared, revealing Annika's sister. She lowered her sword, dragged a pair of goggles down around her neck, the lenses reflecting an eerie green. "Where are your boots, Annika?"

"The bathing chamber. But it's destroyed."

"We don't have extra." She sighed, shook her head. "We'll figure out something. Come back to the laboratory. Have you seen Lorenzo?"

"We assumed he'd be with you," David said.

"No. He left a few hours ago with the troll to retrieve the foreman's body. But I haven't seen him since . . . and he took the suit. I can barely get a word out of Paolo."

They followed her into the laboratory. Olaf lay sleeping on one of the tables, bundled in a swaddle of furs. Beside him, Paolo worked over a sheet of calculations—weeping, Annika realized. The man's eyes were red, his cheeks wet. His tears had smeared the ink.

David sat Annika next to Olaf, took the stool beside Paolo's. Gently, he rested his hand on the older man's shoulder. "Paolo? Are you well?"

"Of course I'm well!" Paolo snapped the response. "Why wouldn't I be well? It is the boy who is gone."

Taken aback by the sudden change, Annika looked to Källa. She shook her head, lifted her hands.

"The boy?" David tried again. "Olaf is here."

"Not him. The other. Lorenzo." The anger suddenly dropped away, leaving his face lined, his eyes confused and tired. "He took the suit."

"Why?"

"He's going to go. Going to go." He tossed his arms up in the air, then buried his face in his hands. "The calculations weren't done. The trajectory is false."

"Paolo." Källa came forward, her eyes wide. "Do you mean the capsule? He's going in the capsule?"

"Yes, yes. He's set the charges." He faced her, frowning, as David abruptly stood and started for Annika. "Is the airship ready, then?"

Källa scooped up Olaf. "Are we supposed to be leaving?"

"The guards will come to take us to the airship at six," Paolo said. "He said the moon will rise on the di Fiore name."

Oh, blast. It was just after six now. Lorenzo had probably timed it so they'd have time to reach the ship . . . but not wait so long that they wouldn't see the launch.

"Källa," Annika said. "We have to take the balloons."

"Yes. I'll be right back for Paolo. We need our coats."

"We need our packs, too." Face stark with tension, David stopped in front of her. "Ideas for boots?"

She thought desperately. "I don't know."

"I do."

He reached down, hauled off his right boot. His foot wasn't what she expected—like a thick cotton stocking. She took the boot.

"Don't put it on yet." He stripped off the padding, revealing skeletal steel similar to his hand. A metallic clank sounded when he set his foot down again. "This keeps it from sliding around inside. It'll do the same for you."

And keep her feet warmer, too. Cozy. She pulled on the second one, her heart filled to bursting. "Thank you."

"I'd only expose my naked feet for you," he said, smiling slightly. "Now, go for our packs. I'll help Källa bring Paolo."

She nodded. The boots rose past her knees, but it wouldn't matter, unless she wanted to crouch. Right now, she needed to run.

Or stomp. Her feet felt heavy, huge. She took a lamp, made her way as quickly as possible back to their chamber. She stuffed everything she could find into their packs, ripped the blankets from the bed, clomped back out to the clearing.

Källa and Paolo were outside, watching David climb up the laboratory's snow-covered roof.

"Do you see him?" her sister called.

"Not Lorenzo!" David called back. "But the other troll is there!"

He was looking toward the capsule tower, Annika realized. She joined Källa, who carried Olaf in a sling across her chest, and a pack across her back. She gave Annika two gas-filtering masks.

"Paolo wants to get him," she said softly.

Annika looked at her in dismay. In two-seater balloons, with no idea when the explosive charges would blow? "I don't think—"

"He's my son." Paolo's voice quavered. "And the final calculations weren't made."

Beneath her feet, a deep rumble suddenly shook the ice. Annika staggered. On the roof, tiny balls of snow rolled down sloped sides. David started down.

The entire laboratory dropped, ice cracking like a cannon shot. Stumbling forward, Annika screamed his name. David took a running leap. He cleared the sudden sheer edge with inches to spare, landing hard in the snow. His legs seemed to buckle, but then he was up again, catching her hand.

"Go!"

They raced across the clearing. Tunnels collapsed with heavy thumps of snow. The cracking of ice sounded like a battlefield. The ground beneath her feet dropped, and she clung to David, terror stopping her heart, but they didn't fall away into a new crevasse— the entire clearing dropped with them. Ahead of her, Källa pulled Paolo up from his knees. Her sister reached the balloons, glanced back at Annika.

Two balloons, only one with an engine. With an older man and a child with her, there was no question which one Källa should take. Annika pointed, heard the buzzing of the small engine from the other balloon as she climbed into her own seat. She began to pedal, waiting while David helped settle Olaf into Paolo's arms. As soon as he was in, she released the tether—even if the ice dropped to the center of the Earth, they wouldn't fall with it now. She saw Källa engage her propellers, pedaled harder, David joining her. Annika lifted the altitude flaps, and they rose slowly into the air. Källa met her eyes, then banked south. Toward the tower.

Blast it. If Lorenzo wanted to escape, he had a troll.

Annika shook her head, but pulled the rudder to the left and began turning south. More crevasses had opened all along the glacier, she saw. Steam poured through the fissures, and even over the propellers and the cracking ice, she heard the whistling of the pressurized steam escaping through tight cracks. The tower rose ahead.

Annika peered across the distance. "The capsule's gone!"

"It dropped into the borehole just before the first blast!" David called back.

And must be still in there, plugging the hole. No steam rose beneath the tower yet. Annika's heart galloped in her chest. "What happens if it doesn't launch?"

"Then he roasts—Good God and da Vinci!"

A burst of steam erupted beneath the tower. The capsule streaked upward, moonlight glinting against steel and leaving a wisp of steam from its tail.

And was gone. So fast.

Her mouth dropped open, and she met David's astonished gaze. From the other balloon came Paolo's whoops and shouts, Källa's wild laughter.

Unbelievable. It had worked.

Annika leaned forward, searching the sky. Except for the moon and stars, only darkness. "Can you still see him?"

But David wasn't looking up. He was looking farther south, past the tower, where a column of smoke had begun pouring from the ice, lit from below by a beautiful orange light. The volcano, erupting.

Lorenzo had woken the witch.

"Källa!" David shouted to her sister. "Stay out of that ash! Go north, into the wind, then around to Vik!"

Alarm tightening her face, Källa nodded. Below them, the rumbling beneath the ice grew louder. Thunderous *crack*s split the air. Pedaling as hard as she could, Annika threw the rudder full over. Terror slicked her back in cold sweat.

David shouted again as they turned north. "Use your masks!"

Källa nodded again, reached for the engine lever. Annika saw her sister hesitate, glancing first at Olaf, then over at their balloon. *Stupid.* "Full steam!" Annika yelled at her. "Don't wait for us! We'll be behind you!"

She stole another look at the eruption before they headed full north. The column of ash and smoke had already thickened, a dark cloud building over it like the cap of a mushroom. The orange glow seemed to be spreading, lighting the billowing steam that rolled ahead in its wake.

They just had to outrace that.

She faced forward again, legs pumping. How quickly could they fly? They didn't seem to be moving much faster than a troll, but when she glanced behind again, they were almost a mile from the camp. Not slow—but the ash cloud had already doubled in size.

A few minutes later, pale flakes began falling around them like snow.

"Your mask!" David called over the whir of the propellers, the rumbling and cracking below.

She pushed down her scarf, buckled the straps behind her head, pulled on her hat again. The mask covered her from forehead to below her chin. The sound of her breathing seemed loud in her ears. A metallic odor tinged every breath, left the same taste on her tongue. Ash fell faster. She could barely see Källa far ahead of them, the glacier below.

A shock of white light suddenly lit the dark. Lightning. David gripped her hand. She couldn't see his face, only the dark glass and round, protruding filters of his mask.

"Can you see Källa?" she shouted.

He shook his head.

Sudden pressure shoved her deeper into her seat, as if the balloon had been thrown forward. A *boom!* followed, like a dozen cracks of thunder. David twisted around to look—and pedaled faster.

Fire streaked by to the left, falling in a steep arc. A burning rock, Annika realized. She waited, waited, panting in her mask and her chest aching, certain that the next would crash into them and ignite the hydrogen, sending them spinning to the ground in a fiery explosion—but there were no more rocks. She glanced back, saw more streaks closer to the plume of ash and steam, but none coming nearer to their balloon. Ahead, she could see the shadowed edge of the glacier, the ridge of mountains beyond. The ash wasn't so heavy now.

"Källa?"

David pointed northwest, higher into the air. Annika glanced over at the glacier below. Their balloon had lost altitude. She pushed down the flaps. No tension. Her heart sinking, she looked back at the assembly. The shaft had broken, the end sheared clean away, the sharp edge burnt black. The altitude flaps were gone.

"David?"

He glanced back. She couldn't see his expression behind his mask. "Can you fix it?"

What did she have? She didn't need the shaft; a rope could lift and lower the flaps. But there was nothing sturdy enough to replace those, except for the rudder—and if she used that, they couldn't pilot the balloon.

Her throat tight, she shook her head.

David looked forward, as if gazing out over the expanse of white. His hand squeezed hers. "As far as we can!"

They pedaled, Annika watching the surface of the glacier coming nearer and nearer. When they were a few feet above it, she held up her hand. David stopped pedaling with her. They touched down a moment later with a soft *thump*.

And they were all right. Not out of danger, but safer.

Annika stepped out, sinking up to her shins in snow. A fine

layer of ash whispered across the top. David shouldered their packs, shook his head when she reached for hers. He pushed his mask up. Grateful to finally see his face again, Annika followed suit.

"Will Källa send someone back?"

"She'll probably come herself."

He nodded, then looked north. "We need to get off this glacier. There are no explosives under the ice here, but God knows what sort of reaction he's set off. Keep your hood up and your mask on. The ash doesn't look so bad now, but the particles are sharp as glass. You don't want that in your eyes or in your lungs, especially since you don't have nanoagents to clean them out."

No, she didn't. She pulled the mask over her face again.

He turned to examine the balloon. "Is there anything on this we can use?"

"That pole." Her voice echoed hollowly in her ears. "To feel through the snow ahead of us."

"Good. What about for snowshoes or a sled runner?"

She crouched as best she could in his boots, studying the cart frame. Just light aluminum tubing. Nothing flat enough, nothing smooth enough, nothing long enough. Not anymore.

"The altitude flaps," she said, and he laughed a little, shaking his head.

"I'll break through the snow ahead of you, then. It's not too deep, so it shouldn't be too difficult."

But it was still slow going. The terrain roughened near the glacier's edge, with sharp rocky protrusions, deceptively stable beneath the snow, threatening a bloody gash or worse if they tripped. Quakes rattled loose shelves of ice, shook Annika's nerves into a shattered mess. They picked their way across the ice, backtracking when they came upon a crevasse. An hour passed, then two. Exhaustion began to settle in, and she had to stop herself from looking out over all the white, had to stop herself from thinking about the position they were in, and focus on putting one foot ahead of the other, testing every single step.

Finally they wound their way down a slope studded with jagged ice and boulders. David paused, slipped his arm around her when she stopped at his side.

He pointed ahead. "We'll hike up on that rise and stop for the night. I doubt we're in danger of a flood here, but it's best to take high ground. Ready?"

She was. The snow deepened as they climbed. Though David plowed through ahead of her, breaking a trail, the heavy boots and the incline soon felt as if she wore cannonballs strapped to her legs. Her breathing was labored when he finally stopped, the inside of her mask humid with sweat.

He set down the packs, drew her against him. Carefully, he slid back her mask, the cold air heaven against her cheeks.

His concerned gaze searched her face. "You're all right?"

As long as she didn't think. "Just . . . out of breath."

"Rest. If you watch for dogs, I'll build the snow house."

She shook her head. "I'll watch for dogs. But I'll help. I'm too sweaty—if I stop now, I'll get cold. I need to keep moving."

Without a shovel, though, there wasn't much for her to do until he'd dug out the base and began cutting blocks out with his steel hand. She helped him stack the blocks in a ring a few feet in diameter. An hour's hard work, though he seemed tireless. Her arms were aching with fatigue by the time she slowly lowered the last block into place from inside the domed house, then smoothed the interior with mittened hands.

As he finished the entrance, she spread out the blankets and lit the small oil lamp. Quietly, she sorted through the packs, searching for the stores left over from when they'd fled *Phatéon*. Di Fiore's men had gone through their things, but they'd have no reason to take potatoes or—

Three pieces of flatbread were left. Annika stared at them, then searched again. Nothing more. Despair and fear thickened her throat. She forced them away.

Källa would come for them.

She stuffed the food back into the packs. She couldn't think of this now. Her mind felt dull. She'd seen too much today, done too much, and she was worn down from exhaustion.

Tomorrow would be brighter. She'd be able to see the way forward better.

David stuck his head through the entrance, met her eyes. Her heart gave a crazy leap of hope. They were still together. And they *would* be all right.

He unbuckled his coat. "It's already warmer in here."

"A little," she said. "But it'll warm up a lot more with both of us."

His smile started, then froze as a quake gently shook the ground. Silent, they braced their hands against the blocks. A few small clumps of snow fell, a few crystals drifted down.

"Nicely built," she said when it stopped. "Did they teach you this in your survival course?"

"Yes."

He grinned, crawled the rest of the way in. It was a tight fit. They'd have to sleep around each other. With his coat beneath them, providing another layer of protection from the freezing ground, and her coat over them, they'd remain more than warm enough.

She waited until he removed his coat, then curled up into a ball. David settled in behind, wrapping his arms around her, tucking his knees against hers. Despite her exhaustion, she wasn't ready to sleep yet. She listened to his breaths, soaked up the warmth of his body.

His breath stilled when a growl grumbled through her stomach. She slid her fingers through his.

"There are a lot of dogs," she reminded him, and felt his tension ease.

He pressed a kiss to the side of her neck. "It may come to that, unfortunately. Källa might have to wait before the eruption stops before she can come for us. It could be a few days."

Or more. She'd heard of eruptions in this region that lasted for weeks. But even if it did, they'd be all right. They were warm. They had food.

"I also have bread in my pack from *Phatéon*."

"Brown?"

"No. It's frozen, though, so at least it will have a better texture." She smiled when his laugh rumbled against her back. "We'll keep it for tomorrow."

"Tomorrow, yes." His voice was slightly rough. "Until then, we'll rest."

Annika closed her eyes, willed sleep to come.

And tried not to think.

David's feet were cold. He couldn't remember the last time they had been. In the boots, he usually didn't notice temperature at all. Now he was toasty beneath Annika's coat, except for his feet, which touched the snow wall. Though the cold didn't hurt, the impulse to bring his legs up beneath their cover and warm his toes against her skin was just the same.

Annika probably wouldn't enjoy waking up that way.

If she wasn't already awake. He listened to her quiet breathing. Too shallow for sleep—as if she were trying not to make any noise and was carefully holding herself still. Probably trying not to think of where they were. Probably feeling the same dread that David did.

She knew this island. She had to know what a dangerous position they were in, though they'd both glossed over it the previous night. Källa might very well come for them and find the balloon they'd left on the glacier, but she couldn't know where they'd headed afterward. Nor would they be easy to spot if she did continue north, especially as they'd taken shelter in a snow house. Though he'd go outside as often as possible, David couldn't stand in the cold indefinitely, hoping to see her in the sky—and Annika should stay inside, conserving her warmth and energy. With nanoagents, David could get by longer on little food, was more resistant to the freezing temperatures.

If they stayed, Källa might not be able to find them. But they could also try to walk back to Vik. David didn't like that option any better. The glacier wasn't large—only twenty miles across—but they'd have to go around it, through the pass, where the rivers would likely be swollen with meltwater, and they'd be in the path of any floods sweeping across the valley floor. Thirty miles through the snow, just to walk clear of the glacier—and then thirty more miles to Vik, across the floodplains . . . and on three pieces of bread.

That bread wouldn't last any longer here, though. Whatever route they chose, they'd have to forage or hunt—and under the ash and snow, the dogs would likely be their only prey.

The dogs would be looking at them in the same way.

With a soft sigh, Annika snuggled back against him. She must have realized that he'd woken. "Just a few minutes more."

He had to laugh. "As long as you like. What are you dreaming of?"

"You."

Smiling, he pushed her hair back. They'd made love yesterday—the greatest pleasure he'd ever known. Nothing could have prepared him for it. Not just the luscious clasp of her body, but her trust, her complete abandonment to the need between them.

Only yesterday. It seemed so long ago, now—too long. Bending his head, he kissed his way up her neck, took a long taste of her mouth. Not to arouse, but the sheer wonder of being with Annika. David could hardly comprehend how much he loved her.

But he sure as hell wasn't going to lose her now.

She looked up when he broke the kiss. "That was better than the dream."

"As it should be." Though reluctant to leave her, he sat up, tucked the coat back against her side. "I'll go out and look around."

"Take my red scarf. Tie it to the pole."

A bright flag that could be seen from a balloon. "Good thinking."

He dropped another quick kiss to her mouth and crawled through the angled entrance. The sun hadn't yet risen. An inch of ash lay over the snow, powdery and light like flour. No trees grew on this slope, and if there was any vegetation, it was all covered. Dark clouds huddled overhead.

To the south, a plume of steam and ash still rose over the glacier, but not the billowing volume of the night before. If any lava still flowed, it had cooled enough to lose its fierce glow. Some of his tension eased away. Lorenzo had triggered an eruption, but not a catastrophic one, and it was already decreasing in strength. His gaze searched the edge of the glacier. No evidence of a flood, but he hadn't expected one in this direction. Most of the damage, if any, would have occurred on the southern side.

For now, he couldn't let himself dwell on his worry for his aunt, Dooley, everyone in Vik. They knew floods might follow an eruption. They knew to find high ground. They knew to stay out of the ash—and nobody lacked for goggles and scarves. If Lorenzo had fulfilled his promise, they wouldn't lack for food, either.

He and Annika still did. Switching to his thermal lens, he searched the barren slope for signs of heat, for a dog or a rabbit holed up in the snow. Anything to bring back to her, to reassure her that they'd be all right.

There was nothing.

A heavy weight settled in his chest. He moved across the slope and farther up the rise. The sun slowly rose, throwing a band of brilliant pink across the eastern sky. He listened for a chirping bird, a bark. Nothing.

Bundled in a blue scarf and fur hat, aviator goggles over her eyes, Annika emerged from the snow house as he came down again. Her gaze swept the slope.

"No tracks," she said.

Not one. "Maybe frightened by the eruption and still hiding under the snow."

"Or there weren't any here." She pulled off her mitten, reached into her coat. "I thawed it, despite the texture. I don't want it to break our teeth."

The flatbread, ripped in half. David shook his head. "I'm infected."

"You still need to eat."

"Not as much."

"You're twice as big as I am."

"And a quarter of it is metal."

"David." Her gaze was warm and steady. "You have to consider the rest."

"Don't say the rest, damn it."

She did, anyway. "This will last us three days. If Källa can't come for us by then, if we haven't found something else to eat, we'll be in serious trouble—and we'll both need to be as strong as possible."

"It can last you six days."

"And by the end of six days, what then? I'm still hungry. And you're dropping into a fever as the nanoagents try to save you from starving."

Certainty filled her voice. David couldn't even argue. He'd gone a few days without before, but never that long. "How do you know that?"

"My mother's infected, too. She got caught out during a storm once, got turned around in her troll. She was raging with bug fever when we found her, and had to put her in the snow to cool her down." Beneath the certainty, the patience, he heard the strain in her words. "You may be the only one who can save us, David, so you will eat this *now*."

God. He knew she was right. He still had to choke it down, feeling as if he stole every single bite from her mouth.

Her relieved exhalation slipped through the folds of her scarf and frosted the wool. "It'll be all right. It takes longer than three days for even us rabbits to starve."

He couldn't think of it. His throat thick, he studied the column of ash again, the direction of the wind: south-southwest. "We probably won't see much more ash here, but it's being carried right over Vik. Källa might not be able to come for us in that balloon until it eases up."

"I know." She moved in against his side. He wrapped his arm around her waist, brought her in tight against him. "Do we try to walk out, or do we stay?"

The question that had tormented him all morning. "I don't know. What do you think?"

"My instinct is always to find a safe place and wait. I know she will come. The question is if she *can*. The ash might disrupt the balloon engine."

"If we left, would it be harder for her to find us later?"

"No. There's only one way to go: through the pass. After she searched this end of the glacier, she'd turn that way. But it might take days. She only has a balloon, and she'd have to come alone or she wouldn't be able to take both of us back."

He'd send Annika off first, anyway. "Dooley might have the clockwork dogs out of *Phatéon*'s cargo hold by now."

"And he'd come, too?"

"Yes, if he can. The steam is still rising—that means the ice is still melting. We're on high ground here, but there's still a chance the pass could flood. And the rivers might be running at spring-time levels or higher."

She nodded. "We don't even try to come this way in the spring. Even in a troll."

"We could avoid them, go back up on the glacier and around the river heads, but I hate to risk the ice."

It would be a rough hike in the summer. Add the uncertainty of deep snow and the eruption, and the glacier could be as dangerous as the rivers.

No doubt, they'd be safer here . . . until they ran out of food. Hoping to discern her thoughts, he studied her profile as she stared out over the glacier. He couldn't see any fear, though she had to be feeling it. She wasn't giving in.

Neither would he. "How far can you walk every day?"

She glanced up at him. "During the daylight hours only?"

Which didn't last long—from mid-morning to mid-afternoon— but they probably shouldn't risk traveling after the sun set, no matter that he could see. And even David would be exhausted after a day of trudging through deep snow. "Yes."

"Perhaps ten miles . . . over flat terrain."

Six days to Vik, at best. If they never had to backtrack, never had to slow. He looked to the clouds overhead. "We'll need to be out of the first snow. It'll be all ice and ash."

"Poisonous?"

"Like the fissure eruptions? Possibly. Probably acidic. When we melt snow to drink, we need to dig deep."

"But at least the snow will dampen this." She kicked at the layer of ash, sending up a fine cloud. "So we won't be walking through it."

"Yes." The masks could prevent them from breathing it, but the dust would penetrate every layer of clothing. "So what do you think?"

She looked to the sky, then out over the glacier again. "Let's wait one or two days—until after the first snow. Maybe by then the eruption will stop and floods won't be such a danger. In the meantime, we'll see if there's anything to eat here. If not, we'll need to go, anyway."

Because they'd have no other choice, except waiting to die.

No choice. David stared out over the barren expanse of ash and snow, fighting the helplessness sweeping over him.

"There's another option," she said.

Hope surged. "What option?"

"You can travel much faster than I can. You go to Vik for help and food, then come back for me here."

That wasn't an option. Even he would be slowed by the snow and the rivers, and would have to avoid that first snowfall. Two days traveling there, at the very least, and two days back. He wouldn't leave her alone for a day. Four was out of the question.

"No," he said.

"I could survive. It's warm in the snow house."

"Not warm enough. Not if you're alone." And if anything went wrong, anything at all, she'd have no way of knowing that he wasn't coming for her—and by then, she might not be strong enough to strike out on her own. "I wouldn't be able to leave you, anyway."

She sighed and nodded. "I wouldn't be able to leave you, either."

But she'd apparently hoped he would, knowing that she might not make it. His arm tightened around her. "We'll be all right."

They couldn't have left, anyway. It snowed that night and through the next day. David ventured outside a few times to dig the entrance clear, but spent most of the day in the snow dome, reading to Annika from his journal. The next noon, the snow stopped. He crawled out and looked south. Only a few wisps of steam and ash still rose from the volcano. No animal tracks marked the fresh snow, though he searched through the afternoon for any sign. When he returned to the snow house, they shared the last piece of flatbread, stuffed their belongings into one pack, and decided to leave the next day.

He couldn't sleep, though Annika faded quickly. She'd been sleeping often to conserve her energy—or because it was waning. And even when awake, she frequently rested with her eyes closed and a faint smile on her lips.

David held her through the night, listening to her breathe. When she woke, he watched her struggle to moisten her dry lips. They'd been digging up snow, drinking plenty of water. But the lack of food was still taking its toll.

She smiled without opening her eyes. "Just a few more minutes while I dream of you."

He couldn't laugh this time. The hungry rumble of her stomach was loud in the small space, and was answered by an agonizing ache in his chest.

His heart was pumping blood that could save her. With a single transfusion, she'd be infected. He had no equipment to do it.

His throat raw, he whispered, "Ready?"

"Yes."

She wasn't. She emerged from the short entrance tunnel and swayed to her feet. He caught her waist. Bending over, she braced her hands on her knees, drew deep breaths.

"Just dizzy for a moment. Too long inside, I think." After a long second, she straightened. "It's already passed."

It would only become worse. He looked to the sky, desperately praying for Källa's balloon to appear in the distance. Nothing but clouds. He wanted to stop now, to send Annika back inside where it was warm, where she could sleep.

But if they didn't go while she still had strength, they never would.

She gripped the pole they'd used to mark the location, offered it to him. When he shook his head, she nodded. "I'll walk behind you?"

"Yes."

With David breaking through the snow ahead of her, they managed a slow, steady pace. He stopped frequently to rest, for Annika to catch her labored breaths. The snow came almost to her knees with every step, and despite the trail he made, despite the strength that allowed her to drive a troll for hours, it was still rough going.

David paused again at two, but not because he'd stopped. Annika had halted behind him, leaning heavily against her pole, the red scarf fluttering. He couldn't see her smile behind the blue scarf, but knew that she was by the tilt of her eyes, the lift of her cheeks.

"I'm so glad . . . I have . . . your boots," she said breathlessly.

He was, too. "You're all right?"

"I was just dizzy again. I'm better now." She glanced toward the sun. "Another hour or two?"

Unable to speak past the ache in his throat, he nodded. He waited for her signal that she was ready before starting off again, listening to the steps behind him, each one seeming to come more slowly than the last. When she paused again a half hour later, gripping her pole, he pointed to the nearest slope.

"We'll camp on that rise," he said.

Annika only nodded. Too out of breath to talk.

She didn't attempt to help him build the snow dome. David thought he'd have to tell her to sit, to let him cut and carry the blocks alone, but she did without a protest, wrapping a blanket around her.

The ragged knot in his chest didn't ease, even when they were inside. She curled against him beneath her coat. "We did well today," she said.

"Yes." Mostly downhill, a relatively easy trek. "Eleven miles, perhaps."

He felt her nod. Her eyes were already closing. On a yawn, she said, "We'll find something to eat tomorrow."

They didn't. Their tracks remained the only footprints in the snow. They'd rounded the north end of the glacier and were finally heading south. Boulders and chunks of glacial ice jutted up out of the snow, smoothing out across the valley floor, rising again to the western glacier. Faint tremors shook the ground twice, dislodging bits of snow that rolled into balls before coming to a stop under their own weight. Annika paused more often, but always started again after a minute or two. She fell twice, and regained her feet before he could reach her side. That afternoon, David stopped an hour before the sun had set, terrified that she would walk until she dropped.

The next morning, she did.

He heard the soft *whump!* as she fell. Heart thundering, he plowed back through the snow. She wasn't getting up this time, wasn't moving. Voice hoarse, he shouted her name, rolled her onto her back. Her eyes opened. Confusion clouded the brown depths before they cleared.

"I'm sorry," she said, and sat up, put her hand to her head. "I think I tripped."

No. She'd fainted. His chest aching, he helped her to her feet, and looked for a place to build a snow dome. They hadn't planned to stop so early, but she couldn't continue like this.

They couldn't continue like this.

He stared down the valley, across the miles they still had to go. They couldn't stop now. She wouldn't be any stronger later. Resolve firmed his jaw. Without a word, he shrugged out of the pack and untied the blankets, and began strapping them to her back.

"David?"

"I'll carry you behind me."

"You can't."

"I damn well can." And would. He picked up the pole, crouched in front of her. "On."

Her voice trembled. "I can stop here while you go ahead—"

"*On!*" Fear and determination made it harsh.

But she climbed on. Didn't argue, didn't insist she could walk. She wasn't heavy, but combined with the pack and the deep snow, the additional bulk shifted his balance. The pole offered a necessary counterbalance and support. Her arms circled his shoulders, careful not to cut off his breathing. It took a few steps to find his new stride through the snow—slower, but steady.

Twice, she fell asleep, and he held her up with his steel arm angled around behind him. He didn't stop until orange streaked the western sky, until exhaustion forced him to a halt. He wrapped her in the blankets before building the dome, and knew a moment of utter desolation and panic when he finished and couldn't wake her. He shook her shoulders, shouting her name, and relief stung his eye with hot tears when her lashes finally fluttered open. He dragged her into the snow house through the tunnel entrance, covered her in their coats. She clung to him, shivering violently, her face against his throat.

"I'm so sorry," she whispered.

"Don't." So rough, it was all that he could manage.

He must have slept. He woke to the sweet pleasure of her hands cradling his face. With clear eyes, she studied him by the dim light of the lamp, a sad smile curving her lips.

"I love you, David Kentewess."

Those very words had once filled his heart with utter joy. Spoken now, they stopped it with terror.

He jerked up to sitting, holding her against him when she swayed. "No, Annika."

"I've had so many dreams of you these past few days," she continued softly. "I've lived a lifetime in them."

"We *will* have a lifetime." There was no other option. David couldn't bear any other option. He gripped her arms, gave a little shake. He had to wake her up, make her see. "It will be better than your dreams."

Her eyelashes fell on a long, slow blink, as if even that was an effort. "Hildegard and my mother will come to Vik. I need you to give her my beads."

To bury them? Not this. God, please not this. He couldn't endure it.

"No."

"David—"

"Don't you tell me this. Don't. God, Annika, you can't ask me to—" The pain splintering in his chest broke his voice. Every breath shuddered, hot and hurting. "I swore that if you left me, I would let you go. But not like this, Annika. Not if you go like this."

Her breath hitched. With gentle fingers, she wiped the tears from his cheek. "You have to."

"I can't!"

His denial thundered in the small dome. She flinched, her shoulders rounding, her body curling in around her stomach as if to hold herself together. Her serene smile crumpled into a desperate, keening sob. "David, *please*. I'm trying to be brave."

He gave his head a violent shake. "Not for this."

"I have to be. I have to. I don't want to end this way, weak and frightened. But I'm so scared. And I don't want to leave you."

"Then don't," he whispered hoarsely. Then no more words would come, only the helpless anguish as he held her, sobbing in his arms. But she didn't even have the strength for that. All too soon, she quieted.

She stared up at him, her eyes red, her voice soft. "Everyone has their time, and even rabbits can't hide when it comes. I have to face it."

"Not today." Determined, he reached for her coat. "Not tomorrow."

"David—"

"Not today, Annika," he repeated through clenched teeth. "Not tomorrow. Not *any* day, as long as I still live."

Shoving her into the coat, he wrapped her in a scarf and strapped on the pack. No dragging her through the entrance this time. He kicked down the side of the dome, hauled her onto his back. She was still strong enough to cling to him.

Every step was an effort. The nanoagents made him stronger, but the strength couldn't last with nothing to fuel it. He trudged on anyway, fighting past the burning ache in his chest, the muscles that shook when he stopped to rest. A few minutes after noon, her arms fell away from his shoulders. David's heart didn't beat again until he felt her thin pulse. Abandoning the pole, he reached behind, bent over and held her against his back. He trudged on.

There was nothing but the next step. The next. And the next. Nothing but moving on. The light faded, but filled with the memory of her falling asleep on the snow, of the terror when he'd been unable to wake her, he didn't dare stop to build a dome. Darkness fell.

His breath was a constant scalding scrape through his throat. His skin was on fire, dry and tight. Too many layers, too many clothes. He stopped to unbuckle his overcoat. Annika slipped from his back, and he cried out, turning to catch her before she fell. Realization roared through him with her soft moan.

He'd been seconds from taking off his coat, from stripping out of his clothes. *Jesus.*

The fever. But he couldn't stop. He had to go on.

Sliding his arms beneath her shoulders and knees, he lifted her up again, against his chest. God, she was so heavy. But there was only one more step. One more.

The next. And the next.

The moon rose, burning against the sky. David glanced up, saw the round face staring down at him with a fishhook smile. Laughing, laughing. He blinked, flipped his lens, and it was just the moon again, the shadows of the craters standing in sharp relief against the gray. Annika's head lolled off his shoulder. He paused, felt for her pulse. They still lived; there was still hope. He trudged on. As if oiled, the moon slid down the sky. Faerie lights danced in the dark. The witches and trolls, released from the Underworld by the eruption, prancing through the snow. He laughed with them, a rasp through his parched throat. Far ahead, mangy forms slunk through the night in a single line, not showing on his thermal lens but their shapes clear.

Dogs. They were trying to hide, but he could see them. A grin stretched his dry lips.

He'd kill one now, and feed it to Annika, and everything would be well. The dogs came closer. Not barking but growling all around him, the moon growing brighter, brighter, huffing down the back of his neck, shaking the ground.

Not the moon.

David turned and found a monster. Too astonished for fear, he stared up into the terrible face. He hadn't believed that anything came from the fissure eruptions, but there was no other explanation for this. Steam poured from giant nostrils, icicles hanging in the ragged beard below. White fur formed a thick ruff around its enormous neck.

A ruff. Perhaps it was a royal troll.

He laughed wildly, until it huffed again and squatted, ejecting a burst of steam. David stumbled back, almost lost his balance.

Almost lost Annika.

His grip tightened, and he steadied, cradling her against him. His vision wavered. He shook his head, tried to clear it.

The monster vomited his mother from its chest.

He stared, disbelieving. *His mother.* Her beautiful face was softer now. Not broken and bleeding, and she wore a coat of fur and homespun trousers instead of a nightshirt stained with crimson. Gray streaked her black braid.

But his mother was dead—and he suddenly realized why she was here, traveling in the belly of a monster from below.

"You can't have her," he whispered.

"David Ingasson—"

"No!" he shouted, backing up. "You can't have her!"

Another woman joined her, her face ghostly pale. "Annika!"

"You can't have her!"

His mother came forward, her dark eyes shimmering. "You must give her to us."

And rip out his heart? A desperate howl tore from his chest, a prayer to the gods that shredded his raw throat. He fell to his knees in a cushion of snow that froze his thighs and crept upward, stabbing ice through his gut. His vision faded. He shook his head wildly, hating the fog.

"David." Her hand cupped his cheek, her skin deathly cold. "Oh, you're burning. Frida, take her."

"Don't. Please don't. I'm sorry, so sorry I didn't keep my promise. But please don't take her. Please." He bowed over Annika's still form, holding her close. His arms shook. "Or take me, too."

"We will. But you have to let her go." She bent her face to his. "We'll help her. We'll help you. Trust me."

David didn't know if he could, but if he held Annika any tighter, he'd hurt her. He couldn't do that. He'd never do that. With a broken sob, he loosened his hold.

He felt her weight lifted from him. And then nothing after that, except the cold.

Chapter Fourteen

The darkness receded from an insistent huffing and swaying. Beneath him, a soft mattress cushioned his back. A firmer body lay against his side.

David opened his eye, rotated his light-blocking lens. Annika looked down at him, her lips trembling, her brown eyes shimmering.

"Are you with us again, then?"

She couldn't be real. His hand lifted to her face. Warm skin. Her tears spilled over, wetting his fingers. She turned her cheek into his palm, her breath shuddering.

"My mother and Hildegard found us."

Trying to moisten his dry tongue, he turned to look. A pale woman with hair the color of rust stood in the troll's hearth chamber. Movement near the head drew his gaze higher. A tall woman—not his mother—climbed down the ladder.

"Aunt?"

He could barely form the word. His aunt nodded. "I am Inga's sister."

Annika's hand flattened on his chest—his bare chest. Only a blanket covered his hips.

"We had to put you in the snow. Or they did, in truth." Annika's voice sounded high and tight, as if skimming the edge of crying. "I was in here, with my sister pouring fish broth into me. It's been two days. I just woke up this morning, myself. Dooley and Källa are outside. They're on the dogsled."

And she was alive. He looked up into her eyes. Her mouth curved on an unsteady smile. God, he'd never thought he would see that again. But she was here, and so was he. Her curls fell over her forehead. Throat aching unbearably, his chest swelling, he brushed them back. Another tear spilled down her cheek and broke him. She was here. Oh, God, she was here. A harsh sob tore from his throat. He drew her down, buried his face in her neck. She clung to his shoulders, crying against him.

"We're all right, David," she spoke past her tears. Her fingers slid into his hair, holding him tight through each wracking sob. "We're all right."

Her soothing murmurs continued. She lifted her head as his shudders eased. Dimly, he was aware that the huffing had stopped, that the others had left them alone. She raised a tin cup to his lips—warm water, and she only allowed him a few sips, but even that was enough to soothe his parched tongue, his raw throat.

"I couldn't bear losing you," he said roughly.

"And I couldn't bear to lose you." She bent her head, a soft kiss flavored with tears. "We're not all the way there yet. They've been pouring broth down our throats, but we need to keep sleeping, slowly eating more."

And he needed to get up. Though shaky, David could sit, then stand. He found his trousers and shirt at the end of the bunk.

Curled up on the mattress, Annika watched him dress. He heard her envious sigh. "I need nanoagents."

Yes, she did. "When we see her, Lucia can perform the transfusion."

"Oh. No, now that we are out of danger, I'll wait until I visit Hannasvik again. My mother will like to celebrate sharing her blood with me—and it gives everyone an excuse to drink and eat too much."

A *visit* to Hannasvik. Not returning to stay. "You won't be able to travel through the New World."

At least not without the bribes that the Society paid during his expeditions through the interior, and those were simply for traveling through the different territories. He could probably find some way to bring her with him . . . *if* he continued that, too.

But he had other options. And he'd choose one that let him stay close to her.

Now, he just had to figure out what that option might be.

"I don't mind," she said. "I like traveling, but I'm ready to be home. Your boots are under the bed."

He glanced down at his steel feet. "Do you have a pair yet?"

"No. But I'm not leaving this troll anytime soon. I've been forbidden."

"By your mother?"

She wrinkled her nose. "Yes."

"Good." He could see that the little bit she'd done since he'd woken had worn her out. He lifted his hand to the beads at his neck. "They came to Vik to find me?"

"Yes. And learned that we were up on the glacier instead."

"So the town wasn't flooded?"

"No. But something else happened. I'll let Dooley tell that story, though. I've heard it three times from him already."

He grinned, strode over to the bed to kiss her. "I'm sure you will soon hear it again."

*   *   *

The muscles in his legs shook when he dropped from the chest hatch into the crunchy snow. Though David was aware of the others turning to look, he ignored them all for the relief of a nearby boulder. They must have stopped near the ocean. He could hear it in the distance, taste it on the air. Rectangular basalt columns stood ahead of him, their sides carved into regular widths, as if with a measuring stick and a sculptor's adze. But it was just nature.

Bludging incredible. The whole damn world was incredible, because he and Annika were still in it.

He started back, his steps slowing as he took his first good look at the troll. By God, it was the ugliest thing he'd ever seen. Mottled patches of hide had been sewn and draped over the frame, hanging loosely. Its enormous, protruding rump steamed. The head was a riot of fur and feathers, and walrus tusks hung over the beard, giving the impression of giant fangs. Though it couldn't have been much bigger than Austra Longears, the illusion that this thing might be living made it seem twice as large, twice as horrid.

"It was almost the death of me when I first saw it," Dooley said beside him.

Speechless, David nodded then glanced at his friend. High emotion had flushed the other man's face. Dooley clapped him on the back, shook his hand.

"Oh, but it's good to see you up and about, Kentewess. I didn't think my heart would beat again when I saw them rolling you naked in the snow. It frightened ten years off of me, only a few days after twenty years had been scared off by that troll."

David grinned. "So I'm only half as ugly. Well, that's something."

Dooley laughed with him. "I figure that after this expedition is over, I'll only have three years left."

He'd no doubt make the best of them. David glanced over to

where his aunt spoke with Annika's mother and Källa. Just behind them stood four clockwork dogs in harnesses attached to a sled. "So how do they run?"

"Faster than a live dog can, and thank God for it."

David recognized the change in Dooley's voice—he had a story to tell. He wanted to hear it, but not yet. His aunt's resemblance to his mother struck him again, a hard spike through his chest. He approached her slowly, couldn't stop staring.

Her gaze searched his face in return. "You look very much like Inga," she said softly.

"Not as much as you, Aunt."

"So I do." Smiling, she gestured to the woman beside her. "This is Frida Kárasdottor."

Without waiting for his response, Annika's mother wrapped him in a hard embrace before stepping back, her small hands gripping his. "Thank you, David Ingasson, for bringing my daughter back to me. I will never be able to repay you. If ever you need anything, I will scour the world to find it for you. If you ever need help, I will sacrifice all of my strength and blood to give it. If you have any enemies, I will hunt them and strip their flesh from their bones. This I swear to you."

Overwhelmed, he shook his head. "I would offer you the same for coming to find us. For helping her when I couldn't."

"She was never in any real danger," Hildegard said. "She'd have clung to life for thirty years, if she had to, crawling into the snow and hibernating until a meal fell into her mouth. She's as stubborn as her mother. Look at that."

David turned toward the troll. Annika hadn't come out, but sat at the edge of the chest hatch with her bare legs dangling over, watching them.

Watching him.

"She hasn't let you out of her sight since she awoke," Källa said.

He could hardly bear to be away from her, either. His gaze on Annika's face, he asked, "How is your son? Paolo?"

"Well. I'm sorry I couldn't come for you sooner."

It didn't matter. They'd come in time. "Where are we now?"

"Coming on about five miles from Vik," Dooley said. "We stopped when you woke. The dogs needed the rest."

He heard Källa's snort. "I'll push the sled the remainder of the way, Mr. Dooley. Go on in with your friend. He can't stand it much longer. Annika can't, either."

David truly couldn't. He returned to the troll, holding her gaze with every step. She drew back from the hatch and stood, making room for him.

He caught her up against his chest, loving the warmth of her skin, the silly bows on her drawers, the curve of her mouth, and the dimple in her chin. "Is this Rutger Fatbottom?"

"Yes."

A footstep sounded behind him. "Turn away, Patrick. I need to kiss her properly."

Slow and sweet, her arms linked around his neck, her lips clinging to his.

At his back, another step sounded. A throat cleared. A female throat. "You're supposed to be resting, little rabbit."

Annika quickly pulled away and scampered to the bunk, where she sat with her face in her hands. Heart thumping, David sat next to her. In a wooden seat across the hearth chamber, Dooley laughed himself into tears.

"In front of my *mother*," she whispered, her cheeks blazing. "That was *so* improper."

He grinned. "And I'm just an ignorant man from the New World."

But he wouldn't do it again. Only proper behavior, from this moment on—and until he had something more to offer her, a promise that he could keep.

Thankfully, Frida didn't look upset, just amused—and was holding his aunt's hand. Hildegard dropped a kiss to her mouth before climbing up the ladder. Such an ordinary, familiar gesture. David had done the same to Annika.

Familiar, but still surprising to see them. David supposed he'd become used to it soon enough.

He braced his back against the steel wall behind the bed, realizing that his short venture outside had left him out of breath. Annika was, too. She drew up her knees and rested her cheek on her folded arms, already looking worn again. Frida stoked the furnace, then sat on Annika's opposite side. She removed her heavy coat, revealing a green tunic, and slipped her arm around her daughter's shoulders.

Frida's gaze moved from Annika's face to his. A wistful sadness crossed her expression, followed by fierce pride. She tweaked one of Annika's curls and said in Norse, "I didn't think I would lose you so quickly again."

"You won't." She squeezed her mother's hand.

David fought the painful twist in his chest. He wouldn't think the worst. Nothing about the future had been settled. He didn't even know yet what they'd find in the town ahead. He looked to Dooley. "What happened at Vik, then?"

"Don't rush into it now." Leisurely, Dooley withdrew his pipe and a small bag of tobacco. "There's only the first telling of it once."

"And yet the second telling always takes longer."

"That is the natural progression of it, as I recall details that I'd failed to mention before."

"Details, or embellishments?"

"It's a true thing that I've fattened up a story or two. But this one doesn't need any," Dooley said. He puffed up a small cloud of pungent smoke. "Well now, then. You and Miss Fridasdottor had been gone two days when di Fiore's ferry cruiser flies in over Vik, and leaves our cargo sitting pretty in the street. Of course we realize that this means you've likely been taken, because we don't imagine di Fiore had a change of heart—though that's what the ferry cruiser's captain says happened. Now, we thought for certain that you were being held at the rail camp."

"Because you didn't know of the glacier camp," David realized.

"We didn't. Now, I've worked up some anger by then. All but steam coming out of my ears, I suppose, as everyone walking at me was suddenly taking another path. But that Captain Vashon, she's got the same bee under her arse. So she comes to me with this flinty look in her eyes and she says, 'Prepare your sled, Mr. Dooley. I'm taking it to the camp and I'm bringing our people back.' And my reply is that she sure as bloody hell isn't leaving without me."

Dooley was working himself up a bit now. Red in the face, chest puffing up.

"Exactly like that?"

"It must have not been much worse as I wasn't slapped for it. So we gather up all the weapons we have, and we're ready to storm that camp looking for you. Vashon was some sort of big cannon in the Liberé war, did you know?"

"I didn't." But David wasn't surprised. Many of the Vashons were.

"So we don't come in straight to the camp, mind you, but looking over the cliffs to the cove below. Getting the lay, she says. That monster whale is floating in the water, and everyone else is sort of moving about. We're watching, trying to figure out where you might be tied up—but we know for certain that they've got you because we can see the troll that you left with, that red ribbon under her nose, standing over two others that are lying on the ground. Then all of a sudden . . ."

Pausing, Dooley took another puff. Annika's hand tightened on

David's—she knew what was coming. She'd heard this before. Her gaze met his, her eyes shining, her lips pressed into a tight line as if holding herself from blurting it out.

Dooley drew it out, breathing a ring of smoke and nodding with satisfaction at its shape before continuing, "So there we were, up on that cliff, looking down at the camp, when a roar sounds above me as if the devil himself were being booted from Hell, riding a streak of burning brimstone across the sky. Vashon clobbers me from behind, throwing me to the ground like she's decided to bash my face open"—he pointed to a cut on his bearded jaw—"but then she's over the top of me, pinning me down, and I'm about to think that I'll need to be telling her about my wife when the world explodes. It goes with a sound unlike any I've ever heard before, even more than when we saw *Pegasus* blow, you remember that?"

David could never forget it. The enormous cargo airship had caught fire over a French port six years before and ignited the balloon. The force had shattered windows on the shops below, set fire to the docks, and had created so much heat that every nearby airship had burst and burned. Altogether, almost two thousand aviators and dockworkers had been killed. They'd called it the worst disaster since Inoka Mountain.

"I remember," he said.

"The rocks beneath us shook, harder than any earthquake I've ever stood through, but not near as long. And then I look down, and I see that there's a crater where the camp was, centered right between the first bunkhouse and the cove. That whale's turned over in the water and the bunkhouses are in ruins. I thought it was a firebomb, though Vashon tells me that it's not, it's not like anything she's ever seen before. Then we see that the ash is coming up over the glacier, so we think the volcano blew a rock."

David had been thinking the same, too, until he realized what it must have been. Astonished, he looked to Annika. "Di Fiore's capsule?"

Brows arched, she nodded wildly, lips still pressed flat.

"We didn't know anything of that, then. We raced down there, searching the remains of those bunkhouses for you, for anyone. But there wasn't a single man who wasn't killed, not a single thing still standing."

All those men dead, and all of them murderers who'd slaughtered the sailors in the whale. He couldn't be sorry, but David would have liked them to receive justice another way—one that made them face up to what they'd done.

And he'd have liked to believe that the capsule *had* reached the moon. But he couldn't be sorry that Lorenzo hadn't succeeded, either—and he was glad that Paolo hadn't tried.

"I don't think that was the destiny he had in mind," David said.

Annika snorted. "But it might be the one he deserved."

Smiling, he glanced at her. "You *are* bloodthirsty."

"A bit." She grinned. "And your Mr. Dooley isn't done."

"For a good hour, we were searching through that rubble, then the ash started falling. Now, we've got our scarves, but not much else, and I've been on enough expeditions with you to recognize the danger we're in if we breathe that. That whale's belly up in the cove, so we can't get into her. So we start along the beach toward Vik as fast as we can, and there're dogs coming from everywhere after us, and we're keeping just barely ahead, when all of the sudden there's a noise from above us. There's di Fiore's ferry cruiser, and men shouting over her sides in a panic, screaming for help."

God. David had to laugh. "The laborers from the glacier camp?"

"The very same ones. Their engine's stalled from the ash, because they never closed up the vents—"

Annika rolled her eyes, shaking her head.

"—and they've killed the crew, so not a one of them knows how to use their sails, and the wind is pushing them out to sea. And so Vashon, she yells up at them to lower their ladder, and they do, but it's a good five feet above our heads and swinging by as fast as they are. So I'm thinking that they're lost, but then Vashon jumps off the sled right into the pack of dogs, and while they're still trying to stop and get their tails turned around, she runs after that ladder like a deer, leaps up and catches hold of the bottom rung, and hauls herself up there. Five minutes later, the sails are out and she's coming back round for me, and has already made a deal with the men."

Awe still suffused Dooley's voice, so David suspected that he hadn't embellished any of it. "What sort of deal?"

"She's got a crew that needs an airship. They've got an airship that needs a crew, and they tell her they're ready to take on all of Castile. By then, Vashon knows we've got to go up to that glacier for you. So she says, you give us the airship to go find our people, we'll fly you to Castile afterward and smuggle you in. At first they weren't happy to do it, especially with that volcano erupting, but then they figure out that it's your girl she's looking to rescue." He pointed the stem of his pipe at Annika. "It seems that she's the one who started all of this. So the captain of the airship—the Castilian who was acting as captain, that is—he says that Miss Fridasdottor is the one who helped him, so he'll help her in return."

Pride swelled through David's chest. He looked to Annika. The cut across her temple hadn't completely healed yet. "And you thought you weren't brave. That you've never done anything that matters."

She shook her head, the color in her cheeks high.

"So we head back to Vik," Dooley continued, "and there's Källa, flying in, though her balloon has next to nothing left and ash in its engine, too. We figure out that you're somewhere north on that glacier. Källa insists that you'll hole up and wait, that you know we'd come. They're cleaning out the engines as fast as they can, the old chief bellowing a full day and night, and that gray snow is falling. We're all set to leave the next morning when a monster walks into town."

"This troll?" David guessed, remembering his own reaction.

"The very same. It gave everyone a terrible scare. If not for Källa, Vashon would have likely put a rail cannon on it."

"I'm glad you didn't," Annika said softly.

"And that's a feeling we all share. So we work it out that Vashon will take the airship up over the glacier, look for the spot you went down, search for where you holed up. Frida here says, 'No, they've got it all wrong. Annika will hole up until she needs to go—and then she'll go despite her fear.' So we decided to run up through the pass, looking for you, as we all agreed that's the route you'd take. And it took us two days, but, there we were."

And thank God for it. "Is the airship still in Vik?"

Dooley shook his head. "Vashon ran into us the next morning, saw that we had you. She'd have flown us in to Vik, where your aunt Lucia still is, but we saw that there was nothing going to pry Annika away from Frida, and I didn't want to fly you into Vik and be murdered when you woke and found I'd taken you away from her. So Vashon's gone on to Smoke Cove, to spread the word about Heimaey and to see if there're any men at the station who want to fly with them back to Castile—and at this moment, I wouldn't want to be where Komlan is standing. I suppose they'll be there a few days, to sort out who is going and who is staying. There're more men at the station camp than that ferry cruiser can carry at once, so they'll be making several trips. Vashon says she'll look to see us in Smoke Cove on her second trip, if we'll be taking a ride back to Johannesland."

"And if I want a job again," Annika said.

David's heart gave a heavy thud. "Do you?"

"No." Her fingers threaded through his. "I don't know where I'll be. I hope it's close to you."

His throat was tight. "I'll find some way to make sure it is."

"I'll not be going far, either," Dooley said. "After my heart stopped palpitating upon seeing this troll, I realized I might stay a while, record a few folk tales."

"Mr. Dooley asks many questions," Frida said dryly.

"And she doesn't answer a one."

She smiled slightly. "Perhaps that will come."

"I think it should," Annika said in Norse. "Sooner than later."

Her mother arched auburn brows, answered in the same language. "No more hiding, little rabbit?"

"For a while. But not in the same way. These stories, these trolls—they worked to keep people afraid, but now that people are coming anyway, I worry that they'll do us more harm than good. They almost put a *rail cannon* on you, Mother."

"I'm not all that pleased by the thought of it, either."

"And if we continue on like this—if people believe we are witches and ride in trolls—it's easier to hurt us when the time comes when we can't hide any longer. It's easier to think of us as monsters who must be killed. But if they know the trolls are only machines, and there is no magic or secrets, then we are just women. Then we aren't any different from the people in the New World. And you know we aren't—you told me so before I left, and it was true. Not for everyone. But it's true for most of us."

She nodded thoughtfully. "It won't be easy, rabbit."

"No. It will take a long time, I think. But we can start small, here. And never back down."

Dooley puffed on his pipe, his gaze following the exchange between the two women. He glanced at David.

David shook his head. Yes, he understood some of it. No, he wouldn't translate.

But he would stay and help them . . . whatever form that took.

Annika had to admit relief that the airship wasn't in Vik. She wasn't feeling strong enough to fend off the looks and questions from the crew. For now, she just wanted to be alone with David.

He was the strongest person she'd ever known—not because of nanoagents, but his sheer will. He'd carried her for a full day and most of the night through the snow. The fever must have started that day, as it hadn't yet become a full-blown bug fever with pustules and a rash, which almost always ended in death. That morning, when she'd finally struggled up out of sleep, her mother had described how they'd found him, cradling her against his chest, burning with fever. She'd been devastated, imagining his terror—and then his naked vulnerability when they'd had to put him in the snow.

But they'd arrived in time, and he was already recovering more quickly than she was.

He was also apparently determined to be absolutely proper—though by whose standards, Annika couldn't guess.

Aside from a light peck, she shouldn't kiss him in front of Frida or anyone older than she was—it was disrespectful to ignore them, and when David kissed her, Annika couldn't think of anyone else. But although her mother might be concerned for Annika's heart, there was nothing improper about taking someone to her bed or sleeping in the same bedchamber.

As soon as they arrived in Vik, however, he moved into a small house with Dooley and Goltzius. Annika didn't want to share Rutger Fatbottom's hearth chamber with Hildegard and her mother, even though it would only be a temporary arrangement. It remained unspoken, but Annika knew that they were all waiting for her to regain her strength before they traveled to Smoke Cove. Though Källa asked her to stay in the house she shared with Olaf and Paolo, Annika felt too awkward to accept, knowing that Paolo still celebrated his son's trip to the moon. In the end, she decided instead to join Lucia, who shared a house with Maria Madalena and her nurse, with the added benefit of pleasing her mother with the assurance that she was so near to a physician, and that David visited often.

Courting, Lucia said. Annika didn't know how that could be true when he never came alone, always with Goltzius or Dooley, and she never had a second of privacy with him.

After two days, Annika was so frustrated that she felt always on the verge of a scream. She filled the hours with sewing. The next day, Källa, her mother, and Hildegard drove Rutger Fatbottom to the rail camp, where they would see if the trolls could be salvaged. David joined them, as did Dooley. Annika was forbidden. She stitched a seam and plotted about how to find a private moment and a bed. Or the floor. It didn't matter.

But though her heart lifted when she saw Austra Longears and a second troll follow Rutger Fatbottom back into Vik, by David's expression she knew not all had gone well. No one told her to return to the warm house when she ventured out. David came to her, gathered her against him.

"What happened?" she whispered.

"The dogs found the camp," he said, and that was enough, Annika was glad she hadn't seen what they must have. "We chased them off, built a pyre—but there wasn't much left. And there's more."

Something that had made Källa angry. Annika could see it in her sister now, the long strides, her face set in stone. She passed them without a word. Annika glanced up at David.

"On the opposite side of the cove, we found the remains of the ships the whale had taken. *Freya's Cloak* was one."

Ursula Ylvasdottor's ship. Throat tight, Annika's gaze found her mother, emerging from Austra Longears. Frida had known the woman better than Annika did—but she appeared less grieved than worried as she opened Rutger Fatbottom's chest hatch.

David took a deep breath. "And then Källa said that Paolo had already offered her an airship, so she would continue doing what Ylvasdottor had done for Hannasvik, bringing in cargo and supplies from Norway. Hildegard . . . disagreed."

Ah. Anger on top of grief. A dangerous combination for them both. "They fought?"

"Yes."

"Did they finish?"

"I don't think so."

So they'd only been interrupted while driving separate trolls. Annika gripped his hand as Hildegard dropped through the chest hatch. Frida looked through after her, met Annika's eyes, shook her head.

"We need to hide now," she said.

He laughed a little. "That bad?"

"Yes. Warn Dooley. He doesn't want to be dragged into it." She pulled him toward the house, where Lucia stood in the door. "We'll wait inside, where it's safe. David is about to learn a bit more about his new family."

Frida soon joined them, and they waited at the table, listening to the storm of shouts outside. Annika still hadn't had a moment alone with David, but she sat next to him, which was almost as good, and was relieved when the conversation turned to leaving for Smoke Cove.

"We'll return for the last troll tomorrow," Frida said. "If we can repair his legs."

Annika winced. "It was only one hinge bolt."

"And I imagine you had reason."

"I didn't want to die."

"I suppose that is reason enough." With a smile, her mother looked through the window, where the second new troll stood. She sighed. "It pains me to see them so naked."

Naked, but more clearly a machine. "Mine will stay that way."

Frida nodded. "And what of that whale? We could salvage a century's worth of equipment from him."

David shook his head. "As soon as everyone outside of Iceland discovers what happened, you won't want them to associate that whale with your people in any way."

"I suppose that's true. It's a pity, though." She glanced at Annika. "Will you be taking your naked troll home?"

"Only to visit. And perhaps in the spring, when I can take David up to bury Inga's beads."

She felt his sharp gaze on her, but didn't look away from her mother. Frida nodded, then regarded him thoughtfully.

"You are much different from your cousin. And your aunt." Who were still shouting outside. "More like your mother, in many respects."

"And my father, too," he said, and smiled a bit when Frida shrugged.

Oh. Annika remembered doing the same once. But when she opened her mouth, David shook his head and looked to her mother again. "Did you know Inga?"

Frida's eyes softened. "Yes. I spent the first part of my life with her."

Beneath the table, David took Annika's hand. "Will you tell me about her? I don't know anything of her life before she left."

"I will be happy to, David Ingasson."

Their last day in Vik dawned late, and not very bright, but since Annika knew that David would be on the ladder behind her as she drove, it was an absolutely perfect morning. A week in Vik, and not a minute alone.

Yet she was more in love with him than ever. Just as during the first night in *Phatéon*'s wardroom when she'd discovered how well she liked him, long conversations over the corner of Lucia's dining table only deepened her fascination, her appreciation for everything David said and did.

And those hours only deepened the ache of wanting him, needing him. Her guts were well and truly riveted. She loved and savored every small touch between them—and was desperate for more, desperate to have David to herself.

Soon, she would. She all but danced, tightening bolts and checking the coal level, stoking the furnace and waiting for her to steam. Finally, she emerged onto the street again, where the others had gathered while the trolls heated. Her gaze quickly found David, who was helping Lucia into Källa's troll. His aunt had volunteered to watch over Olaf while she drove—Källa breaking ahead of them to reach Smoke Cove as quickly as possible, where she intended to help Paolo smooth over the chaos that must be left in Lorenzo's wake. Frida, Hildegard, and Annika would follow at a slower pace.

Frida pulled her close, kissed her cheeks. "We will stop at Thor's Spring tonight."

An eight-hour trek. "All right. But don't be concerned if I fall behind."

Her mother's wry gaze flicked to David. "I won't be too concerned," she said. "But do rest often."

"Do not promise anything, Annika," Källa said from behind her. "Just say that you will be in bed."

"Källa!"

Her sister grinned, slipped her arms around Frida. "Do take care of my mother."

"I will try." Frida rubbed her shoulder. "She will come 'round. She is only afraid to lose you again."

"I know. It will be a while before I can find a proper airship, anyway. Until then, Paolo would like you both to come to the station house. He should be there for some time while he begins work on the southern peninsula. I believe he has invited everyone in Vik to stay there, in fact. But we would be especially pleased by your visit."

"We will come."

Källa drew a deep breath. "Perhaps ask Lisbet if she'd like to visit. Tell her of Olaf. And if she can't . . . I'll understand."

Frida nodded, watching after her as she left them, climbed into her troll. Hildegard approached, her eyes narrowed.

"Did I hear her worry that Lisbet would not come?"

Frida smiled slightly. "You did."

"Ridiculous. Lisbet is not even a hair as stubborn as you."

"And hurt more easily."

Hildegard's expression softened when she glanced back at Frida. "Then let us hope they are not fools to waste as much time as we did, yes?"

"I was not the fool."

Oh, Mother. Annika prepared for another storm, but Hildegard only threw her head back with a laugh—then hauled Frida up for a hard kiss. Oh. Annika averted her gaze out of respect, saw everyone else staring, wide-eyed . . . and none of them half as astonished as Maria Madalena. Her mouth had dropped open, her eyes rounded. She looked to her nurse, who had begun to smile.

Hildegard set Frida back on her feet, leaving her mother laughing after her as Hildegard stalked to her troll. At the chest hatch, she paused, looked back. "You were well worth the wait, Frida Kárasdottor!"

She climbed in. A second later, Maria Madalena raced after her, holding on to her lover with one hand, her skirts hiked high in the other. "Wait! Oh, wait! Let us ride with you, instead!"

With a grin, Frida slanted a glance at Annika. "Tell Mr. Dooley to hurry. He's apparently intending to keep me company as I'm driving."

As was Goltzius. "And what will you tell him?"

"All but the location, most likely."

"Mr. Goltzius is family to Hanna's husband, and he will report what he finds."

Frida's lips pursed. "Will he?"

"Yes." And it might behoove them to stop telling stories of witches and trolls, but a story of some sort still needed to be told. "I think that he will like to hear that her descendants have been caretakers of this island, keeping others from staking claim on this land. His people will have more reason to defend ours if we are family—and if they are coming anyway, we ought to create as much common ground as we can."

"Who is clever? Perhaps I will also not mention the murder, then, and only say that Hanna liberated the Englishwomen." Frida kissed her cheeks again. "Thor's Spring, little fox."

"Safe journey, Mother."

Wearing a smile, Annika joined David. Both he and Dooley were regarding Goltzius with concern. Goltzius was shaking his head.

"I am happy for her," he said. "I truly am."

"Happy for her doesn't mean you can't be sorry for yourself." Dooley clapped him on the back. "But love will come around again."

"I'll wait before looking for it again."

David met her eyes. "I don't think it waits until you're looking."

No, it didn't. Oh, but she was looking now. With a significant lift of her brows, she glanced toward Austra Longears just as Frida's troll gave a huff.

"I suggest that you don't make her wait, Mr. Dooley," Annika said. "She's likes to talk as she drives."

"Well, then." He offered a tip of his hat to Annika, then a nod toward David. "We're off. We'll see you when."

She felt David's gaze on her as she walked ahead of him, as she climbed into the troll. In the next moment he had her back against the wall, his mouth opening over hers in a desperate, deep kiss. She returned it with every pent-up emotion of the past week, every bit of joy that he was there, that he touched her again.

With a groan, he dragged his lips from hers and held her, his breath ragged. "I need you, Annika. So much. Being proper this week has been hell."

It had been, though a wonderful sort of hell. She pressed kisses to his jaw, his throat. "Then why were you?"

"I wanted to put everything in order before I came to you. You said you wanted to be near to me. Are you certain, Annika? Because I can't let you go."

Her throat tightened. He *hadn't* let her go. He'd saved her by never letting go.

She'd never let him go, either. "I'm certain."

"Then tell me where you hope to go, what you hope to do. And I will do all that I can to be with you."

She hoped to be with him. But, no—that was not all that she hoped. "I intend to drive this troll into Smoke Cove, to tell my aunt Valdís that she was right about me. I will walk it through the street, and come out of the chest hatch, and the people will see that I am flesh and blood."

"No hiding?"

"No."

"And then?"

"I thought I might accompany you on your survey." She grinned against his mouth. "I can act as a guide—and it is much easier to get around by troll."

"We aren't finishing the survey. Not the one we intended. Dooley, Goltzius, and I have all changed our goals."

Oh. "Where will we be going then?"

"Not far from your home. I wanted to stay close. So I will be working with Paolo, surveying the southern peninsula. I could use a guide with a troll."

She would love that. "Based in Smoke Cove?"

"Yes."

"And when you're done?"

"I'll stay in Iceland. This island can keep me busy for the rest of my life."

Traveling throughout her home? But not just driving a troll. "I have enough fabric for the rest of my life."

"And bows?" His hands slid to her bottom. "You should make undergarments and sell them. If they affect everyone the same way they do me, you'll soon be a rich woman."

She laughed. "And if they don't?"

"Then you can just wear them for me."

"I'm wearing some now," she said softly, and watched the desire flare in his gaze, felt the tightening of his body. "And I feel like a wolf."

He bent his head. "The troll's in the middle of the street."

"I know. It's so improper—"

His mouth captured hers, and the need twisted inside her. She buried her fingers in his hair, clung as he lifted her. There was no time to waste, and no time at all, only the huff and the heat of their breath, the tug of a bow and his groan upon finding her wet, her cry as he slid deep. There was nothing but his arms wrapped around her, the drive of his body, his urgent words of love in her ear.

Nothing but David—and so much more than she'd dreamed.

Epilogue

The volcano slept, as it had since Hanna and the English-women founded their village. In the first years, the women hadn't worn beads. The names of those who'd died had been inscribed on large stones at the base of the mountain. Annika didn't know when or why the first woman had buried her mother's or her sister's runes, but the tradition had begun in the first generation.

When the time came, Annika didn't believe that her soul would need help finding her family's. She didn't believe that burying the runes helped the dead at all.

She did believe that it helped those still living.

David had gone quiet when she'd started Austra Longears up the path. Here and there, patches of snow still lingered, but most of it had receded with the spring. She'd approached the volcano from the south, and they'd spent the previous day trampling through the rock arches and soaking in the steaming springs that stank of sulphur but were heaven to bathe in. Later, as she'd lain in his arms, he'd read the runes at her neck, asked her to tell him about each woman. She had, and of the women in his line, too.

He still had not been to Hannasvik, though Annika had visited twice since they'd returned to Smoke Cove to begin work with Paolo—the last time returning with Senhorita Neves and her nurse, who had decided that the small fishing town was more to their taste than the isolated Hannasvik. Perhaps emboldened by their time there, or simply tired of hiding, they lived openly together—not flaunting their relationship, but not concealing it, either. Simply living. A month later, Lisbet had joined Källa at the station house—and then moved in with Valdís twice, after two loud public rows.

So far, none of the locals had spoken out against either of the couples. Some of them, Annika was certain, enjoyed the lively fighting. Dooley had told her that several fishermen had placed bets on when Lisbet would return to the station house.

However long it took, no one wagered that Lisbet would give up and go home again. Källa refused to, unless her son could go, too.

Annika would have wagered everything she owned that would eventually happen. Sooner or later, she was certain that the women of Hannasvik would invite David and Olaf to the village. Several of the elders had already come to meet them. Naked or in skins, trolls had become a familiar sight in Smoke Cove.

Already, her small world was changing. Annika didn't know what would come of it, or how long it would remain peaceful, but such a fine start gave her endless hope.

And for now, the rest of the world didn't seem concerned about the goings-on in Iceland. Though word of Lorenzo's whale and the horror at Heimaey had reached the New World, they'd not heard much about it. The newssheets that Vashon brought rarely mentioned either di Fiore, but were filled with news of the civil war brewing in Castile, where small groups of rebels had carried out devastating attacks against the queen's police.

Annika still wished that she'd been brave enough to give over a few coins—but was so, so glad that she'd taken other risks. And she wasn't sorry that any of it had led to this.

She stopped the troll at the edge of a small clearing marked by a natural stone arch. Taking David's hand, she led him up the gentle slope. A breeze stirred as they approached the ring of sixty stones, each one inscribed with a name. She knew where Hanna's stone lay, but took the long way around, pointed out Jane's.

"This is where mine will be buried." She paused, frowned. "I suppose our children's, too. The line has always passed through the mother—though if they wish it, they could choose Hanna's, since that is your line."

"I don't care what they choose," he said gruffly. "If God has any pity at all, I'll be dead before a single one of those runes is buried, and I'll never know where they lie."

Annika hoped that the gods would have pity on her, too—she felt exactly the same way.

She led him on, stopped in front of Hanna's stone. The black soil at its base was soft, with tender shoots of grass poking through.

"Here," she said.

His breath shuddered as he lifted the necklace over his head. He held the runes cupped in his palm, looking down at the ground. Moisture pooled in his eye. His throat worked, but he didn't speak. Annika didn't know if he could.

When he looked to her, she drew the knife sheathed at her thigh, made a small cut on his thumb. "Place a drop of blood over each name before you bury them. Then speak your prayers and good-byes."

"What do I say?" His voice was hoarse.

"Anything you like."

"There is too much."

"We're in no hurry."

He crouched in front of the stone. Whatever he had to say, he didn't speak it aloud. Tears dripped steadily down his cheek, soaked into the ground. After a while, he simply stared at the small hole he'd dug in the soil without making a move to place the runes inside.

"I've been wearing these for so long," he said quietly. "I feel that when I bury them, she'll truly be gone. I've waited to do this for twenty years. Now that I'm here, it's hard to let her go."

"You aren't letting her go. Everything that you said to her, everything you feel for her and remember about her, you'll carry away with you." Annika's mother had told her the same when her grandmother had died—and it had been true.

David nodded. With a deep breath, he pushed the runes into the soil and covered them.

He stood, lifted his gaze to the sky. His eye closed, and another long breath filled his chest. Twenty years, and a promise finally fulfilled. She couldn't imagine how much less he must weigh.

His gaze found hers, then. His hand cupped her cheek. "I had a lot to say—not least of all, thanking her for leading me to you."

Oh. Annika's vision blurred. She turned her head, pressed a kiss against his palm. "I'm grateful for that, too."

His arms came around her, drew her in against him. She held him tight, loving his strength, his gentleness, his warmth. His chest rose on another shuddering breath—release, she thought. His hand smoothed up her spine.

"Is that Hannasvik?"

She glanced over her shoulder, following his gaze. From this distance, the lake was a glint in the sun, but he could likely see the rounded earthen houses, the fences, the trolls. "Yes."

"Can they see us up here?"

"Not without a spyglass. But they knew we were coming, so they might look—and my clothes are difficult to *not* see." A crimson trouser and lime-green jacket, the sleeves lined with blue bows. Annika grinned when he laughed, nodding. She reached into the small pocket at her waist. "The women have something for you, and I want to give it before we leave this place. Lower your head."

After giving her a quizzical look, he did. Annika raised her arms, slipped the runes over his neck. "David, son of Inga, daughter of Helga, daughter of Sigrid, daughter of Ursula, daughter of Hanna."

Lips parting with astonishment, he felt the beads at his throat. "There are two strands."

"I asked them to add the second. David, son of Stone. I didn't know the other names, but we can carve them. I know he was important to you—"

She didn't finish. He caught her up, his mouth covering hers. A hard kiss, no finesse, pure emotion. He set her down again, her face cradled in his hands, his lips against hers. "I love you, Annika Fridasdottir." It was rough, urgent. "I love you. And I thank the gods every day that a bird didn't shit in my eye at the port gates."

There wasn't enough room inside her ribs for her heart. It squeezed painfully tight as he spoke, left her without any breath.

"I didn't even dare look up," she whispered. "I always felt so small. About to be crushed."

"And now?"

She would stand up to anything. "I feel like I'm part of something that matters. With Hannasvik. With you."

"And without you, nothing matters at all," he said gruffly, and his lips met hers for another long kiss. Annika clung to him, smiling against his mouth.

He always said the most wonderful things.

That night, ribbons of green shimmered across the dark sky, backlit by brilliant stars. Annika almost missed seeing the lights, but an idle glance through the eye louvers sent her rushing out in her chemise and drawers, her boots unlaced, and she was through the chest hatch before David managed to pull on his trousers. She looked up. A moment later, David wrapped his arms around her, and the warmth of his body kept Annika from shivering.

Pinks and blues danced through the green. With a contented sigh, she tilted her head back against his shoulder. "Does it look the same through your lenses? Or is it more beautiful?"

"Different—and I can't see the lights at all through some of the lenses. But when I can, they are just as beautiful."

"And they truly don't know what causes it?"

"Truly," he confirmed, and she heard the smile in his voice. "Now tell me: When it's no longer a mystery, when you know exactly what causes them, will you be as enchanted? Will they still be as beautiful then?"

"Oh, yes. Even more so, I think. People are the only things that don't always improve upon knowing what makes them up. Well, people and sausage from a manufactory."

His laugh rumbled against her back. "*Any* meat from a manu-factory."

"I wish someone had told me that four years ago." She laughed with him, then settled back against his chest. "But the rest is true. Look at the sentinels guarding the New World—or a troll. Naked or covered, it's awe-inspiring on first sight, isn't it? But then you realize that a band of women carried salvaged equipment across an island and built the trolls with nothing more than hard work and ingenuity, and a hundred years of maintenance brought them to this point. A troll is so much more incredible, knowing that. It's true of so many other things, too—including your volcanoes."

He dropped a warm kiss to the side of her neck. "Yes, it is."

"And also true of the people I love."

His teeth scraped her skin, raising gooseflesh the length of her body. Never cold with him, but shivering anyway. "Is that so?"

"Yes. My mother, for one. As a child I loved her, despite know-ing so little about her. But now, knowing everything she has done, how stubborn she can be, how blind, how strong, how clever . . . knowing her as a woman, I love her so much more. And there is you." She slid her hand the length of his forearm, laced her fingers through his. "You were a mystery to me at the port, and I wanted to know more about you then. But I didn't lose interest as I came to know you; you are so much more fascinating to me now. And the more I learn about you, the more I love you. Yet I have barely scratched the surface. When you write in your journal, I cannot wait to know what it is that you've been thinking, and I can never guess. When you look at something, I always want to know how you see it. I suspect that when we are gray together, I will still not know all of you. But even if I do, even if the mystery is completely gone, I won't be any less in love. I think that I'll be astonished by every small thing that has come together to make you the man you are—and I'll still feel the wonder and joy of knowing you love me, too."

"Annika." His voice was rough. "You spin my world upside down every single day."

"Do you want me to stop?"

"Never."

Smiling, she turned in his arms, looked up into his face—and when she was gray, Annika hoped that David would be the last sight she ever saw, his gaze burning with love. She hoped that the very last thing she ever felt was this wonderful, riveted twist in her gut, and the touch of his warm lips.

His mouth covered hers. She closed her eyes, opened up to the heat of his kiss.

And the rest of the world melted away.